See Naples and Kill

Gregory Dowling

See Naples
and Kill

ST. MARTIN'S PRESS
NEW YORK

Library of Congress Cataloging-in-Publication Data

Dowling, Gregory.
    See Naples and kill.
    "A Thomas Dunne book."
    I. Title.
PR6054.0862S4 1988 823'.914 88-15828
ISBN 0-312-02277-8

First published in Great Britain by Grafton Books, A Division of the
Collins Publishing Group.
First U.S. Edition
10 9 8 7 6 5 4 3 2 1

For my parents

See Naples and Kill

One

The film, Alain Delon and a gun against the whole world, was pretty boring after the first few slaughters. I thought to myself that if only I had one of those remote control things I could change channel and find something marginally less stupid, or at least less noisy – or even turn off. As it was, to accomplish such life-renewing changes I would have to get out of my armchair, pick my way across the battlefield of the floor, with its dead beer-cans and bottles and greasy plates, and then push a pretty stiff button. So I stayed sitting.

The doorbell rang.

Well, I did it. I staggered over and just got my finger in before yet another person had his head blown off for irritating Alain Delon. Then I had to go down the stairs to the front door, cursing the primitiveness of a second-floor flat un-equipped with intercom and door-opener.

My brother was at the door.

'Oh, hello Gigi,' I said. It's short for Luigi, and he's always tried hard to suppress its use. He has almost succeeded – except, of course, in the family.

'Hi, let me in.'

'Yes, of course.'

He pushed in past me. 'Upstairs, yeah?'

'Yes, second floor.'

He went on up so quickly that I looked outside for a moment before closing the door, half expecting to see pursuing Indians, or gangsters, or policemen. Particularly policemen. But all was as quiet as could be expected from a West Dulwich side street at eleven thirty pm.

I followed my brother on up. He walked straight in and sat down in the only armchair. He dropped the raincoat he'd been carrying on to the floor, but kept the briefcase on his lap as a nervous person might do on the underground late at night.

His expression, however, started to be a little more relaxed. He undid another button of his shirt – the next would practically reveal his navel – but, as usual, he didn't take off his jacket.

'Well, hello,' I said.

'Yeah. Yeah. Hi.'

Nobody, I suppose, would have guessed from our exchange that two brothers of Neapolitan origin were meeting up again after about two years. And not many people, looking at us, would have guessed that we were brothers either.

In fact we're only half-brothers; my father married twice – one Neapolitan, and one Londoner. They both died: one from cancer, the other in a car crash. I can remember neither. Gigi takes after my father and is thus entirely Italian in appearance – dark-skinned, -haired, -eyed. I take after my mother, the English one, and am thus pinkish, blond, and blue-eyed. And yet in many ways I'm more Neapolitan than he is. He was born just a few years after my father and his first wife came to England, when they were very keen to adopt the ways and customs of their new land. So they frequently talked English even between themselves (probably rather like the couple in *Casablanca*, mind you – 'What watch?' 'Ten watch.' 'Ah, such watch!'), and drank tea with milk and watched – with utter incomprehension – cricket on television. My father's second wife, however, died less than a year after I was born, and my father's mother came out from Naples to help bring me up. She, of course, didn't speak a word of English – and in fact in her twelve years in England only learnt about ten, two of which, from my father, were 'Tuddanam Otspurras' – so until I went to school I practically only heard Neapolitan around me (apart from a few useful short Anglo-Saxon words which Gigi, six years older, took it upon himself to teach me).

The six years between us and the difference in our upbringing explain why we are not so close. I expected Gigi to start straight in on an explanation of why he'd called, and when he didn't, I did my duty as host.

'Can I offer you anything?'

'Got any beer?' He had a thirsty look about him despite the coolness of the April night. Part of it, of course, was due to his habit of always dressing underneath his coat as if for a Mediterranean summer – the open, very open, shirt and the light jacket and trousers.

'Some cans maybe.' I went into the kitchen. 'How did you know I was living here?' I called out.

'Oh, got in touch with Zia Peppina.' An aunt of ours who lives in Tooting. 'What d'you come to London for anyway?' he asked.

'Work. So I hoped.' I came back with a can and a glass and gave them to him. He put the glass on the floor – quite reasonably, there being three or four already rolling around there – and drank from the can. This was quite in keeping with his generally dishevelled look, but both the action and the look were uncharacteristic as I remembered Gigi. Usually all the casual touches in his attire are quite clearly deliberate – the open shirt to show off his gold medallion and chest and the unshavenness to show off his masculinity – but this time something in his overall attitude made all these things look unambiguously sloppy. The jacket was rumpled and he hadn't even got cufflinks, I realised. 'Business' must be bad.

I didn't ask anything yet. He drank his beer and said, 'What are you doing then?'

'Nothing now. I lost my job last week. I was doing translations for a firm that exported to Italy. Translating letters mostly, both ways – from English to Italian and vice versa. Anyway the director thought he knew a bit of Italian. You know, he'd been to Italy a few times, north and south, and had learnt a few things like "buongiorno" and "grazie" and he obviously wanted to show what a linguist he was so he kept asking me, "Are you sure you're translating into good Italian and not just southern dialect?"'

'Was he right?'

'Course he wasn't.'

It wasn't a dumb question actually. Gigi could only speak Neapolitan, never having had any opportunity to learn 'correct' Italian. And even that he spoke stumblingly. He'd gone through a fairly common phase of not wanting to talk the parental language as it wasn't what all the other kids at school talked. This had only changed when he met Pasquale, son of an ice-cream manufacturer in a neighbouring village, who had been in England just a few years and who became a close friend of Gigi's. I, on the other hand, hadn't had much choice of whether I wanted to talk it or not, as there was no other way I could wheedle sweets and treats from my grandmother. We'd also been able to go relative-visiting in Naples more often when I was small – once a year, anyway – since business had picked up for my father. (It didn't last.) And then I'd been able to do Italian at school, so I was fluent in both the dialect and the language. In case you're wondering, Neapolitan is different enough from Italian to be pretty nigh incomprehensible to most Italians from about Rome upwards.

'I got a bit fed up and felt like telling him to translate the bloody things himself, but in the end I decided to show him I knew the difference so I translated a letter entirely in Neapolitan for him to see. I was going to do it in Italian as well and let him compare. Only I left the Neapolitan one on a desk and the secretary sent it off. To a firm in Florence.'

'Didn't understand a word, I bet.'

'Well, no; in fact it turned out that the manager in Florence was a Neapolitan himself.'

'Bit of luck.'

'Not exactly. He must have thought we were taking the mickey and he, er, he broke off dealings with us. With them. And they were quite important customers.'

'Pretty dumb fing to do.'

'Well, he riled me. It was as if he was making out I was some *scugnizzo* from the *quartieri* who could only just spell his name.'

'Wouldn't have been far wrong. That's what Dad was.'

'All right then. Let's just say this bloke got up my nose.'

'So now what you gonna do?'

'Don't know. Look for another job.'

'Go back to Radney?'

'There's nothing there now. We had to close the restaurant down, you must have heard that. Too much competition. It was losing even while Dad was alive.'

'Oh yeah,' he said, without much interest.

He'd never liked Radney. We were both born in Bethnal Green, but whereas I'd only been eight when we'd moved to Radney – a little town (or big village) north of Oxford – he'd been fourteen. Three years later he'd disappeared back into the Big City. He had undoubtedly decided to follow the example of Pasquale, who had run off a month before Gigi. The friendship between the two had always been disapproved of by my father, Pasquale being quite clearly a good-for-nothing lout. My father's grim prognostications – 'he'll go to the bad' – and my grandmother's weeping lamentations over her lost Gigino seemed all too justified as a year went by with no news of him. Then he rolled up in a Mercedes, wearing an expensive suit and escorting a clearly expensive young lady. 'Business, business,' he said in explanation of his new-found wealth, and would give no further details. He could give no address either because the nature of his 'business' apparently required frequent moves. Over the years he appeared at not very regular intervals. The cars, suits and girls changed, but the air of opulence didn't. And yet there were indications that we only saw what he chose us to see, and that some of the longer intervals between his appearances could be explained by his not being in possession of one or more of those three impressive items. Zia Peppina, on one of her visits to Radney, said she was sure she had once seen him selling shirts at a very temporary-looking stall near Waterloo Station. This would, of course, explain the obvious brand-newness of those three items every time he turned up – the suit's knife-edge creases, the car's shininess, and the girl's devotion.

Mind you, this was the most charitable explanation given of the intervals – and certainly not the one my father gave.

'Anyway,' I said, sitting on the only other chair the flat possessed, 'to what do I owe, etc? How are things with you?'

11

'Yeah. Er, yeah. Like.'

He seemed to think that he had said it all.

'Really?' I said.

'Can I have a look round the flat?'

'Go ahead. It'll take you about five seconds. There's this room, the kitchen and the bathroom.'

He went and looked at the bathroom and the kitchen, still carrying his briefcase. In the kitchen he studied with surprising attentiveness the simple wooden table by the window. 'It's not an antique,' I said.

'Nah, but it's good and strong innit? That's what you want.' He put the case down on the floor and shook the table. 'Yeah, feels firm.'

'Well, I only eat off it, you know. You wanting a dance floor?'

He didn't answer. He looked out of the window. 'Whose garden's that?'

'The people on the ground floor. Not that they use it much.'

'Let's have another can,' he said. He took one out of the fridge and then went back into the living-room and took possession of the armchair again. 'You know,' he said, 'I bin thinking of Radney.'

This really surprised me. 'What?'

'Well, not Radney itself. More the country, like. You remember that empty house we used to go to? You know, near the wood?'

'Yes.'

'Still there, is it?'

'Yes. But what's put it into your mind?'

'Oh nuffink. Nuffink special. Still empty, is it?'

'As far as I know. Not been there for years.'

'Good. Look, can I doss here the night?'

'Yes, of course. Er, as you can see I've only got the one bed.'

'Yeah. Bit small this place, innit?'

'Well, you see what you can get on an unqualified translator's salary. Or on the dole.'

12

'Yeah. Well, if you must come and live in Dulwich. Bloody garden suburb innit.' He had never gone that much for trees, which made his recent pastoral effusion all the more perplexing.

'A friend put me on to it. And it's convenient and I like the area, and anyway this is West Dulwich, practically Norwood.'

'Suppose so, but it's posher than you've been used to, I'll bet,' he said with the tone of one used to anything and everything. 'Right, I'll doss on the floor – if you can make a bit of room.' He looked pointedly at the chaos.

'Of course. Sorry about all this. Just imagine if Nonna Carmela' – our grandmother – 'could see it. I haven't felt much like tidying up recently. Nor like doing anything, really.'

'A bit down like, yeah?' His eyes shot curiously towards me. These sudden penetrating glances were a characteristic of his; people who didn't know him well often thought him slow, and I think he cultivated this as an image, but these glances were a clue to his essential – well, the best word I can think of is the Italian *furbizia*, which is a cross between sharpness and knowingness. A pretty important word in Italy, particularly in Naples.

'You know,' I said, 'just lost my job and – and – '

'Oh yeah. Zia Peppina told me you got a girl. Out in America or somefing.'

'Yes.'

'What's she like?'

'Fine. And the latest from her was a letter enclosing a photo of her marriage to a Mormon missionary. Very picturesque.'

'Ah. Tough, eh?'

'Yes.'

'They're the ones who go around in pairs looking like the Osmond brothers, in they?'

'Yes.'

'Well, she must have been a bit of a berk then.'

'Give me time and I suppose I'll think so too. Not just yet

though.' I started excavating an oasis of order in the corner of the room. He sat watching.

'Listen,' he said when he'd finished the beer.

'Yes?'

'Listen . . . I suppose you must be wondering a bit what's brought me here.'

'Well, we are brothers but yes, well . . .'

'And why I come in like I had the old . . . somebody after me.'

'You did seem to be in a bit of a hurry.'

'Well, you're not to let on to no one that I'm here. Get me? No one.'

'I see. What no one in particular mustn't I let on to?'

'It's not the old Bill, so don't fink it. They don't want me.'

'Well, I didn't think . . .'

'Don't give me that, Jan. I know what everybody's always thought about us. You're the bright college lad and I'm the disgrace to the family.' He paused. 'Except that in my time I've had more money in me hands than Dad made in his whole life.'

'And except I never went to college.'

'You did A levels and that. And you would of gone if Dad hadn't needed you in the restaurant. Anyway look at all these books,' he said, waving a hand at my two shelves of tattered paperbacks (a few Penguins, an Italian novel or two, a lot of science fiction) and an occasional art book. 'But I'm not in trouble wiv them, OK?'

'Yeah, if you say so. So who?'

'Look, less I tell you, less you need to keep your mouf shut about, right?'

'But you *are* in trouble, yes?'

'For a bit. Just a bit. Just need to keep low for a bit and then – well, if you call the killing of a lifetime trouble . . .'

'Killing?'

'Killing like money, dough, bread. Right?'

'I see. Some very smart business deal.'

14

'Yeah. You got it.' He sat back in the chair looking pleased with himself.

'And you'd like to lie low here, yes?'

'No, no. Don't worry. I just came here in a bit of a hurry like. I wanted to go somewhere they wouldn't know about. And, er, I'm a bit short of the ready just at the moment so I couldn't get a room or anyfing. Couldn't even get enough petrol to get me out of London. But don't worry. I'll move on tomorrow. If you can lend me a spot of money. Just enough for petrol and, er, to keep me going for a few days.'

'You know I've just lost my job.'

'Yeah, but Zia Peppina told me you'd had some factory job before, on a night shift, too. They can pay pretty well, can't they, and you're a careful sort of bloke. Hundred quid? Or make it two? You won't lose out, mate, I can tell you.'

I had a few hundred pounds in the bank at that moment, it was true, but I could think of better things to do with it than give it to someone who behaved as if he were on the run from Al Capone.

But then this someone was my brother.

Only half-brother.

Yes, but Neapolitan half-brother. What would Nonna Carmela have said?

'Yeah, all right. A hundred and fifty. I'll write you a cheque.'

'Fanks, Jan. If you can give me some in cash, too.'

I suppose it's time for a parenthesis on my name. When I was born my father was clearly going through one of those moments when he'd sit and dream of Naples – Vesuvius and Santa Lucia and contraband cigarettes and the rest of it (he'd even play *O Sole Mio* on the tape recorder in the restaurant, and the customers would assume it was just the usual kitsch stuff put on for them) – so he wanted me to be called Gennaro, the name of Naples's patron saint, and of about a third of the city's male population. My mother stuck out for something she could pronounce, so they translated it. Or did their best to anyway. Thus my full name is January Domenico Esposito.

15

I mostly introduce myself as Jan and let people make what they like of it.

He put the cheque and the two ten-pound notes in his pocket, then said, 'You ain't got a spare mattress, I suppose?'

'No, sorry.'

'Well, if you can give me some blankets or somefing, I suppose I'll be all right. You ain't got anyfing to eat? Bit of cheese or somefing?'

'I can open a tin of beans if you like. Haven't got much else just now.'

'That's all right. You do that. Anyfing on the telly?'

'They're doing a season of Alain Delon films. With subtitles, mind. But half the dialogue is "urgh" and "aah" and "wham" and "splat", so it doesn't really matter.'

'Sounds all right.'

He switched on and I went into the kitchen to 'cook'.

We ate beans on toast on our knees and watched the end of the film. When Alain Delon had killed everybody except the girl (and he looked as if he meant to do something about that pretty soon), Gigi said, 'I fink I'll crash out, all right?'

So he curled up fully dressed (I wondered no longer at the rumpled state of his jacket) with a few blankets and a spare cushion. I went into the kitchen to wash up. One of my recent acquisitions, before I lost the job, had been a Sony Walkman, and this was an ideal occasion to put it to use. (Not that I hadn't found two hundred other occasions in the last week.)

I wondered what Verdi would have thought of a full performance of *La Traviata* put on to entertain someone scrubbing saucepans in a dirty suburban kitchen. I hoped he wouldn't have minded too much so long as my attention stayed more on the music than the chore.

I'd practically finished the pans, and Mirella Freni was somewhere in the middle of my head putting her problems to me, when a hand touched my shoulder. I leapt a couple of feet – from Paris to Dulwich.

My brother pulled the headphones off and brought his face

close to mine. The translocation from the Parisian *salon* was complete.

'Listen,' he whispered.

'I was.' Mirella was now discussing her problems, in a distant crackle, with Gigi's left hand. I switched off the cassette.

'Ssh. There's someone outside the front door. You go frough there' – pointing to the flat's main room – 'and if they come in don't let on there's anyone else here.'

'Hell. Who is it?' There was no third floor, so anybody outside had come to see me – or him. And the front door downstairs was often left open.

'Don't worry. Just – just act natural wiv 'em. You don't know nuffing about me.'

'Well, that shouldn't be too difficult.' I unstrapped the Walkman and put it on top of the fridge. Then I went out to the main room of the flat, whistling as casually as possible the aria I'd just been listening to. When I got to the door I stopped. I could hear nothing beyond it. I puckered my lips again for my version of Verdi but realised no noise was coming out. Indeed my heart was thumping louder.

Who needs brothers? I thought. Even half-ones.

There was a sudden knock at the door.

'Yes? Who is it?'

'Open please.'

'Just a minute. Who are you?'

'If you don't open it we will open it.' It was a high-pitched male voice, and it wasn't English. The accent was the one all foreigners imitate (and have done from Chico Marx onwards) when they wish to portray an Italian, be he Milanese, Roman or Sicilian. That is to say, it was a Neapolitan outside.

'It's locked,' I said, and I guessed that this retort would probably not entirely crush them.

'Do you like-a dees door, meestair?' (This represents more or less the way he spoke: I leave the reader to imagine him using this accent for the rest of the conversation.)

'Well, er – ' Oh hell. I had one moment of panic in which I

17

felt like running into the kitchen to get big brother to go and sort them out. Then I said, 'Look, I don't know who you are but I'm going to call the police.'

'While you call them, we break the door. OK?'

I went over to the phone and lifted the receiver. It gave the usual irritating merry tinkle.

'Say goodbye to your door, mister.'

'Look – look – can't we be reasonable? Who are you?' My finger was rigid in the 'nine' hole.

There was a sudden crash and the door shook. (At the same time I seemed to hear an answering crash – or thump – from the kitchen. Was Gigi practising karate chops, or just throwing himself around in an ecstasy of fear?)

'One more push I think,' the voice said cheerily.

My finger still hadn't moved in the dial. I looked at the door and decided he wasn't exaggerating. 'I'll open, I'll open.' I picked up the smaller chair – more, I suppose, to make myself look like a normal nervous householder than because I thought it would do any good. I opened the door with one hand and cowered behind my shield.

Two

There were two of them outside, instantly divisible into the Door Destroyer and the Talker. One was tall, burly and menacing. The other was short, neat and bespectacled.

Then the big one spoke, and I realised that my divisions had been wrong. His was the high-pitched voice I'd heard. 'Put your chair down or my little friend could use that knife.' I only then saw the knife in his companion's right hand. 'At the moment it's only a precaution.'

I put it down but his little friend didn't put away his knife. 'Er, look, I don't think . . .'

'Quiet,' the big one said. They both pushed into the room, me backing away the while. The big one was dressed in black – black raincoat, trousers, pullover and moustache – just so there could be no doubt of his being the baddy. The piping soprano voice should have been ridiculous, I suppose, coming from this dark hulk, but I didn't laugh. Indeed, it was unpleasantly jarring rather than anything else, like seeing a crocodile wearing lipstick: you instantly realised there was something not quite right about him. Mind you, for me it was wrong enough that he was in the room with me. The little one looked like an average bank clerk with his grey suit, striped tie and large spectacles – except for the knife, of course.

'You aren't Esposito's brother,' the big one said, looking hard at me.

Well, if he said not. 'No, I'm, er, I'm borrowing this flat. From January. What's he been doing?' Lying somehow seemed the thing to do.

'Are you alone?'

'Of course. Look, just what's this all – '

'Silence. My little friend will become angry.'

Seeing that the big one was Brawn *and* Brains, presumably

the little one was just Stabber. I looked at him again. He was a smiling Stabber. He hadn't stopped since he came in.

'He doesn't look angry,' I said.

'No. Never. It means nothing. We will look around this apartment.' He spoke to his friend in quick Neapolitan, from which I gathered his friend didn't understand English. 'Let's see if he's in the other rooms.'

I did my best to register no comprehension. 'Listen, why d'you want to look around? I tell you, I'm alone. Why don't you believe me?' Then I added, a little tardily perhaps, 'And anyway, what right d'you think – '

'Shut up, mister. I tell you, my friend gets angry. *Vero, no? T'incazzi?*'

The little one nodded and smiled wider. Then he stepped around me and went into the kitchen. I waited for some sound of recognition – the knife thumping into flesh, a frying pan whamming on to a skull, perhaps even a 'Hello, how are you?'

There was silence. Then his voice, 'Gianni, *viene 'cca.*'

Gianni pushed me in front of him into the kitchen. The little man was waving his knife towards the open window. The table, which moments before had been full of clutter but had at least been neatly aligned along the wall, was now empty of clutter but was apparently trying to climb out of the window. The little man indicated a rather old but stout looking rope attached to the leg which seemed eagerest to escape. The rope, of course, went up and out of the window.

'Do I go after him?' the little man asked, still in Neapolitan.

'Well, see if he's anywhere around. If not, come back here.'

The little man looked towards the window as if trying to decide something. Gianni said, 'Go down by the stairs. We don't want to attract attention.' The little man nodded, with relief I was sure, and went out by the front door. He still hadn't put his knife away, I noticed.

Gianni now turned to me and said in English, 'No more lies.'

'And if I said that's my fire escape?'

'I laugh – ha ha ha.' The laugh was even higher pitched

than his conversational tone – rather like the laughing song from *Die Fledermaus*. 'Very funny. English sense of 'umour. Very good. Now where is the bastard?'

'I don't know. I told you I'm borrowing this flat from January Esposito. I'd never seen this other bloke before. He said he was January's brother and could he stay, so I said yes. Then you turned up. I don't even know where he got the rope from. Must have had it in his briefcase or something.' I noticed the case had gone. Presumably Gigi led the sort of life in which one never went house-visiting without the means of abseiling from the window when conversation got boring or embarrassing.

'Where's 'e gone?'

'I don't know,' I said. 'He didn't tell me anything. Just to keep you out.'

'You were not very – very capable, eh?'

'I'm not really used to this sort of stuff, you know. I'm a chartered accountant.' I wasn't quite sure why I added that.

'Give me somating to drink.'

'Please,' I added, but only under my breath. I went over to the sink and started to fill a glass, but he made a clucking noise with his tongue, opened the fridge and took a can of beer out. He went to the next room and sat in the armchair. I thought how easy it would be now just to run out of the front door and away to a new life. But, well, a psychiatrist might call it running away from things. And it was my flat. I stayed standing.

'Look,' I said, 'you've seen he's gone, whoever he is and whatever you want him for so, well, why don't you go too? If you go now I won't tell anybody about you, not the police nor anybody, and we'll just forget it all. All right?' I sounded like a new teacher desperate to be liked.

He didn't say anything, just sipped his beer. His left hand drummed on his knee. The door opened and the little man came in. He had his knife but not his smile out. '*Niente*,' he said.

'I guessed so,' Gianni said in Neapolitan. 'We'll just interrogate this one. But I don't think he knows anything.' He turned to me and said in English, 'Where is Gennaro – or January, 'ow you call 'im?'

'He's – he's on holiday. In Reykjavik.'

'Rek – ?'

'Iceland. What do you want him for?'

'We want to meet all friends and relatives of dear Luigino. Particularly relatives 'e goes to 'ide with.'

'How did you know about January?'

'We knew Gino 'ad a brother somewhere this way. 'Is girl told us. And there's only one Esposito in this part of London in the telephone book. Gino don't 'ave so many people to go to. 'E's small-time, you know? 'E made a big mistake when 'e mixed wid us.'

'You're, er, big-time?'

'Yes. I think Gigi didn't know 'ow big, you know? 'E's going to find out. 'E's finding out now. But we make the questions. So shutuppa.' Even clichés sounded sinister in his wheedling soprano.

'What questions? There's nothing else to say.' I was getting agitated because the little man had moved behind me, the last place I liked to have him, apart perhaps from at the bottom of my bed.

'Did 'e show you anyting?'

'Like what?'

'Like a cassetta. A recorded cassetta.'

'Shall I look around?' the little man butted in, in Neapolitan as always.

'I don't suppose he'll have left it behind,' Gianni said, 'but yes, go ahead.' Then, in English, 'Did 'e?'

'No. Why should he?' I felt slightly more at ease now the little man had moved away to look around. Then I heard him 'looking around'. Fifty books crashed to the ground. 'That's hardly bloody necessary,' I said. 'What's he doing?'

'Shutuppa,' Gianni said. 'Is that your coat?' He was pointing to the one Gigi had left by the armchair.

'Er, yes.' A little lie here and there gave me the feeling I was really putting myself out for my brother.

He picked it up and said to me, 'You're lying again. I've seen Gino wid this coat.'

'Oh.' Another fifty books went to the floor. I moved towards the little man. 'What the hell do you think you're doing?'

He saïd something rude to me which I did my best not to understand. 'Look, don't you speak English? Stop it.' Suddenly the knife was under my nose. At least there was no need to hide my comprehension of this. I moved away. Gianni said gently, 'Rafé, remember the neighbours.' He was going through the pockets of the coat. 'Too many *caramelle* – 'ow you say?'

'Caramels?'

'Sweets. Too many sweets Gigi eats.' By way of demonstration he dropped twenty or so sweet wrappers on the floor.

'At least he keeps the wrappers in his pocket,' I said.

'Ah,' he said, ''ere is somating.' He pulled out a small notepad. '*Vediamo*.' He flipped through it, but it was all empty. He stared hard at the top sheet which, as far as I could see, was as blank as every other sheet. 'Give me a pencil,' he said.

'Why?'

'Give me a pencil,' he repeated, without looking up.

I found one. He took it and started shading the paper with rapid light strokes. I realised that he must have seen the indentation of whatever had been written on the previous sheet and was now bringing it out. He stopped and stared. His left hand started drumming again. I could see faint white lines in the midst of the grey: it looked like a map.

'Radney,' he said. 'Radney is written 'ere. Where is it?'

'I don't know,' I said.

'Look at it.' He didn't let me take it but turned it for me to see. It was a very crudely drawn map and showed in approximate fashion the way to that empty house near a wood that Gigi had mentioned earlier in the evening. It showed the turning off the main road from Oxford to Radney – though

23

Oxford was not mentioned – and then the narrow lane that led off that minor road up to the house.

'I don't know, never heard of it,' I said again.

'Here are some cassettes,' the little man said behind me. He'd come across my not very extensive collection kept, for want of a better place, in a row under my bed.

'OK, look through them. It's a TDK, ninety minutes long.' He switched back to English and asked me, "Ave you a road map or an *atlante* anywhere?'

It was not worth lying so I said, 'I think there's a small atlas among those books. Er, the ones now on the floor.'

'Get it.'

'Look, why the hell should I?'

'Raffaele,' he said softly, like a mother lullabying her baby, and there was a prick at my neck which was presumably caused by Raffaele's knife which was presumably in Raffaele's hand, even though half a second before he'd been on the other side of the room.

I got the atlas. Gianni looked through it and Raffaele searched the cassettes, opening each box and dropping the cassettes on to the floor.

'Has your friend ever thought of getting a job cataloguing a library?' I asked Gianni.

'Shutuppa,' he said automatically, and went on studying the map.

After half a minute Raffaele said in Neapolitan, 'I've found five TDKs of ninety minutes. Shall we listen to them?'

'OK. Quickly. It's at the beginning of the first side so we only need to listen to a minute or so.'

Raffaele stabbed the EJECT button on my cassette machine, rather as if he took it for my belly. He put the first cassette in and closed it and stabbed the PLAY button. He looked a bit disappointed as the opening bars of a Strauss waltz sounded merrily around the room. Perhaps he'd expected blood.

He changed cassettes in the same, grievous-bodily-harmful way – perhaps even more so because I murmured 'Careful, please'. Beethoven's Pastoral Symphony filled the room. I

24

think I'd never heard the music with more wistful yearning. I don't know how it struck them. We then listened – in the same rather surreal fashion – to the opening bars of Verdi's Requiem, a Mozart piano concerto, and *Rheingold*. Even the fact that Gianni tapped his hand on his knee at one point didn't make the atmosphere that of a Victorian musical evening.

Raffaele switched off the Wagner and said, '*Niente*.' I expected him to rip the entrails out of the machine now, but he went over to my bedside table and started going through the drawer instead.

Gianni said, 'Here's Radney. Near Oxford. I'll look better on the maps in the car. We go there.'

'Have a good trip.'

'You come wid us.'

'Very kind and all that but – '

'Shutuppa. And stop talking like the cool *milord inglese*. I know you're shitting in your pants, so why pretend? Let's go.'

This was pretty wounding to my pride, unless I chose to be snobbishly flattered at his likening me to a milord, something nobody had ever thought of doing before: however, it – the pants-shitting – was so nearly the truth that I could merely react with impotent hatred.

He said in Neapolitan, 'Leave it, Raffaele. He's got the cassette with him. We're going to get him at his hide-out, or whatever it is.' Gianni showed him the map. 'He must have had this for a reason. It's a good chance, anyway. We'll take this one with us. Otherwise he'll talk.' He put the map into his pocket.

I had to take some action and quickly. My eyes flickered around for a possible weapon. But then suddenly I was pinioned with my arms behind my back by Raffaele.

'I'll get the rope,' Gianni said.

Half a minute later my wrists were tied tightly, still behind my back. Gianni then frisked me to check I was carrying no weapon. He found nothing but bus tickets, which he added to the sweet wrappers and other débris on the floor. The room

25

hadn't been exactly tidy before, but one could see that these two had called all the same.

Now, if I remembered rightly from films, the correct thing to do in this situation was to possess myself secretly of a piece of broken glass or a sharp stone or a dagger of oriental design.

Strangely enough, the one destructive action Raffaele hadn't committed so far was to break a glass – or reduce any of the walls to sharp-edged rubble for that matter. He'd thrown the books and cassettes around; he'd kicked the beer cans . . . The beer cans. And their ring openers.

I'd cut myself on a ring opener about a month previously.

Gianni was telling Raffaele to go down and check the street out. They had a shy reluctance, it seemed, to be observed escorting me into their car. As Gianni gave his orders I picked out on the floor the ideal ring top, its metal tongue curled beckoningly towards me. I gazed.

Raffaele went on down the stairs.

Somehow I had to get down on to the ground next to that treasure. Could I convincingly faint, overcome by terror?

No.

Well, would a 'Whoopsadaisy' and an Oliver Hardy skid and thump carry conviction? Damn it, why hadn't I – or they – eaten any bananas that evening?

Gianni was coming over to me.

No. Whatever I did had to seem caused by him, not me.

'Why the bloody hell should I go with you?' I said, not moving. I measured the distance to the ring.

Gianni seemed to consider recourse to his usual method of overcoming my reluctance – a quick summons of Raffaele and knife – but then said, 'Shutuppa and move.' He gave me a slight push with one hand.

'No,' I said and stayed firm. My heart was thumping hard again as I thought of all the possible nasty things he might do or have done to me, whether with Raffaele's help or not.

'You bastard. Move-a.' This time he really whammed me with his shoulder; I pitched towards the ground giving an entirely unfaked yell as I did so. I hadn't thought what having my hands tied would mean in a fall. I saw the floor curving up to smash my unprotected face. I twisted so that my shoulder bore all the brunt that my knee couldn't. And it was some brunt. When I'd stopped juddering I could hear that the room hadn't yet. Bottles and plates vibrated like a soprano on a long note. All the same I'd been fairly lucky and missed the nastier objects, crushing just a few Frederik Pohls and an Edmund Cooper under my ribs.

At least I could be sure it had looked convincing.

The effect of my entirely unplanned mid-fall twisting was of course that my hands were in groping reach of the ring. Indeed, as his foot whammed into my stomach, my fingers touched on a satisfyingly jagged corner, and then closed on it.

'Get uppa.'

I managed to roll over and then jerk myself up to a cross-legged sitting position. 'Er, it's not so easy,' I said. I was sure that as a healthy person in my twenties I ought to have been able to, but at that moment it seemed as unlikely a feat as those triple mid-air somersaults Eastern European acrobats go in for. Mostly, of course, my attention was concentrated on shoving the ring into my trouser waistband.

He hoisted me up with his hands under my armpits. I almost said 'Thanks'. I had managed to lodge the ring just under the waistband so my hands were innocently empty.

We moved to the door and he waited until he heard Raffaele from the bottom of the stairs say, 'OK.' Then he pulled a handkerchief from his pocket and shoved it into my mouth.

'If that 'ankerchief moves, I push you. OK?'

That was a very nasty thought, and I descended the stairs briskly in silence, dreading at any moment the sensation of his fingers – or foot – in my back. The tongue of the ring dug into my right buttock at every other step. I trusted it was not visible through the jeans. These preoccupations at least kept me from wondering too much about the state of the handkerchief I was half choking on. I could hear the television in my neighbours' flat as we passed. It sounded, from the gunfire, like a war film: *The Guns of Navarone*, *The Wild Bunch*, or something similarly cosy.

Raffaele was at the front door, peering into the street like a nervous bank clerk on the lookout for the manager. Except – again – for that knife. Still there in his right hand.

'Let's go,' he said in Neapolitan. ('*Jamme*' – one short decisive-sounding word.)

I was prodded into the street. There had to be some law-abiding Dulwich citizen on the way home from a party or the theatre, surely – with all there is to do in London, surely . . . There wasn't.

Their car was about ten yards down the road with the doors – front and back – already welcomingly open. Presumably Raffaele's work. I didn't notice what make it was. I hardly ever do. It was just a car, a bloody car, about to take me off to Radney or Naples or a convenient ditch. I was pushed into the back. I settled myself on the seat as comfortably as my trussed arms allowed me – that is to say, in a posture one could imagine recommended as an exercise by a particularly sadistic finishing school – and spat the handkerchief out. But then Gianni leant in and shoved me. 'Down. On the floor. Stay there.'

The next moment I was kissing, pope-like, the dust of the floor. Owing to lack of space my body was jack-knifed, with all the boniest parts taking the strain. And people make love in cars, I thought rather oddly.

I heard them get in and slam the door.

'If you make one move to get up, you're dead,' Gianni said from the driving seat. He translated this for Raffaele who said, more or less, 'You bet', and smiled. At least I imagine he did.

I twisted on to my side so that I could breathe something other than cigarette ash.

'Do we call on the Salisbury first?' Raffaele asked. The hotel name (as I presumed it to be) was Italianised – or Neapolitanised – in his pronunciation to Saleezebooree.

'No. What do we want to do that for? We'll go straight to this Radney place and hope to get him asleep.'

'All right by me.'

They then started a discussion of the route to take, studying a road map. I only half took in this conversation. My attention was on other things. I'd started the ring retrieval operation as quietly as possible. As I turned I'd realised the thing was now attacking the flesh at the *bottom* of my left buttock – much further than my hands could reach. It had somehow got inside my underpants. This was just not fair, I thought. Not bloody fair. I could have cried.

I rubbed my buttocks against the bottom of the seat and felt it move slightly. Slightly. I pushed again and then arched my legs to make a space between the trousers, underpants and the flesh, and to allow the force of gravity to work. For some seconds my mind, my will, my soul – everything – were concentrated on an area of about four square inches at the top of my right leg. Indeed, I *was* my right buttock.

Then I felt the thing tickle down in the direction of the small of my back. My fingers closed on it like piranhas.

I realised, as I breathed a sigh of relief and took cognisance of the rest of my body again, that I was sweating all over – in every part of the body that possessed pores, from the little toe to the ear lobes. Indeed, this had no doubt aided the operation vitally, lubricating the slopes. I bent the tongue of the ring back and forth until it snapped, providing a reasonably sharp edge. It struck me now that my relief was perhaps a little exaggerated; I was reacting as if it were all over and it just remained for me to get out and call the police. I was going to feel pretty silly if it turned out I couldn't even reach the rope with the ring.

And I couldn't.

I bent and twisted my wrists in all directions with the ring held by one extremity between index finger and thumb – and then finally, with my right hand crooked at an impossible angle, I felt the ring touch something which could only be the rope.

At this moment the car engine started and we moved off. I started sawing. I didn't expect quick results, but trusted that persistence would pay off. The engine covered any noise.

During the first few minutes of the drive Gianni and Raffaele spoke only to decide on directions to take, Raffaele map-reading, presumably with a torch. I had vaguely taken in that we were making for the A41, wherever that was.

After some minutes Raffaele said, 'Do we take him all the way to this Radney place?'

'No, of course not. When we get out to the country I'll choose a side-road and you can finish him off. But outside the car. Remember it's rented.'

Three

So many complain about the impossibility of getting out to the country from London. Suddenly I found myself wishing I lived somewhere really attractive like Limehouse – or the Tower of London. Who wants trees?

Then I thought of something slightly reassuring. They were wanting to go in the direction of Oxford, which of course meant crossing or circling London. This gave me half an hour or so before we reached anything like countryside. More, if we found a really nice accident or traffic jam.

The way I'd twisted my wrists, the rope was cutting more into them, I felt, than the ring into the rope. And my stretched fingers ached with their minute but lacerating task. There was nothing to do but grit my teeth and keep at it. I could already sense the roughening of one twine. By the time we reached Radney I might have got through it. One twine, that is . . .

I kept at it. I usually like to do such repetitive mindless tasks to the accompaniment of some light music – Strauss waltzes or Beatles songs. Here, however, the situation provided its own accompaniment of terror. Every time the car pulled up at a traffic lights or crossroads or whatever, my heart missed a beat which my teeth provided. And as a permanent *sottofondo* I felt pain – and this in steady *crescendo* too. Once more my whole being became concentrated in one minuscule part of the body, and it was not a nice place to be. I imagined the *wrists* fraying away, layer by bloody layer, and then the hands dropping off, clasped in an attitude of fervent gratitude for their release.

I noticed after half an hour or so that things had changed outside; there was no longer the gentle stroboscopic effect of light, dark, light, dark. It was universally dark. We were in the country. I could still hear other cars, though.

At the same time I realised there was a definite frayed point in the rope. I kept at it – the same boring biting bleeding task.

I strained my hands and they suddenly jerked apart. I lay completely still for a few seconds allowing the ring to fall from my fingers. I then worked the rope off both wrists. The hands did not drop off with it, but I imagined the rope was rosily bedecked with a few soft souvenirs of its lodging place.

Now, whatever I did, I must not arouse suspicion. I had two advantages. They didn't know that I knew that when they stopped I was to be killed (though I suppose they didn't think that I would think it would be for a picnic). And my hands, though bloodied (in parts), were unbound. I had to make sure I made the best of both of these advantages.

The car turned off on to a bumpier road. After a few seconds there was only our engine to be heard – and my heart. Then the car and engine stopped. My heart almost did too. I didn't move.

They sat quite still for a few moments, no doubt checking the loneliness of our position. Then Gianni said, '*Vai.*'

I was lying with my head on Raffaele's side of the car. The light went on as he opened his door. He was presumably then going to open my door and pull me out by my head until my throat was far enough out of the car for there to be no risk of bloodying the upholstery. This could be done in quite a short space of time. My best chance lay in immediate action.

I jerked up and round so I was facing the door. I was going to wham it into him. Gianni said, 'Keep still', but didn't turn round, secure in the knowledge that I could offer no real resistance, and perhaps not wishing to see his colleague at work.

I grabbed at the door opener – and the window opened a fraction. If there's one thing that really irritates me about cars it's the way every model has to have its new gimmicky way of doing things: seatbelts you undo by turning on the radio, doors you open by pulling at the seatbelt . . . Why the hell a simple door handle, perhaps made of brass, can't be universally accepted on all models, I'll never understand.

I stared desperately, trying to work out where the opening mechanism was. In a usual situation (with good daylight and the book of instructions) it would take me no longer than a minute or so to solve the problem, but here things were different. I was convinced I was going to lose the effect of surprise. Gianni had realised something was wrong and was turning round, and Raffaele seemed to have halted outside.

Then Gianni, no doubt on seeing the situation, shouted, '*Presto!*'

This was perfect. Raffaele had been on the point of backing away but at this he reached for the door handle; as he opened it I shoved with both hands. He staggered back, missed his footing and then fell.

I scrambled out and ran – naturally enough in the opposite direction to which the car was pointing. Footsteps started up immediately behind me.

There was almost complete darkness. I could just make out the thick blackness of the hedges on either side against the more diluted blackness of the sky. The road was uneven and I could only pray I didn't trip or twist my ankle.

I heard the car engine start up, and I glanced behind me. I had one confusing glimpse of the car headlights thrown across the road as the car performed a wild hedge-tearing turn. Raffaele seemed to have given up running.

Two seconds later, something in what I'd seen but hadn't quite registered made me turn again.

This time it registered. Raffaele, now silhouetted against the direct glare of the headlights, had stopped running in order to take double-handed aim with a gun. The BANG sounded in my ears as I flew through the air to the side of the road.

I pulled myself to my feet, reasonably whole and free of bullet wounds, and started running crouched along the side of the hedge. I made less of a target that way, I imagined.

The car was suddenly very loud and the hedge was alive with light and shadows – I had acquired a shadow myself and it was becoming rapidly denser. The car was almost upon me.

A gate appeared like a gift from heaven. I was approaching it sideways and I trusted that even so I'd manage to do something I'd almost invariably failed to do on previous less urgent occasions – vault it.

I picked myself up from next to a cowpat and realised I'd done it. The gun went off behind me, and almost contemporaneously I heard the car smashing into the gate. And thirty seconds earlier they'd been worried about a few drops of blood on the seats.

On the other side of the field was a wood. If I reached that . . . Well, they'd be too scared of the bogies to come in after me, wouldn't they?

I was, it seemed, slightly fitter than both of them, and by the time I reached the first trees – gasping, choking, clutching one side – the gap between us had widened satisfactorily.

Something one tends to forget in situations like this is that when one talks of going for a walk – or a run – in a wood, one invariably means along a path. Most of an English wood is filled between the trees with brambles, nettles, and other vicious vegetation. This is what I now found myself fighting. Perhaps the darkness helped; I'm sure if I had been able to see the under- and overgrowth that I'd taken on I'd have given up. But somehow I made progress, even though I left a good deal of myself on the way.

Eventually I felt that I was deep enough in to stop and listen. They were running around the edge of the wood, obviously hoping to catch a glimpse of me. I'd been making a fair deal of noise, but this had clearly been difficult for them to locate, what with the fluttering and scuttering of various unnamed beasties that I'd stirred along my route. Now silence returned. Even Gianni and Raffaele seemed to stop their prowling. Pins and needles crept into my left leg. I didn't move.

This complete silence lasted two minutes at least, during which I felt the whole wood begin to gang up on me. Something that wasn't a pin or a needle crawled with far more legs than can have been necessary up my right calf. My sweat-soaked shirt began to feel very cold and clammy. And my dear old wrists reminded me of their presence.

Then I heard Gianni's voice. 'We'll have to go in after him. Or at least one of us will. I'll go round and see if I can catch him on the other side of this wood.'

I wondered if this could be a trick, but then remembered that Gianni didn't know I could understand him.

'So I go in after him.' Raffaele didn't sound all that happy. It was either the brambles or the bogies that were worrying him. I was sure it couldn't be me. I felt like shouting at Raffaele to tell his boss to muss up *his* suit for once.

Then I heard Raffaele crawling into the undergrowth, and Gianni walking quickly along the side of the wood. Raffaele sounded about twenty feet or so away, and there was no chance of his seeing me. I waited until it sounded as if he were fairly well into the wood before I moved. I swept all creepy crawlies off me, stamped my left foot twice and then turned and went back the way I'd come. The going was slightly easier as I'd thrashed out a sort of path, but there were still quite a few nasty invisible things around to clutch and tear at me like fans at a pop concert.

Raffaele could no doubt hear me but probably didn't guess that I was going back to the field. When I peered out into the open, Gianni was nowhere to be seen. I scrambled out and ran across the field back to the gate. I reached it entirely unpursued.

The front of the car was rather mixed up with the gate, but not cripplingly so. Of course, the obvious thing now was for me to get into the car and roar away to freedom. There was just one snag. I can't drive.

Unbelievable. Absurd. Everybody can. It's like not being able to walk or talk. Yes, yes. Well, I've never learnt.

I'd returned to the car in order to put it out of action, so that I had some chance of getting to my brother before they did. Equal chance, in fact. I'd really have liked to set about it with a pick-axe, but it looked as if the car didn't carry one. I stared at the enormous machine. Immobilising it had seemed such an obvious, easy course of action as I ran across the field, but now I'd reached the bloody thing and had only my bare hands (and perhaps one beer can ring top) I felt a bit stumped. There was almost certainly some undramatic method with wires and things – the mechanical equivalent of Mr Spock's flooring people by pressing two fingers on the back of their necks – but I knew that such subtle fiddling was not really my thing. I hadn't even been able to open the door, after all. No, something simple and savage – and deeply satisfying. Why *wasn't* there a pick-axe?

I thought of the way that cars chucked over cliffs in films always burst into flames. The countryside here offered few cliffs, but flames must be available.

Yes, the car was equipped with a cigarette lighter. And one that didn't require a degree in engineering to operate for a change; just a matter of turning the ignition on. I took the keys out of the dashboard and opened the boot. There was a full can of petrol there. I found out how to open the bonnet (a button under the dashboard) rather more easily than I'd found out how to open the door earlier on. I opened it, and then splashed the petrol over the engine. That would warm it nicely, ready for frying. I stood back, then realised I'd been rather parsimonious, treating it as if it were expensive olive oil going on to a salad. I sploshed some more on.

The cigarette lighter worked first time and I used some pages from a London A to Z as a spill. An orange flame tore rapidly through the northern suburbs of London. I scrambled out and chucked a flaring Ponders End into the bonnet, and turned and ran. There was a noisy WHOOSH behind me and the lane shook with white and orange light. I didn't allow myself the luxury of looking round yet, but kept running. When I reached a bend in the road I glanced back: it had settled down, after its one moment of Cecil B. De Mille spectacle in glorious Technicolor, to a steady pulsing bonfire – not too flashy, but determinedly destructive all the same.

My exultation calmed to a more sober satisfaction which, I suppose, was right. After all, I wasn't a mindless vandal, was I?

Was I? I mean, even if I had found it the teensy-weensiest bit amusing, they had tried to kill me, hadn't they? So what the hell. I ran on into the darkness.

I kept to the road as being the easiest terrain to cover and the most likely to take me somewhere useful. After five minutes and the onset of a stitch, I slowed down to a brisk side-clutching walk. I'd guessed they would probably decide to return to the main road, so I'd chosen to run in the opposite direction, hoping it would eventually take me to a land flowing with milk and honey and all-night trains. It was most likely, I felt, to end in some tiny village. Still, I might be able to pick up some means of transport in some way or other. I'd think about the way or other when the problem arose.

Now I had other things on my mind. I began to apply my mind fully to all those questions that I'd had to relegate to second place so far. Like, who were they and what did they want and what had my brother been up to? All of which could only be answered with the vaguest guesses – apart from the first, to which the answer was very short and simple. But big-time ones, it seemed, while my brother was only a small-time one, if one at all.

Well, whatever he was, he was clearly 'mixed in a funny business', to use my father's mildest phrase when talking about Gigi. So I wouldn't go to the police until I'd heard his explanation – hoping, that is, that I got there in time to ensure him the possibility of giving me one. Stopped him getting his head blown off. We might not be the closest of brothers, but I wasn't going to be the means of his finishing up in a coffin or jail.

Not that I thought he could have done anything really, *really* bad. I mean, he was small time, wasn't he?

The road went up and down and round and about, rather like my thoughts, and apparently with as little prospect of any conclusion. On the side of the roads, fields gave way to woods, then fields again, with no sign of a building anywhere. The hedges and trees, as is usual in the dark, all looked as if they concealed knife-clutching maniacs, but having had to deal with knife-clutching non-maniacs, I didn't let it trouble me too much. I was more bothered by a wind that was plastering my wet shirt on to my back and letting me know just how cold a spring night can be in England. Added to which I was aching in a hundred parts of the body with a hundred different kinds of ache. All it needed to do now was . . .

And on cue it started raining.

Well, it would clean me up a little, I thought, desperately seeking a bright side to look on.

Another bright side struck me. It was several hours since I'd last depressed myself by thinking of Valerie. I clearly ought to have more of this life-style – it was as good as the foreign legion.

But now, of course, I'd let her slip into my mind and, as usual, hundreds of happy memories slunk in craftily after her, each one a tiny idyllic snapshot of sunny moments together, carefully composed to contrast in the most depressing way possible with the lonely, rainy present: the pair of us together in a pub garden, in the zoo, at her flat, in Hyde Park, in a rowing boat . . .

Hang on, I thought. We've never been in a boat together. The image had tried to pass itself off with all the other olde worlde golden-hazed moments on the grounds of artistic rightness. It was clear that my memory was turning itself into a gallery of David Hamilton-like gooey pictures with very little relation to the actual facts. I mean, could I really imagine Valerie in a rowing boat? It had always taken long enough to persuade her to get on to a moving staircase.

Then imagine her reaction to an account of the events of the evening. Screams of horror and fright, which, while momentarily flattering to one's swaggering He Man image, always ended by irritating.

I realised there was something white on the side of the road ahead. A signpost. Indeed, the name of a village.

THRUBTON NEMPWELL.

The road went round a bend and I saw the first houses, all modern red brick cubes with white porches. So what did I do now? Wake some Thrubton Nempwellian and order him to drive sixty miles across country at once? Or phone for a taxi?

Clearly nobody was awake in any of these houses. It was gone two thirty, after all. I noticed, leaning against the side of one, a bicycle. Unchained, unpadlocked, and with its lights fixed.

My ethical debate did not last long and, half a minute later, I was whizzing through the village imagining the conversation in the post office the next day: 'Can't even leave anything out here in Thrubton'; 'My Dad always said as how they never even had to lock the front door when he was a nipper.'

Obviously I was not going to get all the way to Radney on the bike, but it would at least get me quite quickly to the main road and the possibility of a lift. It was in perfect working order, and for the first minute or so I enjoyed it . . . The wind and rain became momentarily part of the general invigorating sense of movement, and not just nature out to get me. And it was a relief to be able to see the road ahead of me even if the shadows of the trees were pretty sinister in the way they all swirled round to get up to who-knew-what behind me.

About twenty minutes later I came to a wider road, which had a sign for Aylesbury. I left the bicycle in a ditch with a vague – very vague – idea that one day I might come back and restore it to the anxious villagers of Thrubton Nempwell, and I started walking. It's difficult to be taken seriously as a hitchhiker if you're on a bike.

I started feeling cold again – cold and wet and not all that cheerful. The thought that I might be picked up by Raffaele and Gianni in a hijacked car I decided to ignore until it happened. Thinking too much about the possibility would only depress me, and it wasn't as if I had any alternative. Cars and lorries passed at odd intervals. They occasionally hooted but they did not stop. I suppose I was a pretty odd figure at that time of night, under a steady drizzle with mud-bespattered torn clothes. It was after three thirty when a lorry hooted; I was about to make a rude gesture when I saw that it was pulling up.

I ran – squelch squelch.

The driver leant over and opened the passenger door. 'Get on in,' he said. 'Banbury all right?'

'Great. Th-thanks.' My teeth were chattering.

'What's wiv you then?' He was a very thin man with a high-pitched cockney voice. I'd never seen a thin lorry driver before. 'Lost your wi?'

'Er, yeah. Er, no. I missed my bus. So I started walking.'

'Where from? Land's End?'

'Feels like it.'

'Looks like it an' all. 'Ere, I've got a spare pullover you can put on instead of vat one. Can't do nuffink about the trousers though, mate.'

'That's really very kind.' I found the pullover behind the seat and took off my pullover and shirt together.

'Me missis always kits me out like I was goin' to the Norf Pole. Don't worry about it. I'll turn the 'eating on. 'Ave a bit of chocolate.'

I accepted that gratefully too. It was good to feel dry in at least one part of my body, and the heating was having its effect on the bottom part as well.

'You a student?'

'No.'

'Oh, I fought what wiv you going this way. Well, you see I was going to Oxford once and I picked up this bloke, green and pink hair, razor blade in 'is ear – you know, the lot – and 'e wanted to go to Oxford. I fought, Cowley or round there like. But no, to the bleedin' university. I said, they let blokes like you in then? and 'e said 'e was professor of history. Bleeding professor, know whar mean?'

'Yes.'

'Anuvver time, picked up a bloke, middle of August, carrying a pair of skis you know? an' 'e . . .'

I wasn't required to make much conversation. I was given what seemed like a complete list of his passengers to date. After a few minutes I was too drowsy to take in what he was saying. The last passenger I remember was one who had told him that he was the Ayatollah Khomeini's younger brother and I agreed that this seemed unlikely. No doubt his next passenger would be told of 'this bloke, pissin' down wiv rain, cloves all torn, idiot expression like . . .'

It was getting on for five when I recognised the turning off for Radney. I asked to be put down and the driver said, 'You sure mate?' almost as if he thought I might just be trying to get away from his conversation.

'Yes. I live near here.'

'Oh. Just fought, you know, you'd got lost already . . .'Ere, keep that pullover.'

'Thanks, but I couldn't.'

'Ah, go on. I don't need it.'

'Well, thanks. I mean thanks a lot. Um, keep mine. Not a fair swop, I know.' Mine was half-way to becoming a scarf.

'Don't worry about that.' He pulled up. 'You're lucky it's stopped raining. See yer.'

'Yes. Thanks again. You've been really kind. 'Bye.'

I climbed out. I had about half an hour's walk before I got to that empty house near the woods where my brother was probably hiding. The quickest way was certainly across the fields. It was also the wettest and the easiest to get lost in but, given the possibility of Gianni's and Raffaele's arrival, it was perhaps the safest for all that. And I did know these fields fairly well. Or used to.

I climbed the nearest gate and set squelchily off. I wondered what had brought this empty house to my brother's mind. It was an ancient cottage with only half a roof and rotten floors and it stood (well, more or less stood) at the bottom of a wooded hill a couple of miles from Radney. Gigi and Pasquale and various other friends of his used to go there to smoke cigarettes and talk about sex and generally be Men. I, who had only left Radney six months before, hadn't been there for two years or more, and Gigi can't have been for about fifteen. So it was an odd place to choose as a hide-out, however temporary. There must be more comfortable ones. Maybe he'd been reading Christopher Robin recently.

I reached the foot of the hill on the other side of which was the empty house. I could either go round it or cut up and over. In terms of distance the up and over route was obviously much shorter, but it was through a wood, and even though I had played Red Indians and Space Monsters in every square inch of it, I felt I'd had enough of woods in the dark.

Then I heard a car driving down the road towards Radney. Of course it could have been anybody but, well, it reminded me of the urgency of the situation. I entered the wood and was instantly dripped on by every bud, twig, and branch. It was as if they'd been waiting for me.

I took a path I remembered fairly well, but nonetheless had to grope every inch of it. The ground was slightly less soaking than the fields had been, but the busily dripping trees were doing their best to remedy that.

I remembered how, as a child, I'd secretly followed Gigi on his way through these woods to those meetings in the empty house that intrigued me so much, and how more than once I'd found him unexpectedly waiting round a tree to clobber me and send me crying home. I'd seen him play the same trick with a yobbo from a nearby village too; one moment the yob was chasing an apparently terrified and fleeing Gigi, and then suddenly he realised he'd been led into a trap as Gigi – and Pasquale who appeared suddenly – let fly with a catapult and a store of apples placed there for that purpose.

Yes, he'd waited for me behind this very tree, I remembered, slapping the trunk affectionately.

And I stopped and thought hard. The wood dripped on me and around me with a sound of persistent and sinister gossip.

I took a path that went off to the left and moved more quickly. If the car I'd heard had contained Gianni and Raffaele, by now they'd have reached the entrance to the track that led towards the old house and would be bumping along it. Then they'd reach the gate up to the house. And there . . .

Yes, that was where I had to make for. If I was remembering correctly, this path would bring me to where the footpath ended on the crest of the hill just above that gate. I was now running in a low bent position, my arms out before me to protect my face from the savager trees. The path began to climb more steeply and at points was slippery. Soon I was scrabbling on all fours, grabbing at roots and branches to pull myself up. Occasionally they came away in my hands and I fell back, knees and shoes slithering through leafy mush.

Above and ahead of me, shifting patches of grey broke the blackness. The sky was trying out the effect of a little light. A bird twittered tentatively somewhere to my right, another one took it up, the first one repeated it more confidently and suddenly they were all at it; they may have thought I was a talent scout from a BBC wildlife programme.

But their ululatory exhibitionism did not cover the noise of a car being driven slowly – presumably along the bumpy track.

I came out of the wood into the grey half-light. I'd gone wrong somewhere and the gate was some fifty feet to my right. The car, however, was almost directly below me, its headlights off. The ground dropped steeply in front of me. As I watched, it came to a halt and the engine died. Presumably they didn't want to risk being overheard, even though their map must have told them they were almost a quarter of a mile from the house.

I stepped back in among the trees and watched as Gianni got out of the side nearest to me. Then Raffaele got out of the other side. They looked around and started walking towards the gate. The birds twittered on. And the trees dripped on.

I knew I had to get to the point above the gate as quickly as possible, but I couldn't risk running along outside the wood, so it was not easy. I found myself forced to take paths that led back into the depths of the wood. At least there was more light now so I could move faster.

Then to my left I saw my brother. He was lying at the edge of the wood between two trees and he was looking down the hill. I was seeing him from behind and it was difficult at first to make out what he was holding. I approached as Mohicanlike as possible from an oblique angle and I saw the rifle. His chin was resting on a brown cushion. He was wearing a thick green anorak and there was a black waterproof sheet under him. To his right I saw a thermos and a tupperware sandwich box. He was clearly well prepared.

He raised the rifle and stared down the sights.

'No!' I cried and dived forward, knocking the gun to one side.

Gigi's face was a collection of amazed circles for one second and then he pulled the gun from my grasp and jerked his elbow up into my face so that I fell back into a clump of nettles. 'You stupid bugger,' I heard him say.

When I sat up I saw him aiming again. This time I kicked at the barrel and sent it swivelling to one side. It went off and birds flew up in every direction, protesting noisily at this vulgar interruption.

Gigi's face was furious as he prepared to fire again. I glanced down the hill and saw Raffaele and Gianni staring wildly around, each with a gun in his hand. They didn't shelter behind the car, presumably because they didn't know where the shot had come from.

I pulled at Gigi's shoulder, saying, 'Come on, let's run.' Gigi's gun went off again, but uselessly.

Another shot sounded and Gigi let out a sharp cry and dropped the gun. It slithered some feet down the hill. I pulled Gigi so that he rolled over into the cover of the trees. His face was twisted in either pain or hate – perhaps both.

'Come on,' I said, 'come on – come on!'

He got to his feet and clutched at his right shoulder. There was a nasty red mess there. I pulled at him again, as I could see through a gap in the trees Gianni and Raffaele scrambling up the hill towards us.

We started running. After a few yards Gigi said, 'The box!' and seemed on the point of returning for it, but I pulled at him again. Was he really going to risk his life for a few sandwiches?

We kept running to the left, in the direction of the old

house. As we ran, conflicting feelings went through me; on the one hand I felt stupid and guilty, on the other I repeated to myself that I couldn't just let Gigi murder people, even if those people were Raffaele and Gianni. I hoped Gigi's wound wasn't serious because otherwise I knew the feeling of guilt was going to win. Things wouldn't be helped if he got killed now, either. Nor if I got killed, come to think of it.

At a certain point Gigi gasped out, 'Down there,' and took his left hand momentarily from his right shoulder to indicate a path off to the right. I took it without asking why. We could hear Gianni and Raffaele as they entered the wood behind us.

After a few steps Gigi said, 'Stop. Look under there,' pointing to an innocent patch of undergrowth. I bent down and touched metal. I pulled out another rifle. 'Hell, you're ready for anything,' I said.

'Except you. Shut up and fire it.'

'I don't know how.'

'Don't be dumb. It's ready. Just pull the bloody trigger.'

I couldn't see Gianni or Raffaele, could just hear them approaching.

'Go on. You know what the trigger is, don't you?'

I pulled it. As the shot died away and the birds made their formal protests, I heard Gianni's and Raffaele's footsteps falter, then halt.

'All right,' Gigi said. 'Just let 'em know we've got it. Let's go.'

We had the advantage of knowing this wood well and this, added to the fact that their pursuit now lost a little of its eagerness, helped us greatly. We were soon running across an open field beyond which was a lane with Gigi's car.

'You'd better drive,' Gigi said when we reached the car.

'Er, sorry, but I don't know how to.'

'You're a bloody marvel, in yer. Jesus.' He got into the driving seat. 'All right. Chuck the rifle under the back seat. Let's get away and then have a look at this bloody arm.'

We drove off in silence. When we'd put a sufficient tangle of lanes and minor roads between us and them, Gigi pulled up at the gate of a field. There was nobody around. 'You'd better do somefing to my arm. If you can, that is.'

The wounded shoulder was on the other side from me, so I got out and walked round to his side. I thought for one horrible moment that the shoulder was oozing out pus, but then realised it was the stuffing of the anorak bulging out. There was quite a nasty red patch beneath this.

'Can you, er, get the coat off, or do you want me to cut it off?'

He gritted his teeth and then squirmed out of it. He pushed his pullover and shirt off the shoulder, beyond the wound. It was a nasty mess, with bits of the pullover and shirt stuck in the blood, but perhaps not as serious as it looked. The bullet had clearly passed on.

'You've been grazed – well, a bit more than grazed, I suppose. It should be stitched, I reckon, but I'll do what I can now. You should be all right. Have you got a first aid box?'

'In the boot.'

I cleaned it up and bandaged it. Still Gigi remained silent – not an 'ouch' nor even a sharp intake of breath. That would have been sissy. (I bet he'd been tattooed on the other arm or somewhere.) When I'd finished he sat back and said, 'And now mate, fanks. Fanks for everyfing. You've been bloody great. Just what I needed.'

'You didn't think I was going to let you murder them? In cold blood?'

'What's it to you? They're bleedin' murderers themselves anyway.'

'Yes, but . . . Look, you can't just go around . . . Oh hell, I mean . . .'

'It's me or them, mate. And it looks like it'll be me now, fanks to you.'

'Go to the police,' I said rather hopelessly.

'Ah piss off. What d'you come for anyway? Just when I got everyfing just right.'

'You'd prepared it all, hadn't you? Every step of the way.

46

You knew they'd come to my house, they'd find that map . . . Hell, you'd gone to some trouble.'

He looked almost pleased with himself for a second. 'Yeah, well, you don't get nowhere if you don't make the others play the game like you want it.'

I could only admire his cunning. The notepad part struck me particularly; that was a really professional detail, as there's no surer way to fool someone than by making him think himself very clever. I remembered the pleased expression on Gianni's face as he carefully shaded the pad with his pencil. This clearly had been the riskiest part of the plan, in that there was always the possibility that Gianni might not have noticed the indentations on the pad, but anything more obvious in the pocket would have been suspicious. Gigi had judged perfectly, and thus brought them to the perfect trap – a lonely place where there was no risk of witnesses and where he could have them surely in the sights of his gun as they clambered over the gate.

But my admiration didn't make me forget my grievances. 'You ask me why I came along. Well, why d'you bring me into the business anyway? Why'd it got to be me you went to see? You know they were going to kill me.'

'I hadn't fought of that. D'you mean it?' He really did look dismayed.

'Course I do. It was just lucky I understood them. They didn't guess I was your brother so they were talking away in dialect in front of me. But, hell, it was a near thing.'

'Sorry about that. I thought they'd just, you know, tie you up or somefing.'

'Or something. Great. Well, thank you, Gigi.'

'Ah, shit, I'd got to be some place someone could cover me while I scarpered, hadn't I? And I'd got to have someone who knew where Radney was.'

'Oh, so you thought I'd say, "Oh yes, you'll find him in this little house here, take the number 10 bus and give him one for me."'

'No, but you know, you might let somefing out. And they'd

believe in me pissing off to Radney a bit more if they saw me, you know, going to me bruvver when I was on the run. You know, they'd fink I was turning to the family in me hour of need. So a hide-out near Radney was likely like.'

'But they didn't even know you were from Radney.'

'Oh, bloody 'ell. Jean was supposed to let out somefing about that. When she told 'em about me bruvver – you.'

'You mean, you'd got a whole chain of people they had to follow. Kind of complicated, wasn't it? And why couldn't you let me know what you were up to? I could have played along.'

'Well, didn't fink you'd like it much.'

'Yes, well, I don't say you were completely wrong there.'

'See? And anyway, people act better when they don't know they're acting, if you see what I mean. And they had to believe I was running scared. You know, from one place to another, desperate like. It makes people more careless – like you saw. If it hadn't been for you, I'd have had them, no sweat. And anyway, what are you complaining about? They didn't kill you, did they?'

'No, but I'm not too well, thank you. Who are they anyway?'

'Oh, you know, blokes.'

'Big time, they said. And you're small time.'

Gigi laughed – a quite genuine amused laugh. 'Real big time. Big bloody Ben.' His laugh became almost a snigger. 'And I'm just a flowerpot man.' He started the engine. 'Come on, let's go.'

'Yes, you'd better get to a doctor or something. Let's go into Oxford.'

'Nah. I'm going back there.' We drove off.

'Hell, why? D'you think you'll find them there?'

'No, course not. I aint stupid. And I don't go in for OK Corral shoot-outs. That's for amateurs. When I go for me bloke I play it safe.'

'You do this sort of thing often?' I was really quite shocked.

'Course not. I'm not a bleedin' hitman. Just, you know . . . Oh shit, you don't know nuffing about me, nuffing about them – you don't know much about anyfing when I come to fink about it – so what's the point? Just you mind your business, I'll mind mine, know wharmean?'

'So why *are* we going back?' I said after a pause.

'That bloody box. Jesus, I just hope they left it.'

'You that hungry?'

'It's got the bloody cassette in it.'

'Ah. The cassette.'

'Yeah. Don't ask me about it cos I'm not gonna tell you. All right?'

'Not really. But if that's your attitude.'

'It is, mate.'

We returned without further discussion to the previous parking place and cautiously crossed the field and entered the wood. Despite his assurance that nobody would be around, he told me to take the rifle.

By now it was full daylight and there was even a sort of sunshine. What with the burbling birds and bursting buds, I felt we should have danced across the field, but the gun put a damper on things. I tried carrying it casually, but realised there was no way I could make it look like a bunch of flowers or an umbrella even, so the only thing to do was to assume a wary attitude and hope that any onlooker would take us for hunters.

We got to the top of the hill without incident. Gigi's thermos, black groundsheet and cushion were all there. The gun and the sandwich box weren't.

Gigi expressed his feelings very briefly. Then he turned to me, 'Fanks again.'

'And thanks to you too.'

'Piss off now cos I might – I might . . .'

I turned, but then thought of something else and turned back. 'Hey, do I guess that you don't really need my cheque and money? Was that just part of the helpless act? Because I've got about 10p to get me back to London.'

He pulled out his wallet and dropped the cheque and two

ten-pound notes on to the ground. I was a bit surprised and thought that maybe he was really quite big time after all.

I picked them up. 'So long, Gigi. See you some time and you'll tell me what it was all about, yes? I suppose those two aren't going to give me any more trouble?'

'Them? They've got what they want. Fanks to you.'

'All right, all right. I can take so much gratitude. See you.'

I walked back down the hill. When I was at the bottom of the hill I suddenly thought to myself that I'd go and have a look at that old house. Two could play at being Christopher Robin.

I walked along the side of the hill until I reached a path I knew that brought me directly over the hill to the cottage.

It hadn't changed. It still looked as if it shouldn't be standing, and as I gazed at it I remembered that strange furtive thrill that had always passed through me when approaching it as a boy; the cottage had symbolised for me the mysterious world of Big Boys. I'd frequently been caught eavesdropping and had received many thumpings from my brother. On one occasion Gigi's friend, Pasquale, had seen to my punishment and now, as I stepped through the low doorway, I remembered with a kind of sickness the look on his face as he ordered the others to strip me ready for my rolling in a clump of nettles – chosen by him. I was surprised by how clearly I remembered this, something I hadn't thought of in ages. Pasquale had been a thin but tough-looking youth with a dead pale face, made paler by the darkness of his hair and stubble which even at that age was thick; his voice sounded permanently hoarse, but decisive. Nobody ever laughed at his heavily accented English – at least, not twice. On that occasion his Italian accent had been stronger, perhaps with relish at what he was ordering to be done. The others had perhaps wanted to protest, but Pasquale's natural leadership had carried the day, and they'd even laughed as I scrabbled tearfully out of the nettles, my skin aglow with pain. Pasquale's expression had remained one of pure enjoyment –

not all sadism, some of it the savouring of power. Anyway, it had cured me of visits to the cottage for some time.

These happy childhood memories were with me as the cottage's familiar odour groped clammily at my nostrils. I looked around. There was no sign that Gigi had even visited the place. It had not really formed part of his plans; it had simply been the bait, and the trap was to have been sprung at the gate where they were more off their guard. It hadn't been sentimentalism that had made Gigi decide on the place, just practicality. There aren't very many totally secluded, empty places in London suitable for a double murder, so if he had to go to the country he might just as well choose somewhere that he knew.

I was glad to think it wasn't sentimentalism: the thought of anybody getting sentimental about anything connected with Pasquale was not nice.

I left the cottage and set out towards the road to Oxford.

Four

I got a bus to Oxford and the train to London. On the train I did my best to wash with British Rail soap and towels, but the results were superficial; that is to say, I covered the surfaces of the floor and sink with bits of soggy grey paper towels. Then I returned to my seat and, in between trying to doze and trying to read a newspaper and trying not to be suffocated by the burnt rubber smell of the brakes, I puzzled over Gigi's various assertions: 1) The men had got what they wanted and so would be no more trouble. 2) The men wanted Gigi's blood. 3) Gigi was a big timer but not a hitman. 4) The cassette was . . . was very important.

It all seemed to come back to that cassette – the cassette which was now in *their* hands. Thanks to me.

When the train pulled in to Paddington I was feeling worse than when I'd got on. I hadn't slept, I hadn't read, I hadn't got over my guilt. However much I dwelt on Gigi's careless involvement of me in the business, I kept remembering that bang, that sharp cry of his, and that nasty red mess on his arm. A few inches to the left and . . .

Somehow Gigi's general all-round culpable behaviour seemed vague and insignificant in comparison with that sudden searing messy moment. Indeed, the bang kept getting louder in my memory, his cry sharper, his expression of pain more intense, and the blood – well, the blood became a red Niagara, drenching the trees like a scene from a Dario Argento film.

And a few inches to the left . . .

I'd prevented him from committing murder, it was true, but hell . . . Two inches to the left . . . BANG! AAAH! Half an inch to the left . . .

And the cassette. Lost for ever. At that very moment they

were probably chuckling over it (or dancing to it or singing along) in the . . . the Saleezebooree.

The name came to me quite unexpectedly. And I realised I hadn't told my brother this name. How stupid of me. If I had, it might have given him the chance to go along and finish off the morning's work properly.

No, perhaps all things considered it was better that I hadn't told him. After all, I could go along and pinch the cassette back just as easily, couldn't I? Without killing anyone perhaps.

I went towards the phone-boxes in the station, forgetting that they are of course the last place to expect to find a phone book. In the end I tracked one down in a pub, the landlord conceding it to me as if it were an autographed copy of Shakespeare's plays.

The Salisbury Hotel was in Bayswater, not more than five minutes from the pub. So, after a pint and a sandwich I strolled along. On the way I bought a blank TDK cassette at a hi-fi shop. The Salisbury was in a rather peeling terraced street, where every other house was a hotel or bed and breakfast place. The Salisbury was perhaps the smartest – or rather, the least dingy. It occupied only one house and didn't look the sort of place that would run to a restaurant or a bar, or to a large staff – which last was possibly a good thing from my point of view. It was definitely not a big-timers' hotel. I went on up the steps into the entrance hall feeling a little nervous – half hoping, indeed, that I'd discover that Gianni and Raffaele had left.

At the desk, a plump Pakistani girl of about eighteen was reading a magazine and drinking Coca-Cola from a can. 'Yeah, can I help you?' she said with a London accent.

I discovered that for some reason I'd decided to use an American accent. 'Yeah, hi. Do you have any single rooms going? For the one night, that is.'

'With or without bathroom?'

'Er, without.'

'Yeah. Number 15. Twelve pounds a night.'

'That's fine.' I hoped no real American passed by as I was sure my accent was doing a tour of the fifty states. 'I left my bags at the railroad station. I'll get them later. Say, out of curiosity how many rooms do you have?'

'Twenty-two. Why?'

'Oh, just wondered. Some friends of mine are coming over later and I kinda thought it would be nice to be together. Are they all occupied?'

'Nearly all.' She had turned most of her attention back to her magazine, to what was either a photographic report on some major battle in the Middle East or a series of stills from a rock concert video.

'Listen, my friends are coming over in a few days and they're interested in getting to know Europeans – not just Britishers, because we're going on a tour of Europe and so we'd like to meet up with as many people as possible from France, Italy, etc, who could give us tips on things, you know. D'you have many French or Italians here?'

'Sometimes. Here's your key. First floor.'

'Any Italians or French or, you know, Spaniards here now?'

'A couple of Italians on the first floor. Unless they're Spanish. A lot of Germans around, too.' Her attention had now gone entirely to the magazine.

'Oh, what are these Italian guys like? Nice people?'

'Just two blokes. One of 'em's always smiling. Little bloke.' She turned a page.

'Sounds very nice,' I said. 'Well, so long.'

At the end of this conversation I wasn't entirely sure things had gone as I'd wanted. I hadn't really intended to take a room – that had merely been a conversation opener to loosen her tongue – but when it had started to look as if I'd committed myself to the room (the room that cost only ninety pence less than what I had in my pocket), then I'd started to feel nervous about pressing her for too much information. I hardly wanted her to be telling Gianni and Raffaele as soon as they came in that there was a blond young man in filthy clothes who'd been asking questions about them and who could be found in Room 15.

Well, the consolations were that there had been no desk formalities, no register to sign, so if I wanted I could always do a runner later. After all, I was up against bloody murderers, so a, teeny-weeny little crime on my part should surely be acceptable. And if they were still there, there was presumably no better way to observe them than to be in the hotel myself.

I went up the stairs quickly, noting the reassuring lack of any other staff. There was also a complete lack of anything that might have helped to add a touch of comfort or atmosphere; the stairs and corridors were all completely blank.

Room 15 turned out to be a box that had been constructed around a bed. It was completely blank too. There wouldn't have been room for any ornaments. As it was, the wardrobe, sink and waste-paper basket took up ninety per cent of the space unfilled by the bed.

I sat on the bed trying to decide exactly how mad my venture on an off-chance was. Well, I suppose the easiest way to find out was to get to work, whatever that meant. To start observing, spying, etc. Straightaway.

First of all I lay on the bed in a purely business-like way, just to see whether it really was worth twelve pounds. It felt pretty good, but any horizontal surface probably would have done then. I decided to give it half a minute of fair trial. Then half a minute on my other side . . .

I woke up after six o'clock. I'd heard a voice going down the corridor – a high-pitched voice I recognised. It had come into my dreams and made things pretty nasty – me and the Ayatollah Khomeini and a cassette and this voice singing '*Ah! fors' è lui*' from *La Traviata*, and lots of blood.

I went over to the door. That is to say, I got off the bed and from there pressed my ear to the door.

Yes, it was Gianni, and Raffaele was replying to him, and they were going towards the stairs.

I opened my door the tiniest fraction and saw them go

around the corner and down. I couldn't hear what they were saying, but I was sure it was nasty.

Now, which room had they left? Was there any way of telling? At that moment Raffaele said something quickly and I heard him coming back up. I closed the door and heard his quick steps pass on down the corridor. The key turned. I opened the door the merest crack to confirm what my ears were telling me and then closed it again as he came out, pulled the door to, and walked back towards the stairs. I opened the door again and saw, just before he rounded the corner, that he was now holding an umbrella.

When in England, I suppose. But I bet it had a knife hidden in it somewhere.

I climbed over the bed to the sink and washed, more to wake myself up than for any other reason. I seemed, in fact, to have fallen into an acceptance of dirt as my natural state of being. And the sink was only large enough to wash one finger in at a time anyway.

Then I stepped out into the corridor and looked up and down. There was nobody around, and all the doors were closed. I sauntered over to the door Raffaele had used – Number 18 – and tried my key on it. It didn't work, which was, I suppose, reassuring in a way. It was a possibility I'd always wondered about in hotels and never had the gall to test.

I went down the stairs. The girl was still reading the magazine and the can of Coca-Cola was still on the desk. As I watched she took a sip from it. It was obviously quite full. She put it back near the edge of the desk.

I was on the lowest step and she clearly hadn't heard me. I took off my pullover and slung it over my shoulder: it was just about warm enough for this to be a reasonable thing to do. I walked over.

'Hi,' I said and handed her the key.

She hung it up. 'Bye,' she said.

'Tell me, where can I get postcards round here?'

'Lots of places.'

'Oh, er, thanks.' I allowed the pullover to slip off my shoulder but then caught it and swung it back up. It caught the Coca-Cola can just glancingly and it rocked for half a second and I thought I'd bungled it. Then the can made its decision and clattered on to the floor, spreading its dark glistening mess.

'Oh, I'm so sorry,' I said, bending down to pick up the can. 'Is there anything I can do? Gee, I'm sorry.'

'Doesn't matter,' she said. 'I'll get a cloth.' She slipped out from behind the desk and went through a door at the end of the hall. I leant over the desk and changed the keys on the hooks marked 15 and 18.

She came back with a cloth.

'Look, I'm really sorry. I'll go get you another can.'

'No. Doesn't matter.'

'No, I really will. I'm so sorry. Bye.'

I went out and bought a new can, a ham sandwich and two postcards. This brought me to only five pence more than the price of the room.

'Here you are,' I said. 'I'll go and write these darned cards now. And sorry again.'

'Thanks. You shouldn't have.' And, given her figure, perhaps I shouldn't have. She picked the key from the hook and I tried to look casual as I prayed for her not to look at the number on the key's plastic tag. She didn't.

I went on up, opened the door of Number 18 and slipped the catch so that it wouldn't lock on re-closing. I then went down again. She'd started the second can already. 'Say, this key didn't seem to work and I looked and you've given me Number 18.'

'What? How's that?' She looked at the key and then at the hook. 'Oh. Must have got 'em mixed up.' She didn't seem over-surprised. I had relied on her total absorption in her magazine to explain all, and it seemed I'd been right. She gave me my key and I went back up.

I went straight into Number 18. I slipped the catch back so

that the door locked. It would give me a little more warning – one and a half seconds perhaps.

The room was larger than mine. It contained two beds and enough floor to walk on without having to go sideways. There were two suitcases on the bed, both open and obviously recently packed. I walked straight to the window and opened it to see about the possibility of an escape route.

The room looked out on to the road which was quiet but not deserted. There were one or two people around, looking as if they were trying to remember which their hotel was, and one or two cars. But I could have chosen worse roads to climb furtively out of a hotel window on to – and indeed, the one or two people might be sufficient to make Raffaele think twice about using his gun, or his knife. The drop, too, was feasible, if I had the time to scramble out and hang down from the sill. And now that I'd locked the door, I'd have two and a half seconds at *least*. I could probably light a cheroot as I did it.

I left the window half open. The buzz of traffic that entered made it more difficult, of course, to concentrate on the silence of the corridor, but on balance it seemed the wiser course to take. I started going through the suitcases. I tried to disturb the things as little as possible, picking them up and putting them back with great care. I amused myself – or rather, attempted to divert my mind from the overall terror that was making me freeze each time any street noise remotely resembled a creaking stair or a turning key (cars changing gear, a baby crying) – by trying to work out which case was whose. As I didn't want to take the trousers out to measure them against my leg it was difficult, but in the end a preponderance of black in one made me decide it must be Gianni's. I was surprised by the number of string vests he'd brought, but then Continentals do seem to go in for such things rather more. Raffaele had a large box of sticking plaster in his case, which I reckoned was unlikely to be for his victims' use. He also had two books of *Topolino* (Mickey Mouse) cartoons, which would have made me smile if a car horn hadn't sent me half-way out of the window at the same time.

But there was no cassette.

I looked under the pillows, I patted the beds, I looked under the beds, in the drawers (this room actually had a chest of drawers as well as a wardrobe), in the waste-paper basket, and I discovered nothing; except for a Vicky cartoon of Harold Macmillan on a very jaundiced newspaper lining one of the drawers.

I could hear my heartbeats getting faster, like a racing commentator as the horses pass the finishing line. And I could feel sweat breaking out on all parts of my body to lend a momentary mushiness to my sticky stiff clothes. The swines, I thought, they must have kept the thing with them, just as Gigi had.

Then I remembered an old spy film in which the laughably obvious hiding place for a secret document had been on top of a high wardrobe. So obvious that I hadn't looked there. I went over to the wardrobe and reached on tiptoes to the top. Amid the fluff-covered insect corpses I touched smoothness, and brought down a cassette in its box.

It was a TDK of ninety minutes, still with its red and white cardboard label untouched. I put it into my trouser pocket, closed the window and moved to the door.

Before opening I listened hard. I could hear nothing. I stepped out into the corridor, and was about to let the door close behind me when I thought of something – the substitute cassette I'd bought which was now in my room. I reached back inside the door and slipped the catch again so the door did not lock as I closed it.

I darted across to my room, unlocked it, picked up my cassette and darted back to Number 18. All I had to do now was leave this on top of the wardrobe and then I could do my runner and go home and celebrate with a cup of tea. And I could put the cassette into my Walkman and bop along to it.

I re-entered Number 18 and went over to the wardrobe. I suddenly remembered that the new cassette still had its cellophane wrapping. My fingers scrabbled at its smooth surface but could make no tear in it. A little voice inside me was telling me about the self-defeating effects of haste but I went on scratching and scrabbling even more hastily. I spurred myself on with a few obscenities too. I was on the point of having a go with my teeth when I spotted the little protruding ribbon on one corner. I gave one neat pull all round – as satisfying as peeling off an ancient scab – and the cellophane was free; I slipped it off and stuffed it in my pocket and reached up and put the cassette more or less where I'd found the other one. I made for the door again.

As my hand was on the handle I heard footsteps in the corridor. The handle was suddenly white hot. I let the catch back up again, but with Fabergéan delicacy so that the metal tongue settled back into the lock noiselessly. I was able to identify the voice that started speaking now as Gianni's. Either his or Mirella Freni's.

And the window was closed.

I made for the nearest bed, which had a generous bedspread that draped all round to the floor. I was under it by the time the key was turning in the lock.

I seemed to have chosen the bed the chambermaid used as repository for the entire hotel's dust. There were whole families of rabbity fluff balls. But for once I didn't stop to wonder where the stuff came from; I was all ears for what was going on around the bed. (It was certainly better not to be nose or mouth for the moment.)

They closed the door and Raffaele said, 'Do we take a taxi?'

'Yes, of course. Close up the cases. And don't forget the cassette.'

'I'm not stupid.'

I suddenly thought that one of the things I always do when leaving a hotel room is check under the bed for anything I might have left there. I hoped – feeble word – I trusted and prayed that they were not so careful.

Raffaele came over to the bed. 'My case . . . Somebody's . . .' I heard him going quickly to the wardrobe. 'No, the tape's still here.'

'What's the matter?'

'It just looks like somebody's been going through the case. It looks different somehow . . .'

'Oh, close it and keep quiet. You're always imagining things. We'll have to pay for this night, I suppose.'

'Yes, I – '

At that moment another key was heard in the lock and both Gianni and Raffaele went quiet – a surprised kind of quiet. Then the door opened very vigorously and suddenly and they both made a surprised 'Who, what'-ish sound (*'Chi, cosa?'*) and then Raffaele said, 'You, but . . .'

'Yes, me. Put your hands on your heads.' The new voice was also Neapolitan and resembled that of someone who'd had a serious throat operation. Despite the command he didn't sound much like a junior school teacher. 'Where's the cassette?'

'But we . . .' Gianni sounded flustered – perhaps terrified. I guessed that the new arrival was either very big or holding something that made him look very big.

'Where is it? Tell me or I start firing. At the balls.'

Gianni sounded more than ever as if this had already happened to him. 'We haven't got – '

'One, two . . .' The contrast in voice pitches made Gianni sound ridiculous at last. I still didn't laugh; the other voice didn't encourage it.

'Give it him,' Gianni said.

'Don't move. Where is it?'

'Here, in this case,' Raffaele said. He'd presumably just put it there.

'Take it out. Slowly. If I suspect a trick I fire before asking a question. Clear?'

Raffaele moved one half-step and I could hear his fingers rustle one second among the clothes. No other sound.

'Put it on the ground and kick it towards me.'

I heard the clack, rustle and swish of this being done.

'Now turn round.'

'But wait – ' The terror in Gianni's voice was open now.

'Turn round. Both of you.'

They did so, Raffaele now speaking quickly, bitterly, urgently. 'I didn't want to do it, it was Gianni's idea, take the tape, it was Gianni, him and that Engli – '

A sudden BANG! interrupted him, reverberating round the room. There was a heavy thud and then a crash which shook the room and at the same moment Gianni started yelling *'Aiuto! aiuto!'* like a soprano going for a top C with energy but not much accuracy; he moved fast in some direction but a second BANG! stopped him and for one fraction of a second he caught that note, then choked and dropped. He kept choking on the floor, but the visitor took two paces across the room and fired again.

There was silence – just the rustling of the visitors' clothes as he bent down, presumably to pick up the cassette. Something suddenly battered into the bedspread and then clattered on to the floor. I only just managed not to cry out.

I heard the man crossing to the window and opening it. There was another moment of rustling and a little heavy breathing. Then I heard the remote thud of his body hitting the pavement. Amid a few voices I heard his running feet.

I lay still for a few seconds, breathing in the dust bunnies. Then I moved my hand forward to grasp the object that had clattered on to the ground by my face. It was, of course, the gun. I gripped it firmly as I scrambled out. It was kind of instinctive, like holding on to the seat when the dentist approaches with the drill.

I'd got out from under the bed on the opposite side from where Gianni and Raffaele had fallen, perhaps with the intention of not having to look at them. But of course I did.

Well, they were dead. Messily so.

I could hear a tumult of voices around me – outside the window; somewhere inside the hotel. I stepped quickly into the corridor and two young men with blond beards who had just come from the staircase stopped and turned and ran back down. I was puzzled, until I remembered the gun in my hand.

I ran straight towards the staircase, wondering why the hell I hadn't gone out of the window too. I heard a whole football crowd on the stairs now, and half a minute before the hotel had seemed entirely deserted. They all sounded excited.

I swivelled and ran back to my room, Number 15. I went for the key in my pocket with the feverish fingers of one hand and pulled out the cassette instead. I dropped it, picked it up, realised I now had both hands occupied, slipped the cassette in between two fingers of the gun hand and searched for the key in the other pocket: that is to say, my left hand was stretched gropingly round to my right pocket, as in some elaborate yoga exercise, except it wasn't all that tranquillising. When I got the key out, people had already appeared at the top of the staircase. I waved the gun vaguely at them, having to tuck my right arm over my left to do it so that it turned from a yoga exercise into one of Houdini's more complicated stunts. They got the point, however, and I entered my room and slammed the door. I dropped key, cassette, and gun on to the bed.

I clambered over the bed to the window. On this side of the hotel it looked out on to a dim backyard with dustbins. I put the cassette firmly back in my pocket and scrambled out on to the sill.

The jar as I hit the ground was such that I half expected the building to come down on top of me. I picked myself up, ran to the wall and managed to climb on top. Another brain-shivering jar and I was in another backyard. The door out of this one led into the reception of another hotel. It was a blonde girl at the desk here, and she stared at me. For the first time I wondered what the hoarse-throated fellow had done to the receptionist girl at the Salisbury to get the master key or whatever it was off her.

I didn't stop to make conversation. I smiled vaguely and ran on through.

'From the Salisbury,' I heard her saying to a guest, as if that explained everything.

Once in the street I soon lost my traces – indeed lost myself, until I found myself by Bayswater underground station. At one point I heard a distant siren but I saw nothing to alarm me.

Five

When I got back home – finding the front door open from the previous evening, something I'd quite forgotten to worry about – I went into the bathroom and started filling the bath and then stared in the mirror and tried to imagine what the identikit picture of me in the morning paper would be like. I wondered too what would be written under the picture: 'BRITAIN'S MOST WANTED MAN', perhaps; or, 'THIS IS THE MAN WHO TERRORISED A LONDON HOTEL', and perhaps a word or two about my accomplice. 'Scotland Yard', it would continue, 'has fortunately been able to identify the fingerprints the man so amateurishly left on the gun with those of a stolen bicycle in Thrubton Nempwell and those on a science fiction novel borrowed from Radney local library in 1981 and later left in a pub in Oxford. An arrest is considered imminent.'

Was I staying away from the police still because I didn't want to 'shop' my brother or because I didn't want to shop myself?

Well, perhaps the cassette would help me come to some decision about what my next move should be. I'd listen to it in the bath on the big machine. A bath is a good place to consider one's problems. One can't panic in a bath. It's not like a shower where one can always start thinking of *Psycho*.

So, when all was ready I switched the tape on and stepped into the bath. There were a few seconds of silence, then the sound of a conversation which had started off-tape.

Two men were talking in Italian. One of them was clearly English, though his Italian was grammatically correct and reasonably fluent. The other had what could be described as an educated Neapolitan accent.

Italian voice: You parked like last time, I presume, round the corner.

English voice: I came by taxi this time. You know what it's like trying to park round here.

Italian voice: Fine. I only mention it because precautions are always best – for you and for us. Well now, you've studied our terms?

English voice: Yes, and I agree to them.

Italian voice: Good, good. Now you appreciate that this will be a rather special operation. We hope to be able to achieve the death within those days you've stipulated, but if it proves too difficult to arrange we trust you will accept a later date.

English voice: Well, er, on condition that . . .

Italian voice: Oh, of course our charges will be reduced in that case.

English voice: And you'll inform me beforehand if you have to postpone the killing.

Italian voice: Certainly, certainly. Now we ask for a fifty per cent down payment now, and the rest on completion of the operation. If the operation has to be postponed, we will ask only a further twenty-five per cent.

English voice: That sounds all right.

Italian voice: Fifty thousand dollars this week then. To pay into that account of which I gave you the number.

English voice: Could I meet the, er, operative first?

Italian voice: I'm afraid that is quite impossible.

English voice: But you'll tell me exactly how and when it's going to be done?

Italian voice: That is also rarely permitted. We usually accept only limitations of the sort you have already stipulated – a set period of a few days, an area.

English voice: Well, if those are your rules . . .

Italian voice: You must realise we are professionals; we keep our reputation because we never bend our rules for anyone.

English voice: I see. Well, I suppose you're right.

Italian voice: We are. Now would you like a drink? A Cinzano?

The conversation passed from the choice of aperitif to a more general discussion of the relative merits of various Italian wines. If I had switched on only at this point no doubt I would have found it casual and tedious enough, but with the knowledge of what had gone before it came across as deeply horrible. Still talking about wine – the Englishman championing the wines of Tuscany and the Italian going for the Veneto – they left the room and the recording stopped.

I let the tape continue to roll, on the off-chance that there might still be something else later on; the water got cold around me as I reflected. My first thought was that I'd never drink Tuscan or Veneto wine again, but my second thought was that that was a very silly thing to think, if only because it would certainly turn out not to be true. Having got that out of the way I asked myself what Gigi had to do with all this. What had he been doing with this cassette? The only answer that came to me I didn't like, so I thought up another question. What was I now going to do? I had evidence of a murder being planned – a very expensive murder, and so almost certainly of some very important person. Not that that made the murder any more serious than if it were a matter of some tramp having his throat cut, I told myself. But all the same it did add a kind of sense of urgency to the whole thing – and it's not often one feels a sense of urgency in a bath.

Maybe the cold water helped; I found myself shivering. I turned on the hot tap and swirled the water around me.

So what to do, what to do? The usual feeble thing perhaps – go and see big brother about it. It was certainly a way of putting off a lot of awkward questions with the police ('Now about this bicycle, Mr Esposito . . .'), and Gigi might have some idea about who the designated victim was. And it was, after all, only fair on Gigi – or if fair was the wrong word, it was at least the fraternal thing to do. There was no knowing how deeply he was involved and what I might be landing him in if I went to the police.

As I came to this typically procrastinatory decision, I felt a slight lessening of tension. The water slopped comfortingly warm around me. All that was missing was a rubber duck.

After a couple of minutes I got out and towelled myself and thought about how I could find Gigi. It might not be so easy. He had found me through Zia Peppina; I could always try and see if it worked the other way round.

When I was in my pyjamas and had a glass of cheap wine (Veneto in fact) by my side, I phoned my aunt. As always, as soon as she'd recognised my voice she switched to Neapolitan.

'Gennaro. It's such a long time.'

'I know, I know. I must come round some time.'

'And how's the job?'

'Oh, so so. Could be worse.' Well, I could have been thrown out of the window by the director, I suppose.

'And, oh, what's the name? Your *fidanzata?*' (You only had to be seen talking together to be *fidanzati* for my aunt.)

'Valerie.'

'Yes, yes. Valeria. How is she? A good girl, I think. Very *simpatica*.'

'Oh, she's in America at the moment. She's fine.' She'd been smiling on the wedding photos at any rate. I could explain all that another time. 'Listen, *Zia*, I was wondering if you'd seen or heard of Gigi at all recently. I'd like to get in touch.'

'What a strange coincidence. Only yesterday – or was it the day before? – Gigi rang asking about you.'

'Really?'

'Yes, I was so pleased. Brothers should keep in touch. Family, you know. It's important. You must both come round here. We'll have a real spaghettata. And a good chat. And some *scacciata*. And . . .'

'Yes, yes. It would be lovely. But do you know how to get in touch with Gigi?'

'He gave me a number to call back. You see, I couldn't find your number or address. And I told him I knew I'd put them down somewhere. And I thought they were on top of the fridge. I keep a notebook there, you see. Well, it's out of the way. And it's handy in the kitchen. It doesn't get covered with other things, you see, so I can always get at it. Next to the fridge I keep my cleaning things, you know. Just where the door opens, you see. But I couldn't find it, so I thought to myself . . .'

I knew there was no hope of interrupting her. The only thing I could think of was imitating the pips to indicate my time was up, but she probably wouldn't hear me. When she'd finished the geography of the house and the reasons for it she said, 'But you were wanting Gigi's number.' It's amazing the way she never actually forgets what she was first talking about. One only needs patience with her – and a completely free timetable.

'That's right, *Zia*. If you've got it.'

'Yes, it should be here by the phone. Well, some I keep on the fridge, you see, and some by the phone. It depends, you see.'

I didn't ask on what, I just waited while she told me. Then eventually she gave me the number.

'Mind you, Gennaro, he said it was only a temporary number. But then, you know how it is with Gigi. Oh well . . .'

I thanked her, promised I'd come round soon and eat some of her *scacciata* (I would too), said that I'd give her all news of Valeria (I would too – eventually) and all news of Gigi (this was a little less likely), and that I'd keep praying to San Gennaro (this definitely – I needed all the help I could get).

I rang the number she'd given me. A female voice with a strong London accent answered, repeating the number.

'I'd like to speak to Mr Luigi Esposito please.'

'Who are you?'

'This is his brother.'

'Well he aint 'ere.'

'Oh, do you know where I could find him?'

'You could try later tonight. But not too late, love, know wha' I mean?'

'Er, yes. Before midnight OK?'

'Yeah. But not after. You could be interrupting, know wha' I mean? 'Ere, you don't sound like Gino's bruvver.'

'Well, I am. Bit younger.'

'You're not from London, are you love?'

'No.'

'Well, never you mind. You talk just any way you like.'

'Thanks, I'll try and remember that.'

'Actually you sound quite sexy.'

'Oh, er, thanks.' I couldn't return the compliment as she had a voice like a dentist's drill. I said goodbye and hung up.

The idea of watching the news came to me, but looking at my watch I saw there wasn't a bulletin on for another hour. I finished my wine. A clunk from the bathroom told me that the tape had finished. I tried the other side, running it fast forward and stopping it at various intervals. It seemed to be all blank. I listened to the conversation on side A again and felt depressed rather than chilled this time. Just depressed at not knowing what to do about it all, not philosophically depressed at the thought of how much evil there is in the world. Maybe I should have felt so, but I didn't. I suppose I knew anyway.

I ate something, played a bit more of *La Traviata*, and felt momentarily stirred by Violetta's nobleness. If I were in an opera at least I'd be able to make music of my problems. Then I looked at my watch and saw I'd missed the news. I phoned Gigi's friend again and he still wasn't back. She said she'd get him to phone me and I thanked her. She said she'd also get him to tell her all about me – 'and I mean all, ducky'. I told her not to be disappointed if it wasn't all nice, then, feeling too tired to do anything else, went to bed. If he did phone, I'd wake up, I thought.

He didn't phone. I woke a little after eight which, since I'd gone to bed before ten, was not bad going. I phoned the lady again but there was no answer. I went out to buy a newspaper, and when I saw the headlines bought three. As I was leaving the shop I had a sudden doubt whether this suspicious act might not be proclaiming my guilt to all in the shop. Glancing round, however, I saw there was someone even more furtive than myself, taking down a copy of *Men Only*.

By an exercise of willpower I didn't read them until I got home. I had rather improbable visions of myself going guiltily pale – or flushed – in front of crowds of gazing strollers as I looked at the account of my misdeeds. When I got back I spread them all out on the kitchen table.

The double murder had made the front pages of *The Times*, *Telegraph* and *Guardian*. There were no identikit pictures, however. The two men's names were given in full – Raffaele Fusco and Giovanni Barra. Only *The Guardian* went so far as to hazard a description of them as 'possibly involved in the Neapolitan underworld'. The papers all agreed that two men were involved in the killing: one a young blond American (I felt momentarily cheered by this testimony to my powers of mimicry) who had taken a room at the hotel as a guest; and the second a large man, Italian in appearance, who had stunned the receptionist in order to steal the hotel's master keys. There were only very vague descriptions of him given by two people in the street who'd witnessed his jump from the hotel room, whereas the receptionist had given quite an accurate account of me, down to my filthy shoes. That magazine's war coverage, I realised, couldn't have taken up quite as much of her attention as I'd thought. The last sentence in *The Daily Telegraph* stated that the police, of course, did not rule out that the man's American accent was assumed.

The only thing I could think of to comfort myself was that I'd gone out to buy the papers in completely different clothes.

I went out for a walk round the park, feeling that if I didn't force myself to go out and face people straightaway I might turn into a complete recluse – become one of those people discovered after decades alone and decrepit in a stinking flat. I took the Walkman with me and listened to the conversation again. I occasionally tapped my fingers and jerked my head convulsively in order to look normal – like all the other headphone wearers in the park, that is.

I tried this time to identify where the conversation was taking place. I could hear a vague noise of traffic outside and there was a voice outside the room – presumably in the street – that kept repeating a certain cry. I did my best to tune in on this voice only, and to ignore the conversation above it. At one point I thought I'd identified the cry as that of a London newspaper seller – that consonantless staccato yelp, 'Ee-ih-a-ar!' Then I realised I was trying to hear this. There was one moment when the conversation paused and the cry was heard on its own. I listened to this three times and I identified it almost certainly as the cry of a Neapolitan flower seller: *'Du milla lire 'o mazzo!'* she said, more or less. 'Two thousand lire a bunch.' So the conversation almost certainly took place in Naples or thereabouts, although it was not of course impossible that it took place in New York or Buenos Aires or Sydney – or any other city with Neapolitans (which meant *any* city, Peking and Moscow included and no doubt Mecca too).

I now wondered about the Englishman's voice. Did I think I'd heard it somewhere before just because I'd played it so many times now? No, that wasn't the kind of *déjà entendu* I was getting. But where, where . . . ? At school, on the radio, at the local shop, on holiday, on an advertisement . . . ? It was like when you meet one of your local shopkeepers out of his shop and you know his face well and wonder if he's a film or TV star.

I realised that thinking too hard about it would just make me confused, so I took the headphones off and tried to listen only to the birds and kids and cars for the rest of my walk.

When I got back I dialled that number again. The same piercing voice answered, repeating the number.

'Hello, this is Gino's brother again,' I said.

'Hello, love. Was that you at crack of dawn this morning?'

'Er, just after eight, yes.'

'Thought it might be. I told Gino you'd phoned and he, well, he wasn't very nice, you're right. What was it he called you? Oh yes, cock-up artist. Nice from a bruvver, no? And he didn't want me to answer this morning. I shouldn't worry, love. He's very changeable, you know.'

'So you've no idea how I can get in touch with him?'

'Bit difficult now love. Didn't I say? He's gone off to Italy. Niples.'

'What? When?'

'This morning. It was like he just decided over breakfast. I mean, I fought he'd come to stay for a bit this time, but no, this morning all of a sudden he just said "gotta go" and rang up straightaway for a ticket. Left for Eafrow an hour ago. Or was it Gatwick? Really dunno.'

'You don't know when he's coming back?'

'Never do love. Never tells me nuffink. I only know he's gone to Niples 'cos I 'eard him on the phone. That's the way he is. Turns up every so often and never tells me where he's bin, or how long he's staying. I mean, he only turned up a few days ago, you know, and acted like he was gonna stick around for a bit. You know, all over me. And I mean all over. Then, suddenly, just like that, ta ta love, send you a postcard – no, not even that. Just a goodbye kiss and he's off. Leaving me all on me lonesome.'

'I see. I'm sorry.'

'You alone too? Perhaps we could, you know, meet up?'

'Er, no. I think I'd better be off to Naples too.'

'Cor. You are shy love.'

'Well, Heathrow anyway. Or Gatwick. Whichever. Bye.' I put the receiver down in a flustered state. Things were getting all too much here in London and I thought of my brother winging his way to blue skies and seas and the seductive curves of Naples's bay. As always, viewed in imagination from a distant dirty suburban kitchen the city became transfigured – became the sort of happy operatic place promoted by ice cream advertisements in which such details as dirt, drugs and destitution didn't figure. The kind of place where all problems get solved.

Or at least get put in perspective. And Naples – in *fact*, not imagination – is the best place on earth to go if one wants to learn how to relax and not bother too much about things. The

73

ultimate laid-back city. One only needs to look at the way the city lies back on its pet volcano to appreciate that.

So I made my decision. I went to Naples – or got the hell out of London, whichever way you like to put it. I was on a flight from Gatwick to Rome the next morning.

Six

I felt some of my worries get whisked away in the slipstream of the plane as it left the runway – the worry at least of getting a tap on the shoulder with a truncheon. Flight – literal flight – gave me the usual sense of happy liberation, which I like to think of as a momentary ride on the wings of the spirit that breathed on Beethoven as he wrote *Fidelio*, but which probably owes more to the drinks trolley brought round by the hostess. Anyway, I knew I'd made the right decision and be blowed to the cost of the ticket.

I might even find a job in Naples, after all. And if I did, there was a friend of mine staying in a bedsit in Clapham who would be pleased to take over my flat in London unofficially and thus keep up the payment of the rent. I could consider myself reasonably fancy-free for the moment.

From Rome I took the train down to Naples, arriving at about half past two. The city greeted me as I got off the train in its usual fashion: bashing me on the ear-drums. Noise, noise, noise: of engines and of voices, in every gear and every pitch, at every speed and tone, and always, always, above and around this the sound of the musical instrument favoured by Neapolitans even over the mandolin – the car horn.

Your first thought on leaving the station is that everyone in the city has come out to shout and honk you a welcome; when you see that this is not the case (of the hundreds of people, only twenty or so are interested in you, all of them taxi drivers), you imagine that some major disaster must have happened that very instant. You soon discover, however, that this is the normal noise level of Piazza Garibaldi, and you're left to wonder what it must have been like when the last earthquake *did* happen. Perhaps things went unusually quiet. I don't know, I wasn't there, and relatives who've told me about it – and it's not difficult to get them to do so – didn't mention the noise; Neapolitans don't notice it.

I got my usual moments of cheap satisfaction from being able to tell the pidgin-English-speaking taxi drivers what I thought of their special pre-fixed rates in their own vernacular, and I made my way, rucksack on back, to the Corso Umberto to catch a bus. I'd decided not to stay with relatives, as their southern hospitality would certainly impede my freedom of action; so I was going to a *pensione* in Via Roma which a friend of mine had told me about; apparently it was cheap, clean – and of course bloody noisy.

Crossing Piazza Garibaldi was as perilous a venture as any I'd been through in the last few days. Neapolitans make Romans seem like model drivers; indeed, the effect of arriving in Naples from Rome is always to make one remember Rome as a quiet orderly place, on the lines of Leamington Spa or Cheltenham. But I got to the Corso, and after one look at the buses and 'queues' I realised there was no way both my rucksack and I could travel together on public transport, so I walked. I got to the Via Roma and Pensione Risorgimento some twenty minutes later.

The landlord of the *pensione*, which was on the third floor of a massive eighteenth-century *palazzo*, was a figure in tune with his environment. He too was built on large lines and looked in need of some kind of restoration; the elaborate ceiling of the *palazzo*'s staircase gave signs of caving in despite the scaffolding, and his belly similarly oozed through the holes of his string vest and out of the triangular unbuttoned gap at the bottom of his shirt. He used no stick but clutched at each object of furniture available as he accompanied me to my room.

He hadn't asked to see my passport, despite the law which makes it mandatory for hotel owners to do so – perhaps because of the law. Naples is like that about bureaucracy; it's one of its nicest characteristics. Thus I felt no need to let on that we could be speaking in Italian. I suppose a little deception like that was part of getting into my new role as superspy. It all helped my anonymity.

'Beautiful room, beautiful room. Fifteen thousand lire.'

'Fine.'

'How long time you stay?'

'Oh, two or three nights for the moment. Perhaps longer.' If I got a job.

'You must say me. Many people want rooms, many many people.'

'Yes, of course.' I doubted this. It was the end of April, long past Easter, and Naples is never that full of tourists even in high season. They go to the surrounding areas – Sorrento, Amalfi, Capri, Ischia – and perhaps go on a coach trip to Naples, getting off the coach just long enough to snap the view across the bay towards Vesuvius, and then jumping back on again before anyone can mug them. 'It depends on, er, how much I like the place. I'll let you know later.'

'Naples very beautiful. Very very beautiful. But people – bad you know. You stay in beeg streets, not leetle streets. Beeg streets yes, leetle streets no.'

'Yes, of course.'

He opened the room and I looked round it and said, 'Fine, lovely,' and he shuffled off.

The room was strictly functional: bed, straight-backed chair, desk, wash-basin with two taps, of which only the one marked FREDDO worked. I went and looked out of the window. It gave on to one of the many long straight alleys that lead off Via Roma towards the Vomero hill and the Castel Sant'Elmo. Viewed from here it appears quite picturesque, all festively a-flutter with washing and full of bustling life, but when one goes up the alleys and has a look at what people are living in, it loses its picture-postcard charm. My father was from this area, and one sees why he liked Bethnal Green. Many of these buildings were still encased in scaffolding from the 1980 earthquake, but there was little sign that anything was actually being done to them. The scaffolding was probably considered a good enough solution for the next few centuries.

I had a quick wash and then I put my Walkman into a shoulder bag and left the *pensione*. I walked in the direction of the Cathedral. I wasn't going there to pray to my patron saint – since he's called upon to solve most problems in Naples, he's got more than enough to do already – but to find a street nearby where a flower seller sold bunches at two thousand lire each.

The Cathedral is in a main street that cuts a wide swathe through the tightly packed warren of Naples's *centro storico*. The Via Duomo itself has many elegant and expensive shops, but leading off it are narrow, dark streets that take you into a different, though equally animated, world. As there were no flower sellers to be seen on the 'beeg' Via Duomo itself, it was this bustling world of 'leetle streets' I had to tramp around.

The area offers a rich study in social history: now it is almost entirely *del popolo*, but a glance beyond the market stalls, behind the rubbish and the washing, reveals the former splendour of many of the buildings – at least, of the buildings that line the not quite so 'leetle' thoroughfares, those wide enough for a car to squeeze past a pedestrian (the narrower alleys have always been slums). The architectural style is mostly Naples's speciality – battered baroque. The palaces all look rather bemused by their present usage – swarms of children in courtyards, knocking the noses off statues with footballs, washing hanging from curlicued corbels, *motorini* leaning against marble columns. The many churches could all do with some face-treatment, and all the domes look in need of a good barber. The general impression is of too much being crammed into too little space. Cars and motorbikes pass by at top speed and volume, driving the pedestrians into doorways; the shops, with crazily crammed rickety stalls, spew their goods on to the street (God knows where all the stuff gets put at night); children are everywhere, and from the age of about six or so upwards they're mostly on motorbikes, four or five of them to a saddle. And in case anyone feels the scene is still a little desolate, the town council sees to it that all remaining space is filled with uncollected rubbish.

I had started my search at about three thirty, and it was gone five when I came across an old woman sitting on a stool surrounded by flowers. It was a nice splash of colour in the dark alley; the only other colour around was the occasional magazine cover or sweet wrapping in the ankle-deep litter. The street was about three minutes' walk from the Cathedral and, indeed, was just behind the Via Duomo, on a turning off the Via San Biagio.

She was shouting '*tre milla lire 'o mazzo!*' I put my Walkman on and played the cassette at the appropriate point. There was no doubt; it was the same voice. Just the price had gone up. There was only one thing to check now. I went over to her and bought a bunch of begonias. I asked her, 'Are you always here?'

'Morning and evening.'

'I mean, you don't have another stall? I, er, I might want to buy some other flowers later, you see.'

'I've been here forty years now. I'm not going to move.'

I thanked her and moved away. I now started looking at the houses that lined the street. On the left were high ancient buildings of no pretensions whatsoever. On the right were the backs of some of the *palazzi* on the Via Duomo and these, viewed from here, were not that much more impressive than the ones on the opposite side. They were mostly offices and shops, I guessed, not houses. Indeed, I had supposed from the first that someone who organised a hundred-thousand-dollar killing did not live near the Cathedral, only 'worked' there. In Naples the historic centre, unlike most towns, is not the place to be: if you've got money you go up, above the age and dirt, into the Vomero or Posillipo; you buy a house with a view over the town at the right distance and elevation for the squalor to become picturesque (and how picturesque). Down in the old city you don't get views; the streets are too narrow. I remember my father telling me that in their old two-room flat they never knew what the weather was like, as they could only see the narrowest ribbon of sky. The street where I stood now was topped by a distant blue strip, like faded washing that had gone adrift.

I went around to the Via Duomo to study the entrance of the *palazzo* nearest the old lady. It was a baroque building with a massive gateway leading into quite an attractive court-yard. Next to the doorway was a list of the occupants, all of them commercial. There were three or four names with 'Avv.' in front of them – lawyers. These seemed rather more likely to be the people I was looking for than the art dealers, perfume distributors or accountants.

I started up the stairs, not really knowing how I intended to go about finding out my suspect – nor what I'd do when I had found him out. Rush in and overpower him (and his gang)? Or just go in and scare him (them) rigid with a few knowing wisecracks? Well, when I'd found him out – and seen how big he was – I could act accordingly. Accordingly.

So I plodded up the stairs and paused before each door: I suppose I was studying the doors for clues, like recent bullet holes or bloodstains. Anyway, there weren't any. At the top a man was leaning on the balustrade; he was smoking and staring down into the courtyard. He gave me one curious glance and then went back to his cigarette and stare. I went back down again and, feeling just a little bit foolish, walked out of the *palazzo*.

Well, that had shown them.

I turned to go back in again and do something more resolute; then I thought of the man at the top of the stairs and his embarrassing stare. Perhaps he was a Heavy, just waiting for trouble. (Actually he'd looked rather light.)

I crossed the road and went into a bar and ordered coffee. It was some time since I'd drunk real *espresso* and it was good, if not exactly oceanic in its quantity (about half a thimbleful). I would have ordered another, ignoring the shocked looks of those who consider two cups of coffee the prelude to a nervous breakdown, but I remembered my financial situation.

I stood and idly watched the doorway across the road and wondered if I was likely to come up with any plan more positive than another door inspection. A few minutes passed during which nothing happened – nothing other than the ceaseless flow of vociferous traffic, that is. Then somebody came out of the *palazzo* and started walking down the road in the direction of the Corso Umberto.

He looked English, although there was no particular detail in his dress or manner that I could have put a Sherlock Holmesian finger on. He wasn't holding *The Times* or a Blue Guide, nor was he even badly dressed. There was just an English aura about him – upper- or middle-class English. He was tall, he wore a light-coloured suit and was tanned; the tan was the shiny bronze of a northern face rather than the permanent darkness of a southern. And there was something, something familiar about him that had made my glance linger into a gaze.

Then I saw the man who'd been smoking at the top of the staircase emerge from the building too and stare out after him. He seemed to be trying to decide on a course of action, probably whether to follow him or not. He fiddled with his cigarette for a second or two and then went back into the building.

Well, if he wasn't going to follow him, then perhaps I should. It would give me something to do at least, and even if this hint of suspiciousness turned out to be completely unconnected with my business, I could consider it good training.

So I set off down the Via Duomo behind him. He was walking at a fairly swift pace, but without seeming to hurry. I stayed on my side of the road, ready to jerk down towards my shoelaces or dive suspiciously into a shop doorway at the slightest twitch of his head. But he gave no twitch, and as far as I could tell was not looking into shop windows for furtive reflections either.

At the end of the road he turned right into the Corso Umberto. I got a little left behind here in crossing the road, which is never a simple sauntering affair in Naples. Nonetheless I could still see him ahead of me. It was lucky he was fairly tall.

We made our way towards the Piazza Municipio. We twice had to cross roads reminiscent of scenes from Ben Hur, and then we were walking underneath the great grey bulk of the Angevin Castle. I wondered if he were going to get a boat to Ischia or Capri, but he walked on past the embarkation point. The pavement got narrower and the pedestrians fewer. I hung further back and wished my hair weren't quite so glaringly blond. Why hadn't I brought a Balaclava helmet? He passed below the red and grey magnificence of the Royal Palace and then turned left to cut across the little garden where couples necked amidst pines and palm trees. I hurried along to catch up. By the time I'd cut through the garden he'd reached the top of the hill. I walked up after him and the coastline came into view ahead of me as a hazy grey smudge. He was still walking briskly along this panoramic road. When he reached the semi-circle where Umberto the First stared regally out at Vesuvius as if daring it to erupt, he stopped and had a little regal stare himself. I was going to look pretty silly if he'd only come here for this. I stopped and did a tourist impersonation too.

It was, after all, a view worth stopping for. The bay lay below us with boats scattered here and there like an untidy child's toys. Vesuvius loomed like a battered grey hat over the smoky grey tangle of the port, and the coastline stretched to the right of Vesuvius in a long misty curve; if one squinted really hard one could imagine one saw all the way to Sorrento, with the irregular shape of Capri floating mirage-like on the horizon at its tip.

Eventually, however, he started walking again, continuing along the now descending road. We turned right and the Castel dell'Ovo came into view, the picturesque little port of Santa Lucia nestling at its foot with its waterfront restaurants and its smuggling boats; maybe he was going to have dinner there and enjoy the mandolin-strumming tenors singing that second most famous of Neapolitan songs – the one about the port itself. But no; he passed on without even a glance. He took advantage of a break in the traffic and crossed the road. He entered one of the hotels.

I didn't go in straightaway. It was the kind of hotel, I felt, where the desk staff would take one look at me and tell me that if I'd come to clean the toilets I should use the back entrance. While I watched, a man in tattered jeans, perhaps American, entered; ten seconds later and his body had not come shooting back out. I realised that, as with so many big hotels, it was manner that counted, not clothes. Anglo-Saxons were not, after all, expected to dress well. So I assumed the scornful air of one who was only staying at the hotel because no *cinquecento* villa of sufficient size with sea view had been available for the week, and I strolled into the hotel's entrance hall.

This was about the size of an airport lounge and in its architecture and furnishings was a cross between a Roman bath and a Victorian withdrawing room. Tourists sat in deep leather armchairs and talked loudly to show they weren't intimidated by the marble pillars and potted plants. I walked past the desk without giving the minions there a glance. The Englishman was nowhere to be seen, presumably having gone up to his room, so I walked over to one of the armchairs and sat in it with what I hoped was the air of a London club member who would then put out his hand for his ironed copy of *The Times*. I reached out instead for a copy of *Oggi* on the nearby table, flicked through the usual five pages of photographs of various members of the Monaco royal family and glanced at an article about the forthcoming English royal visit to Italy. When I felt I'd established my right to be there I glanced around myself. There was a middle-aged English couple sitting at a table with empty teacups in front of them and I went over to them.

'Excuse me,' I said, 'I couldn't help hearing you were English. I just wondered if you could tell me whether the tea's, er, safe or not.'

The woman looked at me. 'Safe?'

'I mean, is it good tea or not? I've had some bad experiences, you know . . .'

The man said, 'Know what you mean. Can be a risky business abroad. But this stuff's all right. At least it's not tea bags.'

'Oh good.'

They asked me to sit down and we got into the usual chat of foreigners abroad – where are you from? here on holiday? first time? how long for? – to all of which I gave tourist-like answers. I inserted into the conversation something about how many English people there were around, to which they agreed, saying something scornful about the tourists they'd seen at Sorrento who were only concerned with finding English beer. I tut-tutted over this dreadful parochialism and then said, 'By the way, I saw someone earlier, an Englishman, and I'm sure I know his face. Tall, bronzed man. Healthy-looking, if you know what I mean.'

'Oh yes, Brendan Cullop,' they said together.

'Of course. I knew I knew his face.'

'Couldn't believe it when I saw him,' the woman said. 'Here in the same hotel, with us.'

'Not that strange really,' her husband said. 'Sort of hotel he would be at.'

'No, but, I mean. In the *same* hotel.'

'And I must say I can never see what all the fuss is about. He's only a playboy.'

'Well, he's done some pretty daring things too,' she said. 'You know, the desert – and – and the North Pole, and . . .'

'Well, he's got the money, hasn't he? I mean, if I had the same money . . .'

'You'd be straight off to the North Pole, I know, dear.'

'Well, if I had the time. A business doesn't run itself, you know. I mean, he's got it made. Just a playboy.'

'Yes, but here. In the same hotel.'

'How long's he been here?' I put in.

'He arrived yesterday evening,' the woman said. 'We saw

84

him arrive. Couldn't believe it. Came into the hotel all on his own. But they obviously knew him.'

'Just can't see what all the fuss is about.'

I made my excuses and left them. I went over to the desk and asked the young man there in English, 'Is Brendan Cullop in?'

'Yes.'

'Could I call through to his room?'

He indicated the phone booth at the side of the desk and said, 'Dial 339.'

'His room number?'

'That's right, Sir.'

I entered the booth and dialled. His voice answered after a few seconds. '*Pronto.*'

'Oh, er, hello. Is that Mike?'

'Sorry?'

'Mike? Is that you, Mike?'

'No, I'm sorry. This is Brendan Cullop speaking.'

'Oh, gee, I'm sorry.' I'd put on my appalling American accent again, I discovered. 'That isn't room 239?'

'No, this is 339.'

'Gee, I'm really sorry, Mr Cullop. *The* Brendan Cullop?'

'Brendan Cullop. Goodbye.'

'Oh, yeah, goodbye.' I hung up. My guess had been proved right. Brendan Cullop's was the voice on the tape.

Seven

I walked along the Via Partenope. The sun was going down behind the cluttered hill of Posillipo across the bay and a carpet of silently shimmering, shifting gold coins was spilt out over the sea. To my right the occasional car rushed towards me from the endless flow of the seafront road, Via Caracciolo. I paid no attention. I was listening in on my headphones to that conversation again – that killing conversation. And there was no doubt about the voice. I'd heard Brendan Cullop interviewed twice on television, and that was why I'd found the voice vaguely familiar. His voice was quite distinctive, somehow both leisurely and incisive, what would once have been described as 'cool'. Indeed, it was this coolness that made half the horror of the conversation – a murder was being ordered like a dry Martini.

I'd seen him on television firstly in a programme about gambling, and secondly on the news after his actress wife had committed suicide. In the gambling programme he'd been interviewed at Monte Carlo coming out of the Casino after dropping a couple of grand at the tables. He'd been cool about it, saying that he'd had worse experiences at sea, which the interviewer of course took up as he'd been intended to do, asking if he gambled for the same reasons he went sailing round Cape Horn or in the Roaring Forties. Cullop answered that he'd never thought about it; he'd never thought about why he . . . and there followed a list of some of his more heroic and expensive adventures. He just did them. The interviewer provided the 'Because they're there' cliché and Cullop stared at him with the unrufflable disdain with which he no doubt stared at a Roaring Forty, to show that he knew the line was a cliché, and that he as occasional poet (*Or Lose Our Ventures, This Nettle Danger*) was above such things. In the interview about his wife's suicide he was caught coming out of the cemetery after the funeral: he said simply that he hadn't seen Melanie for over a year, he was very sorry it had happened as they'd had a very fine relationship that had taught both of them a lot about themselves, and that she was a very beautiful and loving person. Another bounder of a reporter had asked if he felt at all guilty and he'd said very briefly, 'One always does,' and walked away. He knew how to choose his exit lines.

There was no denying the man's overall fascination: he had looks, bravery, a certain amount of intelligence, coolness, lots of money and superb media sense. He was in and out of gossip columns but never squalidly. Nobody had even managed to hang a drugs story on him, though there were plenty of stories of his big binges – mostly with champagne. He'd even managed to take the tame domesticity out of his surname so that Cullop's no longer meant only the chain of supermarkets founded by his father but also the mountaineering and camping shops in his name; and of course he admitted quite frankly and disarmingly that he'd only lent his name and a little advice – he was no businessman. To which, of course, the subtext was, 'not like my boring old father'.

And this was the man who was paying to have someone murdered.

And Gigi . . . I walked a little more slowly and stared out to sea. A certain word had come back to my mind and I realised there was no way of expelling it this time. I had to chew it over. Blackmail.

I'd chewed nicer things in my time – like putty in mistake for chewing gum.

It was the only explanation I could think of for Gigi's possession of the tape. After all, he'd flown to Naples on the man's trail.

But without the tape. Well, perhaps he was going to bluff. Perhaps he thought that he just had to say he knew about it to make Cullop gasp 'Foiled', and hand over his entire estate.

But Brendan Cullop was big time. Really big time when you put him with his Dad. You don't get much bigger than supermarket-chain owners, not now that most of England's been turned into supermarket-chain precincts – and what little bits haven't mostly contain hairy people tramping around in Cullop boots and sleeping in Cullop tents. Gigi Esposito might have got too big for Radney, and might even have become fairly big for Bethnal Green, but he was some way still from the size of clout that could pull down medieval city centres and get knighted for it.

I walked all the way to Mergellina and hoped that the view there in the last light would take my mind off things. Via Caracciolo was a perfect curve of white lights and at the end of its curve, across the dark sheen of the bay, the humped shape of the Castel dell'Ovo rode out to sea like a determined tug pulling the brightly lit ship of Pizzofalcone behind it. Vesuvius's outline was even hazier now against the evening sky – just a distant dream of a Christmas pudding with a spoonful scooped from one side; orange lights were scattered like smarties around its lower slopes.

I remembered gazing at this view with my father and Gigi, all of us chewing *torrone* (nougat). Then Gigi had seemed very big (I must have been about ten, he sixteen) and if he had said he was going to take Vesuvius home with him I'd probably have believed him. Well, the view had remained the same but it looked as if I'd grown up.

And Gigi – had he changed, or was it just that none of us had ever known him?

I said to myself, the first thing to do is to find him, and then we could have it out man to man, brother to brother. I could start by visiting all his favourite haunts, all the bars and *osterie*, etc, I knew him to be a regular customer of. I saw myself entering sleazy bars in sleazy quarters where everyone fell silent and stared hostilely as I moved towards the bar. I saw myself shaking taciturn barmen by the throat – then I realised with a slight sense of anticlimax that I'd only ever heard him mention one place, a small pizzeria in Via Pigna Secca.

I took a bus and went there. Nobody went silent as I entered – a rare occurrence in Neapolitan eating houses I should imagine – and Gigi wasn't there of course. I resigned myself to sitting down and eating one of the best pizzas in Naples – which means of course the world – and I decided I'd start work properly the next day.

Eight

The next morning after breakfast (a gooey cake and a *cappuccino* standing up in a *pasticceria*) I made my way again to that *palazzo* in Via Duomo. I instinctively turned first to the bar opposite to have a procrastinatory cup of coffee, but again I remembered my financial state and I entered the building.

I went up the stairs and reached the first door, which had a plaque: Avv. Vincenzo Amedeo.

I put my finger towards the bell, but before pressing it I thought of the cassette in the Walkman in my shoulder bag. I recalled the film *The Sting*, took the cassette out and slipped it inside my underpants. After all, I was not likely once inside to get much of a chance to put the headphones on and compare voices, so it might as well be kept where it was fairly unlikely to be disturbed.

I rang the bell.

'*Chi è?*' a tinny female voice said from the grille next to the bell push.

'Hello,' I said in Italian, with a heavy English accent, 'I'd like to speak to the *Avvocato*.'

'*Ha l'appuntamento?* 'Ave you the appointment?'

'Well, yes.' I spoke in English. 'My firm made one.'

'What time?'

'This morning.'

'I 'ave nothing wrote about an appointment.'

'Oh, look, I've come all the way from England, not just to talk to a wall. Please let me in where we can talk in a more reasonable manner.'

'One moment.'

There was silence. I noticed a spy-hole in the door and briefly toyed with the idea of putting my eye to it and saying 'peekaboo'. Then the door clicked a few times and swung open. I stepped in. A very large man appeared from behind the door. He was dressed in a grey suit and looked about as welcoming as the door had looked ten seconds before. He had Victorian side-whiskers and a moustache. His certainly hadn't been the voice I'd heard.

He asked me in Italian with a thick Neapolitan accent to give him the shoulder bag. There was a '*per favore*' at the beginning of the sentence but that wasn't the tone.

'Sorry?' I said. 'I don't speak Italian very well.'

A woman appeared from the nearest door. ''E ask if you would like to put down your bag. And also your coat per'aps.'

'Oh, I see. Well, if you like.' I suppose it was slightly less rude than frisking me. I handed him the bag, took off my lightweight anorak and handed that to him too. 'It is a little warmer than England,' I said chattily. 'Mind you, I'd been expecting it really hot. You know, our idea of Italy – sun and sea etcetera. And I come and find it cloudier than London.'

'Yes,' she said. 'Come into the office.'

I followed her. She was rigidly perpendicular in her body – and not much more flexible facially. A lady who was above such foolishnesses as weather chat, it seemed. I gave a glance around the office. Dark bookcases frowned down on all sides; behind their glass fronts reposed respectable and not very browsable-looking volumes in dark leather. The furniture was similarly respectable and uncosy. The man with the Victorian whiskers came in behind me, his hands now empty. I wondered if he'd looked through the bag, and if so what he'd made of the begonias, which were still there from yesterday. He stood – or hulked rather – by the door.

'Now,' said the lady, going to the other side of the desk, 'please explain.' She sat down, her body making a perfect right angle of itself, and waved to me to do the same, which I did, a little more obtusely (angle-wise). Her hands fingered a file on the desk, as if they couldn't wait to be back in there, tidying life up.

'Well, we wrote to you months ago from England. Er, Computer Office Aids is the firm. You remember?'

'No.'

'Oh, hell. I've got a copy of the letter – at least I think I have, in my bag. Do you think . . . ?' I said, turning to the heavy. He didn't move. He probably didn't understand English.

'Please,' said the lady, 'we are very busy. Come to the point.'

'Well, I've come to see the *avvocato* and ask if he wants to buy any of our computers. Marvellous helps in legal offices, you know. With torts and soccages and precedents and all that,' I said speaking quickly, relying on her ignorance of English to cover my ignorance of law – and computers.

'Please, Mr, er – '

'Thrubton, Nempwell Thrubton.'

'Mr Trabbaton, I have no note of your letter, I do not think *l'Avvocato* will be interested, so I suggest you to leave. Thank you for your visit.'

'Now please, I've come all the way from England. I really would like to hear that from the *Avvocato* himself.'

'That is not possible. He is very busy.'

'Oh, come on now. Five minutes, it'll take. Which door is it?' I got up and went briskly to the door on the left. The woman didn't discompose her geometrical neatness for one moment, just said sharply, '*Paolo, fermalo.*' My hand was on the door handle when Paolo's hand reached my shoulder. Well, again, it was better than the scruff of my neck.

I rattled the door handle before I was jerked away. Paolo let go of me and I said loudly, 'Now just what sort of treatment is that? Really, I don't think I've ever – '

'Mr Trabbaton, I told you, *l'Avvocato* must not be disturbed.'

'But, hell, throwing me around the room. Is this a lawyer's office or a dockside bar?' I kept my voice high. Paolo stayed close, and seemed to hulk more bulkily.

The door to the left opened and a man came into the room. He was in his fifties and had gold-rimmed *pince-nez*. '*Che cosa succede?*' he said. I could not instantly identify the voice with the one on the tape: it was not that sort of voice.

'*Avvocato* Amedeo?' I said. 'Listen, I've been manhandled by this thug here, just because I came to keep our appointment. I think – '

'*Un momento*.' He spoke in rapid Italian to the woman, asking who I was. She told him, précising my waffle into two neat sentences. He turned back to me. 'We 'ave not receive no letter.' The accent was dreadful.

I said in slow, but not quite so bad Italian, 'But that's impossible. Can I come and talk about it for a moment? I've come a long way.'

'I can give you two minutes.' He waved me through the door into his room. I entered, resisting the temptation to waggle my finger at my nose to the lady. He stayed behind for a moment, talking quickly and quietly to her. I couldn't hear a word without making my eavesdropping blatant, so I went over to the window. It gave on to a narrow alley; indeed, the building opposite was so close it looked as if one could almost reach out and touch the ancient closed shutters on the windows: in reality it was probably about eight feet away. I'd lost my sense of direction and wasn't sure whether it was the flower seller's alley. I could hear Amedeo still talking, so I turned the handle to open the window and look out. At that moment he broke off the conversation so I stepped away from the window and tried to look casual.

He went straight over to his desk. I noticed he had a heavy limp. He sat down, looking over the top of his *pince-nez* at me. The room was furnished in the same heavily respectable style as the outer office, but if anything it wasn't old-fashioned enough for him. There should have been cracked portraits of the firm's founders on the walls, desks with ink-wells, and a grandfather clock ticking away in a corner. Doubtless it was he who had insisted on Paolo growing mutton-chop whiskers. I felt distinctly silly talking about computers to him, and not only because I didn't know anything about them.

'Er, your secretary told you who I was, yes?' I said, still in my slow Italian.

'She did.' He gazed at my open shirt. 'You are a salesman for a computer firm.'

'Well, are you interested?'

'Signor, er – '

'Thrubton.'

'Drabbitoe, I suspect you may have come to the wrong place.'

'But our letters, and you wrote back . . .'

'I have never heard of you.'

'But don't you remember? In February it must have been. We wrote to most established lawyers in the Naples area.'

'I certainly don't recall it. And I am quite sure I can have expressed no interest. I can see no immediate use for a computer. I already possess a pocket calculator which I never use, and have no desire for a larger, more expensive toy.'

'But it's not just a toy, it's . . .'

'For me it's a toy.' He took a cigarette from a packet of MS, but didn't offer one to me. It should have been snuff for him, of course. 'And I am a lawyer, not a child. Now I hope I have made my position clear. Would you please tell me who sent you?'

'My firm, of course. They gave me a list of all the lawyers they'd heard were interested in our products.' I realised I'd said this rather too fluently (from the linguistic point of view), so I repeated the last part of the sentence, 'correcting' it with a mistaken gender.

'Could you give me the name of your firm?' He had a pen poised.

I said, 'Certainly. Computer Office Aids, Thrubton Nempwell, near London.' Damn, I'd forgotten that that was supposed to be my name, not a place. Could I convince him that my parents had been fierce local patriots? But then I saw that his pen hadn't moved.

'You write it,' he said.

'Of course.' I did so. I gave it a London address, somewhere in Belgravia, adding Thrubton Nempwell as my name.

'Thank you,' he said. 'We will look into this.' He gave me

another long stare over the top of his glasses, very much the Victorian headmaster.

I said, 'Yes, I'm sorry if we've bothered you.' I wanted to get away before he decided to have Paolo administer six of the best.

'No bother. But if you will now leave me to my work.'

'Yes, of course.' It seemed I had better try elsewhere. He was so clearly a respectable lawyer who had only seen me in order to have a sneer at the twentieth century and was now anxious to get back to his tedious Giovanni Doe disputes and cases. There was just the minor detail of the hulker in the outer office to arouse suspicion; but perhaps lawyers in Naples needed such protection. Maybe I'd better leave and go to the next lawyer in the building. While I paused I heard the flower seller's voice outside, '*Tre milla lire 'o mazzo!*' I looked over to the window which, though unbolted, was still closed.

'You're sure you couldn't give me a few more minutes just to look over our brochures?'

'Signor Droopytoo, I'm afraid this is quite impossible.'

And suddenly I knew I was right. The sentence he'd just uttered ('*purtroppo questo è proprio impossibile*') was almost exactly the same as one I'd heard on the tape countless times now, and I recognised every syllable – the way the '*s*' in '*questo*' became almost '*sh*', and the way he stressed the third syllable in '*impossibile*' so heavily. Normal enough pronunciation for a Neapolitan, true, but the similarity was too exact for me to have any doubt. All I had to do now was say, 'Well, if you don't want a computer from us, could you do us a nice murder?' and watch him throw up his arms in gasping amazement. I felt very tempted, but realised I would gain nothing. Probably his expression of weary respectability wouldn't alter at all.

I decided it was better to leave before he got suspicious; suspicion would probably mean more than just a hand on my shoulder. So I mumbled some form of apology and went out through the secretary's office. She looked at me as she'd look at a rat who'd nibbled the right angles off her favourite files, and said, '*Buona sera.*' The whiskered hulk thrust my jacket and bag at me, making it quite clear that he'd prefer to be beating me over the head with them. He accompanied me to the door. As he opened it, I suddenly thought of the begonias, and was about to offer them to him, but on reflection – or rather a glance at his expression and breadth of shoulder – decided not to. I left, feeling I'd accomplished something, if only three people's hatred.

It was a great relief to be able to pull the cassette out once I was outside. A little old lady who was just turning the corner of the staircase as I fished it out gave me a nasty stare. That made it four people.

I walked back along Via dei Tribunali listening again to that conversation. It wasn't that I had any doubt; I suppose I listened to it more to congratulate myself on my brilliance in having identified both speakers within twenty-four hours of my arrival in the city. Half-way down the road their voices started to drag like someone doing a bad impersonation of Yogi Bear and I realised the batteries were going. I bought four more and changed them over, as usual putting the two spent batteries into my pocket with the two unused new ones, in order to infuriate myself when I next had to change them.

As a reward for my brilliance I wandered around the second-hand bookshops near Piazza Dante, and I bought an illustrated book on the tombs of Tino di Camaino. The thought of tombs like these might take some of the sting out of getting killed.

I took the book back to the *pensione*. The landlord shuffled out and gave me a suspicious stare and waved his duster about, as if to make it clear that *some* people in this world had to work.

In my room – which had indeed been cleaned – I sat on the bed and looked at the book. While I was staring at the tomb of Queen Mary of Hungary, I began to think of the fact that I knew now who the two murderers were – or at least the murder planners – but not who the victim was. Which could be pretty important, particularly for the victim, who was after all not likely to get a tomb like this one.

I put my book down and my eyes wandered to the window, and I noticed absently how similar my view was to *Avvocato* Amedeo's. This was not at all strange, of course, as ninety per cent of the windows in the *centro storico* of Naples probably had the same view – other windows very close opposite. But I remembered just how close the windows had been opposite Amedeo's office, far closer than the building opposite here. And the shutters had been closed and, if I remembered correctly, looked as if they had been closed for some time. This last of course might just be an after-impression given by my memory of the age of the shutters; I couldn't actually remember give-away details like cobwebs across the bolts. But it made me think. It particularly made me think of the fact that I'd turned the handle of Amedeo's window and had thus left it (providing nobody else had touched it since) openable from outside.

At midday I was back where the old lady brought her touch of spring to the city alley, whose inhabitants otherwise could only tell the seasons by how long the washing took to dry. She was getting up to go off for lunch, but she looked questioningly at me first, as if thinking that I might have come to complain that the begonias I'd bought had faded in the wash. I gave her a reassuring smile, and as soon as she'd rounded the corner I began to study the house opposite Amedeo's office. Quite probably it was a house that had been evacuated after the earthquake; the inhabitants were probably now living in one of the vast 'temporary' caravan sites on the outskirts of the city. The door, naturally, was locked, but I saw that the shutters on one of the ground floor windows were loose, and the window behind was open. It would be quite an easy matter to get in, if I picked the right moment.

I went round to Via Duomo and had a sandwich and a beer. I glanced at *Il Mattino* but really watched the *palazzo* opposite. After ten minutes I saw the tall lady from the office come out into the street: she was wearing what seemed to me, on this Neapolitan April day, a rather unnecessary fur coat; perhaps it was one way of softening her angles. She walked off in the direction of Corso Umberto. A few minutes later Paolo came out and walked off down the road. Another minute passed and then Amedeo came out, followed by another big man whom I hadn't seen before; his arms hung slightly away from his body like a cowboy's when itching for the draw – or perhaps more aptly, like a suspicious gorilla's. Amedeo stood at the side of the road with the gorilla just behind him. He glanced at a newspaper, ignoring the presence of the gorilla with perfect nonchalance. A car drew up driven by Paolo; Amedeo and the gorilla got in, and they drove off in the direction of Porta San Gennaro.

I finished my beer and went back to the alley. I gave a quick look up and down and saw no one was around. The people going down Via San Biagio certainly didn't bother glancing down this dark alley as they passed. So I pulled the loose shutter open and then hoisted myself up to the window. A few seconds later I was inside what seemed to be a kitchen. I left the shutter half open so as to provide a little light.

Everything had been taken out of the kitchen it seemed, except for the wall fittings. Even the light bulb was gone.

The door ahead of me seemed to be the flat's front door and gave immediately on to a staircase, which was completely dark, of course. There was an overpowering smell of damp mixed, I suspected, with that of human shit. I started walking carefully upwards, my hand on a flimsy banister. I remembered that Amedeo's window was on the same level as the second floor here, so after two flights of stairs I tried the door on the right.

It opened without any problems, and as I entered I kicked something metal. I bent down and felt for it on the rough wooden floor. It turned out to be the door's lock. Someone had been here before, presumably by the very same route.

I moved over to the vague cracks of half light that indicated the window. I shuffled forward so as not to trip over anything and my feet twice kicked things that rolled with little tinkling noises. I opened the shutters – which protested noisily – and the room became visible in musty grey light. It was bare except for a broken sofa against one wall, torn newspapers in a corner and several syringes on the floor. Drug addicts must have used these disused flats as doss houses – perhaps still used them.

I stared out towards Amedeo's window. It was closed, of course, but not shuttered. I could see into its respectable interior. All I needed now was a jungle creeper or chandelier and then I could swing over and fly feet first through the window, landing coolly amidst a tinkling sparkle of glass.

I had a look around the flat. It didn't take much looking around as there were only two rooms and a toilet. All I discovered, however, was the origin of the stench and a few more syringes.

I tried the flat opposite. The door there opened just as easily. By leaving the doors of both flats open I could provide enough light to look around in here too. In this flat there were blankets on the floor, some empty cans and some food débris that was unappealing but not all that old. There was also some furniture: two chairs and a table and an empty wardrobe. No chandeliers (or jungle creepers) however. I toyed briefly with the idea of tearing the door off the wardrobe, but when I fingered its wood and thought of the drop to the alley, chucked in the idea.

I went back to the first flat on tiptoes. It was probably the sight of the blankets that had got me on edge. But I couldn't stop the floorboards creaking.

The floorboards . . .

I bent down, brushed a few syringes and a matting of dust away and studied the floor. One or two boards seemed fairly loose.

I set to work, and some minutes later I'd managed to prise one free. The amount of grunting and groaning on my part and creaking and cracking and twanging on the wood and nails' part had made rather a nonsense of my earlier tiptoeing. The plank was about nine feet in length, one foot wide and an inch or so thick. It should do, I felt.

I started to ease it out of the window. Amedeo's window was slightly higher than this one, and I wondered how I could stop the plank slipping; then I thought that once I'd pushed his window open, I could rest my end on the outside sill against the bottom of the window frame.

As I continued to push the plank out, I looked at the various windows that gave on to the alley. So far no questioning face was to be seen at any of them, but I still wondered whether I wouldn't be better off coming back that night – or giving up the whole idea.

But coming back that night would have three possible disadvantages: the presence of the local junkies, the fact that Amedeo's shutters would probably be closed, and the fact that instead of just being scared I'd be terrified out of my wits.

Giving up the whole idea, of course, did not have these disadvantages, and indeed had so many advantages, I wondered why I kept on pushing the plank across the gap. Because the gap was there, I suppose, as Cullop might say on a bad day. Anyway the plank reached the window, which was formed by two interlocking 'doors' that opened inwards. I just had to hope now that no-one had turned that handle back again.

I gave the window a sharp push at the bottom. The two sides of the window quivered. I raised the plank – it seemed to me the kind of thing I'd seen strong men do in circuses in their drum-rolled finale – and I pushed at the centre of the window where the handle and bolt were. Either it was very stiff, or someone had rebolted it. Then suddenly it flew open and the plank jerked forward and downwards, landing with a crash on the sill. I just managed to keep hold of my end, and fortunately did not go flying after it, like Bugs Bunny forgetting to let go of his bowling ball.

I arranged the plank and gave it a few tentative shakes and pats for the sake of reassurance. As the result was anything but reassuring, I stopped doing it and decided to get on with

100

the acrobatics without delay. I put my shoulder bag more securely round myself and clambered up.

It was impracticable to do it on hands and knees, I realised, so I had, literally, to walk the plank. There was one very nasty moment in the middle when I felt the thing buckling under me like a spring bed, but I got across.

Once in the office I pulled the plank in after me. Then I got straight down to my search. I suppose I was looking for something like a folder with a big name on it, GUYS TO BE RUBBED OUT. I went over to the desk, which had a respectable-looking confusion of papers on it. Nothing seemed pertinent – but then perhaps everything was. I really couldn't know. It was obvious I should have brought a camera along to microfilm the lot.

I picked up a desk diary and flicked through it. Just names and places; nothing to indicate whether the people named had been or were to be shot or stabbed or strangled at those places. I looked ahead to the next couple of months. I pulled my Walkman out of my shoulder bag. It was a model that could also record, so I started to dictate the appointments for the next few weeks on to the tape, after that conversation. It seemed a reassuringly business-like thing to do, and I sat in Amedeo's chair while I did it and wished it could swivel. The main difficulty was in daring to pitch my voice at a business-like and recordable level.

None of the people's names, all Italian, meant anything to me, but here and there I recognised a restaurant's name – though they were certainly not restaurants whose menus I'd ever dared to look at. Some of the places were quite mysterious, like 'Via. Merc. Tor. 11' – if they were places, of course.

I was putting the book back on the desk when a piece of paper slipped out from its back pages. I retrieved it from the floor and opened it out. It was a photocopied map of a small town with long straight roads. There was a cross in red ink at the top of the map. I hadn't even had the time to take in any

of the names on the map when I heard someone putting a key
into the lock of the outer door – a sound that had scared me
rigid but three days before and which had no less an effect
now.

Nine

I shoved the map into the diary and dropped it on to the desk. I then threw the Walkman into my bag and rushed to the window. I heaved the plank on to the sill and pushed it out.

I couldn't possibly make it, I knew, unless the person went into one of the other offices first. The plank thumped on to the opposite sill and I stopped for one moment to listen. I could hear nothing. I was sure that the outer door hadn't opened yet. So what was whoever it was doing?

I didn't stop to ponder but clambered on to the plank. I just managed to pull the windows more or less to behind me – this involved a most nasty twisting of my body – and then I ran (well, it felt like running to me) across. I landed with a thump on the floor; I pulled the plank in and closed the shutters.

Darkness.

I stood still and breathed in the rarefied ordure and allowed my eyes to grow accustomed to the dark. It was almost cosy.

Then I heard a noise downstairs and it stopped being cosy, and became again a room in a dark smelly house. With a shuffling Thing downstairs.

What I'd heard had been a muffled bump, and listening very hard I could imagine I now heard furtive footsteps. Then they stopped. The bump had probably been someone entering the house by the same way I'd entered. Had he gone silent because he'd then heard me? But I had been absolutely silent at that point. Maybe I'd left some indication of my presence, like the unwonted tang of my anti-perspirant. I waited.

So did the Thing.

I waited some more.

Likewise the Thing.

Then when I felt I was going to crack up unless something happened I heard footsteps start up the stairs. I picked up the only object of any useful size, the floorboard, and I stood by the door and stared out into the blackness.

The blackness became less impenetrable, became greyness. The footsteps rounded a corner and the stairs and walls became visible, with jumping, shifting shadows. So whoever it was had a torch, which meant he'd see me and I'd just see a blinding dazzle, out of which no doubt a spectral voice would issue orders.

The last corner was rounded and the full beam shone up the stairs, revealing – I noted strangely – a very bad painting of Vesuvius and the bay on the wall. I was about to step backwards into the room, but then decided that was only putting things off, so stepped out on to the staircase holding the board rather uselessly in front of me. The beam hit me full in the face and I said, 'Go on then, riddle me with bullets.'

'Pardon, do you repeat?' the dazzle said, in a strong Neapolitan accent. The voice wasn't too spectral, I noted.

'Nothing. Could you take the light off me?'

And he did so, shining it quite unexpectedly on to his own face for a moment. 'Now you can see me also.' It took me a second or two to recognise him, then I remembered the man I'd seen smoking at the top of the stairs in Amedeo's *palazzo* the previous day. He was carrying no weapon.

'You,' I said.

'You recognise me?'

'I've seen you.'

'And I you.' He pointed the torch behind me in such a way that I wasn't dazzled.

'Good. So can I presume you're not going to riddle me with bullets, or are you just lulling me into a false etc?'

'Sorry? You speak too fastly. I don't understand all.'

'We can speak in Italian if you prefer,' I said in Italian. I leant the plank against the wall.

'Ah, you speak very well,' he said in Italian too.

'Well, if we're going to swap compliments, I feel I ought to invite you in, only, er, we're spring cleaning at the moment.

104

You know, polishing the underside of the floorboards.' I paused, 'Er, you don't live here yourself, do you?'

'Live here? Are you mad?' He sniffed significantly.

'Well, somebody does and the smell is part of the proof. There are blankets and things through there.'

'Tramps,' he said, 'or junkies. Let's talk somewhere else.'

'You are lulling me, aren't you?' I said to myself in English. Then in Italian, 'Are you with Amedeo?'

'No. Don't worry.' He didn't ask what I meant.

'All right, I'll come with you,' I said. 'In fact, let's go quickly. Someone from Amedeo is probably on his way here.'

'I don't think so.'

'How the hell do you know?'

'That was me with the key. I heard someone inside the office and I knew he must have broken in by one of the windows as I'd been watching the entrance. So I fiddled with a key in the lock, hoping that it would send the intruder back the way he came. Which could only be this way. So here I am.'

'Very clever. I'll claim for the damage to my nervous system, however.'

'Let's go. I can't stand this stink any longer.'

We climbed out into the street, and a passing old lady muttered something about dirty drug addicts and why didn't they bring back the death penalty. We walked briskly into the Via San Biagio and went in the direction of the Gesù Nuovo. Out in the daylight I was able to observe him more clearly. He was some years older than me and had sharp southern features. He was slight of build, and dressed with that casual elegance or elegant casualness typical of so many young and not so young Italians. He dusted off his clothes with quick nervous gestures that suggested a fastidious nature.

'Where are we going?' I asked.

'Have you eaten?'

'Well, a sandwich.'

'Come and have something more substantial.' He turned into a side road and we made towards a small *trattoria*.

105

'Well, in fact,' I said, 'I'm, er, I'm not sure I can afford – '

'It's very cheap, very cheap. In fact, I'll offer.' This seemed to be a snap decision on his part.

'No, no. I couldn't possibly – '

'I insist.'

It was one of the strangest lunch offerings I'd ever received. We hadn't even swapped names yet. 'Well, if you're really sure, thank you very much.'

We entered the *trattoria*. The waiter gave a nod of recognition to my companion and we went over to a table near the kitchen. There were only about ten other people in the restaurant, but as usual it sounded like a full football crowd. To add to this impression the walls were covered with posters of the Naples football team, one wall being entirely devoted to pictures of Diego Maradona. The customers, however, if one really listened, were mostly talking about food.

'I'm Franco,' he said, 'Franco Longo.' His eyes were darting around the restaurant as he said this, as if hoping to find someone less boring to talk to.

'And I'm Gennaro. No, it's true.' I explained my origins briefly.

'So you're Neapolitan.' His eyes came to rest on me – or, at least, fixed me intently for a couple of seconds before darting away again. When they alighted on me I was disconcerted by their fixity, as if for those two seconds I could see another face behind his.

'Half.'

The waiter came and took our order. Franco recommended the *spaghetti alla carbonara*, and I said OK. We said we'd choose the second course later.

'Right. Now we know each other's names, I expect each of us wants to know what the hell the other is up to,' I said. I didn't lower my voice as I said this, since I would thus have been inaudible. But a glance at the other tables showed that nobody was paying the slightest attention to us. Only the footballers on the walls had their eyes on us.

'Exactly.'

'With the possibility that we find out we're deadly enemies and both have to go for the knives.'

'Or I just leave you the bill.' He smiled. It was a bit difficult to imagine him really being a deadly enemy. 'I hear the Neapolitan accent now. It's curious from under that blond hair.'

'I can speak dialect too, if you prefer,' I said, doing so, 'in fact, rather more easily.'

'No, no. I can't take it seriously. Not with those Nordic features. But let's come to the point. What were you doing in Amedeo's office?'

'Looking around,' I said, reverting to Italian.

'That is obvious. What for?'

'You couldn't tell me who you are first?'

'One of us has to speak first. I asked you. And I'm paying for the lunch.' His fingers drummed on the tablecloth. At one moment he seemed entirely casual, almost languid, and then some small gesture indicated an inner tension. Mind you, even his finger-drumming was done elegantly.

'So I'm supposed to deliver myself into your hands for a bowl of spaghetti.'

'Not just any bowl. Peppino's spaghetti. And you appreciate that I could quite easily have called the police and had you arrested.'

'So I've got to trust you because you're not a law-abiding citizen.'

'Exactly. Like you.'

'Yes.' I picked up a bread stick and nibbled it thoughtfully. 'I suppose you're right. We malefactors should stick together.'

'Round here it is the custom. They call it the Camorra.'

'Mind you, there's not absolute solidarity among Camorristi. I seem to have read a lot about gang murders – hundreds each year.'

'Yes.' His face had lost all trace of humour and his eyes fixed on me, again troubling me with that impression of another face behind his mask. It was clearly not a topic he liked joking about – reasonably enough, I suppose – but I had

107

the impression that his attitude was determined by something personal, rather than by general moral principles.

The waiter brought the wine and Franco poured two glasses out.

'All right,' I said. 'I don't know what I was looking for and that's the truth, but I have a brother who seems to be mixed up with this Amedeo fellow and I want to know how and why.'

'Mixed up?'

'He had a tape of a conversation between Amedeo and somebody else, an Englishman.'

'Cullop?' (He pronounced it Cool-lop.)

'That's right. How did you know?'

'I didn't know. I guessed. What was the conversation?'

I had to be careful now or I could be landing Gigi in embarrassing situations. 'It wasn't very clear. But it sounded suspicious.'

'Yes, I'm sure. Where is this tape?'

'Er, my brother's got it. I heard it in England.'

'So you came straight out to Italy to break into *Avvocato* Amedeo's office. I see.'

'Well, er, not exactly. I came out here, you know, to, er, come to Naples, and seeing I was here . . .'

'Walking past his office this morning, you said, "How convenient" and in you went. *Dai, andiamo.*' These last two words were accompanied by a flinging gesture of one hand which managed to be both languid and expressive (of disbelief).

'I spoke personally to Amedeo yesterday. I went in and – '

'And interrogated him fiercely. Did he go down on his knees and beg for mercy?'

'Well, not exactly. Mainly I just wanted to check the voice on the tape was the same.'

'Where did your brother get this tape?'

I was getting a bit fed up. 'Look, I've answered all the questions so far. What about you answering a few? I mean, when I know who you are, I may be more willing to answer a few more questions.'

'Or just answer the same ones a little more completely.'

'You have a very charming way of calling someone a dirty liar.'

'Please! I just think you could be a little more explicit. Anyway, let me show you how. I'll tell you about myself. I'm a journalist, and I got interested in Amedeo after those hotel killings in London. Probably like you.'

I didn't choke on my wine or shout, 'I confess it all'; I stayed looking at one of the many photos in which Maradona was caught in action, his body twisted in mid-air and his features screwed up in a maniacal grimace. 'Well, in a way,' I said. 'Tell me what you mean.'

'You know, those two men murdered in a hotel. Bayswater. *Acqua del Golfo*. All the newspapers made some sort of half-jokey comment about what a suitable place for a Neapolitan to die. I knew the men. Or I knew something about them. They were Amedeo's former bodyguards. Two hired men from Torre Annunziata, which is where Amedeo's from originally.'

'I see.' There had been something concentrated and bitter in his tone which stopped me from making any jokey comment, half or otherwise.

'And so am I. You know Torre Annunziata?'

'Well, I know where it is. I've never visited it.'

'No. It doesn't come very high on tourist itineraries. Many tourists go through it on the way to Pompeii and Sorrento. But one bored stare and then their train's off to more picturesque places.'

'You don't sound all that fond of it.'

'Of course it has all my happy childhood memories – all two, or is it three of them? – and I've got friends there; but let's say that now that I live here I don't often feel homesick. Torre Annunziata has all the problems of Naples, without any of the compensatory picturesqueness. Extraordinary levels of unemployment, delinquency and drug addiction.'

'Now you're making me homesick,' I murmured.

'So I thought a little investigation into what's behind the death of those two could stir some waters.'

'I see. The police have made the connection between the two men and Amedeo, have they?'

'They've got equal access to the evidence, if they want to use it. Really want to. Since it happened I've been keeping an eye on Amedeo's office. I discovered that, very fortunately, the office at the top of the stairs is closed for some reason – holiday or restoration or something – so I could stay outside their door and watch the stairs without being observed. At least until you came along, whatever you were doing. I've just been staying there and watching Amedeo's door. Seeing who's visiting it. And taking photos. I have a lovely one of you going down the stairs.'

'Me? But . . . You could have told me.'

'And this Signor Cullop who has been twice. The first time he came I followed him back to his hotel and got his name. He is famous, I'm told. A colleague on *Il Mattino* tells me they're going to interview him this afternoon.'

'Oh, yes? He's known in Italy too then?'

'Well, not so far, but he sounds like the sort of person *Oggi* and *Gente* would feature if they knew about him, so *Il Mattino* could start a rush. He hasn't any connections with the Royal Family by any chance?'

'Not that I know of.'

'That would make it front-page stuff, with this royal visit next week. Royal families are always big over here, even tatty artificial ones like the Grimaldi – especially them, in fact.'

Our spaghetti arrived. We wished each other '*Buon appetito*'. After a few mouthfuls he said, 'Good, no?'

'Very good.'

'Now, tell me about this tape and how your brother got it and what it says.' You can't refuse me anything after spaghetti like this, he seemed to imply.

'You're a journalist,' I said.

'I've already told you so.'

'So it wouldn't be much use asking you to be discreet about anything I tell you, would it?'

'Writing about matters like these you learn pretty quickly about discretion, in fact.'

'Yes, but discretion about the wrong people probably. Discretion about the big bastards. I want you to be discreet about me, little me.'

'OK. You become "reliable source". Very simple. And I'm not intending to be discreet about Amedeo, you know. I've not been spending the last few days observing him just to be discreet.'

'You were observing him pretty discreetly, mind you. Is he big?'

'That is also what I want to find out. But I'm not going to be scared. I'm out to get him. So help me.'

'It's just that when he's got, I'm, er, a little worried about other people getting got too. Not only me, there's my brother too.' And I took a huge mouthful of spaghetti that would give me at least half a minute's respite.

'I see. Well, convince me that your brother deserves discretion.'

'He's my brother,' I said – without most of the consonants.

'What?'

I swallowed the last strand. 'All right. I don't know where he got the tape, but those two men that got murdered came to my flat in London looking for him and the tape, so perhaps he pinched it from them. But he didn't kill them.'

'No, I'm sure he didn't. That was Amedeo.'

'Who is Amedeo exactly?'

'Well, that's the interesting thing. Only a year ago – or less – most people would have said he was a has-been, but now . . . Well, I at least am not so sure. You presumably know what's been going on with the Camorra over the last few years.'

'Well, more or less.'

'The rise of Cutolo and all the gang warfare that came out of that. Daily murders and the rest of it.'

'I've read it up,' I said. I read Italian news magazines when I could, so had a vague idea of what he was talking about.

Cutolo was the man who had created, while in prison himself, the *Nuova Camorra Organizzata*, transforming the Camorra from something local and almost medieval into a vast modern organisation on a par with the Sicilian and American Mafia. In doing so he had smashed various small Camorra 'clans'; the NCO itself was now being broken up, both by the phenomenon of *pentitismo* (grassing) and by the creation of other organised clans, in particular the *Nuova Famiglia*.

'Well, *Avvocato* Amedeo was linked with one of the clans that got eliminated. A clan from Torre Annunziata. He had represented various members of the clan in court and so on. Then in the late seventies the clan got smashed, all the main members of the family dying in various nasty ways. Amedeo himself was shot in the legs, possibly only as a warning, and it was then that he took to travelling with bodyguards. He seemed, however, to have left the gang world – or rather it had left him. He was on his own and had to be happy making an honest living as a lawyer, if such a thing is possible; and he kept his bodyguards only out of nervousness, since there was no longer any real reason for anyone to be after him. So it seemed, at any rate. So it seems, in fact, to most people. But there's the mystery of those two murdered bodyguards who left his service some months ago.'

'Do you know why they left?'

'Well, er – ' He seemed a little hesitant. 'I know they weren't happy to leave. And there's also the rumour about the man they call 'o Rauco.'

'Sorry, what rumour's this?'

'Oh, he was a Camorra killer, one of the best so they say, in the Torre Annunziata clan for whom Amedeo worked. He disappeared from Naples some years ago and many people suspected it was a case of *lupara bianca* – you know, when Mafia or Camorra victims just disappear to become part of the foundations of some new block of flats or motorway – but anyway, nobody did very much about his disappearance, mainly because nobody cared that much. He didn't have family, nor any real friends. Then some months ago he was

112

seen in Rome having lunch with Amedeo. So I've heard. But nobody as far as I know has looked into it. He was only a minor killer and, in fact, nothing had ever been definitely proved against him.'

''o Rauco. Nice and sinister.'

'Yes, they go in for these nicknames. The man apparently has an unnaturally deep voice – like someone after a throat operation.'

I suddenly remembered the killer's voice in the Bayswater hotel – as deep as an open grave.

He continued, 'Some of the names are more horrible. 'o Animale. 'o Pazzo. And many of them live up to their names, too. I've seen some things . . .' He allowed a leisurely but significant pause. 'But I think this rumour's worth a little investigation. Particularly when we note the way Amedeo's wealth – new house in Posillipo, villa at Ischia – just keeps on growing. All in all, I feel the need to know more about him.'

'How well do they pay you for these articles?'

The waiter removed our bowls and Franco said, 'I don't have to tell you that it's not a question of payment. You yourself aren't here for profit, I know.'

'Well, at this moment I'm engaged in scrounging a meal,' I said, and poured myself another glass of wine.

'Yes, but you didn't break into Amedeo's office to find something to eat.'

'No. I never go housebreaking without entirely worthy motives.'

'Don't try and be funny. I can see you're an honest person. So help me.'

'Listen. I think – I know – we could get on well. I like you, which I suppose means, which does mean, I trust you, so I'd like to help you. But as I've said, it's not only me who's involved. Give me your telephone number and as soon as I'm sure – that is if I ever am sure – that I can help you without getting my brother into too much trouble, I'll give you a ring. I'll tell you all I know. Which at the moment is not very much, in fact. But anyway I promise. And, since I've decided

113

that I'm not going to give you anything now, I suppose I'd better turn down the next course.'

'Oh, come on, sit down,' and he threw his hands out in a languid gesture of generosity.

I'd only made half a move towards getting up in fact, but I completed it. 'No, no. You accused me of being honest, so I suppose I have to show I can be now and again. Give me your number.'

He did so, writing it on a piece of paper. The waiter came up and looked questioningly at me. I said, 'I'm afraid I have to go but my friend – '

'I'll have the veal, Sandro.' The waiter moved away. 'Well, this looks like pathological honesty. Either that or just running away.'

'I'm not going to be far. Tell me, by the way, about Cullop. Who's interviewing him?'

'Someone from *Il Mattino*. I told you. A chap called Carlotti. Why?'

'I just wondered. How did *Il Mattino* know he was here?'

'They keep an eye on the big hotels, of course.'

'I see. What time's the interview scheduled? I wouldn't mind having a word with him myself, before or after.'

'If he'll let you. I think Carlotti said at three thirty. Tell me now where I can find you.'

I gave him the name of the *pensione*.

'You have no relatives here?'

'Yes, but you know how it is with relatives. I'd never be able to get anything done with them forcing food and drink down me.' At Zia Ciccina's, whenever I visit it, I never get up from the lunch table before four o'clock, and then only to stagger over to a sofa. And Zio Carmelo spends his whole time arranging trips to Vesuvius or Capri; the island, of course, is very pretty, but is one of those places where only the postage stamps cost the same as elsewhere; and as for Vesuvius, I feel I've got to know its present brooding self well enough and am not keen on being too close when it changes mood. I like it on the postcards best.

'I suppose not. But be careful. Remember you're not in London with your friendly bobby on every corner (*con i vostri bobby simpatici ad ogni angolo*).'

'You've never visited London, I presume, but I take your point.'

'Are you sure? You don't seem a very careful sort to me. A little too impulsive, and that can be dangerous. You understand?'

'I understand.' I thought of Gianni and Raffaele. 'I'll do my best to be calm and rational. At least as calm and rational as everyone else around,' I said, looking at the other customers. One man was banging his fist on the table as he insisted on the necessity of not grating cheese too long before a meal. Another man was flinging his arms up in disgust at something his companion had said about inflation. And three men at another table were all shouting together: one would have said they'd reached some crisis if it weren't for the fact that they'd been shouting together since we came in – apparently about where to buy oysters.

'A calm Neapolitan's a dead Neapolitan,' Franco said, 'and that's what you'll become if you're not careful.' He tossed back the last of his wine with a gesture of finality; he obviously felt this was a neat note to end the conversation on, so I thanked him again and left.

Ten

I found a phone box in Piazza Carità and phoned Cullop's hotel. I was eventually put through to Cullop's room. His voice came over the line, loud and clear, suave and evil (or so it struck me at any rate). 'Cullop speaking.'

"Ello, Signor Cullop. Dees eeze *Il Mattino*.' I used a fairly heavy Neapolitan accent. 'I am Carlotti.'

'Oh yes. You're the journalist coming here, isn't that right?'

'That is right. But I 'ave a problem. Would it be possible for me to come a little earlier? You see, my programme is changed.'

'Well, all right. Three o'clock?'

'Yes, that would be fine. Oh, er, the photographer will come some minutes later. Just to, er, 'ow you say, take a quick snap or two.'

'OK. See you then.'

'Goodbye.'

I put the phone down. I couldn't believe how easy it had been.

I went back to the *pensione* to get a notebook and pencil for my journalist disguise. The owner of the *pensione* said in Neapolitan to someone in his kitchen, 'This English chap, in and out, in and out, let's hope he doesn't start playing music too.' I wondered briefly if they had regular trouble with English people playing loud disco music, but then thought that the English were no more likely to be guilty of it than the Italians, and besides, in Naples, who'd ever notice?

I entered my room and extracted the notebook and pen from the rucksack. I sat on the bed and had another look at the Tino di Camaino book, to assure myself that it really had been worth the money. I'd have to steer clear of the bookshops for a little while, however, if I wanted to avoid having to call on relatives for charity. While I was studying the book I heard music from next door: Elgar's Enigma Variations. It was a bit of a surprise.

It was not easy to hear through the wall with the traffic noise from outside, so I stepped into the corridor and listened through the door. Just out of curiosity. Then suddenly the door opened. A short man of about forty in a shabby corduroy suit stared rather suspiciously at me.

'Sorry,' I said, guessing him to be English, 'I was just listening to your music.'

'Oh, I see. Thought I heard someone outside so decided to check. You're English, are you?'

'Yes.'

'So am I. Jolly good. Here on holiday?'

'Well, yes.'

'How nice. I live here.' He said this as if he expected a round of applause for his courage in facing the Neapolitan jungle. He had a very precise, just slightly pompous voice. I could imagine him speaking Italian without at all altering his accent; that would be giving in to the foreigners.

'Really? That must be nice too,' I said. 'I, er, I must – '

'Oh, if you want to come in and listen, please do. Just about to make some coffee. Nescafé, you know.'

'Oh, thanks.' He made it sound like a special treat.

I went into his room.

'Good old Elgar, eh?' He pulled out an electric kettle from under the bed. 'This is probably the only electric kettle in Naples.'

'I expect so.'

'Sit down,' he said, waving me to the only chair.

'Thank you.'

He bent over the kettle; he was one of those people who hope to hide their baldness by pushing long strands of hair over the tops of their heads, and he succeeded in hiding it about as effectively as telephone wires hide the view from a train. I always promise myself that I'll never stoop to this, but I sometimes wonder if those who do it said the same thing

117

themselves once; after all, I can't imagine anyone not having noticed the silliness of the pretence on other people's heads.

I looked around the room. It was more or less the same as mine but there were various little indications of his more permanent residence in the *pensione*. Apart from the kettle, there was a row of books on top of the wardrobe, and a couple of framed photos on the chest of drawers. One of these photos showed an Oxford or Cambridge college group, the other a large Victorian building – almost certainly a public school. The music came from a radio-cassette recorder by the window. A copy of *The Times* lay on the bed, three days old; I was glad it wasn't the day before yesterday's. The only thing that seemed to be missing was a picture of the Queen.

'There we are,' he said as he straightened up from the kettle. He sat on the bed. 'Well, it's nice to bump into somebody English. A bit of news from home. My name's Jameson, Martin Jameson.'

'I'm Jan,' I said, as usual preferring a little anonymity.

'Isn't this music just too wonderful?' The Nimrod variation had just begun. 'They don't know Elgar abroad, you know. Not at all. Such a pity. I teach here, you know. Teach English in a language school.'

'I see. Must be very interesting.'

'Well, you know, it's nice being in Italy. Cheap wine and all that, ha ha.' His laugh was practically a direct statement – 'this is humorous.'

'Yes, of course. Do you like Naples?'

'Well, it's very interesting, of course, but it's not, well, it's not northern Italy. I was in Tuscany before, Lucca: that's so beautiful and, well, civilised. Marvellous churches, marvellous buildings and, well, Tuscany, you know. But I had to change schools.'

'Been here long?'

'Six months, more or less.'

'In this *pensione* the whole time?'

'Very difficult finding a flat, you know. And this place is quite cheap, central, and, er, clean. And Don Gaetano – the owner, you know – is quite a character when you get to know him. I'm *il Professore* for him.' A little laugh to show how little the grandiose-sounding title meant to him.

'I see.'

'He always says how he likes my taste in music. I may have made an Italian convert to Elgar and Vaughan Williams. Quite a little coup, you know. You here long?'

'Oh, don't know. A few days. Just wandering around.'

'Very nice, too. Of course you mustn't miss the Archaeological Museum, or Capodimonte, or –'

'No, I've got a guidebook.'

'And do go to the church of San Gregorio Armeno. A little baroque jewel. Rococo almost. Quite exquisitely absurd. I tell you because it might not be in the guidebook. Not so well known, you know.' While pouring out the coffee, he chattered away about the various things I must not miss, revealing a pretty extensive knowledge of the city's sights and monuments, in particular those that struck him as exquisite or too too absurd or quite stunningly awful. He didn't stop at any point to find out whether I in fact cared at all about baroque art and architecture. I drank my coffee and half listened to him and half to the music. Then I realised he was asking me something. 'Sorry?'

'Where are you from?'

'Oh, er, London originally. Bethnal Green.'

For once he didn't say 'That's nice'. He said, 'And, er, what do you do?'

'Well, I'm unemployed at the moment.'

Again he didn't say it. 'Oh, looking for a job here?'

'Well, you never know.'

'I could introduce you to our director. He's, er, he's not English.'

I felt that I was supposed to murmur 'poor chap' or something.

'He's Italian. Very nice chap, of course. Um, they might be needing someone for some external courses. You know, teaching in factories and things. Ever done any teaching?'

'Just a bit.'

'Oh, what?'

'Er, some French. At adult evening classes.' I wondered whether my urge to lie was becoming pathological (I'd once taught Italian at evening classes), but then decided I was probably right to cultivate anonymity, even if only for the sake of practice.

'Oh, well, that should hold you in good stead. It's not everyone who can teach languages, you know. Quite a skill. But then all teaching is really. I've been doing it since I came down from Cambridge, you know. In England and abroad.'

'Really?' I said. 'Um, thanks for the offer. It would be very kind of you – introducing me to your director, I mean.'

'Tomorrow all right?'

'Yes, I think so.'

'Tell you what, why don't we have a pizza together tonight? Then I'll have found out from the director when you could see him.'

I agreed to this and we fixed a meeting time. He might be a little pompous in his manners, but his offer was kind and could prove very helpful. I got up and went towards the door, having a look at his books on the way. There was a green Michelin guide to Italy, a few Penguin Dickens, a complete paperback set of Anthony Powell's *A Dance To The Music of Time*, and several books by and about Baron Corvo. I pulled one of these down, blew some dust off it and looked at it. 'You seem interested in this bloke.' I spoke a little absently.

'Oh yes. Such a character, you know, such a character. Quite unique. You really must read him if you never have. An English eccentric abroad.'

'I see.' I put the book back. He probably wanted me to say, 'Like yourself', but I didn't.

'Well, now, see you this evening.' He changed the cassette as I opened the door. 'Walton's *Crown Imperial*,' he said. 'Marvellous stuff. And what with the thought of this royal visit, you know, I find I'm always playing it. So looking forward to it – as indeed the Neapolitans seem to be. Going to be very exciting.'

'Yes, of course,' I said. 'Well, see you later.' The music followed me into the corridor and I imagined him standing up and saluting. A lonely sort of person, I thought.

Eleven

At three o'clock I was at the hotel. My notebook and pen were in my shoulder bag and I trusted that these and the acceptance of a glass of whisky would be sufficient disguise. I crossed the reception hall, which seemed to have grown overnight from the size of Gatwick to that of Heathrow, and I went over to the desk. It was a different man there, fortunately.

'Signore?'

'From *Il Mattino*,' I said. 'Come to see Mr Cullop.'

'One moment. I'll ring.' He did so, and after a few seconds nodded to me. 'He says to go on up. Room 339.'

I took the staircase to give myself more time for mental preparation. As always I had no master plan, was just playing things by ear. But talking to Cullop was undoubtedly the right thing to do, and what better way to interrogate him than by being a journalist?

I tapped at the door of 339.

'*Avanti*,' shouted a voice, that even in this one word proclaimed its Englishness.

I entered. The room was only marginally smaller than the reception hall below, it seemed to me. Two windows with balconies framed Capri and the sea, which had decided to turn a gorgeous blue at that very moment. Cullop was standing on the balcony, his hands pressing down on the railing. It struck me as a rather posed stance – the challenger of the waves staring out into their azure distances. He'd probably even put his white suit on with this picture in mind. And then being bloody Cullop the sun had come out for him as well.

'Good afternoon,' I said.

'Ah, ciao,' he said, and came into the room, closing the windows behind him. 'Can I offer you a drink?'

'Yes, thanks. A whisky would be very nice.'

'Sit down.'

I did so, looking around. It made a nice contrast with my *pensione* room, everything – bed, window, chairs – being four times as comfortable and ten times as large; and there were of course many things which were completely lacking in my room, such as television, fridge, carpet, telephone, quiet (now the double-glazed windows were closed). In case one couldn't be bothered to go over to the window there were a couple of nineteenth century paintings of the view towards Vesuvius, with picturesque urchins laughing in the foreground – they'd probably just picked the painter's pocket.

He opened a cabinet and poured the whisky. He was slightly taller than I'd expected from my long-distance views of him yesterday, just as good-looking and deeply tanned. I think he knew what a fine contrast his teeth made against the tan, so he went in for strong Charlton Heston type smiles. He must have been in his late thirties, but apart from a line or two around his eyes, seemed younger than me. His clothes were as pristine and as wrinkle free as his skin. 'Ice?'

'No thanks, neat.'

'Well, fire away,' he said when he'd given me the drink. He sat down in the armchair opposite me, his legs crossing and still no wrinkle defiling the trousers.

'Mr Cullop, you are a famous man – '

'Brendan, please. You're Ben, aren't you?'

'Beniamino, yes. Of course call me Beni.'

'You don't look very Italian, you know.'

'My mother was English.'

'That explains how you talk so well. I was rather afraid I might have to give the interview in Italian. Not quite up to that really.'

You managed to order your murder without any problems, I didn't say. I said, 'Thank you very much. I manage. Now, Brendan – '

'Are you going to record us or just take notes?'

I hadn't thought of recording the interview. I said, 'Yes, of course, my tape machine.'

'Good. In all the interviews I've given to reporters with

notebooks I've ended up saying things I know I never said, if you follow me.'

I took my Walkman out, carefully ran it forward, and then put it on the table between us and started it recording.

'Now, Brendan, why have you come to Naples?'

'Well, Benny, I love Italy. I love its cities and its art and its music and its, er, people. You know, people smile more here?'

'I see.' This was the usual Michelin guide tat. 'So you come quite often?'

'Yes. About once a year. This year, in fact, more than once. I always stay a few days in Naples and then go over to Ischia where I have a small house.'

About as small as one of his father's supermarkets, I imagined. 'What made you choose Ischia?'

'Oh, it's a little jewel, of course, and well, so many interesting people have lived and live there.'

This, of course, gave me the lead in to, 'And you're one of them yourself.'

'Oh no. I've done a few interesting things perhaps.' His light modest laugh irritated me because it was so *un*irritating. He really did sound modest, the bastard.

'Well, yes. What makes you decide to take so many risks in your life?'

'Without the risk of death one doesn't fully appreciate life.' I don't know how he did it, but he managed to make it sound as if he were saying it for the first time.

'I see. Have you any plans for a similar expedition now?'

'I'd like to know the jungle. I've got to know the sea in most of its moods, the mountains, the Arctic, and I've crossed the Sahara, but I've never really dared the jungle yet. It's another challenge, you know. And I don't like turning down challenges.'

But you won't do your own murders, you yellow belly. 'But you've nothing like that planned in Italy?'

'No. I'm on holiday.' He gave me a fully relaxed smile. 'Can't be "the hero" full time, you know.' And the ironic inverted commas made this remark – which should have been the most irritatingly smug so far – sound convincingly self-deprecating. There was something about his ease of manner which communicated itself, so that I felt almost inclined to own up to my little jape. I told myself, however, that I must not succumb to his playboy charm and I forced my hackles back up. 'Tell me about your, er, personal life,' you decadent capitalist slob.

'Lady friends and the rest of it. I know.' He sounded humorously resigned.

Of course you're desperate for your privacy and you only agreed to this interview because you thought I'd ask for your opinion on the meaning of life. 'Well, yes. And any enemies?'

'Sorry?'

'Well, do you think in your life in the public eye you have made any personal enemies?' Anybody you want killed, you slimy hypocrite, and cut out that charming smile.

'Well, I, er, I suppose one always has one's critics, and not being perfect one has always hurt someone somewhere, but, well, I've never actually thought of myself as having *real* enemies. I hate nobody, at any rate.'

So you're killing whoever it is for profit. 'Your, er, emotional life?'

'The papers have reported quite extensively my relationship with Sally, and I'd just like to say we're both very happy. But I don't like talking too much about my private life. It's not that interesting – for other people.'

'So is, um, a marriage likely?' He wouldn't believe in me as a journalist if I just dropped the subject.

'Who knows? Though I think we are as married now as we ever can be.'

'I see. What about relationships with your father?'

'My father is a very hard-working man who helped me a good deal when I was younger and who has come to accept the way of life I've chosen.'

'How, um, financially dependent are you on him?' I was about to add 'if you don't mind my asking', but again remembered my role.

'With the Brendan Cullop stores and those two books about my expeditions I do all right. If I were a businessman, I could, of course, be very rich, but, well,' light laugh, 'you know, I live as I want to live.'

I looked around the room with what I hoped was a sardonic eye and said, 'Yes, of course. Now, have you any long-term ambitions?'

'To be at peace. And you can be at peace with the world, you know, in the middle of an Arctic storm. I wrote one of my poems about the experience.'

I managed to resist asking him to read me the poem. But the annoying thing was that this didn't come across as sounding as pretentious as it should: he was somehow able to make it quietly convincing – almost.

'Really,' I murmured. I felt that to break the spell of his charm I'd have to shout 'You murdering swine!' and throw my whisky at him.

The phone by the door gave out a long buzz. The internal phone presumably. I gripped my whisky tighter and watched him as he rose – one lithe movement, without even touching the arms of the chair – and went over to the phone.

'*Pronto*, oh, but . . . Send him up then.' He put the receiver down. There were faint corrugations in his brow.

'That'll be my photographer,' I said quickly. 'I told you he'd be along later.'

'Yes. Yes, you did.' He didn't sound entirely convinced.

'I'd better go and help him.' I was about to say something about carrying his tripod but I thought better. 'He, er, he can never find his way around anywhere.'

I walked quickly out of the room, ignoring his 'But just a moment – ' I was half way down the corridor when I remembered the Walkman on the table. With *the* cassette. I turned instantly and started back. But I heard him moving towards the door too and my mind just flipped. Without any reason in the world I found myself tapping at the door next to his. Possibly I thought he'd rumbled me and would straightaway strangle me.

A female voice said, 'Hello?'

I heard his hand on the door handle and said, 'Room Service' and opened the door without waiting for an answer.

I was inside before Cullop opened his door. A girl with long blonde hair stared at me from the bed. She was lying there reading a magazine. She was, at least, fully dressed.

'Er, hello,' I said.

'Hello. What do you want?' She was American.

'I, er, look, um, just give me a couple of seconds.' To invent a story. And to listen to the sounds outside. I heard Cullop step outside his room, pull his door to, and then walk down the corridor, presumably in search of me.

'What for?' She didn't look the sort to start yelling in panic, at any rate. She lay there quite composed. I had the feeling that she knew perfectly well what to do if I started any 'funny business'. She was about twenty and attractive in a healthy, sun-tanned sort of way. I could imagine her being a judo black belt. I stayed by the door.

'Just to get my breath back,' I said. Cullop's steps faded, but he'd presumably be back as soon as he'd realised I was nowhere about.

'What from?'

'I'll, er, be going straightaway.'

'Yeah, but why did you come in here in the first place?'

'I made a mistake.'

'Yes, you did. Like you said you were room service. And you don't seem to be.'

'Not exactly.'

'You're English, aren't you?'

'In a way.'

'In a way. Not exactly. Yeah, you sure sound English. But not room service.' She was still quite calm, almost amused.

'Look, sorry, sorry, sorry. Wrong room. I'll be going. 'Bye.' I walked out again and went to Cullop's door. It was locked. While I was trying it I heard the girl's door open. She stood there watching me, probably choosing her moment to spring. 'Another mistake?' she said.

'Look, I swear I don't want to give any trouble. I'm not a thief or anything like that.'

'You're sure of that? You wouldn't mind me calling up someone to check?'

'Don't do that. Look, I can explain.' I was desperate to be away now, and be blowed to the Walkman.

'I think you'd better. Why don't you come back in here?'

'All right.' Anything to be away from the door. She walked back in without even looking to see if I was following. I was, in fact, though not sure why. Well, she had a very attractive figure to follow, I suppose, in blue jeans and a pullover that looked as if it was made of pink candy floss.

She went over to an armchair and perched on the arm. It was a good compromise position – not entirely relaxed and friendly, and yet neither sleeves rolled up and legs flexed for a flying kick. She gazed at me, her arms half-folded. 'You don't look like a thief, I suppose.'

'Thanks. I'm not, I'm really not. In fact quite the opposite.'

'You're a cop, are you?'

'Well, I didn't mean . . . All right, I suppose I might as well admit it.' I was straw clutching.

'Wow.' She said it without any major revolution in her expression like a raised eyebrow or lowered lip. I gazed at her steady blue eyes and her 'tell me more' face and decided I could make an ally of her. She looked a good sort to have on one's side. After all, she could probably throw Cullop out of the window.

'Listen,' I said, 'do you know the person in that room?'

'The guy next door? He's some kind of celebrity, isn't he?'

'Well, yes. He's Brendan Cullop.'

'Oh yeah. I knew I'd seen his face.'

'Well, I'm watching him.'

'Oh really? Why's that?'

'Well, it's a little complicated. But, look, can I trust you?'

'What kind of question is that?'

I moved a little further into the room. She unfolded her arms. 'I'd like to feel I can trust you,' I said.

128

'I'm the one who should be saying that, I reckon. You came into my room. And tried to get in next door.'

'Yes, I'm sorry. Look, this is quite unorthodox and I don't want to involve you in something that doesn't concern you . . .' I went over to the window, as if checking for eavesdroppers.

'In what?' she said, shifting her position in order to keep me under surveillance.

'What's your name? I think it would help if we introduced ourselves.'

'Sarah. Sarah Ryan. And I'm twenty-five, from Los Angeles, unmarried, was brought up Methodist – anything else you need to know?'

'I'm Jan,' I said. 'I'm from London. Are you here on holiday?'

'Yes, I am. This is one of the funniest social chats I've ever had. Are all English cops like this?' She paused, then added, 'Or English thieves?'

'I'm not an ordinary cop. Er, not a thief either.'

'No, I guess not. Ordinary at any rate. But go on. Why are you watching this Cullop guy?'

'Afraid I can't tell you that. But could I have a look at your balcony?'

'Go right ahead.'

I stepped out on to the balcony. Cullop's balcony was some five or six feet away. Too far to jump – at least, for me to jump. Doubtless Cullop would do it while lighting a cigarette. And at that moment Cullop stepped out on to the balcony. He must have returned without my hearing him, and from the fact that he was talking to someone in the room I presumed he must have met up with the real *Il Mattino* interviewer.

He saw me. 'You, but what the – '

I dived back into the room and made towards the door. Suddenly she was off the chair and coming towards me.

'What's up?' she said, grabbing my arm as it made to open the door.

Fortunately I didn't follow my instinct, which was to smash

out at her. I'd have probably ended up in the sea if I had. 'Cullop coming – hell – lemmego.'

'Well, let's listen to what he's got to say to you, why not?'

'All right.' She relaxed her hold on my arm and opened the door. Cullop was outside and as soon as he saw me he said, 'Just what the hell – '

I decided I'd listened to enough and darted round the side of him and down the corridor. He was after me in an instant – so I heard, because I didn't look. At the end of the corridor I saw the lift doors closing and I dived through the gap at the very last moment, feeling like Indiana Jones. The lift went down. There was only one other person in the lift, a room service boy with a tray and the remainders of an afternoon tea. He said, *'Pianoterra?'* and I nodded. I said in English, 'Just made it.' He smiled uncomprehendingly back. The lift, though making no other stops, was not very quick; I could imagine Cullop thundering down the stairs even faster than us – hang-gliding down them, perhaps. I said to the boy, 'Do you speak English?'

'A little.'

'I'd like to give you a small tip,' I said, fishing out a two-thousand lire note.

'Thank you,' he said with a puzzled smile as he put it in his top pocket. He didn't ask any questions about it.

'Nothing you've done, of course,' I said, 'but for what's going to be done.' He clearly didn't understand, which was probably a good thing.

The lift doors opened – and there was no Brendan Cullop. Presumably he'd decided it wasn't worth it. Having keyed myself up for the big moment when I'd shove the boy – crockery-laden tray and all – into him, I felt almost disappointed. I could hardly ask for the tip back, and the alternative – pushing him over anyway – I toyed with for only half a second. I gave him a nod and as much of a smile as the loss of a Walkman and two thousand lire permitted and left the hotel at a brisk pace.

130

Twelve

The rest of the afternoon I spent in the sun up in the gardens at Capodimonte reading newspapers and news magazines to find out whatever possible about the present state of Camorra warfare and to find any possible clues as to Amedeo's involvement. I didn't learn all that much, though I did find out about the lottery number that hadn't come round in years and was thus causing regular bankruptcies in Naples. I also rang up relatives from a bar to ask if they had any news of Gigi: I said that I was in Rome and hoped to be able to come down and see them. As usual their hospitality even at that distance was overwhelming; they practically wanted to feed me spaghetti down the line. None of them had heard or seen anything of Gigi.

At seven thirty, as arranged, I went for a pizza with Jameson. (He was the sort of person one tended to think of by surname only.) At that hour, of course, the daily ritual of the *passeggiata di sera* (evening walk) was at its height. The pavements of the Via Roma were as solid with people as the road was with traffic; they were all dressed in their casual elegant best, apart from a few *scugnizzi*, darting in and out of the traffic with the same contemptuous coolness with which they darted in and out of the crowds. It was the only time in the day that the sound of voices was almost as loud as that of traffic: voices chatting, gossiping, laughing, and – noisiest of all – greeting each other. The greeting cries seemed to be the same in volume whether delivered at a foot's distance or across the traffic-packed road – cries of 'Ueeh! Pasquale!' or 'Ola!' or 'Ciao!', which were lengthened by Neapolitan cadencies to operatic extremes. It's easy to hear why Neapolitans produce so many songs; their normal conversation is half-way to being the close of a Rossini first act.

We turned off the Via Roma, Jameson saying, 'Awful at

this time, isn't it? I mean, they're only showing off their clothes to each other.'

'Well, it's a lot livelier than an English town.'

'Yes, I know, awful, isn't it? There's the pizzeria.'

The pizzeria had only just opened and was, of course, empty. Neapolitans never eat much earlier than eight thirty. The waiter led us to a corner table. There was a painting opposite us which showed the *pizzaioli* standing in the middle of the Bay of Naples and cooking the pizzas over the crater of Vesuvius. We sat down and immediately showed our un-Neapolitanness by lowering our voices to suit the ambience. Jameson said, 'I like eating now, it's so peaceful', and I said, 'Well, yes, it's certainly that.'

Jameson chatted throughout the meal. He told me about the school he'd taught at in England, and whose sons they'd had there and how different teaching was in Italy and yet how similar in many ways. He told me what a responsible job teaching English was, and how the other teachers didn't take it at all seriously; they were either young louts come over for a year in the sun with cheap booze or girls looking for Latin lovers. I wondered why only girls, but he didn't enlarge. He told me how excited all the English community – except his fellow teachers, of course – were about the royal visit and how much in-fighting there was to get an invitation to the party with the Royals. I didn't ask him if he'd got one because I knew that if he'd had one it would have been the first thing he'd have told me. He asked occasional questions about me and I was vague in my replies. He raised his eyebrows slightly on learning that I'd not been to university, let alone to Oxford or Cambridge – but then not having been at all was probably better than having been to the wrong college. When we ordered our pizzas, I admitted to knowing a bit of Italian and explained that my father had been Neapolitan, but I didn't say how much I spoke. I wasn't keen on breaking my anonymity completely.

He drank almost a litre of white wine with his meal; he only

132

ever drank white, he said, as it didn't give him hangovers. He didn't actually get drunk, but his voice got louder; soon we were talking almost as loudly as the waiters.

After a cup of coffee and a grappa (which I decided to go mad and have because, after all, I was going to see his director the next day and have an interview for a job) we left the pizzeria. The first customers other than ourselves entered as we left.

The Via Roma was still quite animated; one or two prostitutes were already hanging around on the street corners. One of them called out to us, and Jameson quickened his pace. I heard her saying to her companion that we were certainly '*finocchi*' – queers.

When we entered the *pensione*, Don Gaetano came to the door of his room and peered at us. We could hear an American soap opera behind him. Don Gaetano pointed his belly and finger at me and said in Italian, 'Are you called Esposito?'

'Yes.'

'You speak Italian then? Why didn't you say so . . . A friend has phoned for you.'

'Oh yes?'

'Franco, his name is. He says it's important.'

'Oh, can I use your phone?'

'Yes. It's in Naples, isn't it? Two hundred lire then.'

Jameson went on down the corridor and I followed Don Gaetano's lumbering body back into the room. In one corner two members of an excessively rich American family were talking quietly to each other prior to hurling the Ming vases which were clearly on the sideboard for no other purpose. Don Gaetano shook his belly in the direction of the phone.

I dialled the number, Don Gaetano counting the number of turns my fingers made.

Franco answered, '*Pronto.*'

'January here. Do you mind if I speak in English?'

'No, no. I've tried to find you all afternoon,' he said, also in English.

'Really?'

'Yes, I forgot to tell you at lunch. You know you have been followed this morning. When you left Amedeo. The big man with the big arms followed you.'

'What?'

'Ah, I asked myself if you knew it. You didn't see him then.'

'No, I didn't think of it. How stupid of me.' And to think I'd wondered scornfully at Cullop's foolishness in not checking in windows for furtive reflections.

'This is what I told you. Not to be so – so impulsive. To look around you, no? You don't know the world in which you're involving yourself. Just this I wanted to tell you. And to remember now they know where you stay.'

'Oh hell.'

'Yes. So be careful. Don't walk down any dangerous streets – don't walk down any streets, that is.'

'Just wait for them to come here.'

'Well, be ready. Is there a fight in the room with you?'

'No, just the television.' The first Ming vase had gone. 'They've not come for me yet.'

'So you think. Be ready.'

'Yes, yes. Don't worry.'

'No, but you start to worry. All right?'

'All right.'

'Ciao. *Statte buone*.'

I was about to reply with the same Neapolitan formula, but decided I didn't want Don Gaetano to realise how much Neapolitan I spoke. I said, 'Ciao' and put the phone down.

Don Gaetano kept his eyes on the television, which was now showing an advertisement for toilet rolls with music from Beethoven's Seventh Symphony, and said in Italian, 'Everything all right?'

'Yes, yes,' I said.

'Two hundred lire please.'

I thought of telling him to put it on my bill (it was rather less than 10p) but instead fished the coin out and handed it over. He pocketed it and said, 'Why didn't you tell me you spoke Italian?'

'I don't speak it very well,' I said, keeping my accent plummily English – the sort of joke accent they use to dub Laurel and Hardy films (*Stanlio e Ollio*).

'But you're Neapolitan.'

'No, no. My father Neapolitan, my mother English.'

Don Gaetano waited for the end of the advertisement and then turned to me and said, 'Signor Jameson is a very nice man. Very polite and kind. He has never given us any trouble all the time he's been here.'

'Oh really?' I said, wondering if this was a polite way of saying, 'We don't want *your* sort here.'

'Six months here, you know, and no trouble.'

'Yes, very good.' Was I supposed to go along and ask Jameson for tips on behaviour? I said *'Buona notte'* and left Don Gaetano watching an advertisement in which a baby's nappy addressed the viewer in a high-pitched voice.

As I reached my door Jameson peered out from his room and said, 'Everything all right?' I could hear Elgar's Violin Concerto behind him.

'Yes, yes. Just a friend saying hello.'

'Oh, you've got friends here? Relatives perhaps?'

'One or two.'

'How nice. Coffee?'

'Well, no thanks. I'm a little tired. Goodnight.'

'Goodnight.'

I closed my door and went over to the bed where I sat and thought. Amedeo, of course, had not believed for a moment that I was a computer salesman and so he had had me followed. And I'd not noticed anything despite the fact that the man who'd followed me was, in Philip Marlowe's phrase, about as inconspicuous as a tarantula on a slice of angel cake. So now they knew where I was.

Why was I such an interfering fool? My brother had called me a cock-up artist, and it wasn't a bad definition.

What the hell had I thought I was trying to achieve, barging in on big criminals and mass murderers and engaging them in chit-chat? And had I in fact achieved anything?

Nothing except the possible friendly alliance with Franco – and perhaps with that American girl. And even she might have had her doubts about my identity as Super Cop after seeing me run like a scared rabbit just because somebody had raised his voice at me. Well, the faint possibility of her support was something to keep in mind, all the same, for the next time I went along to have it out with Cullop.

I went over to my rucksack to get a pullover out. The pullover was on top and came out easily. I thought to myself, 'That's funny,' and then wondered why I'd thought that. I snatched at the thought before it flipped over my mind's Niagara, and I stared at the rucksack and remembered that the last time I'd opened it the pullover had been entangled with a shirt, like a snake fighting a ferret.

I emptied the rucksack. Nothing was missing, but then nothing was worth taking. I examined my pile of five science fiction novels on the small table beside the bed. They were all still there, and as far as I could tell in the same position as before I'd left, but then that was likely enough. My money and passport, etc, I'd had with me in my shoulder bag all day so that was safe. Even as I thought this I panicked and made a grab at the shoulder bag to check. They were still there.

So there was just the evidence of the pullover. But I was sure all the same. Someone had searched the room.

Thirteen

Whoever it was could have found nothing of any importance, except clues to my character and financial state such as holes in my socks and safety-pinned turn-ups in my jeans. But all the same, the thought of someone going through my things made me feel vulnerable. Indeed, I even opened the wardrobe and looked under the bed for bogies.

I dismissed the idea that it was just a hotel thief, highly desirable though it would have been to discover one (a little one) cowering in the wardrobe. It was Amedeo's work, however indirectly.

The fact of being in a hotel room made me think of Bayswater. I thought of that unseen big man with the voice like Satan gathering phlegm, and I thought of him in this room flipping through my underwear. I found I was sweating – and I still hadn't put my pullover on.

Next door the Elgar stopped abruptly in mid bar and I heard Jameson come out of his room and close the door. He walked past mine in the direction of the lavatory. It was round the corner at the end of another corridor. His footsteps halted uncertainly as he reached the corner, and I remembered from the previous night how the corridor was kept unlit. A few seconds later his footsteps proceeded briskly out of my hearing and I heard the distant CLUNK of the lavatory door.

I realised that my sharp attention to every noise was an indication of how nervous I was. I was on tenterhooks, whatever they were.

Then I was niggled by a curious thought. What had that pause been when Jameson reached the end of the corridor? I remembered how the night before I'd stood there myself looking for a light switch. I'd eventually found it on the opposite wall from where I'd been looking.

I heard the lavatory flush and Jameson went back to his room. The Elgar recommenced.

I left my room and tapped at his door.

'Oh, er, *chi è?*' (Well, 'key ay' was what he said.)

'It's me, from next door.'

'Come in, come in.'

He was sitting on his bed reading an Anthony Powell novel. He had a mug of coffee by his side.

'Sorry,' I said. 'Would you mind if I borrowed a book?'

'Of course, of course. The music isn't disturbing you?'

'No, no. It's lovely.' It's not disturbing you? I thought of asking; he was reading a novel, after all. I went over to the wardrobe and took down *David Copperfield*.

'Oh, er, it's rather long,' he said.

'It's all right. I've read it before. Just like to look at some bits again. You can have it back tomorrow.'

'Oh, I didn't mean . . . Keep it as long as you like, of course. Awfully good stuff, you know. Micawber's marvellous, marvellous. Er, tomorrow, you said? Right, goodnight, goodnight.'

'Goodnight and thanks.'

I went back to my room with a kind of fierce satisfaction inside me, still mixed of course with the general trepidation that hadn't left me since Franco's phone call. I had been right: the *David Copperfield* had a film of dust just as the Baron Corvo biography I'd looked at that afternoon had had, but the dust was all on the bottom of the book. That was the curious thing that had half struck me as I was putting the biography back.

The only explanation was that the books had recently been put on the undusted surface of the wardrobe top. It was, of course, possible that Jameson had just re-organised his room, but thinking of his groping inability to find a light switch in a corridor necessarily used by residents every day, I rejected the idea. No, Jameson was as new to the hotel as I was.

I recalled Don Gaetano's strange conversation, and it struck me that the only purpose behind it could have been to insist on the fact that Jameson had been in the *pensione* for six months. Presumably Don Gaetano had been bribed – or terrorised (as who wouldn't be by that Voice?).

I packed my rucksack, putting the pullover back in and putting on my anorak instead. It looked as if this was going to be another of my hotel runners. I was becoming quite an expert.

Or was it? Could I learn more by sitting tight (indeed, getting drunk might be the only way I could summon up the courage to do it) and waiting to see what Jameson was up to? He had, after all, learnt a little more about me this evening – like the fact that I was called Esposito and had friends and relations here – and would presumably want to communicate this to his superiors at some point.

So I sat on the bed and waited. I picked up my Sheckley novel and even turned a page occasionally, but it was mere show (for all the watchers I hadn't discovered perhaps, behind the two-way mirror or looking through the cracks in the ceiling). I was attentive only to the sounds from next door, and I was so impaled on my tenterhooks that I didn't enjoy a single note of the music. An hour or so later he turned the Elgar Sea Songs up a little higher and I moved to the door, my ear aquiver like a car aerial on the M1. Yes, I was right. His door opened very softly and then closed just as softly. He didn't lock it, no doubt afraid of making too much noise. He moved off down the corridor – at least, so I imagined; I heard no footsteps.

After some twenty seconds I left my room (locking it and pocketing the key) and tiptoed down the corridor towards the *pensione*'s front door. From Don Gaetano's room came the sound of a game show. A contestant was about to answer his final question on, it seemed, the history of washing-powder advertisements, and there was a suitably dramatic drum roll. It suited my mood too as I stepped quickly across that part of the corridor visible to Don Gaetano. Clearly he was absorbed in the drama of the game because he raised no interrogative cry. I reached the front door and I waited till the contestant answered before putting my hand to the knob. He got the answer right and the thunderous applause covered the noise of the door opening and closing.

Below me now I heard the distant thump of the door into the street. I ran down the stairs and out. I saw Jameson walking down the road in the direction of Piazza del Plebiscito. I followed wishing my anorak had a collar I could turn up. The road was still fairly animated, though there were fewer pedestrians about. Prostitutes were at the corner of many of the roads leading into the *Quartieri Spagnoli*. Jameson did not look back, however, and as far as I could tell was as slack about shop window glancing as Cullop and I had been. I kept about fifty feet behind him nonetheless.

He crossed over at the end of the road and entered the brightly lit Galleria Umberto. There were quite a few people sitting and chatting at the various bars, though as usual the first impression on stepping into its cool heights was of a sudden cathedral-like peace after the noise and buzz of the traffic. I guessed, from the occasional long-dressed woman, that many of those drinking had just come out of the San Carlo opera house on the other side of the Galleria. *La Sonnambula* had been performed, I remembered from a poster. I hovered at the entrance and watched Jameson make his way to a café table at the far end of the Galleria. A man waved a hand towards him. It was Amedeo. I went into the nearest bar from where I could watch and be fairly sure of not being seen. Jameson sat down at the table with Amedeo and started talking. Amedeo seemed to be alone, but then I saw the two large men from the office at a table nearby: the gorilla and the Victorian Elder. They had glasses of beer in front of them. They weren't talking, just staring around the Galleria. I wondered if Amedeo had been to the opera, and if so had he taken them with him. Somehow I couldn't imagine them listening enchanted to Amina's last great aria.

I drank a beer at my bar and kept watching Jameson and Amedeo. Amedeo was sitting in an elegant but casual pose, with his legs crossed and his hands lightly joined on the table.

140

He scarcely looked at Jameson, as if uninterested in what he had to say, and while I watched he reached for his drink only once. Jameson was hunched over the table, his small head pushed out towards Amedeo like a tortoise's, and he fidgeted with his drink as he talked. I had the impression that Amedeo despised his informant, and I was with him on that. Mind you, I didn't go all that much for Amedeo.

I didn't see what could usefully be gained by watching them, so I finished my beer and went back to the *pensione*. I made it to my room again without being observed. The last song was coming to its close next door.

I decided it would be safer to go now, and I picked up my rucksack. Then I thought of Don Gaetano: if he'd been terrorised into his lies to me then it would be unfair to go without leaving the money for the room; if he'd been bribed to do it – well, I could just hope that the example of my honesty would touch him with shame and make him lead an honest life ever after. I put three ten-thousand-lire notes on the bedside table.

As I walked past Don Gaetano's door his voice called out sharply, '*Dove va?*'

I opened the front door quickly. I heard him waddling across the room at his top speed. He called out again, '*Ma dove va?*' I yelled back the first thing that came into my head, something about the music being too loud, and then ran on down the stairs. He kept shouting, '*Ma dove va? ma dove va?*', as if it were an incantation that might pull me back up.

Below me I heard the door into the street being opened and I halted where I was, at the top of the flight of stairs that led down into the courtyard. I heard Jameson say quietly in his Stanlio and Ollio Italian, 'What's going on here?' and I retreated round the corner. There was someone with him and that someone now raised his voice and shouted up the stairs, 'What's happening, Don Gaetano?' It was a Neapolitan voice, probably the big gorilla's.

Don Gaetano yelled down, 'That young Englishman's leaving.' I thought of the thirty thousand lire I'd left with sudden resentment.

I heard the henchman start up the stairs and I acted on impulse. The scaffolding made the staircase narrow in parts, so I hadn't put my rucksack on my back; it was on the ground in front of me now and I picked it up in both hands, jumped into full view at the top of the stairs and hurled it down.

I saw, for one instant, the gorilla man raising his huge arms defensively, then there was just a noisy tumbling confusion as he fell back to the courtyard with the rucksack on top of him. The rucksack seemed to have hit him with a resounding explosion, but a second later, as I stared at him sprawling underneath the rucksack like an overturned tortoise, I realised that that had been the gun in his hands going off. Plaster from the ceiling fell around me to confirm this.

I was at the bottom of the stairs in two wild leaps, ready to do all sorts of vicious things to him, but I realised it wasn't necessary. His head must have struck the ground with great force and he lay still. I saw Jameson standing by, his hands raised to his face in a trembling attitude that would have been comic in any other situation. From above, Don Gaetano's incantation became frenzied: '*Ma cosa succede? ma cosa succede? ma cosa succede?*'

I picked the gun from the prostrate man's fingers, and pushed my rucksack off him.

'Don't – don't – don't – ' began Jameson, his hands a-flutter. He looked like something out of Beatrix Potter.

'Shut up,' I said. I stared down at the man on the ground. He was still alive, which some inner dispassionate voice told me was to be considered a relief. I looked again at Jameson and pointed the gun at him. It was just about manageable in one hand, though no doubt two hands were advisable for firing it accurately.

'Don't – don't – ' he said again.

Other voices were now to be heard from the other floors of the *palazzo*. I realised that I'd better be going, and quickly. It struck me that if I were to be stopped while running from this scene, I'd make a better impression if I weren't holding a smoking gun. And I was scared of the thing anyway.

But I'd be rather more scared of it in Jameson's hands.

'You're coming with me,' I said and I gestured menacingly with the gun again.

'Please, please, don't – '

'Go to the door,' I said, 'quickly.' I could hear people coming out on to the stairs.

He went over.

'Open it.'

He did so. I put my rucksack on to one shoulder, threw the gun into the furthest corner of the courtyard, then ran to the door, pushing him out in front of me. 'Come on,' I said to him.

'But – but where?'

'We're getting away from here.' And I pointed up the nearest side alley.

'But these streets are dangerous,' he said. 'I – I never go up – '

I didn't argue the point. I grabbed his arm and pulled him. He ran with me up the dark street. It rose steeply and with the rucksack on my back I was soon panting painfully. I kept my hand on Jameson's arm, but he made no attempt to break away.

I took the first turning to the right underneath a house held up with scaffolding. Somebody came out from the scaffolding and Jameson said, 'Oh my God, who is it – ?'

'It's a prostitute, you stupid berk,' I said, and we walked on past her, without looking too hard at her. She presumably had her reasons for choosing the darker streets to ply her trade.

'Where – where are you taking me? Must we – must we stay in this area?'

'Until we get far enough away, yes.' I hadn't decided where I was going yet. I thought of the underground station of Montesanto which wasn't very far, but rejected it as too obvious. I had a vague idea that there was a way up to the Vomero hill by crossing the Corso Vittorio Emanuele and

143

taking a staircase, and I thought of making for it. There is always something reassuring about going upwards. 'And I want to ask you a few questions.'

'Look,' he said. 'I – I didn't want to get involved in all this. I really didn't. Oh my God, you must believe me.'

I could feel him shaking. 'Well, you'll have to tell me about it. Why you did get involved?'

'I had no idea he had a gun, you know. I – I thought he was just going to ask you to go along and see the lawyer, you know. Mr Amedeo.'

'Just give me a polite invitation, RSVP. Of course.'

'Look, please, I – I don't know why they want you. I don't know who they are. You do believe me, don't you?'

I looked at him. His face was screwed up plaintively, a few of his strands of hair were hanging down from his left ear to his collar like long-dead flowers. He inspired pity not loathing. I said, 'Not one hundred per cent. But you can keep trying. What were you telling Amedeo just now?'

'What? When?'

'I saw you,' I said. 'In the Galleria. Discussing the opera perhaps.'

'No, no,' he said quickly.

'Silly Eye-tie music, I forgot.'

'Look, can't we go somewhere more salubrious and talk – er – civilly about the whole thing?'

'Like two English gentlemen, of course. Only I'm half Neapolitan and so I'm only capable of waving my arms around and sticking stilettoes in people. And you're a shit, not a gentleman.'

'Look, I say – ' He pushed his hair up with a fussy offended movement and I felt – illogically – a bit embarrassed at what I'd said.

'All right, where can we go?' I asked. He was certainly right about the insalubriousness of the area. The streets were lit – or not lit – in such a way that one suspected skulking figures in every doorway and round every corner; slimy things, mostly paper, clung to our feet as we walked, and every so often piles

144

of rubbish hulked drunkenly against the walls. We saw few people: one, an obvious junkie, shuffled towards us out of a doorway, and Jameson gripped my arm instead of the other way around; I kept walking firmly forward and the junkie, after a bit of menacing play with one hand in his coat pocket, decided to slink back to his doorway. I hadn't been too terrified. It could only have been a knife and I'd have pushed Jameson into it anyway. A couple of prostitutes in short skirts and fishnet stockings which looked about as sexy as Don Gaetano's string vest, called out to us from another doorway and someone shouted an obscenity out of a house window. Otherwise only cats (or worse) moved, scratching at the rubbish and whipping away into the darkness as we approached, like shadows when a torch is dropped. The houses mostly had their windows shuttered and only a vague and persistent murmuring gave any clue to the teeming population one knew to be packed into the buildings that leaned and bulged in on us threateningly.

'Well,' he said, 'why don't we go back to my little flat. I, er, I don't really live in the *pensione*, you know.'

'No, I guessed that, after I heard you take five minutes to find the light switch for the loo.'

'Oh, I see. Not very clever of me. But I – I didn't want to get mixed up in all this. Oh, it's too horrible. I should have refused.'

'Why didn't you?'

'Oh God, it's all so awful. I suppose I'll have to tell you. But please, let's get away from here. Let's please go to my flat.'

'Oh yes. No doubt to find Amedeo and friends all sitting around waiting.'

'No, no, no. Oh dear, what a thought. Please believe me, I don't want to have any more to do with Amedeo.'

'And why did you have to "do" with him in the first place?'

'I'll tell you. When we get to my flat. I'm – I'm too nervous here.'

I decided to trust him. He really did seem pretty shattered

by what had been going on, as if he'd involved himself in something more serious than he'd expected – which made him a boon companion, after all. 'Well, a cup of cocoa in a cosy armchair would be nice,' I said, 'but just because you've decided to have no more to do with Amedeo, what makes you think he's decided the same about you? Isn't he going to want to know what happened back there? And he's not going to get much of an account of it from your friend on the floor.'

'Amedeo doesn't know where I live. I moved flat only a week ago without telling anyone. I did it really to try and find a little peace. He gets in touch with me through the school and so at least I know that at home I'm safe. Nobody knows where I live. Not even the school.'

It didn't sound a very sociable way to live, but I wasn't looking for knees-ups at the moment. I said, 'OK' and then, because it seemed a unique opportunity to use the remark, added, 'But no funny business.' He said, 'Of course not,' and we made our way out of the warren of the *Quartieri Spagnoli* and up the hill to the Corso Vittorio Emanuele. There we walked along to the *funicolare* station.

A quarter of an hour later we were walking through the streets of the Vomero, which, if not all that much cleaner, were at least wider, so that the rubbish wasn't quite so noticeable. Large blocks of modern flats lined the streets and there was even an occasional tree. We hadn't talked much on the journey. As we walked into the station he'd said, 'Let me give you a ticket,' and I'd thought it was the least he could do but hadn't said this, just a brief 'Thank you'. On the almost empty *funicolare* he'd suddenly come out with, 'God I'm so sorry – ' but had then broken off. I hadn't tried to prod.

His flat was on the third floor of a modern block and was clean, compact, comfortable and characterless. This was not only because he'd just moved in but also because he was clearly the sort of person who never imposes his personality on his environment. Indeed his room at Don Gaetano's had been positively cluttered with his belongings in comparison with the empty shell here. A few books on a shelf, a few

146

cassettes in a corner, and everything else in cupboards. I guessed he'd have three of everything – three plates, knives, forks, etc – not so that he could have two guests, but so that he only needed to wash up once a day. There were no pictures, possibly because the only two he had were both at Don Gaetano's. The furniture was functional and sparse. It was more like a cheap hotel than Don Gaetano's had been.

I went to what looked the most comfortable chair, put my rucksack by its side and sat down. I asked him, 'What about all the stuff you've left in the *pensione*?'

'I know, I know. I'll have to go back. I – I do hope the police haven't been called. Oh God, it's all such a mess. Why *did* I get involved?'

'I don't know. Let's have a drink and you can tell me.'

'You don't want cocoa? Oh, er, was that a joke? Sorry, I see, well, I've got some white wine.' He went to the kitchen and brought a bottle and two glasses.

'Right. Tell me what Amedeo wanted to know, what you told him and why.' I could see he would burble unless I took a firm line.

'Well, Amedeo told me he wanted to know who you were and what you were doing in Naples. So he wanted me to introduce myself to you in the *pensione* and, er, get to know you. Really, it all seemed quite harmless. I mean, the only, er, thing not entirely honest was my telling you I lived in the *pensione*, but as Amedeo said, I had to make your acquaintance casually. But as to all the rest, well, we, er, we chatted and naturally I asked you questions about yourself. I honestly did mean it about the job, you know. And of course it's still possible.'

'If Amedeo doesn't have me killed first.'

'Oh, well, I don't really think . . .'

'As for all this entirely honest stuff, you know perfectly well that Amedeo's a crook.'

'Well, um, I – I really don't know very much about him at all. I don't want to know. And he didn't sound menacing about you at all.'

'Of course not. And his way of getting to know me was perfectly normal, wasn't it? Paying someone to spy on me.'

'I didn't do it for money.' He sounded quite offended.

'Oh? So why? And by the way, what about going through my stuff?'

'Oh God, yes. I'm so sorry. Look, I really am ashamed. I suppose I'll have to tell you why I did it.' I noticed his hands were going up to his face, Squirrel Nutkin fashion again, and I suddenly thought, My God I hope he's not going to cry on me. He didn't; he dragged them down his face with a gesture of tiredness and said, 'Amedeo is, well, blackmailing me.'

'I see.'

'Go on then,' he said with sudden anger, 'ask what about.'

'Not if you don't want to tell me.'

'Oh God, what does it matter now? Your opinion of me can't really get much worse.' He poured himself another glass. 'Amedeo first got in touch with our school because he needed some translations done. Oh, just legal letters and articles, you know. So I did them and that's how I met him. He seemed quite a – well, quite a gentleman, you know. He took me out to dinner and said he had some other letters to be translated for which he needed somebody discreet. He was still awfully charming and polite. I said, well, yes, of course, thinking it was just private legal matters and all that. It turned out they were addressed to some chap in America who was involved in some big tax fraud. He was, well, I suppose you could describe him as a gangster, in fact. I didn't understand what the letters were all about, I confess, but I told Amedeo I'd rather not get involved with it and he – and then he told me he'd got – oh, this is most embarrassing . . .'

I didn't say anything, just waited.

He sipped his wine and resumed. 'Well, some weeks before this, coming back from Castellammare where I teach in a factory, a boy got talking to me. On the train, you know. Quite – quite naturally. He started the conversation, in fact. And – and, well he, he came back to my flat. Oh God. You do see – I get lonely occasionally, like anyone else.'

'Yes, yes,' I murmured, staring into my wine, my face possibly redder than his.

'Well, I never saw this boy again. Amedeo told me that the boy had come to him claiming that he'd been seduced by me – ' The words came out as if the wine were sour. 'He wanted redress. And he was only fifteen. And of course there were people who'd seen the boy come into my flat. Oh, it was all obviously a put-up job, and the boy is as corrupt as any of them, whatever his age, but what could I do? Amedeo said he thought he could persuade the boy to accept a little money for his silence and he would do it if I agreed to, well, to help him with his letters and such now and again. So, well, I had no choice. I mean, I'm a teacher, you know. You do see, don't you?'

'Yes.' I suddenly remembered the photograph in the *pensione* of his old public school and thought how unhappy he must be to have left that – the rows of boys with 'nice' accents and manners, the comfortable study with tea and muffins – and come to this – the lonely flat with tapes of Elgar and yesterday's *Times*; the teaching job in noisy classrooms on the Via Roma, and in factories in Naples' grimy suburbs, with unsympathetic mocking colleagues. I couldn't ask him why he'd come abroad, I could only make guesses – perhaps unjust ones. I realised how important it was for him to believe in the dignity of the teaching profession. I said, 'Yes, I see. Did you ever think of leaving Naples?'

'I'm tired of always leaving places. And I'm respected at the school – by the students at any rate. Many of them ask particularly to have me, you know, when they enrol. It's – well, I find it a heartening thing. And the director appreciates me. It's all right for you. You're young.'

'Has Amedeo bothered you a lot?'

'Until today it had only ever been translations and things like that. I suppose he needed to have someone on hand, someone he could rely on to be, well, discreet. So he picked me. As I say, it had always been letters and documents, and

149

then this morning he rang me at the school and told me about you.'

'What did he tell you?'

'Well, that you were at the *pensione*. I was to, er, to get talking to you and if possible, have, um, a little look at your things. You know, anything that might tell me something about yourself. But you really did make things difficult for me.'

'I'm sorry,' I said.

'Oh, you needn't be, I – Oh, I see. You were joking.'

'More like savage sarcasm, in fact. Did Amedeo tell you why he wanted to know about me?'

'No. Really, I haven't any idea. I did protest, you know. I said I didn't want to do it and he said – well, he threatened me in his, um, charming way.'

'And this evening, what did you tell him?'

'Just your name. And the fact you have relatives here. And, er, that you seem quite a nice sort of chap.'

'To which he, of course, said, well then we *must* have him along to make the party go. Hence your return complete with thug.'

'I tell you, I had no idea he would take a gun out. He was just going to ask you to go along and see Amedeo. What could I do?'

I had to agree that there was little Jameson could have done. He hadn't had the advantage of being at the top of the flight of stairs with a heavy rucksack in his hands – and of feeling bloody. Or at least not quite the way I had felt bloody.

'So now,' I said, 'what are you going to tell Amedeo?'

'I don't know, I don't know. But I can't go back to him now. Not after that – that gun had been pulled.' He made it sound like some obscene sexual practice.

'So you'll be wide open to his blackmail,' I said.

'Let him,' and he put on a Churchill expression, but it only lasted for about two seconds and the raised paws and Squirrel Nutkin look came back. 'But, oh dear, the – the shame, you know. The shame. And I've gained such respect – with my students, you know. Oh dear.'

'Well, why not help me to destroy Amedeo first?'

'What?'

'Get him before he gets you.' I hadn't known this was my aim, but as I said it I thought it sounded pretty good.

'Oh, er, and how do we do that?' This question, uttered in his fussy voice, made me think perhaps it wasn't quite so good. He didn't really sound or look like a gang buster – and I only felt like one because of the wine and the late hour.

'Well, of course, we'll have to work out the details,' I said.

He poured himself another glass and refilled mine. 'I just want to be out of it all. Maybe I will leave the city. Perhaps go to Greece. I've sometimes thought of it. I read classics, you know. But why, why should I have to? Oh God.' He looked straight at me for a moment, something he wasn't prone to doing. 'And how are you mixed up with Amedeo? Why does he want to know about you?'

'It's complicated. But really I've come to Naples looking for my brother who seems to have got himself involved with Amedeo. And with Brendan Cullop. You know the name?'

'Vaguely. The son of the supermarket chap, isn't that right?'

'Yes. And my brother had got hold of some evidence that Cullop was in touch with Amedeo in order to plan a crime – a murder, in fact.'

'Really? And who?'

'Who was to be killed? I don't know. That's one of the infuriating things. And I don't know what my brother meant to do with this evidence, but I want to see Amedeo and Cullop incriminated.'

'I should think so. And, er, where is the evidence – and what does it consist of?'

'Ah. Well, that's where the catch is because I had it and I, er, lost it.'

'Oh. Where? If that's not a silly question?'

'No, no. I left it with Cullop.' It was definitely a silly answer.

'Oh.' A pause. 'I see.' He looked very puzzled.

'Um, it was all a bit of a mess,' I said.

'And what about your brother? How did he come to be involved?'

'Well, he's the sort of person who does get involved with things. And who usually knows what to do when he is involved.'

'Oh, I see. Your brother, you say?' He sounded a little surprised.

'Yes.'

'And where's he?'

'I don't know.'

'So, um, you're on your own really.'

'That's right.'

'I see.' He thought for a moment. 'And you want me to help you, um, smash Amedeo?'

'Well, yes. If possible. Um, we could sleep on it. I'm feeling really tired. Things might look better in the morning.'

'Well, yes, they might.' Again that note of thrilled enthusiasm was lacking.

'Right. Have you got a spare blanket or something?'

'I have a sleeping bag, in fact. If you'd like this room, I'll, well, I'll have my bedroom. Shall we finish the wine off first?' He poured the rest of the wine out. 'What a pity we can't have any music. The cassette player's at Don Gaetano's, of course. I always like a little Delius at bedtime.' He made the composer sound like cocoa. 'Oh, just one question, you hadn't thought of going along to the police and playing – letting them hear your evidence? I mean, it would seem, er, the logical thing to do, no?'

'Er, well, I'm worried about how my brother is involved, you see. I wouldn't want to be the cause of his arrest for concealing evidence or whatever they call it.'

'Yes, I see. I see. Well, it's all a muddle, all a muddle and I don't know what I'm doing mixed up in it all. I only ask a little peace, and to be allowed to get on with my job where I'm respected – I am, you know, the students ask to have me. And now it looks as if I'll be starting all over again.' He was probably imagining the next badly paid, insecure job in some Greek town, and the cheap flat where his Elgar battled against the bazouki playing from next door. 'Well, let's sleep on it, as you say.'

I got up and went to the bathroom. While I washed he took the rubbish out of the flat, got a sleeping bag from a cupboard, and tidied up fussily. There was, in fact, nothing to tidy up, so fussily was the only way he could do it.

When he'd retired to his bedroom, I unrolled the sleeping bag and laid it out by the window. As always I wanted to read something before going to sleep, so I went over and had a look at his books. There were the early Anthony Powell novels, a few green-backed Penguins and, rather oddly, two Tom Merry annuals. I pulled one of these out with some curiosity and noticed something behind the books. It was a cassette in its case. The cardboard label had written on it in biro ink, 'First Certificate Grammar Drills', and the cassette inside was a ninety minute TDK with nothing written on it.

I wondered why this cassette should be kept behind the books, and this thought suddenly reminded me of something curious Jameson had said: 'You hadn't thought of going along to the police and playing – letting them hear your evidence?' *Playing*, he had said, and at no point had I ever mentioned the fact that the evidence consisted of a conversation on a tape.

I stood there with the open cassette box in one hand and the Tom Merry annual in the other, and my back and neck felt as if they'd developed bristles. I gazed at the picture on the annual cover, where a boy with a monocle had slipped on the ice and a whole group of other boys stood around, slapping their knees and chortling, and I thought hard.

There was no getting away from it: Jameson was not the bewildered innocent he claimed to be. I felt pretty much like the boy with the monocle, and no doubt Jameson was surreptitiously slapping his knees next door at that very moment.

He was a brilliant actor – and I, admittedly, was a gullible fool. He had turned complete defeat into victory, getting my whole story out of me when I had thought myself to be in the position of victor – Old Brown Owl to his Squirrel Nutkin. Had any of the blackmail story been true? Perhaps, and he was still determined to keep Amedeo's favour and silence. Or perhaps not; he might just be paid bloody well for his treachery. After all, a flat in the Vomero was not so easy to get – particularly on a language teacher's salary.

And now the bristles on my back were melting in the first hot wave of terror and I felt clammy all over. Amedeo – and friends – could well be on their way. Jameson had slipped out fifteen minutes earlier to take the rubbish down – and probably to make a phone call too.

The sound of a car door slamming in the street below jerked me out of my state of terrified jellified inertia. In two convulsive hand-movements I thrust the cassette back on the shelf and replaced the Tom Merry annual. I then rushed – on tiptoes – to the window, but it gave on to a side-street and so told me nothing about possible nasty arrivals. I stood still for two seconds and listened to the flat. It was saying nothing. I could hear no suspicious noises through the wall from Jameson's bedroom and no suspicious footsteps in the hall – just suspicious silence.

I picked up my rucksack and tiptoed towards the door, holding it defensively in front of me. It had been a good friend so far. I opened the door with infinite care, and stared down the corridor. The light from my room showed me quite clearly its full twelve foot length and the front door at the far end. Immediately to my right was the door of Jameson's bedroom, and getting past that making no noise was going to be the main difficulty. No noise at all, since Jameson was probably awake and chortling (or saying his careful 'ha ha') over Billy Bunter while he waited for his friends to arrive.

As I stared I marvelled yet again at how convincing the

bastard had been. I even wondered whether I shouldn't be feeling the slightest bit sorry for him in some corner of my mind – not a corner that had anything to do with making plans, of course.

I was about to take the first painfully cautious step along the corridor when I suddenly thought of the cassette – and of how stupid I'd been to put it back on the shelf. The action had been dictated simply by panic, by the instinctive but senseless urge to pretend I hadn't seen anything, as if the situation could be repaired by being tidied up. One tenth of a second of reasoning was sufficient to make me realise that I should be taking the thing with me.

I hovered in the doorway in an agony of indecision. Was there time to go back for it now?

And then I noticed the catch on the front door was moving. This answered the question.

Jameson must have left the key in the lock – or somewhere nearby – so that the thugs could come in without bothering to ring or present their cards.

I looked wildly at the rucksack in my arms, but realised I hadn't the strength to make it quite such an effective weapon hurled on the straight. And probably there would be more than one thug this time, prepared to deal with recalcitrance.

The catch clicked open and I instantly turned the light off and closed my door. I slid across the polished floor to the sleeping bag, and plumped it out so it resembled roughly a sleeping form – at least it might do so for two and a half seconds. I could hear soft footsteps padding along the corridor and I slid back to the door, grabbing one of the functional chairs on the way. I trusted it would function equally well as a thug crusher.

I had taken the traditional position for lurkers with raised chairs – just beside the door where I would be concealed as it opened, and from where, of course, I couldn't see who came in. I'd just smash out and hope they were frail.

The door handle went down with the kind of careful slowness that normally brings forth loud creaks, but didn't this time, so I could hear the tense breathing of the man on the other side and could only hope that he couldn't hear mine – nor my heartbeats, nor my knees shaking, nor the sweat dripping from my right armpit. I was a one-man orchestra.

The door pushed towards me and I tried to grip the chair tighter, but my knuckles were already white enough to light the room. He stepped forward, moving towards the sleeping bag, and someone started to come in after him. I brought the chair down on the first man, uttering as I did so a high-pitched whimper that I had intended to be a bloodcurdling yell. He went straight down with a punctured 'Uh' sound; I didn't watch to see him reach the ground but instantly whammed against the door with my shoulder so that it slammed into the other man.

I jerked it immediately open again. I had nothing but surprise on my side, while they had guns and muscles and hard hearts (perhaps I had just a little of the last at that moment too) and I had to exploit surprise while it lasted – about another second and a half, I suppose.

The man in the corridor was just a dark staggering shape, but I could see he was already raising his arms and there was probably a gun in them. I jumped on him, my hands grabbing his wrists and pushing them to one side. There was cold metal there. He staggered back again and I brought my knee up hard to his crotch. I'd quite forgotten I knew tricks like these. I managed to wrest the nasty contraption from his hands at the same moment, and then jumped back and waved it at him. He couldn't see very well perhaps, but he knew I had it.

'Stay by the wall,' I said, and realised I was speaking in English. I said it again in Italian. Jameson's door opened to my right and light flooded on to the scene. I jumped back a step so I had them both in my line of fire. Jameson's strands of hair hung down from his ear like bedraggled pennants: he looked like Peter Rabbit caught by Mr MacGregor. He said, 'What's going on?'

I said, 'Shut up and don't bother to pretend. Get back into your room.' I switched to Italian and addressed the man by the wall whom I could now recognise as mutton-chop Paolo: 'And you, follow him.' My only thought was to clear the way to the front door and the promised land of the safe Vomero streets. I was horribly aware that the man in the sitting room might have risen from the wrecked furniture (or what I remembered from films should be the wrecked furniture) and might be creeping up on me, chair raised, and I could not turn even one instant – not even if Jameson or Paolo suddenly looked over my shoulders and said eagerly, 'Yes, thump him one.'

They both backed into Jameson's bedroom and I said, 'Shut the door.' They did so, and the last thing I saw was Paolo's face with his eyes and mouth squeezed into thin parallel lines of hatred, and his whiskers a-quiver – a Victorian clergyman at the mention of Darwin (or Mr Tod to Jameson's Peter Rabbit). Then the door closed and I could swing round to check behind my back. He wasn't there, but I could hear him gathering himself up from the floor. I just stepped into the room, grabbed my rucksack from where I'd left it by the door and then ran for it. As I opened the front door I heard Jameson's door being opened and I swung the pistol round and fired it towards the ceiling.

The noise was deafening and probably frightened me more than them. Anyway, I slammed the door shut and ran towards the staircase as if I were afraid I'd brought the ceiling down. When I reached the stairwell I slung my rucksack over the banisters and let it drop to the ground floor, wishing I could follow it. It landed with a remote THUD and I hoped I hadn't misremembered about not having any bottles of shampoo or aftershave inside.

I started down the stairs, and after the first flight realised I could do better if I had my hands free to support myself on the banisters as I leapt. I chucked the gun over too. I was then able to leap whole flights: my arms shot down the banisters, supported me as I jumped and twisted a right angle, shot out again, supported my twisting jump again . . . Half-way down – and in mid leap – everything went suddenly black as if I'd hurtled headlong into hell's mouth. Then I realised the lights could only have been on in the first place because they'd been turned on by the two thugs coming up, and they presumably worked on a time switch. It gave some indication of how quickly everything had happened back there. While I hesitated, adjusting myself to this sudden blackness, I heard footsteps above begin to pound down the stairs. I continued jumping, trusting that the design of the staircase remained the same on the lower floors; it didn't after all seem the kind of building to hold quaint architectural surprises.

When I reached the first floor I had a sudden idea and plunged my hand into my coat pocket where the four loose batteries for my Walkman were rattling around – the two dead ones mixed up with the two new spare ones I'd bought that morning. I paused one half-second to lay them on four different steps and then kept leaping. It was a remote chance, but still a chance, and almost certainly a better one than any banana skin could provide.

I was slinging the rucksack on to my back when I heard, just above me, a sudden high-pitched and really quite comic 'ay-a-a-a-ulp!' followed by a series of crashes, terminating in a final expletive. Apart from the last word it had sounded worthy of Stanlio and Ollio.

I picked up the gun and ran out of the building, resisting the temptation to fire it again in general triumph. As I ran down the street it struck me that this was the fourth gun I'd had in my hands in the last four days, and I'd always considered myself a peaceable sort of fellow. Well, I suppose I hadn't killed anybody.

And a little voice inside me said, 'Yet.'

Fourteen

I found a *pensione* near the station where the man at the desk raised neither eyebrow at my late arrival, battered rucksack and snow-white hair (actually, I did find a little plaster in it from Jameson's ceiling). The gun I'd remembered to pack away before descending from the Vomero. This *pensione* didn't bother with desk formalities either.

The sounds of the noisiest square in Naples – which probably means the world – woke me at about seven o'clock the next day, so I got up and left the *pensione*. I went to the market nearby which occupies the area around Porta Nolana (though during the daytime most of the centre of Naples gives the impression of being an open-air market). The stalls were being prepared: metal shutters on shop fronts went rolling up with sudden apocalyptic thunder; vans trundled around, apparently with the sole purpose of providing an object that could be shouted at; crates and boxes were everywhere set down on to the ground or on to stalls with jarring crashes, and anybody without anything particular to do helped the party along by shouting out sudden phrases in dialect that even I found difficult to understand.

There's pretty well nothing you can't find in this market, including the radio that was in your car only two minutes previously. I myself was looking for various articles of clothing. I ignored the genuine Armani belts and Yves Saint Laurent wallets for two thousand lire and the gold watches for five thousand, and I bought myself a beret and workman's apron and a length of rope. I then made my way to a bus stop on the Corso Umberto. The first bus to come was so crammed one half-expected a Vesuvius-like eruption of bodies when its doors opened, but all that happened was that two old ladies stepped down and the fifteen people waiting, myself included, got on. Neapolitan buses defy all of Archimedes's principles.

I got out at Piazza Municipio and made my way to Santa Lucia on foot. I got there at about ten past eight and strolled around the port, watching Vesuvius and the line of the bay towards Sorrento emerge from mistiness to grey solidity in the morning sunlight. It was going to be a nice day.

When I was sure no-one was watching, I pulled the gun from the bottom of the bag and slipped it into the water. There: at least I could be sure I'd kill no-one with it.

And I wondered when I'd meet Gun Number Five.

Just after eight thirty, Cullop emerged from the hotel. My guess about him had been right. He was wearing running gear and he jogged off in the direction of Mergellina. And he'd probably shaved first, I thought, fingering my rough chin.

I went round to the back entrance of the hotel. Sauntering in through the main entrance again would be asking for trouble, I felt. I put on the beret and apron and had a look at myself in a nearby shop window. So long as I kept the beret pulled well over my blond hair, there was no reason why I shouldn't be a Neapolitan labourer.

I walked in through the door at the back and found myself in the kitchen. A couple of cooks and a coffee-bearing waiter looked at me without too much curiosity and I said in my thickest Neapolitan, 'Straight through for the lift, right?'

'Straight through and turn right,' said the waiter.

I walked the way he'd indicated, but made towards the stairs instead of the lift. I had to cross just a few yards of the main entrance hall to reach them, but I was far enough from the desk not to be noticed. As I started up the stairs, I suddenly thought that someone sitting in the far corner of the hall had looked very like my brother. I was about to turn and check but I then thought that that might make the porter I'd just passed look at me, and besides it had been so vague an impression that it was almost certainly not true. By the top of the stairs I'd forgotten all about it.

I reached Cullop's door. I tried it and it was, of course, locked. I knocked at Sarah Ryan's door.

Her voice, rather sleepy, answered. 'Yes, who is it?'

'Er, it's me. Jan. You know, the guy from London.'

'The screwball?'

'Well, yes, that's me.'

I heard slippered feet crossing the room and then the door opened. 'Kind of early, isn't it?' She was wearing a bathrobe, and bathrobes, unlike other forms of clothing, always seem to be saying, 'Hey, I'm really naked underneath you know' – at least to my perhaps rather over-suggestible mind. This one certainly did anyway: it may have been her way of wearing it – the nonchalant knot that flaunted its unintricacy and the casual looseness of the way the two sides met – or it may just have been the fact that it was very short. At any rate I had to force my eyes to remain at a decent horizontal level.

'Yes,' I said, 'I'm really sorry. Very very sorry. I hope I didn't wake you, but it's urgent.'

'No, I was just meditating.'

'Oh, er, sorry if I disturbed you, but you see – '

'Don't worry. I like getting disturbed when I'm meditating. It's kind of boring, you know.'

'Ah. Look, could I come in?'

'Well, I don't know about that. I'm not dressed to receive.'

Various one-liners came to mind, but they were more worthy of the cinematic James Bond than a gentleman, so I repressed them. 'Look, I told you who I was yesterday. You do trust me, don't you?'

'Yeah, maybe, but I was dressed yesterday.'

'Nothing could be further from my thoughts,' I began, persuading myself it was to all intents and purposes the truth.

'Oh, come on in. You don't really look like trouble, I suppose.'

'Thanks.'

Like yesterday, she turned and walked ahead of me with apparent unconcern as to whether I was following or not. I guessed that it was the casualness of one who knew exactly how alluring her rear view was.

She sat on the bed, pulling the robe carefully tight around her legs. 'So let's hear today's story then.'

161

'Well, I haven't much time really. You see, I want to have a quick look in Cullop's room while he's out jogging. He's just left. I expect he'll go as far as Mergellina, but I can't guarantee it, of course. So you see things are pretty urgent. Why don't we talk about it all afterwards?'

'Yeah, sure. We'll have a really cosy tête-à-tête breakfast. You've got some nerve, haven't you?'

'Please, trust me.'

'Who is this guy Cullop, according to you?'

'Let's just say he's involved with the Camorra – the Neapolitan Mafia.'

'Wow.' I remembered that expressionless 'wow' from yesterday.

'So will you help me get across to the next balcony?' I said.

'How? Do you want me to throw you?'

I could quite believe she was capable of it, but I said, 'No, I've got some rope here.' I pulled it out of my shoulder bag.

'Oh, I see. A Tarzan act.'

'Well, not exactly. Let me show you what I've thought of doing.' I thought of saying casually, 'I usually tear up the floorboards in these cases', but decided that would lead to too many tedious questions.

I took off the beret and apron and put them on the end of the bed and we went towards the balcony. Before stepping out she pulled her bathrobe a little tighter, as if preparing to receive the homage of expectant crowds below. The David Hockney blue of the sea hit our eyes. When we were able to open them fully we could see that Sorrento and Capri were sharply clear on the horizon. Below us the traffic roared on round the bend of the promontory; there were hardly any pedestrians, however, and thus few eyes to look up curiously at our balcony.

I indicated the railings. They were formed by parallel vertical bars about four inches apart, with one horizontal bar some six inches above the floor of the balcony and another at the top of the vertical bars. Cullop's railings were the same. 'You see,' I said, 'I throw this rope over his balcony, over the top of the railing and then back under the bottom bar and do the same here and then tie it here so I've got a complete loop, if you follow me.'

'How do you pull it back? Do you want me to go across to the other balcony and throw it you?'

'Ah,' I said, 'good point. Yes, I see what you mean. Well, we just need something long to pull it back here with.'

'Like what? Any suggestions?'

'Yes, yes. Wait, I'm thinking. Anything really, a spade, a broomhandle, a brush . . .'

'I've got a toothbrush.'

'Hang on, yes, if I remember rightly, let's hope it's still there . . .' I went back through the room and into the corridor. I returned a few seconds later with a long-handled mop. 'One of the cleaners must be inside the room making the bed. We'll give it straight back.'

'*You*'ll give it straight back.'

It was a fairly fiddly business, rather like a large-scale version of threading a needle (if that isn't actually oxymoronic). The rope first refused to be pulled under the distant horizontal bar, and then, when it had been so pulled and was dangling down to attract the attention of people in the room below, kept dropping away from the mop's end; it did so twice when I'd brought it to within inches of my outstretched fingers. However, after a minute or so I finally succeeded in making my loop. Sarah leant against the closed half of the window and watched with arms folded and one leg most distractingly crossed over the other.

I pulled the ends as tight as possible so that theoretically the two horizontal stretches of rope should be rigid, and I made a knot with the help of vague memories of cub-scout days and Sarah's forefinger. I looked down and checked that nobody was watching us still. I took the mop back out to the corridor where it appeared not to have been missed. When I returned Sarah asked, 'Done this kind of thing often?'

'Oh, you know,' I said, 'when I've had to.' I resisted the temptation to add, 'Yesterday, just before lunch, in fact.'

163

With the same nonchalance (at least, this was how I hoped it looked) I swung my right leg over the railing and put it on to the lower rope. The theoretically rigid rope bucked under my sole like an electrocardiogram. I gripped the top rope and felt that, too, do its little St Vitus' dance.

'Get a move on,' Sarah said, 'you might be seen.'

'Hanging around suspiciously,' I managed to get out without even a stutter. My left leg and arm joined the others and I swung in the void for a couple of seconds, trying not to move a muscle, just watching the hotel lurch around me and quite expecting to see at any moment gulls at my feet and the sea over my head; then I got as good a grip on myself as I had on the rope and I started shuffling across to Cullop's balcony. I tried not to think about the possibility of the knot coming undone or the railings breaking away.

I reached the balcony a couple of seconds later, feeling rather as if I'd spent a day on a stormy sea. I gave another nonchalant smile to Sarah, who fluttered one hand at me and then turned and went back into the room, all in one beautifully self-conscious movement, as sinuous as a rope slipping over a balcony.

I entered Cullop's room, perhaps in rather more lumpish manner. The room looked the same as yesterday except that the bed wasn't made and my Walkman was now on the sideboard. I went straight over to it and opened it. The tape was still there. I put the machine into my shoulder bag and went towards the door.

The door was locked. It was a door that only needed to be pulled shut to be locked, but one could double-lock it for security with the key and that was presumably what Cullop, the suspicious bastard, had done. So I'd have to go back via the rope. I went out to the balcony.

The rope was no longer there. For one dazed second I looked down, expecting to see it snake-curled somewhere in the street, and thought, My God I had been lucky it had happened afterwards . . . Then I thought of Sarah.

'Sarah, come on, what are you playing at?' I called out,

164

trying to make myself sound like one who could appreciate a jolly prank (or whatever the Americans called it) as much as the next man, and not like one who was wishing in terror that all this was happening to the next man.

There was no answer.

I shouted again, 'Please, Sarah, this is serious. You can't leave me here.'

Still no answer.

I dived back into Cullop's room and ran to the door. I rattled and banged it, and then tried to look more rationally at its lock, but I knew it was no good. I went back to the balcony. The only thing I could think of was swinging myself down on to the balcony on the floor below, but it only took one glance down to decide me against that. While I was standing there trying to come to my next decision (whether to panic or not), Sarah came out on to the balcony. She was now wearing the same jeans as yesterday and a blue and white blouse. She leant against the door in the same position as before and said, 'Hi again.'

'Er, hi. Um, look, do you think . . .'

'I just thought you might like to know that I've been Brendan Cullop's companion for nearly a year now.'

'Ah.' A pause. 'But wait a minute, he said – oh, I see, Sally, Sarah. Stupid of me. But look, you've got to believe me . . .'

'You don't give up, do you? Well, I guess there's no point me sticking around listening to you. I'll go and call the management.' She went back into the room.

Fifteen

So once again my brilliantly devised secret plans had proved not to be worked out to quite the last detail. Probably one of the first rules they teach a secret agent is that when you want to break into your enemy's hide-out it's best not to tell the enemy's girl-friend all about it beforehand.

To do so is the sign of a cock-up artist.

But still, who'd have thought of Cullop's girl in a separate room? Quaint old-fashioned things. Or did he perhaps snore?

But there was no point in going over all this now. I had to plan my next move. The management would possibly have a hotel detective, someone trained to deal with such situations efficiently and discreetly. Would he be armed? Well, in a city where there are children who go from teddy bears to tommy-guns it was not to be ruled out. And he might well not be alone. No, resistance was not a good idea. Maybe the time had come for me to tell all. Brotherly love can go so far.

I just had to hope that I would be believed.

I went back into the room and sat on the edge of one of the armchairs. (Sitting actually in it seemed rather too unserious an attitude.) I thought of various cases I'd read in the papers about people in Italy waiting literally years for trial – waiting in jail, of course – and the only way to get out, if I remembered rightly, was to be elected a member of parliament, something which I felt was unlikely to happen to me. Maybe a teeny bit of resistance might not be a bad idea.

But then, of course, if I didn't manage to escape or if I got caught again, there would be no question of establishing my innocence. I got up and walked around the room, thinking what a pity it was I couldn't enjoy the fact of being alone in a hotel room, the luxury of which I'd never before experienced. And which was likely to be in fairly sharp contrast with my accommodation for the next few days – or years. I recalled descriptions of Naples's Poggioreale Prison as perhaps the worst in western Europe.

A couple of minutes had passed and I now heard voices in the corridor. Sarah was talking to someone Italian, who was making short non-committal replies. I couldn't actually hear what she was saying. Then the voices stopped outside the door.

I waited. There were a few seconds' silence and then a voice said in English, with a heavy Neapolitan accent, 'Meestair, do you speak Italian?'

'Yes, er, sì,' I replied.

'So,' he went on in Italian, 'we'll open the door. You stay in the middle of the room with your hands up. OK? Or we shoot.'

'He won't resist,' I heard Sarah say in English. 'He's not the sort.'

So I'm yellow, am I? I thought to myself fiercely. You just watch then, and I curled my fists up. Then I thought, what the hell, I'm going to punch a gun barrel? and I uncurled them again. I said in Italian, 'OK. I'll come peacefully. I don't want to make any trouble.'

I stood there as he'd told me and said to myself, What's yellow and stands in the middle of a hotel room with its arms raised? The key clicked and the door was suddenly thrown open and a small man came flying in as if he'd been thrown (by Sarah perhaps), landing to the right of the door where he straightened up immediately, training a gun on me. It wasn't a big gun, but it was big enough. He himself made the same impression: he was short but stocky; his face was a leathery colour and texture, with a jet black moustache dividing it into two more or less equal halves.

Sarah strolled in then.

'Thanks so much,' I said to her.

'Any time.'

The man with the gun said in English, 'Madam, per'aps you wait outside? And please close the door.'

167

She closed the door, remaining inside however, and said, 'No, no I'm interested. I'll help.'

He said, 'Please stay there, madam.' He came up to me and pushed the gun into my back and I thought, that's the only thing nobody's done to me so far. He took the bag off my shoulder and tossed it away – fortunately on to the bed – and then patted down my sides. When he'd finished he withdrew the gun; I imagined a red circle indelibly branded on my skin.

'All right,' he said. 'We'll go to the service stairs. I won't put on the handcuffs but if you make one move, I shoot. Understand?'

'Yes.'

'You can put your hands down.'

I did so. He put his gun away inside his jacket and motioned me towards the door. Sarah opened it for us.

'Thanks again,' I said.

'You're welcome.' She stood aside as we walked out.

At that moment Cullop appeared at the top of the stairs. His face was aglow and his shirt had great patches of sweat, rather like a map of Naples and its islands. He stared. 'What's happening?' he said in Italian.

The man replied, 'We found this man in your room. We're taking him down to the office for questioning. We'll wait for the police there. If you want, come down. We don't want a fuss in the corridor.'

Cullop stared at me, his eyes narrowing. He said, 'I'll just wash first,' and he went into his room followed by Sarah who started talking at once.

'Move,' the man said, pointing towards the service stairs.

We reached the stairs without having scandalised any hotel guests. Indeed, if I had scandalised any guests that morning it had been by coming up the main stairs in my apron and beret. We passed just one girl carrying a pile of pillow cases; she gave us a curious stare but didn't stop. At the bottom of the stairs we turned into a long corridor with strip lighting. Large bags of laundry leaned against the walls. At the end of the corridor was a metal door. I hadn't actually noticed how many floors we'd gone down but we seemed to be in the basement.

'OK, stop there,' he said when I reached the door. He pulled the gun out and held it one-handedly, while he fished in his jacket pocket. He drew out a bunch of keys.

'You have your own private jail?' I said.

'It's a store room, but it'll do while we wait for the police.' He put a key into the lock.

A door on the right of the corridor suddenly opened. The man swung round, the gun, however, staying fixed on me. My brother stepped into the corridor with a bag of laundry. I just managed to suppress a cry which might have been of greeting or surprise or pleading – I really don't know. I think, judging from his next action, he would have been about as pleased with me as he had been when I'd shouted out in the woods near Radney. As my guard took his eyes off Gigi and went back to the lock, Gigi swung the laundry bag and sent it flying against his head.

It all happened in a matter of a second and a half, and yet I remember my eyes fixing on that black yawning metal which seemed by some optical illusion to remain fixed, even as the man went staggering towards the floor (rather as a cartoon character's hat and cigar hang in the air when the body's plummeted off the cliff), and I remember thinking that I was going to hear a sudden explosion and that would be it.

But at the end of the second and a half the guard was pinioned in my brother's arms and I'd somehow got hold of the gun. Number Five. Already.

'Open the door,' my brother snapped, and as I dithered, 'Bloody open it!'

I turned the key and opened it. My brother pushed the man through the gap with no more resistance than a few burbled swear-words and then Gigi slammed it and turned the key.

'Gimme the gun,' he said.

I handed it over and he shoved it inside his jacket and said, 'Come on,' and ran towards the door he'd emerged from. I followed him.

A steep staircase brought us out near the kitchens and we ran straight through them, with just an impression of a few staring faces left behind us, and then we were running through the streets behind the hotel. We turned right, then left and arrived in a narrow road. Gigi walked briskly towards a small car, taking the keys out of his pocket.

We drove off and we said nothing to each other for the first minute or so other than 'Oof', 'Phew', and an occasional 'Shi-it' on Gigi's part. When we were a few streets away he said, 'Go on then, say fanks.'

'Sorry, sorry, thanks. I mean it. I was just a bit, you know, confused by it all.'

'I'm not surprised, mate. You've been causing enough bloody confusion around the place.'

'Yes, I suppose so. Er, how did you happen to be there?'

'That's what I'm for, innit, pulling you out of your bloody messes.'

This didn't seem to be a totally fair version of the events of the last days but I didn't say anything for the moment. Gigi said, 'Right, where've you been staying?'

'Why?'

'So we can get your stuff and you can get out of the place.'

'Get out? Why?'

'Look mate, you've just done over a private detective and the police were on their way, and you kind of stick out around here with hair the colour of Marilyn Monroe's. Just tell me where. Then afterwards I'll take you somewhere safe.'

I told him and we drove in the direction of the Piazza Garibaldi. I said, 'How's your shoulder?'

'Oh that? That wasn't nuffink.'

'Oh good.'

We went silent again, probably because we both had too many questions. Eventually I came out with a fairly easy one. 'Where are you going to take me?'

'Wait and see.'

'If I asked you the time you'd say "aha", wouldn't you?'

'If you asked me the time it would only be because you'd blown up Big Ben by mistake or somefink.'

'All right, all right. I cock everything up and you come along with your magic wand, but I didn't ask to get involved in all this.'

'Well, what are you doing here then?'

That was a good question and it reduced me momentarily to thoughtful silence.

We drew up at traffic lights. A boy who looked about ten sauntered through the stationary cars and offered us packets of paper handkerchiefs. Gigi waved him away. Another boy, apparently his younger brother, came up and offered us toy ducks on strings. Gigi waved him away too. Their baby brother then came up with contraband cigarettes and Gigi bought a packet.

'Didn't know you smoked,' I said.

'Well, seems stupid not to here when they're so cheap,' he said, handing the money over. A sudden outbreak of hooting behind us told us that the lights had changed (most of the drivers had probably considered it pretty sissy on Gigi's part to stop anyway just because of a little red light). The toddler, who hadn't finished giving the change, turned and flung his hand up in a gesture of supreme disdain towards the chafing drivers and let forth a stream of abuse, which mostly regarded their departed relatives. He turned back and handed Gigi the money, and then walked away through the now moving traffic, stopping an articulated lorry with one imperious hand.

We moved off. 'Well, let's say I came as little brother interested in what big brother was up to.'

'Nosey bleeder inyer?'

'Well, you know how it is, getting half murdered by people you've never seen before always leaves you a little curious. Oh, by the way I got your cassette back for you,' I added, thinking that at least would make him sit up.

'I know.'

'You what?' I realised I'd sat up. After a pause I said, 'Well, go on then, say thanks.'

'All right, fanks. Got it here then?'

'Ah, well now . . .'

'You left it at the hotel, I know.'

'You're really beginning to impress me, Gigi,' I said.

He obviously liked this and almost smirked. He made a sudden half right turn so I jolted forwards and the hooting ritual started up again behind us. He'd just spotted a car about to leave a parking place, and in the centre of Naples you don't give up an opportunity like that, even if you had no intention of parking, just as a desert animal will drink whenever it sees water. We were, however, quite near my *pensione*.

'Right,' he said. 'Go and get your stuff. I'll wait here.'

I did so. As I walked back with my rucksack on my back I wondered why the hell I should trust Gigi, and whether I wouldn't be better off going to catch a train, but then I thought it wasn't a question of trusting him, but of satisfying my curiosity.

I got into the car again. 'Right, off on the mystery tour.'

He pulled out into the traffic, causing a taxi driver to call on the Madonna, San Gennaro and his mother, and he said, 'We're going to Mergellina. To me boat.'

'To *your* boat?'

He smirked even more and said nothing.

'All right,' I said, 'you win. I'm bowled over by your wealth and power and bemused by your mysteries and I can't be bothered to ask any more questions. Just take me to your luxury villa on Capri and I'll crash out there on the four-poster bed.'

'Ischia as a matter of fact.' And another smirk.

I kept to what I'd said; I asked no questions and only raised an internal eyebrow.

We reached Mergellina. Gigi found a parking place not too far from the port and we walked down to the sea. I followed him as he walked along one of the jetties. He stopped at a slender white motorboat. A small man tanned to the colour of mahogany helped us on to the boat and was paid by Gigi for his not particularly necessary services.

The boat had a small cabin with cushion-covered benches and a table. I thought of saying 'What, no colour television?' but then thought that he'd probably pull one out of a drawer. He started the engine up and we moved out of the port.

Having made my resolution not to give Gigi the opportunity for any more enigmatic replies, I decided to enjoy the trip. As the day was splendid and the boat satisfyingly swift, this turned out to be easier than one might have thought. All I had to do to forget about the events of the last few days was gawp – the Bay of Naples did the rest.

Twenty minutes or so later we passed the island of Nisida beyond which the smoking chimneys of Bagnoli could be seen. I broke our silence. 'You know something?'

'What?'

'That island there's where Brutus and Cassius planned the murder of Julius Caesar.'

'Oh yeah?'

'Yes.'

'And so?'

'Nothing. Just wondered if Cullop ever goes there for his holidays.'

Gigi didn't make any reply to this. We went on towards the island of Procida. We passed to the left of it. I admired the almost oriental picture the brightly coloured houses made along the water's edge, and tried not to look at the sullen mass of the prison at the island's end. The houses became less frequent as we reached the flatter southern end and then we were heading towards the slopes of Ischia. We left the lumpen shape of the castle to our right and made towards the south side, which for some miles was mostly sheer cliff – this indeed was the only reason it hadn't as yet been covered in concrete, though no doubt someone was working out a way to do it.

The coast became gentler and more familiarly hotel- and villa-filled, and Gigi directed the boat towards a little port so picturesque that I expected strains of a mandolin from a dockside tavern to welcome us in. Instead we could hear disco music from a juke-box.

Another mini mahogany man, apparently the twin brother of the one in Mergellina, helped tie up the boat, and was similarly rewarded by Gigi. He seemed to know Gigi.

We took a taxi from the port. I said, 'I don't suppose I have to tell you that I'm pretty well skint.' He made a largesse-scattering gesture and I said, 'Well, thanks.'

The taxi climbed up a steeply winding road; at each bend the driver hooted and the sea flashed back. We passed through another little village with whitewashed houses, a church with a maiolica-tiled dome, and a tree-lined terrace where a few German tourists were photographing the view. The road kept climbing. We finally drew up at a gate beyond which I could only see vine-covered slopes, and we got out. Gigi paid the driver and, I presume, from the profuse thanks, tipped him, and he drove off. We went through the gate and up a steep path between vines, olive trees, and occasional clumps of Indian fig plants. I remembered our morning walk of four days earlier through the dewy (well, in fact, rain-soaked) freshness of an English field and wood. It seemed a long long time ago.

The path twisted to the right where the hill folded back and a high wall appeared before us, topped with the customary welcoming touch of cemented broken glass. We made towards the wrought iron gates beyond which we could see the villa: long, low, and white with a Doric portico in the middle, like a model of the White House someone had accidentally sat on. In front of the gate was a copy of the *Cave Canem* mosaic from Pompeii, with its snarling dog; no modern villa in the surroundings of Naples seems to be considered complete without this.

The real dog made its appearance: an Alsatian, Baskerville Hound-like in size, alternating snarls with barks.

'OK Bobby,' Gigi said.

'Bobby? That's nice and original.' In Italy any dog that isn't called Bobby (well, Bobi to be strictly accurate) is called Dog. 'Er, are you going to go in first?'

'Yeah, don't worry. He's all right when he knows you.'

'He doesn't know me.'

'I'll hold him, don't worry.' Gigi opened the gate and grabbed Bobby's collar. Bobby was thus stopped in mid leap for my throat. I sidled in while Bobby did what sounded like an imitation of 'o Rauco on a foggy day and ripped the air to pieces in front of his face.

'Er, I'll make friends some other time,' I said. 'There aren't any others?'

'No, Bobby's enough.'

'Yes, I'm sure he is. I'll go on up to the house.'

'Yeah, I'll just tie him up.' He did so, attaching him to a chain by the wall. Bobby strained and scrabbled and gargled seeing my throat get away intact. I hoped the chain – and the wall – were stout.

The villa was furnished with cool elegance. A lack of clutter seemed to indicate that it was a holiday villa not a home, but it was by no means bare or merely functional. Gigi went round opening shutters so that the place filled with light. I glanced at the sitting room to the right of the hall. There were cream-coloured armchairs and sofas, looking somehow virginal – untouched by human posteriors; there was a sideboard with a record player and various bottles, and there were a few abstract paintings, the two- or three-colour sort that usually look as if they've been chosen to go with the furniture. I went back to the pillared porch and gazed down the hill to the sea. By a lucky freak of the surrounding hills, no other houses could be seen nearby, just the distant white cluster of the port. Thirty years ago this would not have been so remarkable, but there are now very few stretches of coastline in Italy where people haven't admired the beauty so much that they've just had to build concrete blocks of flats in order to be able to admire it at greater length, and Ischia is (was?) particularly worthy of lengthy admiration.

'Not a bad little place, is it?' Gigi said.

'No, whose is it then? Cullop's?'

'That's right.'

So maybe Cullop *had* handed over half his estate. Or maybe

I'd been wrong all along about the relations between the two of them. 'Are you going to explain?'

'I'll leave that to Bren. Just take it that it was his idea to rescue you from that bloke in the hotel. Not mine, mate, oh no.'

'Well, thanks for doing it anyway. But how? He only saw me at the last moment.'

'He knew I was in the hall and he phoned down telling me to act smartish like. So I did.'

'Yes. Very smartish. Cullop didn't dither either.'

'No, he wouldn't.' There was quiet approval, or admiration even, in his voice.

'Nice of him. He is, um, a murderer though, isn't he?'

'He's a bloody good bloke. You got that tape all wrong, you know.'

'Ah. Sorry. It seemed fairly clear. Are you going to tell me how I got it wrong?'

'Wait till Bren comes.'

'You promise he won't murder me then?'

'Don't be dumb.'

'When'll he be over?'

'Lunch-time probably. Coming over on the car ferry.'

'So I wait with bated breath till then.'

'You can wait just any way you like. I'm gonna watch a film.'

'Oh, is there a cinema here?'

'Nah, on the video. In the bedroom there. There's a whole load of westerns. Clint Eastwood.'

'Ah, yes, I suppose there would be. Well, I'll go for a walk. If Bobby'll let me.'

'Yeah, well don't forget to come back.'

I walked down the steps. Bobby hurled himself forward and choked on his chain. I wondered how many times a day he made the same mistake. Probably every time he saw anything else alive, like a bird or a spider. I walked round to the back of the house. There was a lawn – an actual English-looking lawn complete with croquet hoops; I looked around for Beach

176

the butler. Beyond the lawn was a small swimming-pool with only dead leaves in it. Then there was the glass-topped wall and the slopes of Mount Epomeo rising beyond.

Against the side of the house I found a box with croquet mallets and balls, a cricket bat (no doubt Cullop occasionally flew the England team over for weekends), and some deck-chairs. I decided the last appealed to me more than a walk, so I went and fetched my Robert Sheckley novel from my rucksack, opened one of the deck-chairs and sat in the sun and pretended I was on holiday. Occasional distant gunfire didn't disturb me; it was only Clint Eastwood cleaning up the west.

Sixteen

Brendan Cullop and Sarah arrived some time after midday. I heard their voices coming up the path. Bobby was silent – until I rounded the corner of the house.

'Oh hi,' Sarah said, 'I'm so glad to see you you know I'm really sorry for all that business back there I mean I just didn't know . . .'

'Shut up,' Cullop said, which surprised me a little until I saw he was addressing Bobby. Even more surprisingly, Bobby shut up at once. Cullop was wearing an open-neck shirt under a white linen jacket and light blue trousers. She was wearing what I'd last seen her in. They both looked like something from an advertisement page; despite the suitcases they were carrying they didn't seem at all puffed. I remembered again that I hadn't shaved. 'Hi, Jan,' Cullop went on. 'I've heard all about you from Luigi.'

Gigi came out of the house at that moment.

'Yes?' I said. 'Well, I haven't heard all about you yet and I want to.' I was determined not to be bowled over by his smiles and his easy charm.

'Yes, of course. Let's just dump our stuff and then we can go and have an aperitif on the lawn.'

Well, it wasn't quite the way I'd pictured the interrogation/ explanation scene, but what the hell, this was Ischia in April.

So we sat in deck-chairs with Martinis in hand. Sarah said: 'I just didn't know who you were, I mean no one tells me anything, I'm just the dumb blonde you see. Any moment now and Bren'll send me off to the kitchen while you get on with man's talk.'

Cullop smiled. 'Sorry darling, but you know that I don't talk about everything. I told you that from the beginning. And have I ever made you cook?'

'Just kidding, Bren. But come on, start talking now. I can

see Jan's completely confused.' She said to me, 'He's only let me in on all his crazy plans this morning. On the ferry on the way over. So I'm not too clear either.'

'Let's say I'm still wary rather than confused,' I said. 'You've got my Walkman?'

'Complete with tape,' Cullop said. 'And how did you get the tape?'

'Just came across it in this hotel in Bayswater. And how did your voice get on to the tape? Saying what it does?'

'What does it say what does it say?' said Sarah.

'A business conversation with that lawyer fellow,' Cullop said. 'The one I told you about.'

'Some business,' I said.

'Jan, I'm going to have to ask you to trust me.' He stared straight at me, his blue eyes steady and unblinking. 'I am not a criminal. I mean, otherwise why would I have bothered to have you sprung back there?'

'I know too much, perhaps.'

'All right, so why don't I just knock you off?'

'Well, you don't seem to like doing such things yourself.'

'I should get angry at that, I suppose, but I like you. Yes, the main reason I'm sitting here talking to you is that I want you on my side. I admire your courage and your persistence.'

'Wow,' I said. I looked at Gigi, who was allowing only the faintest half-smile to curl one side of his mouth. 'But not my efficiency, I presume.'

'Well, you're obviously an impulsive sort of person. I like that, too, even if I can see it's got you into a few messes.'

'Just a few. Let's talk about your messes though. Starting with that bloody tape.'

'OK.' He sipped his Martini and then looked up at the sky. 'You know who I am, there's no point in my being bashful about my fame. Let's say I like adventure. Let's say, if you like, I'm an old-fashioned romantic sort of person.'

'All right. Let's say it.'

He shot one glance at me, then looked back up at the sky. 'You know, too, that I don't have financial problems. I'm not one of your fabulously wealthy people, but I get by comfortably.'

I expect this is what all millionaires up to the second richest man in the world say. And the richest no doubt says that of course nowadays no one's really rich.

'Anyway,' he went on, 'you know the things I've done, the polar expeditions, the climbing, the desert, etc. I like it. Now a criticism often levelled against types like myself is that we're pretty useless sort of people. I can understand this: I don't say it's true, but I can understand people feeling like this, and not only out of envy necessarily.' His eyes shot back at me. 'Probably you think the same thing.'

'I, er . . .' He'd succeeded in embarrassing me, the swine. Then he shot one of those quick easy smiles across and I found myself smiling back – quite against my intentions.

'It wouldn't be surprising,' he said. 'I've felt the same thing myself. And some years ago I started wondering to myself what I could do to, you know, help the world.'

'Your old clothes to Oxfam?' I suggested.

'Yes, of course, there's the whole charity business. I greatly admire people who devote their lives to such things, I just know it's not my – my – '

'Cup of tea?' I said.

'Not my scene. I'm probably not good enough for that. My scene is adventure, as I've already said. So I started thinking how I could put this talent, if you like to call it that, to some practical use, beyond occasional documentary films for the BBC. And it struck me that around the world there are quite a few big men, evil men, who never get touched by the law because the law can't reach them. You know the sort of people I mean. People who are too well covered. So I've made it my business to go after them myself.'

'I see,' I said in a neutral tone. 'And what do you do when you've got them?'

'I do what I can to see that justice is done.'

'And what does that usually mean?'

'I think you know. They get killed.'

'They get killed. Passive. Let's try it in the active. You kill them.'

'Sometimes it's necessary.'

'I see. So I was right about you.'

'Hell, Jan, you know the kind of bastards I'm talking about.' He'd leant forward in his chair and was speaking in a tone of quiet, fierce conviction. 'They're people who are not worthy to live, people the world needs to be rid of, and the law can't do it so somebody else has to. It's a necessary job.'

'Do you know who you sound like?'

'Who?'

'A Nazi talking about the Jews.'

He didn't answer for a moment. He was quite still and the other two didn't sip their drinks. 'That's nasty, Jan. I am talking about real criminals. People responsible for filthy cruel crimes. Do you see that?'

'But I don't even believe in the death penalty.'

'That belief is fine as regards criminals who can get caught and put in jail. I'm talking about people at the top who kill day in and day out and will never even see a pair of handcuffs.'

'Like you.'

'Fire to wipe out fire,' he said. 'I feel no remorse for what I've done so far, nor for what I'm doing now. And tell the truth: when you hear on the news of terrorists blowing themselves up with their own bombs, or bank robbers shot by the police, do you really feel sorry?'

I looked at Gigi and Sarah. Gigi's expression was still coolly contemptuous – but towards me. Sarah as usual was unreadable. Her eyes seemed vaguely amused and flickered from one to the other of us.

'Would you mind me saying that you sound just a little bit cracked?'

'Oh, I'm not normal, I know. I'm not an average man.'

'Nobody's average,' I said, 'not even stockbrokers, and it's too easy to get a kick out of proclaiming how non-average you are. Anyway, who've you killed?'

'People you've probably never heard of. Here and abroad. In Bangkok I broke a whole gang.'

'So the place is perfectly clean and decent now. Jolly good.'

'It's a little cleaner. That's all one man can hope to achieve in this world. I don't take any pleasure in killing, you know. I'm not a sadist.'

'You do it for the exercise, I know. So who are you after now?'

'I think you've guessed. The man they call 'o Rauco.'

'And who is he exactly?'

'He's one of the world's top hired killers. He started out as a killer for a small-time Camorra gang and when his gang got busted he got right out of the gang world and set up as a loner. With the help of Amedeo. He obviously liked killing and was very good at it.' He looked sharply at me. 'And if you say "like me", I'll get angry.'

'No, no. I know you don't do it for money.' I allowed my roving eyes to add the subtext, 'you don't need to.'

''o Rauco would kill anyone for money – anyone except Camorristi. He's learnt to stay outside of the Neapolitan gang world. No fool. Most of his killings are done abroad now. Amedeo is his, er, agent if you like.'

'Just how do you get to hear about such people?' I asked.

My brother made a contemptuous snorting noise which suggested that I'd displayed an ignorance comparable with not knowing where the Prime Minister lived. Cullop said, 'It's a question of getting into the criminal world. One hears from someone who knows someone who knows, etc.'

'I see. Like getting a plumber.'

'Anyway, I got to hear about this man and decided I'd go after him. Obviously the first thing to do was to contact Amedeo, and this was most easily done by pretending to want a murder done – after, of course, having had my credentials established.'

'How did you do that? Gave him a list of people you've already bumped off yourself?'

'No. Luigi saw to that. He's got contacts in the London

Italian, er, world and he was able to spread the word to a few people who counted that B. Cullop could be trusted.' My brother gave one of his smirks.

'As a criminal.'

'Ye-es. So Amedeo, who has international contacts, received me, and I put my project to him.'

'And who was the lucky victim you chose?'

'Ah. Well, er, that's not important for the moment.'

'It is for the bloke himself, don't you think?'

'Don't worry. He's in no danger.'

'He knows, does he?'

'No, but it doesn't matter. He won't get killed. I'll let you into all those details later.'

'Later when? When 'o Rauco's got his gun trained on the poor guy?'

'Let's leave that for the moment. I just want to know if you're prepared to help.'

'What do you want me for?'

'I told you. I like you.'

'And you'll probably cause less bloody *casino* if we can see what you're doing,' my brother put in. *Casino* – that most important Italian word, meaning originally little house, and derivatively brothel, and yet more derivatively, confusion, mess, cock-up. Trust no dictionary that doesn't include it.

'Look,' I said to Cullop, 'I didn't get involved in all this for fun, like you.'

'No, but you stayed in it for fun,' he said. 'You didn't have to go to that hotel in London, you didn't have to come out to Naples. At any point you could have opted out. But you like it.'

'Now wait a moment,' I began.

'Admit it.'

I was momentarily silent. 'I haven't been bored. And that's no doubt what the passengers say at the end of a hijack.'

'Boredom's a terrible thing,' Cullop said. He smiled. 'Maybe I should admit that apart from any worthier motive I do these things to avoid boredom. I hate boredom.'

'Awfully honest of you, old chap,' I said. 'You know, at a certain point in all bad films there's a moment where the goody's tied up to a pillar and he asks the baddy, "But why do you want to break open Fort Knox or wipe out London or enslave the world?" and the baddy takes out his cigarette-holder and says, "I'm so terribly bored".'

'All right. I'm a bit of a damned bounder. But admit it, you're attracted by the idea of joining me.'

And he clearly thought I was. 'You're a loony, mate.' And I looked at Gigi and Sarah. 'And you must both be pretty screwy too.'

Sarah said, 'Why don't you listen to what he says? This Row-Co guy really does sound like a pretty good bastard. I'd go for him.'

'You're too deep in it now to get out,' Gigi said. 'It's your own fault.'

'I only went to that bloody Bayswater hotel to get your cassette for you. Didn't even like the music when I got it.'

'Ah yes,' Cullop said, 'the cassette. We were forgetting.'

'*You* might have been,' I said. 'That's not the impression I got about half the gangsters in Naples. Where did it come from first?'

'Amedeo seems to have been in the habit of recording conversations with his clients, an understandable precaution. Two ex-bodyguards of his managed to get hold of the tape, I don't know how. I'd gone back to London for some business connected with my shops and I got a little phone call just telling me about the tape and telling me to expect another call. So I got in touch immediately with Gigi.'

'And I picked up on these blokes straight off,' Gigi said. 'It wasn't difficult. They were hanging around Bren's house and then they went to a pub. And you know, they were talking away in Italian certain that nobody could understand, stupid berks. And they had the cassette wiv 'em. So I kept me eye on 'em and later, in anuvver pub, got talking wiv 'em. They didn't suspect anyfing. I mean, real amateurs. Dunno where they got the brains to fink of nicking the fing in the first place.

184

So first off I nicked it back, no sweat, and then I scarpered. I knew they'd go first to me girl who I'd told 'em all about, then, well, you know the rest.'

'The first corpses in the game.'

'You saw what sort of people they were,' Cullop said. 'You can't really say you wept when they got killed.'

'No, I was too scared. I was under the bed at the time.'

'Ah.' Cullop gave a little laugh. 'When we read the account in the papers we wondered just what you'd been doing at the moment of the killing, but we hadn't thought of you actually under the bed. Luigi identified you from the description, you see. Later, of course.'

'Yeah,' Gigi said, 'didn't fink of it in fact till I was reading the paper again on the plane. On the bloody plane. Then it struck me. Blond hair and all that. Shit, I said. I tried phoning you as soon as I landed but got no reply.'

'I was going round travel agents,' I said, 'finding a cheap flight. Just so I could give you back your bloody cassette. That'll teach *you* to answer phones in future. Your lady friend told me you'd refused to speak to me.'

'Well, how was I to know? I mean, didn't cross me mind you'd've gone back to 'em for more. I fought all you wanted was to be out of it.'

'I did. I do. It was just one of those moments of misplaced fraternal affection.'

'Anyway,' said Cullop, 'was it 'o Rauco?'

'Well, he had a pretty sore throat.'

'Did you see him?'

'Er, one foot.'

'You know it shows how seriously Amedeo took this leak to send 'o Rauco out. I wonder how he got on to their trail?'

'They'd probably left a brochure for the hotel next to Amedeo's safe,' Gigi said. 'I mean, real amateurs.'

'They struck me as being pretty good with their knives,' I said.

'What d'yer mean, good? They didn't kill you, did they?'

'Not quite. There's no need to sound regretful. I'm going

to have another drink.' I might as well profit from the situation while I could.

'Oh, yes, of course,' Cullop said, playing the unrufflable host.

'I'll show you where the bottle is,' Sarah said, rising from her chair. I followed her into the house. I heard Cullop saying to Gigi, 'I think he'll come over,' and then we moved into the kitchen out of earshot.

Sarah said to me as she took the ice-tray from the fridge, 'I'm kind of glad you're not a thief.'

'Oh, thanks.'

'You can't really despise what Bren's doing, can you?'

'I never used the word despise,' I said. 'Disapprove might be better.'

'Oh, I see. Like a schoolteacher.'

'If you like. Or like he disapproved of me just now. Did you see when I said I was going to get myself another drink? He had to check himself from looking shocked at my rudeness. And yet there's the guy breaking all the commandments for fun.'

'Not all of them. The sixth one you're thinking of.' I obviously looked a bit surprised and she said, 'Methodist upbringing.'

'Ah. I see. I'm RC, and we know nothing about the Bible whatsoever. Anyway, you see my point about Cull – Bren.'

'Yeah, well, he went to one of your public schools. And I guess they teach you there that social rules really matter.' She started filling a saucepan with water. 'Guess I might as well put the water on for some pasta. Otherwise we'll never eat.'

'Yes, I can hear where he went. I went to a local grammar school and am thus a foul-mouthed slob, but I haven't killed anyone yet. And I don't want to. You know what's wrong with Cullop: he's read too many trashy thrillers where because the hero knows which wine to drink and how to tie a real bow-tie he's got the right to take on and wipe out the world's unwashed criminals. And I bet he thinks of himself as having a daredevil glint in those blue eyes of his.'

186

'Well, he has, kind of. Slice up another lemon.'

I started doing so. 'I don't know what to make of you. I've got loony Cullop sussed out but you're a mystery. Here am I laying into your boyfriend, and I don't know whether you're agreeing with me or just waiting till I've finished with the lemon to send me through the window. All I know so far is you like his eyes.'

'Bren's a funny guy. You know, I've never known all he was up to, not in detail, though it was clear enough some things weren't exactly, you know, on the level. But he'd never do anything mean. That I've always known and that's enough for me. And he's never a drag, just never. When I first met him I was living with a guy who worked for an advertising agency, a guy who talked about nothing but money money money and how to get it and how to keep it. Well, Bren is really different.'

'Well, for a start he's already got it.'

'Yeah, well so had this other guy, only he wanted more. I've stayed listening to you because I know how most people can't take Bren's being different. He doesn't live by the same rules, so people can't fit him into their usual schemes and that bugs them.'

'Yes, yes, I know. It's the usual Mike Hammer stroke Rambo thing. The man outside society whom we boring little stockbrokers and chartered accountants aren't fit to judge. Well, I'm obviously a stockbroker at heart and I don't swallow it.'

She picked up the tray with the four brimming glasses and looked straight at me with those eyes, so open and so candid that one hadn't the faintest idea what she really thought. 'All right. Well, maybe I'm the dumb blonde like I said, but I do. Bren's a real fine guy. And you've got to admit, you know you do, that deep down you can't help admiring him.'

'I'll go so far as to say it's difficult to dislike him. Trouble is he knows it.'

'Come on, let's go back out.'

I followed her, wondering whether I should follow up my

display of oafish manners by getting completely drunk –
perhaps throwing up as a finishing touch. But then I decided
I still needed my wits about me.

Over the second round of drinks I told them my story in its
rough outlines. They'd never heard of Jameson and I didn't
mention Franco, just that I'd left Amedeo's office in a hurry.

Gigi came out with an occasional exasperated snort at my
persistent up-cocking, but Cullop said at the end, 'You're
either crazy or you've got some guts.'

'He's crazy,' Sarah said, 'as crazy as you.' And she smiled
at Cullop. I, dumb idiot that I was, perked up to think that a
portion of that smile was for me. It was a warmer smile than
Valerie had ever given me.

Cullop said, 'I had the impression that Amedeo was a little
suspicious when I called two days ago. Outwardly he was all
apologies for the blackmail business and full of reassurances
about how he'd had the matter seen to, but I felt that he was,
well, wary. And now, with your having actually talked about
me to this teacher chap, I suppose I'll have to presume the
deal's off.'

'Sorry if I've ruined your chance of a bargain.'

'Well, let's just say that things might have gone a little more
smoothly if you hadn't come along, but,' and he gave his
winning smile, 'I can't blame you for it and it's been worth it
to have met you.'

'Well, look, now you've seen me and had a chance to admire
my talents for getting in the way, maybe I should just
disappear, slip out of everybody's lives again – while we are
all still alive.'

'You realise your position,' Cullop said. 'In England, suspected of involvement with those two killings, and here of
resisting and doing over a private detective. The easiest thing
would be to agree to help us. And don't you agree that
Amedeo needs to be *sistemato*, as they say here?'

'Yes, and you should go straight to the police and tell them
all you know.'

'And that'll never get 'o Rauco.'

'Why don't we just leave him, poor chap, send him a few cough sweets perhaps, I mean, why should *I* – '

'Nobody's going to force you to do anything,' Cullop said. 'Just think it over. You might as well stay here for a day or two and, well, keep thinking it over.'

'All right. But if you think that I'll come over to your side out of embarrassment because I'm eating your food and drinking your wine, I warn you I've got a very high embarrassment threshold.'

Cullop went to the kitchen and started cooking. We had a simple but satisfying lunch of *tortellini alla panna*, followed by Milanese cutlets with side salads. Cullop, of course, was a good cook (I'd been thinking that if the meal had been awful there would at least have been the consolation of knowing there was one thing the guy couldn't do), and food provided a welcome change of subject. At least on this subject, as son of an Italian restaurant owner, I could appear less bungling than usual – with the result that I was chosen to cook the evening meal.

I spent most of the afternoon lolling in a deck-chair reading my novel while Gigi and Cullop got on with cleaning out the pool and Sarah lay on the lawn in a bikini that slowed down my reading rate. (Gigi, who in London fogs goes around with only the two bottom buttons of his shirt fastened, now that he was engaged in physical exertion under a Mediterranean April sun naturally didn't remove his jacket. That would have been sissy.) At around four thirty I finished my novel and I said, 'I'd better go down to the village to buy some food, hadn't I?'

'Yeah,' Sarah said without looking up or opening her eyes. 'Bren'll give you some money. And don't come over all shocked-gentleman-of-course-I'll-pay.'

'Wouldn't dream of it,' I said truthfully.

'Take the car,' she said.

'Er, well, just one problem – '

Gigi looked up out of the swimming pool. 'I'll give you a lift. Cor, I didn't fink there was anyone your age who couldn't drive.'

Cullop said, 'Why don't you go down to the coast for the food, and then you can stop off and have a look to see if Amedeo's come over.'

'Amedeo?' I said.

'Yes. You knew he had a villa here, didn't you? And it is the weekend after all. Friday, at any rate.'

'And what do we do if he's there?' I asked.

'Just come back and tell me.'

I wondered whether it was worth suggesting that they could always try phoning Amedeo's villa, and decided it wasn't. Gigi and I left. We passed Bobby who gave me the usual warm – well, scorching – welcome. 'Doesn't seem to have got to know me yet,' I said.

'Well, you've got to be friendly to him first – obvious I'd've fought.'

'Who looks after him when the villa's empty?'

'There's an old bloke in the village comes up and feeds him.'

'What with? Spare grandchildren?' I asked.

Only when we'd rounded the bend did Bobby's barking fade out. The car was parked where the taxi had dropped us. It was green, and wasn't a Rolls-Royce or a Mini, the only two I can recognise with any certainty. But it was evidently expensive: the dashboard looked like part of the set of one of those films where space crews get eviscerated by streaking red blobs; I half expected Gigi just to type in the co-ordinates for where we wanted to go and then leave the car to it.

'So what brought you and the loony together?' I asked as we drove down the hill.

'You mean Bren? He aint a loony. He's a bloke who knows what he wants.'

'Like, say, Al Capone.'

'Oh stuff it wiv your smart-ass cracks. He's a smart bloke and a real pro.'

'Yes, all right, he's a pro. That's all that counts, isn't it? Doing things professionally – like professional burglars, torturers, killers, child rapists – '

'You gone off your nut? Who are you calling a child ra – '

'Sorry. Forget I said it. Just tell me how you got involved with him and how long you've been involved.'

'You're the loony, mate: child rapist, torturer – round the bleeding bend. I've been wiv him just a couple of months.'

'What did he do? Put an ad in the papers, guide to Italian underworld needed?'

'Bren had been working on somefing in London before this. Don't suppose you've ever heard of Mike La Rocca.'

'No.'

'You're not likely to now either. He was a gang boss in Soho, a really nasty piece of work – I mean really nasty, child prostitutes and that sort of stuff – and, well, Bren sorted him out.' He hooted as we approached a bend, as if in celebration of Bren's achievement.

'And Mike La Rocca is now a quiet CND-supporting social worker.'

'Don't be dumb. Anyway while he was getting mixed up wiv the gang world he bumped into me and obviously liked me. He needed a, well, a guide like you said and I liked him so we got togevver.'

'And you're, er, equal partners, yes?'

'You can insinuate what you like, but we bloody are. We get along fine. We're both independent sort of people, see what I mean. I've never been tied to no gang, but I know me way around 'em and that's what Bren liked about me. Independent.'

'I see. What do you put on your tax forms? Guide round London? And are you going to make a career of it?'

'Could do worse. Not that I go much for careers like you mean careers. You know I've never been one of your nine to five steady job types. I like change. Independent, mate, that's what I am. And I don't owe nuffink to nobody. Clear?'

'And a big-timer.'

He took his eyes off the road momentarily and glanced at me. 'Yeah. I reckon so.' After a few seconds he went on, 'And don't believe anyone who tells you anyfing else. I may've had bad moments but I've always moved among the people that really count, people wiv clout. That clear?'

'Yes, if you really care so much.'

'Don't anyone ever say I'm small, 'cos I aint and I never have been. Clear?'

It was curious to think just how little I knew about Gigi's life. Another world – at least so it had been until Monday last. Those had been the days, I said to myself nostalgically – and then realised I didn't mean it. I wouldn't really have wished these five days not to have happened.

So I was turning out to be another cheap adventurer, ready with the easy sneer for honest nine to five stockbrokers, for people who objected to little things like murders as a way of staving off boredom.

Maybe I should ask Gigi for advice on the best gang to join.

'Tell you one fing though,' Gigi said, breaking in on my thoughts.

'What?'

'I got to admit you've surprised me these last few days. I mean, you might've cocked fings up in general like, but I'd never've fought you'd've kept at it like the way you have. Yeah. Bit of a surprise you're turning out to be.'

'Ah.' And as a confirmation of my general depravity I found I was pleased by this estimation of Gigi's. I had difficulty in keeping my 'Thank you' dry and ironic.

We passed through the village and kept on going down. We were not far from the little port when Gigi pulled up at a lay-by. We got out and Gigi led the way along a path that took us towards the sea. We walked in silence.

'There it is,' Gigi said, pointing. We were at the brow of a hill. There were white houses scattered down its slopes; at the very bottom there was a little beach with three buildings along its edge.

'Which one?'

'The red one.'

It was a bungalow that sprawled out in all directions, like a manic game of Scrabble: it looked rather as if the architect had died after making various rough sketches and it had been decided to build them all, crossings-out included. But it doubtless had a lovely view. The shutters were open, I saw. To its left was an unfinished concrete structure, and beyond that a simple bungalow.

'The shutters are open,' Gigi said. 'Must be there.'

'I suppose so.'

'Right, let's go on down then.'

'What, to the house?'

'To the village, yer berk. Got your shopping to do, aint yer?'

'Ah yes, good.'

'Had yer worried, dinnit?'

We went back to the car and drove on down to the little port. We parked in a road leading off the piazza.

'You go and do the shopping,' Gigi said, 'I'll go and have a drink. Here, have some money.' He gave me two fifty-thousand-lire notes and walked off towards a bar. Presumably buying vegetables wasn't quite in keeping with his image.

I was crossing the square, laden with crammed plastic bags, when I saw Franco. He was sitting alone at one of the two café tables, reading a newspaper. All around him arose the sound of Teutonic chatter, and bare limbs contrasted pinkly with the white tables. Franco, of course, like all the other natives, was wearing a pullover and jacket: the temperature might be in the seventies, but it was nonetheless only April, and certain norms had to be respected.

'Ciao,' I said. 'What are you doing here? You didn't follow me, did you?'

'I didn't know you were here.' He didn't greet me in expansive Neapolitan fashion; maybe they were more reserved down Torre Annunziata way. His eyes looked at me for a second or two and then flickered away, scanning the square with their usual nervous liveliness, as if checking I was alone. 'Do you want a drink?' he said. 'Sit down.'

I sat down. 'Well, this is a surprise,' I said.

'Yes. What are you up to?'

'Ah no. This time I asked first. *And* I'll pay for the drinks.'
I looked at his gorgeous coloured concoction and hoped I
wouldn't regret my offer. Then I remembered the change
from the hundred thousand lire in my pocket.

'That seems fair. All right, I've come following Amedeo.
He came over this afternoon. I saw him get into his boat at
Mergellina and I came over on the *aliscafo*. Just to check this
was where he was coming. And there's his boat, so I was
right.' He pointed to the harbour and I guessed he was
indicating the largest boat – not quite the size of Onassis's
yacht perhaps, but pretty noticeable in a port like this all the
same.

'I see,' I said. 'Very nice.'

'He was travelling with three gorillas. Two of them new, in
fact. Would you have had anything to do with the disappearance of the old one?'

'Do I look the sort of person to be responsible for such a
thing?'

'You don't look it, but I don't know if that means you're
not. I suspect you of having hidden talents. Did they come for
you yesterday?'

'Er, yes.'

The waiter finished taking orders from a German couple
and came over to us. '*Ja, trinken?*'

'I'm not German,' I said, 'and I'll have a mineral water.'

'And I'll have another of these,' Franco said. 'It's your
hair,' he said when the waiter had gone off.

'Yes, I know. Tell me, do you know anything about an
Englishman called Jameson? Linked with Amedeo? Little
man going bald?'

'Yes, I've seen him visiting Amedeo. I didn't know his
name. I didn't know for certain he was English.'

'He is. And he's a nasty piece of work.'

'I see. Are you going to tell me how?'

I told him briefly what had happened the night before, as it
didn't involve anybody but myself and the definite criminals –
not the not-quite-so-definite criminals. The waiter brought us

the drinks. Franco's only needed a sinister curling fume to be the concoction of a mad professor in a comic strip. But at the moment, in his relaxed pose, with his cigarette in one casual hand, he looked the last person ever to have a mad glint in his eyes. He swirled the drink with an olive-impaled stick and said, 'Well. I warned you. Remember you probably won't be so lucky next time.'

'No, I suppose not. And what about yourself? You're not exactly hiding here.'

'Nobody knows who I am. I take care of myself.'

'It seems a funny way of doing journalism though. I mean, just hanging around, watching. Shouldn't you be marching into offices, shoving microphones into people's faces, demanding interviews, asking Amedeo's murder victims' widows how they feel over the corpse?'

His eyes settled on me for one split second and then jumped away again like nervous fleas and he said, 'I'm not – I suppose you've guessed – I'm not a regular journalist.'

'Not regular. Free-lance you mean?' I hadn't guessed anything, in fact. I'd just been speaking in my usual idle fashion.

'It doesn't matter.' He clearly wanted to close the subject. 'And you then? What are you doing here?'

'Um, er, buying vegetables.'

'Very funny. You're here for Amedeo too?'

'Well, er, in a way, that is to say, oh look . . .'

He lit a cigarette with slow coolness. 'You sound confused.'

'Why the hell does everybody manage to make me confused and I don't make anyone? If you'd just throw your arms around a bit, show you're really Neapolitan, I'd feel better.'

'I'm having a drink by the sea at Ischia. I don't feel like throwing my arms around. Is your brother here?' He added this with deliberately exaggerated casualness, holding his glass up in front of himself and gazing at it as if to compare its colour with that of the sea. The languid side of his nature was definitely being cultivated, though no doubt if I looked hard

I'd see a little finger or toe drumming away nervously somewhere.

'Well, er, look, I'd rather not say anything more. I told you why yesterday. Listen, I'll get in touch with you again as soon as I've sorted things out.'

'You sound in need of sorting out.'

'Thanks. Where can I find you on Ischia?'

'You can't. I'm a day tripper. But no doubt I'll hear of you. I'll look in the *Mattino*'s obituaries.'

'Thanks again. Can I ask you one more thing?' I added on impulse.

'What?'

'Are you doing all this just out of curiosity? I mean, just for the sheer hell of it, something to do?' I suddenly had an idea of him as a Neapolitan Cullop; there was his languid take-it-easy air, and there was the mystery about his 'irregularity' as a journalist.

He stared at me with his cigarette to his lips. Then he said slowly and deliberately, 'I am not doing any of this for fun. And if you are, get right out of it. Clear?'

'No, I just wondered, I – ' I finished my mineral water. Franco's casual pose had dropped and all his inner energy blazed from his eyes which were hard and concentrated. Again I had that impression of another face recognisable behind his. He took a puff on his cigarette and then turned to stare out at the square again, still frowning. I felt suitably worm-like. I said, 'Well, I'd better be going. I'll be in touch some time, I swear.'

'I hope so.'

I paid the waiter, picked up my shopping bags and walked away. When I reached the wistaria-draped archway out of the square I stopped and turned. I saw he was still gazing at me. His fingers were drumming on the table. I gave a final wave and walked towards the bar I'd seen Gigi enter, trying to work out why the person who seemed most *simpatico* in the whole business was the one I was refusing to collaborate with.

As I walked up the hill a bus trumpeted elephant-like behind me and I spun round; I was only prevented from shooting it by the fact that I didn't have a gun. I'd be a cold-eyed killer yet.

Maybe that was the reason.

Seventeen

I said nothing about my meeting with Franco to Gigi, nor to the others when we got back. Franco had wanted to be discreet and why should I 'betray' him? And he was going to leave the island anyway, so it could have no importance. I went to the kitchen and decided I'd escape from the world for a couple of hours by preparing the best meal these people had ever eaten. I turned on the radio and found there was a Donizetti opera to keep me company – *Emilia di Ponders End*, or some such title, full of stirring choruses, duets like duels and arias that ended on chandelier-shattering notes. Just right for stuffing peppers to. I rediscovered the pleasure of working in a large kitchen, where I didn't have to make a master plan for the disposal of dirty saucepans, burnt oven-cloths, chopped onions, peppers or finger ends – just let it all pile up for the next morning's poor sucker. As the débris rose behind me, my creations took shape before me and the soprano went mad around me, I could almost forget what we were all up to on this island. A glance out of the window showed Brendan and Sarah (dressed again) playing croquet, and Gigi reading a sports paper in a deck chair – an idyll of rural peace. No doubt if I looked out the other way I'd see Bobby with a kitten slumbering between his outstretched paws.

Eventually the lasagne got put into the oven, the croquet balls and mallets into the box, the soprano into a mad-house and the tenor into a grave, and it was aperitif time. They came in for it, Brendan swinging the cricket bat jocularly and all of them making suitable comments about what delicious smells. I took my aperitif out. Anything to avoid conversation with these loonies. Of course, during the meal I had to sit with them, but I tried to keep the conversation on the subject of what a wonderful meal I'd prepared. At a certain point, however, compliments were exhausted (though I could think of a few aspects of my dressing for the salad that hadn't received full critical appreciation) and Brendan said in a now-let's-talk-seriously voice, 'Sooner or later we'll have to see if our friend Amedeo's up to anything. In fact, I'll have to see if there's any chance that my deal with him is still on.'

'Maybe he's already had it done,' I said, 'as a nice surprise for you.'

'No,' Brendan said, 'that wasn't the agreement. And besides,' with a slight smile, 'I think we'd have heard. No, more than likely he's got scared.'

'Well, if the deal's off, we can pack up and go home,' I said.

'Don't be dumb,' Gigi said, 'if the deal's off it means we're probably the next targets. Amedeo can't afford to take chances.'

'So it's us or him,' I said. 'I think that's where I came in on this story.' And once again that wet English wood came to my mind, and it had – quite illogically, considering what had been going on there – taken on a suggestion of lost innocence for me.

I brought out the sweet course. I could do with a few more compliments and the change of subject that implied.

After dinner I went out to the garden to have a quiet mooch under the stars, and think about life and its meaning and all those other topics that a few glasses of good wine (well, and bad wine too) can convince you you're really coming to profound conclusions about. Behind me I could hear Ella FitzGerald singing Cole Porter songs; the French windows at the back of the villa were slightly open, though no doubt the coolness of the evening would soon cause them to be closed. I walked round the swimming pool which was perfectly still so that the reflected stars lay almost inert, like coins on the bottom. It was the sort of evening that made me wish I smoked a pipe, or at least had a gate to lean on. I walked on to the wall at the end of the garden; the broken glass on the top glittered prettily in the moonlight. There was a wooden door in the wall, closed with two stout bolts. I decided to go for a longer mooch up the hillside where, without the interference of 'I Love Paris', my thoughts could plumb even deeper into life's mysteries.

I pulled the bolts, jerked the door open and stepped outside. The hillside got steeper here and was no longer cultivated. Just right for real Wordsworthian meditation. I started up a rough path; the moonlight glittered on spent hunting cartridges to help me find the way. I began to feel lonely – the sort of self-congratulatory lonely which comes from realising you're far too deep a person for anyone else to understand (which, in turn, comes from the last glass of Orvieto). After a minute or so, and two near trips and a stumble, I realised it wasn't necessary to walk any further to cultivate this feeling, so I sat down against a rock and mused – on various things, from Valerie to Mormons to Americans to Cullop to vigilantes to Camorristi to the unaccommodating nature of Ischian rocks to Cole Porter (just audible in the distance). In the midst of my musings I heard footsteps and instinctively I tensed up, ready to run.

Two figures were coming down the hillside. They were walking with obvious stealth, and seemed to be dressed entirely in black. They hadn't seen me, as their attention was on the uneven ground below their feet. I retreated behind a clump of Indian fig plants and as they got nearer wished I'd chosen a plant I could snuggle up close to. But they passed by me – within four or five yards in fact – without hearing my heartbeats or my knees knocking, and continued in the direction of the villa.

One of them was tall and wide and the other small and exaggeratedly stealthy. The large one was cradling something in his arms, and it wasn't a baby. I suddenly remembered the door was no longer locked and I went cold all through. I rose and started creeping down after them.

I had already guessed that the large one was Paolo and the smaller one Jameson. Jameson, I hoped, would have no gun. They reached the wall and Paolo put his hand to the door. He opened it. They both stepped inside and at this point I started running – still stealthily. I reached the door some few seconds after they'd entered and I peered through. They were walking round the swimming pool, both round the same side. (Jameson, no doubt, was too scared to go off on his own.) At the other end of the garden Ella FitzGerald was singing 'Why Can't You Behave?'

I would have no moment so good as now. I grabbed a croquet mallet that was lying against the wall and I ran. They heard me, and swung round just as my mallet was swinging down. It didn't connect with Jameson's head as I'd intended (because he was the nearest, of course, not because the most dangerous) but with his upraised arm. He staggered to one side, and I jerked the mallet straight back up; it connected with Paolo's gun arm at the very instant that Jameson hit the water, so the sound effects were rather surreal.

I moved straight in on Paolo, while the gun was pointing sideways, with only one thought in my head – and I succeeded; the next moment we were both in the water, in a confusion of limbs and metal. My head was above water for a half second and I managed to get out a 'HE – ', before a tug on my hair pulled me under and filled my mouth with water.

I can't really give a lucid account of the next ten seconds or so. All I know is I didn't enjoy them much. I emerged once more from the water and saw Paolo's face with gritted teeth and bedraggled whiskers and heard Ella FitzGerald sing 'where we two can go' and I was back under before I could hear the end of the line, 'and try settling down'. Suddenly I realised Paolo was no longer entangled with me, and I struggled back to the surface. I was surprised it was such a long way up; I felt as if I'd swallowed half the pool.

Paolo was pulling himself out of the darker side of the pool and there was a confusion of voices on the lighter side – Brendan's, Sarah's, Gigi's, and Ella FitzGerald's.

'*Fermati là!*' Brendan shouted. Paolo, of course, ran on to the open door. He was still carrying the gun. There was a sudden BANG! from Gigi's direction, but it didn't stop him.

A second later he was out of the door. Gigi and Brendan pounded past the pool after him.

I swam towards the side and heaved myself out. I sat on the edge and spat and panted. Jameson was standing in the shallow end, making a rather last ditch attempt to conserve some dignity by adjusting his pullover and patting his hair across his head. He looked around at us.

'Er, good evening,' he said. 'Look, I'm really sorry – '

'Oh shut up,' I said, 'or I'll come in and drown you.'

Sarah said, 'This is the guy you told us about, yeah?'

'That's the one,' I said. 'Never calls without a killer.'

'You must listen to me,' Jameson said plaintively, 'you must – '

'Go on, tell us you thought that guy was just going to invite us to dinner.'

'He looks kind of harmless,' Sarah said. 'Why don't we let him get out of the pool?'

'I think we should leave him there all night. With a brick tied round his neck if possible.'

'Oh dear,' Jameson said, 'I know what you must be thinking, I know, and I can't blame you, but you must listen, you must listen to me.'

'Come on out,' Sarah said.

He climbed out, though with some difficulty. I thought of offering my hand and then letting him slip back at the last moment, but it wasn't enough. There were no piranha fish in the pool.

Sarah said, 'You'd better both come in and get some dry clothes on.'

'Thank you, thank you,' Jameson said. He followed her across the lawn and I followed him. Unfortunately he didn't trip on any croquet hoops on the way. I did.

We were standing in the hall, dripping away, and Sarah was telling us she'd just get some towels when Gigi and Brendan appeared, panting. 'No sign of him,' Brendan said.

Gigi said, 'I'll just go and let Bobby off the chain.'

'Er, you'll close the windows first, won't you?' I said.

Gigi slipped out. Brendan turned to Jameson and said, 'I suppose this is the Jameson fellow you mentioned.'

'That's the one. Sarah wants to give him a change of clothes. I think we should start with a nice tailor-made rope for the neck.'

'And you're the one who doesn't believe in the death penalty,' Brendan said.

'For humans,' I said, 'for humans.'

'Listen, please listen, you must listen,' Jameson started again.

'Let's listen,' I said. 'For curiosity's sake. I just have to know how you explain this one away.'

'Look, it's not a question of explaining it away, it's, it's, oh, look you must listen.'

'We're listening, we're listening,' I said. 'I never like to miss hearing a real artist at work.'

Sarah said, 'We've got some bathrobes you can both put on first. Through there, in the bedrooms. I'll show you.'

So two minutes later we were all in the sitting room. Brendan was sitting astride a reversed chair, leaning on the back towards Jameson – something I'd only ever seen people do in films, which was no doubt where he'd picked it up from. Gigi was sitting with his elbows on the central table looking sceptical already. Sarah was curled up in an armchair in the darkest corner of the room. Jameson and I had both ended up on the sofa, much against my natural feelings, and we sat there in our blue and pink bathrobes (fortunately longer than the one Sarah had been wearing that morning) as if waiting for a mug of cocoa. Ella FitzGerald had come to an end, so I rather expected Jameson to ask for his Delius nightcap.

'All right then,' Brendan said. 'What were you up to?'

'Look, er, presumably Mr – Mr – ' He gestured towards me.

'Esposito,' I said.

' – er, Mr Esposito has told you about, about all this unfortunate business I've found myself mixed up in. And how I came to be mixed up in it.'

'You're not still expecting us to swallow all that poor little victim stuff?' I said.

'But, but that's what I am. I know it sounds pathetic, and God knows I feel pathetic – I feel almost a – a worm, but – a victim – that's what I am. Last night I really didn't know they were going to come round, I swear it, I – '

'You called them. You told them you'd got me there waiting for them, waiting in bed, nice and harmless.'

'I, I swear – ' He did his face-rubbing gesture. 'Oh God, I suppose I have to admit – admit the ultimate shame.'

'The very ultimate?' I said. 'You're sure?'

'You've every right to be sceptical. I confess. I phoned Amedeo. I had to. I'm, well, it sounds silly and melodramatic, but I'm in his power. I had to tell him. My life wouldn't be – Oh, I know you think it's not worth all that much anyway, and possibly you're right. But I, well, I'm not a brave man and I know it. I, I just had to tell him. Let him know. He swore that he wouldn't have you hurt. He really did.'

'He really did. Well, good old Amedeo.'

'And what about this evening?' Brendan said.

'Look, you've got to believe me. There was no plan to have you hurt at all. There really wasn't.'

'And the gun?' I said.

'That was protection, of course. I *know* there was no plan to have you hurt. Paolo – er, the big chap – was told just to ask you some questions. Amedeo is worried, it seems, worried about what you're up to, Mr Cullop.'

'And why did you come along?' Brendan asked.

'To translate, of course. Um, you speak Italian, I know, but Amedeo knew it would be easier for an Englishman to hear if you were telling the truth or not. Er, not of course that I think you'd, um, lie. That was Amedeo, you understand.'

'You are of course such an expert on the truth,' I said. 'And your kinky black get-up?'

'Well, they said we, we had to surprise you. Otherwise, well, otherwise you'd react. Oh, I didn't want to be involved in any of this. I'm sick of it all. It's all getting too much.'

'So why don't you get out and go off to Greece?' I asked. 'Like you said.'

'Oh, it's easy to say.' He sighed. 'But maybe you're right. I've had enough now. I've got to get out. If you – if you could only help me.'

I stared at him in wonder. Then I heard Sarah saying, 'You sound like you've had a pretty rough time of it. What can we do?'

I broke in, 'You're not all going to fall for this rat's sob tale?'

Brendan said, 'I think I can tell when a man's being sincere.' He was resting his elbows on the chair and was holding his hands together at the fingertips – the Sherlock Holmes pose.

'That's what I thought last night when he told me he'd take me to his house and I could stay there safe and sound.'

'Look, I can't tell you how ashamed I am of myself.' There was almost a real (so to speak) sob in his voice. 'I can't expect you to treat me well. I know, I know I acted appallingly, but God, if you knew how I've, I've slept these last nights – or not slept – just thinking about how Amedeo can do what he wants with me, about how he'd take revenge if necessary, and he *would*, he *would*, I know it – and, and then he *did* promise to me you weren't going to be hurt, he *said* so. You must believe me. But listen, now I swear, I *swear* I've had enough. I've seen too much – too much violence. I'm through with him. If you'll help me, if you'll only help me. And, and I can help you.'

I didn't say anything. I looked around at the others. Gigi was staring out of the window with an uninterested expression. Brendan was looking thoughtful, and Sarah was looking frankly compassionate. No doubt she'd been brought up on Beatrix Potter. Finally Brendan said, 'How can you help us?'

'Well, the most important thing is to destroy Amedeo, isn't it? I mean, it's necessary.'

This almost sounded convincing. After all, if he were doing all this because he was being blackmailed, the elimination of Amedeo was one kind of solution for him.

'I see,' Brendan said. 'And what were you just saying about violence?'

'I don't want to have anything to do with it. I wish, I wish I weren't involved. But, but what other way – isn't that what you want?'

'Well,' Brendan said, 'well . . . Really we want some information from Amedeo. That's all.'

'Yes, well, I can help you. I mean, I can help you get on top of Amedeo. So you can question him. He must be broken, his power must be broken.'

'You're making him sound like something out of a bad science fiction novel,' I said.

'But you know what I mean, don't you, you must.'

Brendan said, 'So how?'

'How what? Oh, how can I help you? I, I think you should go straight to him now. Armed, of course. Before he has time to get ready.'

'I see,' Brendan said. 'And what exactly does your help consist of – in concrete terms?'

'I can tell you just how to take them by surprise.' He was leaning forward now, his little face eager. 'Have you seen the villa?'

'Yes,' Brendan said.

'Well, he's there with two, er, two bodyguards. Three including Paolo, the chap who ran away just now. And they're on the lookout.'

'So?'

'So, er, I can tell you where to, where to, well, attack – enter, you know. On the left of the villa – left as you look at it from the sea – there's a shed, you know, you've probably seen it. There's a boat kept in it. And there's a door from that shed into the house. And I've got the key for it. Oh dear, it's in my trousers, shall I go – '

'I'll go,' Sarah said, and she uncurled herself and walked out.

'How do you happen to have the key?' Brendan asked.

'I, well, to tell the truth, at the last moment as I left I just slipped it in my pocket because, well, I must confess, the possibility of coming over to you – of helping you – you helping me – well, it crossed my mind. It was just a desperate thought then, you know, desperate – well, hopeful, you could almost say, the one glimmer of hope I had. I've been feeling pretty black.'

Sarah came in with a pair of dripping trousers and tossed them over to Jameson. He fished out a large key. 'This is the one,' he said. 'You see, if you come down from the hill through the vineyard you can't be seen till you get to the shed.'

'Like you just now,' I said.

'Er, yes.'

'Right,' Brendan said. 'I suppose we'd better move immediately.'

'Er,' I said and stopped.

'Yes?' Brendan said.

'Um, look, what are you intending to do down there?'

'Are you trying to say you don't feel like joining in?' Brendan said. His voice was entirely neutral.

'Well, you know how it is. I'd rather leave things to the police, you know. Let them break Amedeo's mystic power.'

'Hm. I know you can't be accused of cowardice,' Brendan began.

'But you can always hint at it,' I said, 'and try and make me squirm. Let me make my position clear. I don't much feel like going down to the seaside and shooting people, even Amedeo.'

'We're not going to kill anybody,' Brendan said, 'unless – '

'Unless they do anything provocative like lowering their brows at you. I know. Well, I don't want any part in it.'

'Fine. Luigi and I'll go together. Right, Luigi?'

Gigi said, 'Yeah.'

'And you and Sarah can stay here and keep an eye on Mr Jameson. Not that we don't trust you, Mr Jameson – '

'Just that we don't trust you,' I said. 'Be careful how you use his information.'

Brendan said, 'I like risks, but I always take them carefully.'

I looked with some curiosity across at Sarah. I saw she was half smiling at him – with him, rather. She was enjoying the act.

'Good,' I said. 'We'll have the camomile tea ready for when you come back.'

Sarah said, 'I won't do a big act, insisting on coming too. But I'm ready to help out when necessary. You know that.'

'Of course I do.'

Everybody got up and Brendan, Gigi and Sarah left the room purposefully. I was about to follow, but then decided I'd sit back down again. Jameson looked around in embarrassment and then went over to the record player and started looking through the records. I made no attempt at conversation.

A minute later Gigi and Brendan reappeared. They, too, were dressed in black trousers and pullovers, and had bulging bags slung over their shoulders. I didn't ask what was in them. I preferred to know as little as possible.

'Well, wish us luck at least, you bugger,' Gigi said.

'Er, do you want it in Italian? *In bocca al lupo* (Into the wolf's mouth),' I said. 'And let's hope it's not too appropriate.'

There was a longish farewell kiss between Brendan and Sarah, and then they moved to the front door and opened it. Bobby was there immediately, slavering away for human flesh. Gigi grabbed him by the collar and tugged him away from the door. 'You better close it,' Gigi said. 'We'll leave him loose.'

Sarah pushed the door to and Bobby's protests slowly died away.

'Right,' Sarah said, 'so what do we three stick-at-homes do now? Hey, I feel over-dressed.'

'If you want to put your bathrobe on,' I said, 'I've no objections.'

'Wow, you're getting fresh. Tell me, how do you feel now they've gone?'

We walked back to the sitting room and Jameson started looking through the records again. 'I know,' I said, 'I'm supposed to say, "Hell, I can't let those two go into it alone",

208

and redeem myself by galloping up at the last moment when the battle looks lost. Well, I'm not going to. You heard me say why.'

'I heard you. Be really consistent then and ring up the cops and tell them there's going to be some trouble.' She went over to the sideboard and opened a whisky bottle. 'You want a drop?'

'OK thanks.' I sat in an armchair and tapped the arms. She was of course right in a way. I had to work out the way in which she was wrong. I said, 'That would make all my behaviour up to now fairly illogical – a pretty good waste of time – seeing as I only got into all this mess because I didn't want to get Gigi into any trouble.'

'OK, OK, I was only asking. It's your conscience.'

'Do you want me to shoot myself for shame here or outside?' The trouble was I didn't feel too good about things. Logic and my moral sense told me I was right (in a way) but that didn't mean I felt an inner glow of virtue satisfying me with its warmth. I looked over at Jameson, still poring through the records. 'No Elgar or Delius,' I said. 'I've already looked. The only English composers are Lennon, John, and Bowie, David.'

'Ah yes. Marvellous stuff in its way, I'm sure. But not, um, not my, my – '

'Scene, man?'

' – er, my cup of tea.'

'Well, I'm going to put a record on,' said Sarah.

'And I'm going to get dressed again,' I said. I fortunately had a spare pair of trousers and a pullover.

We passed a not very sociable forty minutes or so. Sarah sat with her whisky, half-listening to Joni Mitchell and half-reading a magazine. Jameson tried to look as if he were getting into this new scene (cup of tea) and I sipped my whisky, read a Frederik Pohl novel and alternated between trying to look as if I'd come to my decision after serious internal moral struggles and trying to look as if I didn't give a damn. From the occasional looks I got from Sarah it seemed that either way

I was a louse. When she wanted she could be facially expressive.

The record's second side had come to an end and we were sitting there in uncompanionable silence when we heard Bobby barking.

'Leave it to me,' Jameson said, 'I have a way with dogs.' He was out of his seat and at the front door before Sarah had even got through half of her 'Just hang on a minute.'

I was surprised by this sudden courageous alacrity and crossed the room after him. Jameson threw open the front door and stepped out.

'Just what the – ' I began. There was the sound of a gunshot and Bobby's barking ceased abruptly. Jameson ran in the direction of the gunshot, round the corner of the house. 'Hell,' I said to myself and dithered for a second or two. Sarah joined me. 'What d'you think – ' she began.

'I think we'd better get back in,' I said, touching her elbow in an ushering movement. She resisted. 'Wait a moment,' she said.

'We haven't got a moment – '

Three people rounded the corner of the house: two large men carrying rifles, followed by Jameson.

'Shit, no, we don't,' Sarah said.

Eighteen

'*Alzate le mani*,' said one of the large men.

'Huh?' said Sarah.

'He says "hands up",' I said. 'I think we'd better comply.'
I raised mine.

'Guess so,' she said. She raised hers with deliberate
slowness.

The two large men came forward. They were both wearing
the fashion of the moment – black trousers and pullovers – so
that Jameson's pink bathrobe was rather prettily set off. The
man who had spoken had a thick black beard which, like Cut-
throat Jake's in Captain Pugwash, hid his mouth completely
when closed. When he spoke it was revealed as surprisingly
wide and cavernous. The other man was younger – about my
age – and rather sneeringly good-looking, with black curls
over his ears and collar.

Jameson said in Italian, 'We'd better take them inside.' As
I remembered from the pizzeria, his accent was pure Ollio and
Stanlio.

'What are you saying, you rat?' Sarah said.

'Er, just that we should go inside. I'm so sorry for all this, I
really am.'

'Oh shut up,' she said, 'I don't want to hear any of that
crap.'

'I don't know how you keep it up,' I said, staring at him
almost in admiration. 'Don't you ever slip up and find yourself
telling the truth by mistake?'

'You've got to understand,' he said, 'that I – I don't do any
of this for choice. It's not, not my plan, you know. But
anyway, do please move inside or these chaps will get, um,
will get angry.'

We walked into the hall followed by the three men.

'Now where?' Sarah asked.

'Er, I rather think they want to tie you up or something,' Jameson said. 'But you do see that this is Amedeo's order, not mine.'

'Tell me,' I said, 'are you just improvising now or was the whole thing planned? Were you supposed to get caught by us?'

'Well, er,' Jameson began, 'to tell the truth – '

'Oh, come on now,' I said.

' – to tell the truth,' he continued, 'Amedeo had, um, told me to try and get caught. It seemed the simplest way, you see.'

Sarah was staring, her eyes even wider than usual. 'You mean Bren and Luigi just walked straight into a trap?'

'Well, um, Amedeo didn't want any violence if possible; you see that, don't you? This seemed the safest way – for everybody, you understand, for everybody.'

'You slimy little ratbag,' Sarah began, her hands above her head curling into fists.

'Oh, please, you must see things my way. I know it's not easy, but – ' As Sarah began to move towards him he yelped, '*Fermala!*' and the younger thug stepped back and jerked his gun up threateningly. She stopped and raised her hands again. She kept looking at Jameson, and I realised that the looks I'd been getting before had revealed only a fraction of her capacity for facial expressiveness.

The bearded thug spoke in Italian. 'Don Enzo's going to come up in the van for them as soon as we've phoned. I think we should tie their hands at least.'

'There's no phone here,' I said in Italian, not really expecting that they'd all reel back gasping 'foiled'.

'What?' Jameson said in English. 'You sure?'

The bearded man looked at him, and I guessed his mouth was pulled downwards in contempt under the beard. 'Didn't you check that?'

'I couldn't wander where I liked. They kept me under watch. Well, let's tie them properly to chairs or something and then either you or Silvio can go down and tell Don Enzo in person. Besides, he'd probably like someone else to help keep an eye on the other pair down there.' His Italian was grammatically perfect; there was just that awful English accent – the accent of one who refused to make any concessions to damned foreigners by moving his tongue in silly new ways.

'Silvio will go,' the bearded man said and Silvio shrugged his shoulders in resigned acceptance.

'Just tell me,' Sarah said, 'what's happened to Brendan and Luigi?'

'Oh, I'm sure they've come to no harm, I'm sure there's been no unnecessary violence.'

'I don't know why I ask,' she said, 'since we can't trust a word you say.'

'But I assure you, I've told you I'm opposed to violence, I really don't like it, and I'm sure Amedeo – '

'Jeez, if I got my hands on you I'd give you a few more reasons for not liking it,' she said.

'Actually, Sarah, from what he was saying just now in Italian it sounds as if they're OK – or at least still alive,' I said.

'I wouldn't believe him in any language.'

'Now come on,' Jameson said, 'enough of this silly talk, move through to the sitting room – no, the kitchen. The chairs there are more suitable.' But for his unusual costume, he could have been a form master admonishing fourth formers who'd been larking in the corridor.

We moved through and were made to sit on chairs on opposite sides of the still uncleared table. Our wrists were tied behind our backs by Silvio who produced rope from under his pullover. He took the opportunity offered by the job for prolonged contact with Sarah, until she hacked at his shin with her foot – at least that's what I guessed she did from the sound effects. He drew his fist back with sudden viciousness and was stopped by a sharp order from Jameson, who said in Italian, 'Remember Amedeo wants to talk to them and he won't want them hurt before that. Just finish tying them.' Again the fussy schoolmaster tones. Silvio did the job sullenly, tying us round the waist to the chairs with professional skill and brutality. Only when he'd finished with me did I remember I should have been expanding my belly to make the knots looser; instead I'd been holding my breath tensely. The bearded thug trained his rifle on us with one-handed nonchalance and with the other hand poured himself a glass of Orvieto from the open bottle on the table. Jameson rubbed his hands in fussy agitation; ignoring every physical detail about him, it was just possible to see him as a nervous boxer entering the ring with his trainer.

When we were securely tied the bearded man said, 'OK Silvio. Get down to the villa.' He knocked the wine back and I half expected him to chuck the glass into the cavernous hole in the beard as well.

Silvio pushed his hair back up and looked at the bearded man with what I suppose were smouldering eyes. He said, 'All right.' He looked at Sarah and said to her, 'But you'll see me again, don't worry.'

Sarah said in a bored tone to me, 'Did he say anything worth hearing?'

I said, 'Just fixing another date.'

'Tell him to go screw himself.'

I didn't translate this. Jameson said in Italian to Silvio, 'Quickly, quickly. They'll be waiting.' Silvio walked out with a gait which was clearly intended to be cool and casual, but which was equally clearly an imitation of some film star and about as natural as a defeated candidate's smile as he explains how happy he is about the election result. We heard him leave the house.

Sarah said, 'They've killed Bobby, haven't they?'

'I suppose so.' This was not the most worrying thing on my mind at the moment, but I didn't say so.

The bearded man said to Jameson, 'You take this gun. I'll look around the house and see if there's anything that might interest the boss.' Jameson took the rifle with obvious reluctance and positioned himself by the door. He held it as an inexperienced father holds a baby, as if not knowing which end might cause more mess.

'It doesn't really go with your bathrobe,' I said.

'I know, I know. It's not my sort of thing at all.'

The bearded man said, 'Right, keep your eyes open.'

I said in Italian to him, 'There's some good whisky in the next room if you're interested. Why don't you drink yourself senseless with that?'

'If they talk too much,' he said to Jameson, 'I'm sure Don Enzo won't mind a bruise or two around the mouth.' And he smashed my face with the back of his hand.

I heard Sarah start to speak and I said quickly, 'Don't say anything, there's no point.' It didn't come out all that clearly as my lips and cheeks were tingling with pain, but she shut up anyway.

The bearded man nodded to Jameson and walked out. Jameson said, 'Now I've told you I don't like this business but I must warn you I'll use this gun if I have to, I really will, so please don't try anything silly.'

'Would you mind pointing it away from us at the moment, though,' I said. 'They're delicate things.'

'Oh, yes, of course. Sorry.' He lowered it.

'Rather a change from teaching,' I said. 'Unless you had a particularly tough fifth form to deal with. But really, what would Tom Merry and Harry Wharton say?'

He looked at me with lowered eyebrows. 'You've been looking through my – ' Then he collected himself and said in his eager chatty voice, 'They're jolly good stories, aren't they? I mean, even after all these years I find the characters so unforgettable.'

'Who would you compare yourself with? Vernon Smith, the Bounder of the Remove? Cardew the Cad? No, they're reckless fellows but rather likeable at heart. I'd say Skinner or Snoop or Stott. Or perhaps Bulstrode the bully.'

'Just what are you talking about?' Sarah said, staring at me. She couldn't see Jameson – not that that would have helped her comprehension, of course.

215

'Books no decent English kid grows up without reading. Full of stout chaps who play the game – and others who sneak and lie and cheat and are general rotters.'

'I say,' Jameson said, 'that's a bit – a bit below the belt. I know, I can't pretend to be – well, to be a Harry Wharton, but in my own way I'm trying to – to play the game as best I can. I promise, I *promise* I'll intercede with Amedeo – you know, see that you don't get treated too badly.'

'I don't get you,' I said. 'Each time we strip off a mask there's another one beneath. Don't you ever just enjoy a straightforward evil cackle? Or do you just lie so well that even you believe it?'

'Oh, it's easy to judge,' he said, 'but you must see my situation. I didn't want to get involved – '

'If I hear that again,' Sarah said, 'I'll scream.'

'And just what is your involvement with Amedeo?' I said. 'The way you talk to those gorillas, you sound a bit more than an occasional interpreter. How long have you been with – ' I stopped. The glimmerings of the possibility of the start of an idea had come to me: that cassette hidden behind his Tom Merry annuals. OK, I'd been so stupid as to leave it there, but I did know it existed, didn't I?

'Long enough, long enough to regret it, I can tell you. I dream of – of a nice retired life, you know, far from all this awful gangsterism and – '

'Anyone would think he was the one tied up,' Sarah said. 'If that's the way you feel, why don't you just cut us loose?'

'I have my responsibilities,' he said, 'my word to keep to Amedeo.'

'Make up your mind whether you're his faithful retainer or his blackmail victim,' I said, 'or we'll all get confused.' Talking of blackmail, I said to myself . . . And I thought hard.

Jameson said, 'Oh you can't understand my situation . . .' and kept on in this strain for half a minute or so. I wasn't listening. When he came to a pause, I said, 'You might be interested to know I found that cassette behind your Tom Merry annuals.'

'What?' And the gun jerked up.

'Put that thing down. You know Amedeo wants to find us whole.' He didn't move the gun. 'You'll have some explaining to do if your finger moves on that trigger. Anyway, I'll keep talking and hope you'll see sense. I took the cassette with me.' Everything now depended on whether he had looked behind those books since yesterday, and I stared up at his face in breathless, expectant agony. I added to the torture by asking myself for the *n*th time, Why oh why oh why *hadn't* I taken the bloody thing?

There was a definite expression of alarm on his face. 'And – and so?' he said. He *hadn't* looked there.

Relief overwhelmed me – but fortunately for my poker face I realised almost at once that that was only the first stage in my bluffing. After all, I couldn't be a hundred per cent sure about the contents of the tape. With another prayer to San Gennaro and another curse at my negligent stupidity I said, 'I'm sure Amedeo will be interested to know that there's a second copy of that conversation around.'

'And why shouldn't there be?' he said.

I was right about the tape. The bluff was working. 'Well, I've just remembered something one of those men who got killed in Bayswater said – yes, I was there. He said that they'd got the cassette from the Englishman, it had been all his idea.' I was remembering Raffaele's last cry ('It was Gianni, him and that Engli – ') and elaborating on it. 'Those two men, after all, weren't really the sort to carry out a big blackmailing scheme on their own. You'd put them up to it. No doubt it seemed like an easier way to big money than just bowing and bobbing at Amedeo's side.'

The gun was wavering; presumably he was itching to do his usual nervous face-rubbing bit. I hoped the itch wouldn't communicate itself to the trigger. I had no doubt now that I was right. He said, 'But, but – can you blame me? There I was in his power; the theft of that cassette put things on a more – well, a more equal footing. And then those two men – you know, they'd been awfully badly treated by Amedeo. Sacked over a little matter – not keeping away a journalist or someone who found out about a meeting with this, um, this Rauco chap – you know, when he was making the first deals with him. So how could I *not* offer to help them out?'

It was, of course, impossible to know how much truth he was telling. I discounted automatically all the part that referred to his poor-victim status, and to his capacity for sympathy. Not much was left, but I listened to it with attention. I said, 'Yes, I'm sure Amedeo will understand when I explain things to him.'

'Oh, now you wouldn't do such a thing. Oh, dear me.' He was becoming flustered, like Mrs Tiggywinkle in a pink apron. But still Mrs Tiggywinkle with a gun. 'You see,' he said thoughtfully, 'I can always tell him I had to shoot you because you attempted to escape. You do see that, don't you? It would be a terrible thing – terrible. Who would have thought that I . . . But, well, circumstances could force me to this step. You must see my position.'

'Remember,' I said, 'Amedeo is no fool. And remember too that the moment you fire, your bearded friend will be in to see what's up. Would you like him to explain to Amedeo?'

'Oh dear, what a quandary.'

'Your fault for leaving the copy of the cassette around. Why did you make it anyway?'

'Cassettes so easily break,' he said. He was answering in a tone of absent politeness as if his mind were really on something else – presumably on the question of how to bump me off without putting himself at risk. He went on, 'There's a language laboratory in the school I teach at so it seemed a good idea to take advantage of its facilities.'

So he did actually teach at a school, I thought, with oddly detached interest. I said, 'Just out of curiosity what went wrong with your plans?' Whatever else I did I had to keep him reasoning: if he got panicky with that gun in his hands I could get dead. The best thing seemed to be to keep him talking.

218

'Now why should I tell you?' he asked.

'No reason – or perhaps just to make me more *comprensivo* as the Italians say. You could even make a new friend.'

'Ye-es. Well, it's an awfully complicated story.'

'I'm used to that sort. Go on.'

'Well, I suppose – yes, it'll show you what an awkward situation I got put in. You see, they phoned telling me that the cassette had got stolen. Well now, as you can imagine I was in a bit of a – well, a bit of a tizz, a flurry, you know. Such incompetence. And I thought, you know, next thing they're going to get arrested and start telling everything, so I took a bit of a risk – a calculated risk – and I went along to Amedeo telling him that these two had come to me some days earlier in Naples asking if I wanted to come in on their scheme – as interpreter or something – and I told Amedeo that I'd of course turned it down with, with indignation. I mean, what else could I tell him? And I said that they'd let slip the name of the hotel they were going to – I mean, I made it convincing, saying that, um, it was their cousin's or something, that's why they'd mentioned it, well, you know I made quite a good story of it.' He seemed to expect congratulations. 'Well, he believed it – I mean, you know, I really laid it on, saying I'd been debating for the last few days whether to tell him or not and at last had realised it was my – my duty. And he accepted it all; oh, it was quite a relief. You see, I knew he'd actually set Mr er, Signor, um, Rauco on their trail, and I knew that Rauco, if he found them, would kill without asking questions, so my name wouldn't come out – or so I, well, hoped. It was quite a tense day or two. But, but you do see, I had no choice.'

'No, of course not. Most natural.'

Sarah was staring at me with an 'Is this guy real?' expression, but she didn't say anything.

I said, 'And you do see that you've got no choice here now either. You'd better let us go.'

'Ah, but have you any proof? You see, it'll be your word against mine, and I – '

'I can tell Amedeo where the cassette is now. It's not here, so it's no use looking for it,' I said in perfect truth.

'Ah.' He thought a bit. 'You are putting me in a sticky situation, dear me. I suppose I could, er, try and, well, hit the truth out of you about where it is. Awfully unpleasant it would be, the last thing I'd like to do, but you know – Or better, you might be quite a hardy sort of chap, not like me at all I confess, so I could, er, start on this lady. It would be nasty to be reduced to such expedients but needs must . . .'

'You filthy bastard,' Sarah began.

I cut in, 'Again there's the problem of your bearded friend. He'd want to know why we're screaming.'

'Ye-es, ye-es. Such a quandary. But then, if I let you go what do I gain? I mean, Amedeo isn't going to approve, is he – and you do appreciate my position with him. And what's to stop you going to Amedeo next and, um, telling him this story anyway? You do see my point?'

'Let me do a deal,' I said. 'Cut me loose or let me escape in a natural-looking way – and keep the girl. It'd be difficult to make two escapes look natural, but they'd swallow one. And she doesn't know anything about the cassette, where it is or anything like that, so if she tries talking she's got no proof, and you'll easily outlie her. So let me go and I swear I'll just clear out. Leave Ischia, leave Naples. I mean, hell, I didn't want to be involved in any of this in the first place, and all I ask now is just to get the hell out.' I had been staring over the top of Sarah's head towards Jameson through all this and had consciously avoided glancing downwards. At the end I dropped my eyes briefly and saw that her expression was even more contemptuous than it had been while listening to Jameson, which I wouldn't have thought possible. Still not looking directly at her I said, 'You do see, Sarah, it's just not my problem. Sorry, but there it is.'

She didn't speak.

Jameson said, 'Just a moment', and slipped out of the room. Still neither of us spoke and it was quite a relief when Jameson reappeared – things were at a pretty pass when he brought relief.

'All right,' Jameson said, 'he's looking through the drawers in the bedrooms. I've been thinking and, um, well, maybe you're right. But how are we going to work it?'

'Give me access to a knife or something; you know, we can make it look as if I got hold of one off the table and then took you by surprise.'

'Ye-es. Well, I suppose so. You do swear you're going to clear off then?'

'Like a bat out of hell. I mean, what's in it for me to stay? You'll never hear from me again.'

'Ah, good, well, it's been all most interesting. I mean, I'd say hope we meet again, but it wouldn't really be appropriate of course, ha ha' – again that carefully explanatory laugh – 'but who knows that one day, back in England perhaps, we might meet up, and I hope without any, you know, rancour on either side – '

'Some long-distant time, I trust.' It would look suspicious if I suddenly became over-conciliatory.

'Um, I'll have to fire a shot, you understand, otherwise it'll look, you know . . . But first, here's a knife.'

I took it in one hand and started sawing. Better than beer can tops any day. 'Could you just slip the catch on the window there,' I said, nodding to the French windows that gave on to the back lawn. 'Because when I'm through I'll dive at them and smash them open, only I'll feel safer if I know they'll give. Don't worry, it'll still look realistic if your friend happens along.'

He did so and then returned to his watchful position by the door. I cut through the ropes that bound me to the chair. The ropes tying my wrists were of course much more difficult, but by pressing the handle against a cross bar of the chair I managed to achieve a position of sufficient leverage. Sarah just kept looking at me, her expression unchanged.

'Hurry up,' Jameson said, 'do. Oh, and which way will you run?'

221

'I'll go for the gate in the back wall – the one you came in by.'

'Yes, yes, I see.'

The knife went through the cords and I worked them off my wrists. I did it unobtrusively, however, keeping up the appearance of busy sawing. I said, 'Just another few seconds and I'll be through.' I measured the distance to the French windows with my eye and poised myself. I started another sentence, keeping my voice quiet and concentrated as if I were still intent on the task of cutting. 'No, it's tougher than I thought, it'll take – ' On that word I leapt up and hurled myself shoulder first at the windows; they burst open. I heard a startled cry from Jameson while I was flying through the air. I hit the grass to the right of the windows and rolled over. The gun went off and I knew my suspicion had been right: Jameson had fired to kill and only my precipitate action had saved me.

I came out of my roll into a run, making for the side of the house. I had just turned the corner when the gun was fired again.

I'd remembered rightly: there was an open window here into the bathroom that led off the kitchen. I heaved myself up and through it in a second and a half, landing jarringly in the bath. I pulled the window shut and I listened hard. I could hear the voices of Jameson and the bearded man. Jameson was saying that I was making for the front gate. The bearded man, judging from the next confused noises, crossed the hall and opened the front door.

I got out of the bath. On the wall near the bath was a towel-rail, a wooden rod supported on two brackets. I removed the rod and tiptoed over to the door. I opened it the merest fraction and saw Sarah's face jerking up in astonishment; I urgently communicated the need for silence with one hand. She nodded.

There was a large pile of plates on the table just to her left and, without moving from behind the door, I indicated that she should knock them off with her chin if possible. Given the narrowness of my performing area it was quite an accomplished mime. She looked puzzled, but bent to comply and I mouthed one word: 'Wait.' She waited.

Jameson came in through the French windows. I couldn't see him, only hear him. I gave Sarah the signal and she moved. One vigorous jerk of the head and a sound like something out of a disaster movie. I hurled the door open while Jameson was still in mid-surprised-spin. I smashed the rod down on the back of his head – right on the bald spot – and he plummeted forward, holding the gun, into the still slithering mess of broken plates.

The door opposite flew open before I had time to make a grab for the gun; the thug stood there holding a cricket bat.

We stood at opposite ends of the room for a second or two, he swinging his cricket bat, I my towel-rail: W. G. Grace versus Andy Capp's Flo. Jameson lay between us in his pink bathrobe on the greasy wreckage, like a dead pig on a rubbish tip.

The thug started forward and Sarah – whom he hadn't even glanced at – suddenly shot her legs out so that he tottered. I slammed down with my towel-rail, and it caught his head with a noisy crack that I never want to hear in my life again. He slumped down on top of Jameson, smashing the few plates still unbroken.

I leant against the wall for a second or two, feeling a little queasy. I let the rod drop. I heard Sarah say, 'That's team-work' and I managed a smile and a nod.

Nineteen

I went over to her and started cutting her ropes. She said, 'I'm going to have to say a lot of sorries for some of the things I've been thinking about you just now. You sure took me in. I shoulda known you weren't that sort of guy. Hell, I'm sorry.'

I cut through the last cord and said, 'I meant you to think that. I mean, I meant you both to think it – to think that all I wanted to do was run for it – not far off the real truth, in fact, just that I'm too dumb to act on my real feelings. But I knew there was no way I could persuade him to let us both go, so I had to go for second best and work from there.'

She rose and went over to the two bodies. She pulled the gun from under them. 'Did you know he was going to try and kill you?'

'I guessed that. I mean, he couldn't be sure about me clearing off for good, and I was giving him the perfect opportunity to silence me for ever without it looking too suspicious. No, he's not the kind of bloke I'd choose to go into partnership with.' After a moment's thought I said, 'It makes me wonder about him and Amedeo. Who was blackmailing whom? Funny if we had to start thinking of Amedeo as a victim. Well, I suppose there's no way of ever getting to the truth about anything this bloke's involved with. If he told me it was a nice day I'd get my umbrella out.'

'What bugged me was that it looked like he really believed in all that victim stuff.'

'Perhaps he does. Who knows what's eating him up inside?' I wondered if years ago he'd been passed over for promotion or some new teacher had sat in his favourite chair in the staff room, and ever since then he'd been able to justify every lie or murder he'd committed because he was just a poor put-upon bloke trying to get by. I said in rather feeble conclusion, 'Anyway he gives me the creeps.'

'What are we going to do with them?' She handed me the gun and turned Cut-throat Jake over and I found myself going tense on the trigger. I'd have to be careful. I took my finger off it.

'Well,' I said, 'I suppose we'd better tie them up. You any good at that?'

'I was a girl scout once. I guess though they should have a doctor or something, but I'm not going to lose any sleep over that.'

'Nor me. Let's just get them laid out a bit more tidily. I'll stay here with the gun; you get some pillows to put under them.'

A minute or so later they were trussed, but with pillows instead of plates under their heads. Jameson was coming to and not liking it.

'I don't say they'll never get them undone,' Sarah said, 'but at least it'll take them some time. Now what, Jan?' She joined me by the door.

'Well, I suppose we'd better see what we can do for Gigi and Brendan.' Now, she was asking *me*.

'Yeah, sure.' A pause. 'Thanks. When I think what I was thinking five minutes ago . . . Sorry.'

'Think nothing of it. I've got used to it.'

She smiled, and this time I could think that it was all for me. It felt good. I said, 'Remember Amedeo's supposed to be coming up here with a van or something. Maybe we should wait till he comes.'

'Add him to the heap. You know, I really want to meet this guy.'

'Well, so do I, so long as we stay this end of the gun. Look, why don't we go to where he'd have to leave the van? Take him by surprise there.'

'Yeah, sure. I don't fancy hanging around here; looks too much like a mortuary. Hang on, I'll just get that stick of yours.' She picked up the towel-rail I'd used.

I said, 'Just give me a moment' and ran to the sitting room sideboard where Brendan had put the few things of mine he'd brought over from the hotel. I found the large beret I'd bought that morning and pulled it well on.

'You're really bashful about that blond hair of yours, aren't you?' she said when I reappeared.

'Yes, when I go housebreaking in the south of Italy. I think you should do the same.'

She went and got a scarf and tied it round her head. It was rather more fetching than my hat, I felt. We left the villa by the front door. Sarah went over to a dark shape in the middle of the lawn and bent down. I prepared tender words of commiseration. She came back and said, 'Yuck, what a mess. The bastards. Come on.'

We left the garden and walked along the hillside path in the moonlight. After a few steps I said, instinctively whispering, 'Do you know how to use the gun? Because I don't.'

'I can manage one. Back in L.A. I've done target practice.'

We exchanged weapons and I felt a lot better. I said, 'Did you do it just for fun or did you know you were going to get mixed up in this sort of thing?'

'Where I come from in L.A. it's not that strange a thing to learn to do, you know.'

'Ah, I see.'

'Hell, there I go again, playing up to the usual image you Britishers seem to have of the States – muggings and rapes on every street corner. I just fancied doing it, OK?'

'OK by me.' We reached a point from where we could see the road. 'We'd better squat down here,' I said, going towards a vine that would more or less hide us. We squatted – well, I knelt, she squatted – and watched the road. A motorbike came roaring up but went on over the brow of the hill. When the sound of its engine had faded away I said, 'Er, you'll use the gun for protection of course.' It was resting on her thighs at that moment.

'Of course. I'm not a killer.'

Just hang around with them. No, mustn't say that. 'Sorry, I didn't mean – well, I was just wondering.'

'About me and Bren?'

'No. About what we're going to do when Amedeo turns up.'

'Oh, I see. I'm getting kinda touchy. I reckon the simplest thing would be just to take over the van. Once we've clobbered them. That shouldn't be too difficult if we can get to jump them. I mean, they'll come through that gate, won't they?'

'Yes,' I said, and added unthinkingly, 'good.'

'You *were* thinking I was out to kill.'

I started to um and er but then, after a moment's frowning thought, came out with, 'Well, let's face it, you didn't seem too worried about the thought of Bren doing it.'

'I just recognise that's the way he is.'

'I suppose the daredevil eye-glint excuses everything.'

She swivelled to stare at me directly. 'I've gotten to like you. Don't screw things up.'

'Sorry. Maybe you'd better make me a list of taboo subjects.' She didn't answer, but I saw her eyes full on me – big and unwavering and with their own little moonlit glint. I said, 'Look, I mean it, sorry if I'm, er, speaking out of turn. I think we could get on well together too, but it's just, it's just I like things to be straight, clear. I don't go for Brendan's Rambo-style solutions and that's not what I've got in mind for when we zoom in to the rescue. And I just wondered, well, how far your admiration for him would take you.'

'You do see me as the dumb blonde, don't you?'

'No, not in the slightest,' I said without any hesitation. 'That's what puzzles me actually. You're so obviously an independent sort, ideas of your own and, and the rest of it, that I just don't understand what makes you, er – '

'What makes me fall for a moron like Brendan. Go on, say it.'

'He's not a moron but, well, let's face it, he can be a bit of a poser. Sorry, I'm screwing things up again.'

'No, maybe you're right. But then you've never gone

around with a jerk from an advertising agency. At least Bren poses differently. I guess too that the – the transatlantic gap helps; I mean, where *you* see posing, an ignorant Californian like me sees style.' She smiled. 'With an accent like Bren's in the States, they either fawn on you or yell faggot at you. Well, I don't fawn, but I know he's not – not the other. And another thing that brings me and Bren close is what he told you today – that he can't stand boredom. I can't either. And I've never been bored with him. That means a lot.'

'Well, when he starts palling, remember I know lots of jokes.' I surprised myself by saying this, and then realised I half meant it. Well, a moonlit night, the Bay of Naples, and a blonde (though headscarfed) beauty, what could you expect?

She smiled again. 'Yeah well, I know that you're another guy who wouldn't bore me. I've told you, you have a lot in common with Bren, you really do.'

'Oh hell. Look, for a start, like most weaklings I'm against violence.'

'So is Bren. Deep down.'

'I've never got below the piranhas. Anyway, we're agreed: this gun is just for clobbering, right?'

'Yeah, sure. At least till one of them pulls his gun on us.'

'Let's try and avoid that,' I said with convenient vagueness.

'You want me to call the cops up? Let them do it?'

'Er, no.'

'Right then. Remember that makes you as Rambo as the rest of us.'

'As cowardly, I suppose. Oh hell. What got me into all this?'

'You know that. I've already told you. You've got that same crazy loner thing Bren's got. And I do too.'

'You?'

'Don't sound so surprised or I'll know I *am* the dumb blonde for you. Listen, I may be hanging out with Bren now but that doesn't mean I depend on him. We have a good relationship but, well, when the day comes that I decide to

228

move on or he does, I'm not gonna start screaming for alimony.'

'I never suggested – '

'No, sure you didn't. But when someone like me hangs around someone as rich as Bren there are always people ready to call you gold-digger – or just think it quietly. Well, I've asked for no jewels or furs so far and I don't intend to. Like I said, we have a good relationship, but I know it's not for ever. Nothing is.'

'You could get some good song titles out of that,' I said, and then wished I hadn't. 'Sorry,' I said, 'I don't mean to sound cynical. It's just that everybody I've met in the past few days is obsessed with telling me how independent he or she is. What's wrong with a little old-fashioned dependence or per-manence? I like the old clinging-vine type songs.'

'I got out of all that when I left Eddie, my adman, and met Bren in Spain.'

'Killing bulls, no doubt.'

'No, climbing. He took me up a few mountains. There's nothing like it, you know.'

'And I suppose you can always cut the rope if you start feeling too dependent.'

The conversation was illuminating, but only in a limited way. I was, I realised, as big a sufferer from the transatlantic gap as her. I was unable to supply any background to her in the way I automatically could to an English person the moment he or she opened his or her mouth (place of birth, kind of school, social class, etc). California I only knew from television and films, which meant that for me its inhabitants divided their time between surfing and car-chasing; and the fragments of autobiography she'd given me – Methodist upbringing, ability to shoot, life with an adman – didn't help much to build up a coherent picture. I suppose what was illuminating, in fact, was the very fragmentariness of this picture; as far as I was concerned she really came from nowhere – from no place and no past, and that, I suppose, was what true Independence was all about.

I knew I ought to say, God preserve me from it; but I thought how those memories of Valerie (now well on the way to being a full-length Zeffirelli film) could lacerate me if I dwelt on them, and I couldn't deny the sneaking attraction the concept held for me.

We were silent for a moment or two. I wondered at the strength of her thighs: she hadn't shifted her squatting position once. Presumably the result of hours of meditating with her legs wrapped round her neck. Then she said, 'Since we're getting so kind of friendly, I suppose there's a confession I ought to make. On behalf of your brother and Brendan too.'

'What's that?'

'Kind of silly really. You know in the hotel when that detective guy showed up?'

'Yes.'

'Well, he wasn't.'

'Wasn't what?'

'Wasn't a detective. He was just one of the porters. You see, Luigi knew him and was friendly with him – Luigi'd been living out here at the villa – '

'But wasn't he in London?'

'Oh, we've all been coming and going, you know. But when out in Italy, Luigi always stayed at the villa, and we were either here or at the hotel. And I guess Luigi got to know this guy at the hotel from coming to visit us. Anyway, when I said I was going to report you to the desk, in fact I was going down to tell your brother; I knew he was waiting there for Bren to get back from his run. I went down and told him it was that same jerk from yesterday; you see, I'd told Bren and Luigi the first time you'd shown up.'

'So you knew who I was. I mean, Gigi had guessed the first time, hadn't he?'

'Probably, but he didn't bother telling me. Nor did Bren. I was getting the dumb blonde treatment still. So I was down there telling Luigi that this jerk had shown up again and what should I do, and in comes Bren from his run and they thought up this thing straightaway. I didn't feel too good about it but

230

I said I'd play along. Luigi fixed it up with this friend of his in two seconds flat, lent him his gun and, well, I guess you know the rest.'

'I see. Should have thought really. After all, would a bloke turn up on his own in a situation like that?'

'You can see that Bren really wanted to convince you to join him. You can't blame him for what he did. Well, maybe you can.'

'I can, I can. Was the gun loaded?'

'Oh, I shouldn't think so – No, I don't know.'

'Great. Hey, ssh.'

An engine could be heard around the bend. The headlights made their appearance. They slowed down and came to a stop by the gate.

'Do you suppose it'll be Amedeo himself?' Sarah whispered.

'Well, that's what Blackbeard seemed to say.'

'Whoever it is, hope he's alone.'

'That only means there'll be two down at the villa,' I said.

Nobody got out. The headlights were switched off and we could see the vehicle now as a largish van, no doubt specially chosen for the transportation of trussed victims. We could only see one person, sitting in the driver's seat, but it was impossible to identify him. After a few seconds he sounded the horn – two long blasts and a short one.

'Do you reckon that's some kind of signal?' Sarah whispered.

'Yes. God knows how we're going to answer it.'

She was now squinting along the sights of her rifle.

'Well, that's one way I suppose,' I said.

'Don't worry. Just aiming at the wheels. If he decides not to get out.'

He sounded the horn in the same way again. We all waited quietly. Half a minute later he turned the headlights and engine on and started a turning manoeuvre. Sarah fired and various species of wild life, myself included, leapt startled into the air. The van, after one second's grinding of gears, gave up trying to turn and shot forward. Its wheels were apparently unharmed. It raced along the road under us and around the bend.

'Shit,' said Sarah.

'Yes,' I said. I got up. 'We'd better move.'

'That van is going to turn further down the road. I mean, it has to; there's no other road to Amedeo's villa. Couldn't we stop it on the way back?'

'That's an idea.' I ran down the hill towards the gate, Sarah just behind me. As we reached the gate and as I started to say, 'Well, how are we going to – ' the van roared past in the other direction. Sarah swung the rifle and fired, but too late. It disappeared.

'It's going to be difficult to surprise them,' I said.

'We've got one chance,' Sarah said, 'and that's if we attack them from a direction they won't think of – at least not immediately.' She started running down the road.

'What's that?' I panted out as I caught up with her.

'The sea.'

We heard a car approaching from behind.

'Let's hitch a ride,' Sarah said, swinging round to face it.

'Yes, but perhaps it would be better to do it without the gun.' I tossed the towel-rail into the bushes.

'Gimme your sweater.'

I saw the headlights appear fuzzily through the sweater as I pulled it over my head; I tore it off and was hit by the full dazzle. Sarah grabbed the sweater and swung it over the gun. I started waving wildly and the car slowed down.

The driver leaned out. He was a middle-aged man, and he looked suspiciously at us. I called out in Neapolitan, 'Could you give us a lift down to the sea?'

'I'm only going as far as the next village.' Then he narrowed his eyes yet more suspiciously and said, pointing, 'One moment, what's your girlfriend got under that thing?'

Sarah looked at me, shrugged and then flicked the pullover off and levelled the gun at the man. She jerked it once as an indication that he was to get out. She looked entirely convincing in this role.

232

The man started gibbering but then raised his hands from the wheel. I said in Neapolitan, 'You'd better do what she wants. Get out.'

He got out.

'Go back to that field,' I said. He did so, walking backwards, his eyes on the gun the whole time. I picked up my pullover and we got into the car. Only I found I'd got into the driver's seat. Sarah was holding the gun out of the window, still training it on the poor fellow.

'Er, Sarah,' I said.

'Come on,' she said without looking round, 'let's go.'

'Oh hell,' I said, and turned the key in the engine. I pressed my foot down on something and the engine went off. 'Sarah, we'd better change over. Give me the gun.'

'You'd better come round and take it from me.'

So I got out and walked round. The man was standing way back down the road, his hands still heavenwards. I gave him a smile of vague apology which, if he saw it, no doubt just increased his confusion.

Anyway, we finally got away and roared off down the hill. She was not a timid driver. As we took a bend on two wheels, if that many, she said, 'Are there still guys your age who don't drive? I mean, in L.A. you start before you walk.'

'Well, I'll have to make sure I don't move to L.A.'

'Yeah.' After a second or two she said, 'Poor guy. I hope he wasn't in a hurry.'

'Yes. One more felony to add to our list. Still, with our disguises – '

'Our what?'

'Your scarf, my beret. With them and the fact he didn't hear you speak, and I spoke dialect, I think we're fairly well covered. Hey, be care – oof, very neat.'

The journey, though hair-raising, was without incident. We passed through the little village, which was completely quiet. Some minutes later, when we were just above the little port, we passed Brendan's car, parked in a lay-by. We didn't stop to inspect – we were travelling too fast.

The little port was as quiet as the village on the hillside had been. The bars and restaurants were all shut and there was not a soul around. This was fortunate because, although Sarah had wrapped the gun again in the pullover, to my eyes it looked about as effective a disguise as tying a nappy round the barrel and pretending it was a baby. We ran across the square towards the sea.

She led the way along the jetty and swung herself down to the boat.

'You've got the keys?' I said, as a sudden horrible doubt struck me.

'Sure. We've all got a set. Go on. Untie us. Hey, wait a moment. Go get some of those empty bottles over there – d'you see by the bar?'

I followed her pointing finger and complied. They were wine, beer and Coca-Cola bottles. Still nobody appeared to ask what we were up to. It would have been difficult for me to answer, as I really didn't know. I ran back to the boat.

We moved out of the port to the moonlit sheen of the open sea. Once we were out she slammed full down and we shot forward like a guided missile – a guided missile with a bad case of tremors. I found myself holding on to the side of the boat. The full moon was right ahead of us and the boat's prow rose out of the water as if it had an appointment there. Sarah took her scarf off and her hair streamed back in the wind. I put my pullover on.

'Hey!' shouted Sarah

'Yes?' I shouted back.

'Can you make petrol bombs?'

'Well, I've never actually – '

'You take over here and I'll do it.'

I crossed over, the spray whipping into my face as I rose, and I took the wheel. This, at least, I could drive.

Sarah gathered together the bottles I'd brought along. 'Hey!' she shouted. 'Maybe you'd better slow down a moment while I do this.'

I did so and the world settled down around us; the

bumping, the noise and the wind died, the long white V of our wash rippled itself away to nothing, and we became aware of the peace of the night and the stillness of the sea, on which we were the only moving object. Apart from the chugging of our engine, the only sound was the homely glug-glugging of the petrol as it slopped into the bottles.

Sarah said, 'You're wearing a sweater and I'm not, so let's use your shirt.'

I stopped the boat completely and removed my pullover and shirt. I handed the shirt over and put the pullover back on. She started tearing the shirt into strips, which is not as easy as it sounds.

'You're going to make some lucky man a wonderful wife one day.'

'Oh, come on, everyone knows how to do this,' she said. 'Let's get going now. Not too fast.'

I started the engine up again and we moved along at a stately pace.

'Hey, see there,' she said pointing, 'that's the house.' We were about two hundred yards from the coast and we could see the three buildings apparently at the very water's edge. Only the one on the left had any lights on.

'Yes, that's it,' I said.

'How are we going to work it?'

'Well, presumably you made all those things with some purpose in mind.'

'Throwing.'

'Yes, but – you do remember we're here to rescue Gigi and Brendan, not blow them up.'

'A diversion, that's what I was thinking of.'

'Well, I suppose – yes, it's an idea. But to get the maximum benefit we'll have to split up.'

So after half a minute's discussion I brought the boat towards the shore. The discussion had mostly been about who should land, and Sarah had argued for herself, pointing out that she was the one who could shoot – and it might be necessary. The discovery that the gun was now empty made that an irrelevant consideration, so I was the one who got out bare-footed into the bitingly cold water. I was carrying the gun, because there are other ways to use a thing like that. We were some fifty yards up the coast from the house, and there was the bungalow and the unfinished concrete structure between it and us. The noise of the engine would alert them at once, of course, so Sarah was to wait where she was until I'd had time to get closer to the villa.

One last doubt struck me and I turned back to the boat. 'Have you got matches?'

'Don't worry. There's a cigarette lighter in the cabin. Good luck.'

'Thanks.' I waded ashore.

Twenty

There was a little beach here, with soft sand only sparingly interspersed with sharp shells and bottle tops. The bungalow was on a slightly raised promontory on the other side of the beach. I started running, bent low. A sandy path took me off the beach behind the first house. The shutters were all closed. It was presumably a holiday house. The path wound in front of the next building, the unfinished concrete mess which was protected by an iron railing. It was presumably one of the many such buildings on the island that someone had tried to knock up without planning permission before anyone realised. Perhaps Amedeo had had it blocked: after all, if he could get permission for his monstrosity, he could do anything.

I climbed over the railing and started walking cautiously along the blank side of the house. I reached the end of it and peered out. The land dropped again here to another little beach, and Amedeo's villa gave directly on to it. I could see a windowless side wall of the villa about ten yards away, and nothing else. I stayed completely still. I heard a faint movement and I saw a dark figure emerge from the cover of the villa on the land side. He was carrying a rifle. He walked down the side of the house to the sea. He had a red dot of light hanging from his mouth. He put one hand up from the gun and tossed the dot into the sea.

Somebody tapped me on the shoulder.

Fortunately I didn't yell; I swung round with the gun. It was jerked out of my hands even as I was still turning. There was somebody small and wiry there, unrecognisable in the complete darkness under the roof's overhang. He swivelled the gun expertly and menaced me with it.

At that moment I heard the boat approaching. I glanced out to sea and saw it racing towards the villa on its brilliant gash of foam; it slowed down and I turned away from my mysterious assailant and starting running towards the man by the sea. He was turning away from me, with his gun levelled, following the course of the boat; a flaming white streamer curved through the air from the boat, and then there was a sudden explosion of light.

Highly diverting.

The man fired at the boat. I was almost upon him and only half sensed (visually and aurally) the boat picking up speed again. The man started to move towards the white pulsing of flame and I dived at his legs in a vague memory of a rugby tackle.

He went straight over and I made a knee-tearing squirm up the length of his body and smashed my fist into his head – it was something I'd never done before in my life and I was surprised by how painful it was on the knuckles. He slumped and I was able to wrest the rifle from his grasp. I brought this down on the back of his head, giving him the flat side of the butt.

I then rolled over, and swivelled the gun to train it on whoever it was who'd pinched mine. But there was nobody there.

I jerked round, still recumbent, and saw a white and orange glow of flames at a window of the villa. Beyond this light I could see another man on the beach with a gun – trained on me. I jerked myself up from the ground and ran, bent low, towards the house. The gun went off and I had a sudden – strangely vivid – mental image of the sand being kicked up where I'd been lying.

The boat was coming in again and I saw – beyond the roaring flames, increasing in height and intensity – the man at the other end of the house training his gun on it. I fired mine, and only when it had gone off did I realise I'd aimed it directly at him. In fact I missed, but I caused him to dive for cover.

Another streamer of flame from the boat cut a perfect arc through the air, this time further down the house, towards the man with the gun. There was another explosive roar and then I heard a yell and saw the man, his back ablaze, running to the sea. It was only this moment of devilish light that let me recognise him as whiskered Paolo. Sarah had brought the boat practically up on to the beach, doing God knows what to the propeller, and he ran right past her. She leapt out and started running towards the house.

I darted from my cover and smashed the first window I came to with the butt of the gun. I leant in and opened it, cutting myself as I did so, but only mentally noting the fact. I found myself in an unlit bedroom which I ran across. I pulled the next door open and was in a large room with noise and light, fire and people. This was where the action was. The nearest person was the dark youth who'd tied us up and he was aiming a gun at Sarah. She was at that moment stepping through the large window, which was half framed in flame.

I bashed my gun down on his head with more viciousness than I had used on previous occasions, and he went flying forward, colliding with various little cluttered tables and ending up on a sofa. He was obviously one of those lucky sort of bastards.

I then looked around the rest of the room. It was clearly the main living room, and a richly furnished one. In the far corner Gigi and Brendan were sitting roped back to back. They were both speaking, as was Sarah, but there were other things to pay attention to – like the fact that half of the opposite wall was ablaze, and that a small man had just limped out of a door next to the one I'd come in by.

Sarah ran towards Gigi and Brendan, as I did, and when we got there and saw the knots we both said together, 'A knife.'

'Where's the kitchen?' I said to Gigi.

'Through there,' he said, nodding towards the sheet of flame which was the nearest wall.

'Use some glass,' Brendan said.

There was enough of that around. I chucked my gun down, ran over to the window and grabbed a large triangular piece. I ran back and gave it to Sarah. She started cutting. I ran to the door I'd seen Amedeo leave by. It led to another bedroom which was empty. There was another open door in the right-hand wall which gave on to the room I'd entered the house by. Amedeo had simply darted round behind my back. I suddenly found the other three were in the room with me, together with a lot of smoke.

'Come on,' Brendan said, 'the whole bloody building – ' His face was nastily bruised.

I pushed past them back into the living room. The air was thick with smoke.

'What the hell – ' Sarah began.

'That bloke on the sofa,' I managed to get out before choking. I ran towards him, Sarah following. I took his legs and Sarah his arms. We went back into the first bedroom. Brendan and Gigi had already clambered out of the window. I back-kicked the door shut and realised I was half fainting with smoke and heat. I noticed with a curiously detached part of my mind that I'd managed to keep my beret on.

We climbed out of the window on to the sand, still with the inert body between us.

The whole beach was lit by the flames now. In the crazily dancing light we could see Brendan and Gigi running towards the boat. Amedeo was in it and aiming a rifle at them, and Paolo was pushing the boat out.

We dropped our burden next to the first man I'd stunned. He was slowly dragging himself up, but was clearly far from offering any kind of dangerous opposition. As we ran towards the others, Amedeo's gun went off and Brendan dropped. Sarah screamed and darted towards him. Gigi kept running. I followed him.

The boat was now fully afloat and Paolo was attempting to climb up. Gigi reached him and grabbed him round the neck. I could see but not hear him scream (the fire was now too noisy) at the contact with his burnt back. Amedeo raised his gun again and levelled it towards Gigi. At that distance he couldn't miss; the only risk was of sending the bullet straight through Gigi's back and killing Paolo too. Amedeo probably wasn't all that bothered. I was still running, now splashing through the first waves, and I was, I think, shouting too, though the roar of the flames probably smothered my voice.

There was the sound of a shot to my right, distinctly audible above the flames, and Amedeo was suddenly thrown back as if struck by an invisible fist. He hit the opposite side of the boat and crumpled down out of sight. I turned my head and saw a small dark figure on the beach lowering a gun. I couldn't afford to spend any time staring and working out this extra mystery; I threw myself forward and grabbed Paolo, who was now on top of Gigi. I managed to pull him off. Even in this flickering light I could see the burns on Paolo's back. He had no shirt left, of course. Gigi gave him two savage head punches while I held him; I felt the punches judder up the length of my arm. Paolo's head slumped to one side and I found I was supporting his whole weight.

Gigi splashed towards the boat and stared over the side, his face bewildered. 'Who the – ' he began. At this moment the small figure joined us, no longer holding the gun.

'Franco,' I said, '*ma cosa diavolo –* '

Gigi looked at us both and then gave a facial shrug and ran off towards Brendan.

'Quickly,' Franco said in Italian, 'let's get Amedeo out, then we can take your friend to hospital.'

I dragged Paolo ashore and left him lying on the sand – on his belly. He was already groaning which I felt was a healthy sign. I was suddenly aware of two or three cuts on my body smarting at the contact with the salt water; a long-delayed reaction.

I ran back to Franco's side and stared into the boat. Amedeo was now slumped in an untidy huddle against the cabin door. His mouth hung slightly open but his eyes were staring as reprovingly as ever; I almost expected to be given a hundred lines for disrespect. But then I saw the bloody mess that was his chest. He was dead.

'What are we going to do?' I said.

'We'll chuck him in there,' Franco said, indicating the

inferno behind us. 'Quickly. People can see this blaze for miles around and they'll be coming.'

I looked over towards the others. Sarah and Gigi were bent over Brendan, Sarah cradling his head. Just beyond them the first man I'd stunned was staggering away down the beach. Good for him. I said, 'OK, let's move.'

It was an awkward business getting him out of the boat, particularly since I was taking instinctive but not very logical care to avoid banging his head. We carried him across the beach as Sarah and I had carried the unconscious youth earlier, but in the opposite direction and with the opposite intention. As we got half-way across the beach there was a deafening crash from inside the house; half the roof had fallen in.

The fire was not actually dying but at least it didn't look as if it were going to spread. There was nothing around for it to take hold of. The heat was still intense, but the house was distinctly more skeletal. There were continual cracks and crashes as various parts of it gave way. We swung the body and it flew through the flames, the limbs spreading out like a child's stick-man drawing, before flopping down behind a wall. I was grateful to that wall.

Franco picked up the gun from the sand and threw that into the flames as well. Then we ran over to the group around Brendan. He was sitting, propped up by Sarah, and was clutching his side which was dark and sticky; his face was twisted in pain and shone with sweat in the flickering orange light. I heard him gasp out, 'You see, he thinks it's still on – ' He coughed a painful cough with no satisfaction to it.

Sarah said, 'Bren, Bren, who is it?'

Brendan was clearly trying to utter some words, but only agonised gasps came out.

Sarah looked up at me. 'We must get a doctor – get him to a doctor.' She sounded urgent but controlled.

'Let's get him to the boat,' I said.

Gigi and I did most of the carrying, Sarah fluttering at the side. Brendan groaned once or twice. Franco held the boat still. Nobody asked who Franco was.

Eventually we were settled, though the boat was not exactly ideal as an ambulance. Gigi stood at the wheel, Franco at his side. Sarah was sitting in the cabin with Brendan sprawled out on the bench as far as the cramped space permitted. He was breathing hard and heavy, as if still trying to speak. Sarah's head was bent close to his mouth. I was hovering around trying to look less futile than I felt.

The engine started and I suddenly remembered my fear for the propeller. It must have been all right, however; we moved out to sea. I looked back at the beach. Seen from out here the fire was far less impressive than the smoke above – thick, black and twisted, like an immense Bernini pillar. Paolo, a tiny silhouette against the fire, was getting groggily to his feet. The other man was also showing signs of movement. At the far end of the beach people were approaching; even at this distance their excitement was clear. They were coming along to enjoy the fire.

I turned back and looked at Brendan. His eyes were closed. I asked Sarah, 'How is he?'

'He's dead,' she said. Her eyes were unseeing and one hand was ceaselessly stroking his hair.

I was about to say, 'Are you sure?' but thought that would be stupid. Instead I moved over and, kneeling on the floor, looked closely at him. I felt his wrist. Sarah didn't look at what I was doing, nor did she say anything. Eventually I said, 'I'm sorry.' She just nodded.

Twenty-one

I stepped out of the cabin. Gigi and Franco were not talking.
I said, 'Brendan's dead.'

Gigi said, 'Shit.' Some people have that gift of funeral
oratory.

I said, 'What do we do?'

'Always got to ask me. Look, who's this geezer?'

'He's – he's a journalist.'

Gigi's comment was as succinct as ever. He went on, 'Well,
this'll give him somefing to write about.'

Franco said, 'I'm not a journalist now.'

I said, 'No?' Then to Gigi, 'And he saved your life.'

'I've said fanks. Just I like to know who I'm fanking.'

'He's a friend,' I said, 'all right?'

'You invited him along for the party, did you? Great.
Anyone else gonna spring up from out under a seat?'

'I didn't invite anyone,' I said. I was too tired to argue
properly. In addition to general fatigue I could feel my cuts
and burns aching, and the wind pasting my icy-wet clothes to
my skin. I had no idea it was possible to experience so many
contrasting sensations at the same time, all of them
unpleasant.

'I came of my account,' Franco said, his slow English
further impeded by the chattering of his teeth. 'But don't
worry. I don't write of these things. Remember, I killed
Amedeo.'

Gigi said, 'Yeah, I know. Fanks again.' He turned to me.
'What's Sal doing now?'

'Reading the newspaper, of course, what do you think?'

'All right, all right. No need to jump down me froat.'

'Sorry. Not feeling too good. None of us is, I suppose.'

'Here, you take over, I'll go and have a word wiv her.'

'Yes, but be – be gentle.'

'Oh, I was gonna chuck Bren overboard and then jump on her. Fanks for the tip.'

Sarcasm was obviously catching. 'Sorry again,' I said, 'just trying to be helpful.' I took over at the wheel. 'Where are we heading for?'

'Back to the village, of course. We left the car just up the road from it.' He entered the cabin.

Franco was now crouching down to shelter from the wind and was hugging himself against the cold. 'Well,' I said in Italian, 'are you going to tell me what you're doing here?'

'I still don't know what you were all doing, but never mind. You're three to one.' He crossed his arms and rubbed their upper reaches with his fists in quick vigorous movements. 'It's complicated. But, well, I suppose I can say it was family problems. That's what brought me here, in fact, family problems.'

'Oh yes?'

'My name's Barra, not Longo. Gianni Barra was my brother.'

'Who?' I said, and then realised. The tall man with the high-pitched voice I'd seen – heard rather – killed in Bayswater. That was the facial resemblance that had been troubling me ever since I met Franco. If it hadn't been for the more obvious differences, such as height and – most importantly – character, no doubt I would have tumbled to it long before. They both had the same nervous finger-drumming habit, now I thought of it. 'So you were here for – '

'No, no. I wasn't here for revenge. Even though it now looks that way.'

'No, it doesn't.'

'It will do to the judges.'

'Who says any judges are going to get to hear of your being here?'

'I – I don't know. I might confess. God knows what I might do. You see, I've never killed anyone before.'

'Well, don't say it as if you think I'm the expert. Neither have I. And what you did was save my brother's life.'

'Yes, but I wouldn't have fired that gun if it hadn't been Amedeo. You see that? You see what it makes me?'

'It doesn't make you anything.' I thought, it certainly doesn't make you like your brother, but of course didn't say it. I glanced along the side of the boat, beyond the glimmering of our wake. Amedeo's funeral pyre was just a distant flicker of light against the dark coastline – and then it disappeared behind a headland and only the smoke was visible.

'It makes me – makes me almost like my brother,' he said.

'No, it doesn't,' I said, too quickly perhaps.

'You knew him?'

'I met him. In London.'

'I see.' This was said in an attempt at his old casual nonchalance. But then he added, 'No, I don't. You'll have to tell me when I finish. But anyway, it was on account of Gianni I got involved in all this.'

'Brother trouble. I know something about it.'

'Gianni was no angel, as you must know. But he became what he became, like many others in Torre Annunziata, thanks to people like Amedeo.'

This seemed a debatable over-simplification at the very least, but I let it pass. He was speaking with obviously deep-felt conviction.

He went on, 'It was seeing what happened to Gianni, and others, that made me want to become a journalist. To speak out. Against all those bastards who were telling unemployed kids that the only way to get on was to learn to kill. I admit I used Gianni. I observed him and I got stories from him. Then he became Amedeo's bodyguard and one day I got a story from him about a meeting between Amedeo and the killer 'o Rauco. Gianni and his friend Raffaele got sacked from their posts when the story was published and Gianni was furious – with me, of course. In the end I left Torre Annunziata. It was safer that way. I gave up my job at the *Mattino* too. I didn't have the courage to keep at it. Then I heard of Gianni's death. And I thought what a waste. He was seven years older than me and when I was small I saw him – well, I won't say as a hero, but you know how elder brothers can seem when there's a big gap in age. He was someone who could, well, could do anything, I used to think. And instead he wasted his entire life. Or his life was wasted for him, thrown away – by that bastard Amedeo who'd just bought himself a big villa at Posillipo. So I thought, maybe if I looked into Amedeo and his affairs full-time I could bring the killing home to him, I could do a story that would finish him for ever; it would be a good return to journalism. And it would render some kind of justice to Gianni. So that's how you came to see me hanging round his office. And here. I was hiding out in that unfinished house next to his.'

'I see. And what did you mean when you came up behind me and took my gun?'

'I wanted to find out what the hell you were up to, that's all. I still do. I didn't have any intention of killing anybody. Not till – not till I saw Amedeo. When I found your gun was empty I went round the back of the house to see what was going on from a – a safer position, but the windows were all shuttered there. I made the full circuit of the house and came on to the beach in time to see Amedeo lifting his gun. And there was a gun on the sand near me.'

'Ah yes.' It must have been Paolo's, dropped in his agony. 'A pretty good shot.'

'I know. Gianni taught me to shoot when I was a kid. It was one of the things that made me respect him, you know.'

'I see. You were sensible to chuck it into the fire.'

'I seem to know certain things by instinct,' he said. 'Here's Amedeo's gun.' It was on the floor by the cabin door.

'Chuck it overboard,' I said.

'Before I get tempted,' he said, 'I know.' He did so.

The lights of the little port came into sight around a headland. Gigi opened the cabin door behind us and said, 'Go out to sea.'

'What, why?'

'We're going to dump Bren.'

'What? I thought you were joking when – '

'It's her idea.'

I turned the boat out to sea.

Sarah called from the cabin, 'I want to do what Bren would have wanted.' Her voice was steady, matter of fact. 'I want to get this Rauco guy. You didn't hear his last words, did you?'

'No,' I said. I wondered if he'd said sorry.

'He just said, "it's been fun".'

I might have guessed. The funeral pyre came into sight again on the right. I didn't make any of the many possible cynical cracks. I didn't feel like it.

She went on, 'I guess it wasn't a bad way for him to go.' Clichés can be moving in certain situations – in fact, can be the most moving things to say. 'And burial at sea, well it's what he would have liked. I know. And if we report this . . .' She didn't need to add anything. I had already started thinking again of the prison in Naples – 'l'inferno' as the papers called it.

Gigi said, 'There's a small anchor under the seat. I can tie it round him.' He entered the cabin again. I was glad he was doing it and not me. I could imagine myself getting into all kinds of grotesque embraces with the body as I tried to tie the knots – and I'd feel awkward about asking for Sarah's finger. I glanced into the cabin and saw that Gigi was managing to do it neatly and quickly without Sarah even having to stop her hair-stroking. When he'd finished he said, 'So long, Bren old mate,' and prepared to carry him out of the cabin. Sarah gave him one last kiss and then Gigi brought him out, holding him in his arms like a scene from *Gone With The Wind*. He slipped him over the side without ceremony. He entered the water almost splashlessly. Sarah stayed inside the cabin and I saw her hands go up to her face.

It struck me that when we actually had the time to think about this action – with dry clothes perhaps and a mug of cocoa – we might find ourselves considering it to have been rather hasty and silly. But now – and I started a shrug which turned into a shiver – I couldn't really care.

Gigi took over the wheel and said to me, 'I suppose you

dunno what Bren was trying to get out before he died.' He turned the boat back towards the port.

'Apart from "what jolly fun"?' I said.

'Yeah. Before that.'

'No. What?'

'It was somefing Amedeo said. When he'd got us tied up. That bloody little Jameson runt, lying bastard.'

'Yes, yes. I know.'

'Amedeo was freatening us, like. You know, trying to get out of us who we were. Seems like he didn't know if we were anuvver gang or the police or what, he was shit-scared it seemed, he was gonna start on Sarah when she was brought down, cigarette burns and the rest to get us talking – you can imagine how that got Bren worried – but anyway at one point he said, just sort of casual, like he wasn't really worried about it, maybe he wasn't, I dunno; he said that he hadn't heard from 'o Rauco since Tuesday – you know, in London.'

'And so?'

'And so 'o Rauco probably finks the killing's still on. That was how fings were left.'

'Yes, but surely when he hears what's happened here – I mean, it'll be in all the papers.' I paused, then added, 'With our photos probably.'

'The killing's due for Sunday, Bren said. The day after tomorrow. So there's no guarantee he'll see the papers.'

'Ah, Who's the victim?'

'Well, that's it. That's what I was trying to get out of Bren, but all he could do was cough.'

'You mean, he hadn't ever told you?'

'He liked playing fings close like.'

'If he hadn't wasted his breath making heroic last words . . .'

Gigi shrugged. 'Don't knock him.'

'No, all right.' *De mortuis*, etc. Only trouble was that it looked as if there'd be more *mortui* on Sunday thanks to this *mortuo* – stupid berk. 'What exactly did Brendan say?'

'Just that. Must stop 'o Rauco. Killing due Sunday morning.'

'And we don't know who. Or where. I mean, 'o Rauco operates worldwide, doesn't he? Could be in Rio de Janeiro or Hong Kong.'

'No. It's gotta be somewhere round here, cos Bren didn't have any plans for moving out.'

'That's what you think, but it looks like he didn't tell you every detail of his plans.'

'No, but he'd got tickets to go and see Naples play Milan Sunday afternoon.'

'Ah, I see. Sunday morning, kill 'o Rauco. Afternoon, watch the football.' After a pause I said, 'Do I gather that 'o Rauco and Amedeo don't – didn't write each other daily postcards?'

'Them? They needed each uvver, but you can bet your life they didn't like each uvver.'

Franco was looking very puzzled at all this. I turned to him and said, 'Look, I'll explain everything.'

Gigi said, 'Why don't you just write it all up for the *News of the World*?'

'There's no point in our trying to look innocent in front of Franco,' I said.

'Yeah, all right, shut up now.' We were entering the port, which in the moonlight looked as peacefully charming as ever. 'Listen. You lot get out and go up to the villa.'

'You're running off on your own, are you?'

'Don't be dumb. You lot go up there and get your stuff, then drive over to Casamicciola and I'll pick you up in the boat there. All right? I mean, we'd better get off the island. If one of Amedeo's gorillas gets caught and starts talking, could be dodgy.'

'Yes, could be.'

'All right then. When you leave the villa make for Barano, then about half a mile after Barano at Piedimonte there's a minor road, bit rough like, marked for Fiaiano, I fink. Take that and you won't meet anyone. I mean, just in case like. It goes on down to Ischia Port, but if you turn off left just before the end you're on the road to Casamicciola. Nobody'll fink of us leaving the island from there. I mean, if anyone is on the lookout. Never know. See you at the jetty there, right? Don't forget my stuff, cos I'll bloody need a change of clothes.'

'All right.'

'Just dump the car somewhere in the centre of Casamicciola and walk down to the port, all right?'

'Yes. Is your stuff scattered round the house?'

'No. You know me, I'm always ready to make a quick exit. I mean, you never know, do you? Just a small case next to me bed.'

'And, er, where are we going to go then?' I said. 'Or is that looking too far ahead?'

'Anywhere. Just keep driving,' Gigi said.

'You could come to my flat,' Franco said. 'I share with a friend, but he goes away at the weekend. I have the space.'

'Thanks,' I said. 'You're sure?'

'Of course. One night, why not?'

We were now nestling up against a jetty. Sarah had come out of the cabin. Her eyes were moist but she was keeping her emotions under control. She tied her scarf around her head again. I had to feel my head to realise my beret was still there.

We made it to the car without seeing anyone, and apparently without anyone seeing us. This uphill walk, feeling cold wet cut burnt tired and scared, was the worst part of the journey. We did it in silence, Sarah not even asking who Franco was. Once in the car, and that fraction more relaxed, I did some rapid introductions. She nodded, her face drawn but composed. She started the engine and turned the heating on too. I began explaining things to Franco. I asked him – profiting from the fact that we were talking in Italian – not to express out loud the disapproval his features were showing at Brendan's behaviour. He said he wouldn't be so heartless. He added, with a touch of bitterness, 'After all, what right have I to criticise now?'

The villa was dead quiet when we reached it, but the lights

251

were all on. We crossed the lawn in silence – I forgot to revel in the fact that this was now possible.

Sarah gasped at the sight of the living room. I hadn't appreciated the full extent of the havoc the bearded man had wrought there: everything openable was open – windows, drawers, books, record sleeves, bottles – and the contents strewn on the floor (except fortunately for those of the bottles, most of which I imagined as being now contained by the bearded man). Sarah then managed a shrug of her shoulders.

I went to the kitchen, Franco following me, and I got a surprise. Jameson was lying trussed on the floor. He was looking a bit peeved. Somehow I hadn't thought of either of them being still there. Sarah's knots must have been pretty good.

'What's up?' I said to him. 'Wouldn't your friend help you?'

He said, 'My head, it's about to split, you must take me to a hospital, I'm going to die.'

'I wonder,' I said to Franco, 'if he knows anything of 'o Rauco's plans.'

'I do assure you,' Jameson began, 'I really do assure you – '

'Oh shut up,' I said. 'Let's change our clothes first, shall we, before we get pneumonia.'

'If you could lend me some,' Franco said.

'And, er, me,' Jameson said plaintively.

'I haven't got any myself,' I said. 'I think we'll have to borrow some of Brendan's. Oh hell, they'll be in with Sarah. You keep an eye on this fellow, but don't listen to a word he says.'

I crossed the living room and tapped at the door. She said, 'Come in.' She was sitting on the bed in the same bathrobe I'd seen her wearing that morning.

'Sorry,' I said.

'Oh stop apologising,' she said. 'What do you want?'

'Well, Franco and I haven't got any dry clothes. Do you think – '

252

'Just go ahead. Brendan won't be wanting them.' She managed a smile.

'Thanks.' I went over to the wardrobe she'd waved me to.

'Don't get the idea I've flipped,' she said. 'I'm sure we're doing the right thing. I need something to keep me thinking, to keep me going.'

'Ye-es,' I said. 'Well, we've got that. But, um, you do realise that Brendan's disappearance won't be received like, say, my disappearance would be. It'll be big news, and that'll mean big investigations.'

'Yeah, well we'll think about that when it happens. Right now I just don't want to be bugged by cops and cops' questions. Anyway, who'll suspect me? I don't make a cent out of his death.'

'I see. So after this?'

'After this I think what I'm going to do. But *after* this. Right now we're going for Rauco. OK?'

'Yes, of course. Oh, by the way, we'll have a passenger. Jameson's still here and he may be able to tell us something about 'o Rauco.'

'So we take him with us?'

'I think it'll be best. No time to question him now.'

I studied the clothes. There was a rich choice: trousers, shirts and jackets neatly folded and hung, half of them with discreet and not so discreet tags – Armani, Valentino, Trussardi. Not my sort of stuff at all, though Franco possibly wasn't unused to such things. I took a selection back to the kitchen.

Jameson was now untied and sitting at the table. He was saying to Franco, who was examining his head, 'And you see I didn't want to be involved in it at all.'

Franco said, 'Ah no? I don't see any – anything, er, broken. I think you will be all right.'

Jameson put a hand to his head and said, 'It feels terrible.'

'We mustn't let him escape,' I said. 'He may know something useful.'

Franco said, 'I think his head hurts him too much; he won't run.'

'He *says* his head hurts,' I said, 'which isn't the same thing.'

'But if you hit him with a stick!' Franco said.

'Yes, and a minute ago I'd have said it must have hurt him, but having heard him say it I don't believe it any longer.'

'Now, please,' Jameson began.

'Shut up,' I said. 'You know Amedeo's dead?'

'Yes. This gentleman told me.' The slight stress he laid on gentleman was undoubtedly supposed to make me cringe with shame. He went on, 'It's all so awful really. But violence will breed violence, you know, I've always – '

'Your heart bleeds, I know. Like mine would have done if I hadn't dodged when you shot at me.'

'But I wasn't aiming at you, I really wasn't, I – '

'Shut up. Here, choose some of these clothes.'

I got changed in the kitchen where I could keep an eye on Jameson, who seemed to have run out of lies for the moment and just let forth an occasional moan as he pulled the clothes on, which assured me he was all right and probably working out his next trick. Franco modestly went through to the bathroom and returned wearing a pair of grey trousers and a polo-neck pullover, which both looked as if they'd been made for him – until one noticed the elegantly casual turn-ups. I chose the oldest jeans, a blue sweat-shirt and a loose linen jacket, and they still looked as if I'd stolen them. But Jameson looked even sillier in baggy white trousers with floppy turn-ups and a grey pullover like a girl's dress from the 1960s.

'Let's tidy up through there as much as we can,' I said to Franco. 'And you help,' I added to Jameson. We moved through and started rather feebly picking up the more obvious things from the floor. Jameson moaned each time he bent down – which wasn't so often that it disturbed our work rhythm.

Sarah came in wearing another pair of jeans and a blue pullover. 'What are you doing?'

'Just trying to make it look as if the murder didn't necessarily happen here,' I said. 'For when the police break the place open.'

'OK. I suppose it's not a bad idea.' She set to work too, with quick efficiency. We three had been merely picking up stray wisps of straw from the Augean stables' floor; she whirled around the place with torrential force, and soon, if not tidy, it at least looked less like a scene from *The Day After*.

'OK, that's enough,' she said. 'Let's go, shall we?'

I said, 'Er, don't like to mention it – the washing up?'

She frowned, then said, 'Let's do something I've always wanted to do.'

'What?'

'Chuck it all in the trash can.'

It was an obviously attractive idea. I said, 'Is there one nearby?'

She said, 'Just down the road. A truck comes and empties it every other day, I think. We can make a sack of it all.'

We stripped a sheet off the bed, took it into the kitchen and simply dropped everything – saucepans, dirty plates, broken plates, cutlery, glasses – into it. Jameson, on my instigation, fetched his sopping black clothes and dropped them into the sheet too. Our sense of urgency unfortunately prevented us from enjoying to the full the satisfying simplicity of this mode of culinary reorganisation. I took the improvised sack through the front garden and down the road, aware that if anybody were to see me I only lacked a black mask to be a burglar in an Anton cartoon. I made it to the large square bin at the side of the road and dropped it in with a resounding crash. That, at least, I enjoyed. I hurried back to the house. Sarah said, 'Now we go, yeah?'

'Yes,' I said, 'and quickly.'

'I've got all my stuff together,' she said, pointing to her suitcase by the bedroom door.

'That's all?' I said. 'I mean, you hadn't any other things in the place already?'

'Like what?'

'Oh, I don't know. Family photos, Bibles, Ming vases.'

255

'I travel light.'

Another of her statements of faith – another possible song title. 'Like Gigi,' I said.

'Gigi? Luigi? Like him?'

'Yes, all right, maybe this comparing game's getting a bit tedious. I'll go and get his stuff.' I did so. His case was only a little smaller than Sarah's, but I didn't bother pointing this out.

I said, 'Should we tie Jameson up now?'

'Now look really I say – '

'Shut up.'

'We only have to get him to the car,' Sarah said. 'If he makes a move, smash him again.'

We let down all the shutters and left. It was tidier than my flat in London had been when I left it. I had my rucksack, Sarah her case, Franco Gigi's case, and Jameson nothing – or just his pack of lies.

'Bobby,' Sarah suddenly said.

'Oh God,' I said. 'I suppose we – All right.'

'Well, a dog with a bullet in its head is kind of conspicuous,' Sarah said.

I took my jacket off and gave it to Sarah. I went over and picked him up. He was very heavy, and fairly bloody too. I staggered under his weight. It was my turn to feel like Rhett Butler. 'If you're thinking of giving him a burial at sea, I tell you I'm not walking through the streets of Casamicciola like this.'

'OK. We'll dump him off on the road somewhere.'

We drove off in the direction Gigi had told us, and after a mile or so I saw a deep gully to one side of the road. I told Sarah to pull up and I got out carrying Bobby. I was right: the gully was full of rubbish. For some reason, Italians seem unable to pass steep declivities without feeling impelled to drop their larger items of rubbish into them – or perhaps when they have to get rid of old furniture they actually go out in search of ravines that seem sufficiently picturesque to provide worthy resting places. I slung Bobby over, and after a couple of bounces and a bit of undignified rolling and slithering, he settled down on an old mattress. It looked comfortable. If anybody should ever clamber down remorsefully to retrieve some family antique, there was a chance Bobby would be taken for the victim of a hunting accident.

We reached Casamicciola some fifteen minutes later. Gigi was already there waiting. 'What d'you bring him for?' he said, pointing at Jameson.

'Not for the pleasure of his company,' I said. 'He may know something about 'o Rauco. If not, we can always chuck him overboard.'

'Too good for him,' Gigi said. 'That's where Bren went.'

We boarded, Jameson wisely not attempting any defence of himself with Gigi. Gigi entered the cabin to get changed and Sarah took us out of the port. Franco, Jameson and I stayed outside, nervously watching for any signs of followers. There were none – there was just the sea, the moon, and the lights of Casamicciola.

Twenty-two

Gigi came out of the cabin and pointed at my sweat-shirt. 'What you been up to?'

'Giving Bobby the last rites.'

'Killed him did they? Bastards.'

'Yes. He's probably savaging St Peter's ankles this very minute.'

We picked up speed. The lights of Ischia Porto appeared to our right. Jameson, feeling perhaps a little *de trop*, opened the cabin door. 'My head, you know,' he said apologetically, and entered the cabin.

We were all silent for a while; we watched the isle of Procida approach.

Eventually Sarah brought up what we were all evidently thinking about. 'So what do we do? I mean, about this killing.'

'Got to find out who it is first, haven't we?' Gigi said.

'With our luck,' I said, 'it'll be someone whose death will instantly plunge the world into nuclear war.'

Sarah said, 'Brendan could be so – so thoughtless.' The best that could be said about this as a reproach was that it was no doubt difficult for her to have to make.

'But when did he say?' Franco asked.

'Sunday,' Gigi said. 'That's all. Sunday morning.'

'And today is Friday. No,' he looked at his watch, 'is Saturday already. Is past one o'clock. And we think somewhere near Naples.'

'Yeah,' Gigi said.

'Of course,' Franco said, 'you know who arrives in Naples tomorrow – today, I mean, Saturday.'

'No, who?' Sarah said.

'You don't read the newspapers? Have you not read of the royal visit?'

'Is that starting already?' she said. 'I thought it was later – hey, you don't think – '

'I don't know. Is just an idea. You know, the papers talk of nothing else, the first visit to Naples – '

'No, but Bren would never – ' Sarah began. A pause. 'I suppose it's possible,' she said slowly. 'Are they here till Sunday?'

'They leave on Sunday evening.'

'Well, I guess it could be, but how do we know?'

'Yes,' I said, 'I mean, there'll be all sorts of other people presumably – the mayor, the prime minister, etc, etc. And then again, maybe 'o Rauco's chosen that day because everybody's attention will be on them so he can kill someone else more easily.'

'You 'ave a good criminal's mind,' Franco said.

'Yes, but what we really need to know is Brendan's mind,' I said, 'because he's the one who stipulated the victim – and come to think of it, the day. Would he have chosen the Royal Family? He had to have someone convincing – I mean, someone he could convince Amedeo he really wanted to have killed. Well, would he have chosen them?'

Sarah shook her head. 'You're talking about a whole side of Bren I knew nothing about. I mean, that's not Bren as I knew him.' She paused. 'Except – no, that's silly.'

'What?'

'Well, it's just he'd made one or two Irish friends in New York – you know his mother was Irish – '

'With a name like Brendan, it figures.'

'Well, he knew these guys in New York who were heavily into the whole IRA scene; you know, fund raising and that. Bren was only a, a casual friend of theirs – I mean, he met them once or twice; I never thought he had any political sympathies that way.'

'He didn't have to have,' I said. 'He only had to convince Amedeo he did. After all, few Italians really know very much about the IRA. It's possible. What about you?' I said to Gigi. 'Didn't he ever confide in you?'

'Not about fings like that. He could be bloody close.'

'Well,' I said, 'I suppose we should warn the police anyway.'

'Already,' Franco said, 'the police 'ave 'ad warnings from people saying they are the IRA' (he pronounced it as a word, ee-ra), 'the Red Brigades, OLP, plenty of mad people, you know. We telephone, what do we say? Someone per'aps wants to kill Their Majesty-Highness on Sunday some time – but per'aps they kill someone else, we're not sure?'

Jameson called, rather tentatively, from the cabin, 'Shocking idea, how could anyone – '

'You must know something,' I said. 'Talk.'

'I assure you I would have nothing to do with any attempt against the Crown, the very idea – '

'Oh what's the point?' I broke in. 'I don't know why we lumbered ourselves with him. Shall we chuck him overboard?'

'I could make him talk,' Gigi said.

'Yes, but could you make him talk the truth, and how would you know if he was?'

'You're not really going to throw him overboard, are you?' Sarah said, her eyes wide.

'Well, I suppose not,' I said, 'the Bay of Naples has enough problems with pollution as it is.'

'But we must keep him with us,' Sarah said, 'when we get to town, too. If anyone does get killed on Sunday, he's gonna pay for it, even if we have to get arrested too.'

'Maybe you're right,' I said.

'But I assure you – ' he began.

'Shut up,' Sarah said and he shut up. I was reminded of Brendan's power over Bobby.

'So what are they doing on Sunday?'

'The Royals?' Franco said. 'The yacht arrives tomorrow – today – and they visit various places, Castel Nuovo, Capodimonte, Pompeii, the Opera. On Sunday they go to Capri and spend all day there and then leave in the evening for Palermo.'

'Well,' I said, 'I reckon we should all go to Capri.'

'And do what there?' Franco said.

'Listen for raucous assassins, of course,' I said. Ischia one day, Capri the next – it was turning into a pleasure jaunt.

'Yeah,' Sarah said. 'But just now all I can do is think of bed. Not that I think I'll sleep. I just need to be flat out.'

'Me too,' I said. 'Maybe after a good sleep we'll have more energy for beating the truth out of Jameson.'

'Oh look now – '

'Shut up.'

We all shut up, in fact. Gigi took over the wheel, and we entered the cabin where we could at least sit down. We broke our silence only to protest at Gigi's next proposed precaution: to drop us off at the beach at Capo di Posillipo. He would then proceed to Mergellina, get the car and drive back and pick us up. 'I mean, there's always people around Mergellina, even this time of night. They'd remember if we all get out wiv suitcases and the rest of it. But they know me, know it's my boat so if I turn up on me own, no-one'll fink anyfing of it.'

We had to agree. 'Well,' I said, 'I suppose if we get bored waiting we can always go along to Amedeo's other house and burn that down as well.'

It was thus well over an hour later that we pulled up outside Franco's flat in the Vomero. It wasn't all that far from Jameson's – near enough for Jameson to say, 'Why don't you let me out here? I'll never bother you again, let's forget all about it – '

The flat was scrupulously neat. Like so many Neapolitan houses, it seemed a kind of reproach to the chaos outside the front door. It was in a block similar to Jameson's, and its lay-out was similar too, but it was definitely a home, where Jameson's had seemed a collection of waiting rooms.

Franco said, 'Do you – do you want a whisky or something?'

'I want a bed,' Sarah said. 'Or anything you've got that resembles one.'

'You can have my friend's room,' he said to her. 'He won't mind. Shall I change the sheets?'

'Are you crazy?'

261

'Yes, my friend's very clean. He works in a bank,' he added, without immediately apparent relevance.

'What about him?' I said, pointing to Jameson. 'Who's going to look after him?'

Franco said, 'He can stay in my bedroom. We can lock it.'

Gigi said, 'I'll sleep outside. I sleep light, so if he tries anyfing . . .'

So Sarah went to the main bedroom, Jameson to Franco's bedroom, Gigi used a sleeping bag in the corridor, and Franco and I dossed down on the two sofas in the living room.

I was woken the next morning by the sound of voices in the room: Sarah's and Franco's.

Sarah was saying, 'Well, I didn't hear anything.'

'No, I didn't too. When do you think – '

'What's the matter? Ouch,' I said, sitting up and discovering I had a crick in my neck. I remembered just in time that I was naked, and so didn't fling the sheets off.

'Your brother and that little man have walked out,' Sarah said. She was dressed. Franco was in pyjamas.

'What? Why? When?'

'Don't know. Must have been pretty damn early.'

I looked at my watch. It was gone eight thirty. 'I wonder what story he told this time,' I said.

'Who? Jameson?'

'Yes,' I said. 'I mean, I don't see Gigi and him getting together otherwise. Perhaps he convinced Gigi he knows where Amedeo's secret treasure hoard is. Ow, my neck.' I rubbed it hard. 'Or perhaps they've just gone down to wave Union Jacks.'

'Oh, yeah. The yacht must be getting in now.'

Franco turned on the radio. A Beethoven symphony filled the room. 'Too late for the news,' he said. 'But they arrive early, it's true.' He turned the radio off.

Sarah said, 'They did change the day though, didn't they? I was thinking about it in bed, and I'm sure it was tomorrow they were supposed to arrive.'

'Yes, yes,' Franco said. 'It caused big troubles. But they

had to change the day during the week because of naval exercises or something. NATO. Even your Royal Family gives way to NATO. The Mediterranean belongs to America now, after all.'

'Don't look at me,' Sarah said. 'I didn't buy it. Shall we have some coffee? I guess there's no point worrying about Luigi. Nothing we can do.'

'No,' I said, 'and he knows how to take care of himself.'

'I have that impression too,' Franco said. 'He's different from you – that is, I want to say – '

'Don't try and apologise,' I said. 'Cock-up artist are the words you're looking for. Ouch.' I rubbed my neck again. 'Can't even be trusted to sleep without breaking my neck.'

'I'll give you a massage,' Sarah said. She did so while Franco made the coffee, and I did my best to think of it as a medical necessity and forget the fact that it was a beautiful blonde rubbing my naked body. One of the things a gentleman does not do – as I'm sure Jameson would have been happy to inform me – is make advances to a girl whose boyfriend's body the gentleman has helped to send to the bottom of the sea the night before. So we made no small talk.

I dressed and, most psychologically refreshing, I shaved before going through to the kitchen for coffee. After my first cup I said, 'Why don't we go and see what the Windsors are up to? At Pompeii or wherever they're going.'

'You English,' Franco said, shaking his head.

'I'm sure there won't be only English people around,' I said. 'Not if magazines like *Oggi* are anything to go by. And anyway, who knows, 'o Rauco might be there too. Testing the ground.'

'I thought we said we'd go to Capri,' Sarah said. 'That's where they'll be on Sunday – tomorrow that is.'

'Well, I've thought about it,' I said, 'and I'm not so sure . . .'

'No, I think Gennaro is right,' Franco said. 'It is best we keep – we keep our eyes on them . . .'

'They'd be so relieved to know,' I murmured.

'Well,' Franco said, "o Rauco may be – may be following. At Capri I don't think we can find him now. No, we must follow them too. After all we must do something. At ten o'clock they arrive at Pompeii. We go there, all right?'

'That's fine by me,' I said. 'I've never been there.'

'You understand that the *scavi* – the excavations – will be closed. Your Royals cannot visit them with the common people, oh no.'

'Do I gather you're strictly a Republican?'

'With a small R, please. I'm a communist, after all.'

'You're not, are you?' Sarah said, staring at him almost open-mouthed.

'An Italian communist,' I said to her. 'Don't worry. They're the cuddly variety, they don't bite.'

'Wow. I've never met a real Commie before,' she said.

'If you like I give you my autograph,' he said. 'You can show it to your friends in America: the communist who was killed trying to save the English Royal Family.'

We went by public transport to Pompeii. The roads in and out of Naples were likely to be clogged, Franco said, whereas the train – the Circumvesuviana – was almost always prompt, royal visits or not.

We were standing all the way. Here and there people were talking in Neapolitan about the Royal Family. Franco said, 'I never understand why are all these people so interested about your queens and princesses.'

'Mostly in their hats as far as I can tell,' I said. My neck was beginning to ache again.

'Well, it annoys me,' he said. 'There are so many more important things.'

'I know,' I said. 'Dallas and Cicciolina and Maradona.'

'Ssh,' he said. 'You mustn't name the name of Maradona in vain. Not in public.'

Sarah looked puzzled and I said to her, 'And neither shalt thou ask aloud in public who Maradona is. Naples's second patron saint.'

'First,' Franco said. 'All the children are called Diego now, not Gennaro.'

Sarah said, 'I was just gonna say it doesn't bother me – all this enthusiasm, I mean. What's wrong with a little romance now and then?'

'But this is very expensive romance,' Franco began excitedly. He was hampered by the fact that he only had one hand to gesticulate with. 'This costs the people millions of pounds every day, every hour – '

Sarah went on, as if not hearing Franco, 'What I can't take in is that Bren should have wanted to put them in danger. I mean, it's tough enough to take in that he should have wanted to put anyone in danger. But why them, if it is them?'

'I think I know why,' I said.

'Why?'

'It made it more exciting.'

She looked hard at me and I sensed I'd offended her. But then she said sadly, 'I think – yes, it's possible.'

'It's probable, I'm afraid,' I said. I remembered his last words and added, 'What fun was it otherwise?'

'But other people . . . Oh Bren, Bren.'

'There must have been easier ways to catch this bloke,' I said, 'but I think he fancied the – the big final scene. You know, jumping the bloke just when he's got the victim in his sights, his finger on the trigger. Like in all the best films. The only trouble with a scheme like that is you can't afford to be slapdash – and, and well . . .'

'Bren was slapdash.'

'Well, Sarah, let's face it, at the villa he wasn't exactly busting a gut to find out what Amedeo was up to. Croquet on the lawn, aperitifs and swimming. As far as I could see, he didn't even look at a newspaper to see if they were following up the Bayswater story.'

'Bren never liked the press much. He only gave that interview to the *Mattino* to keep them off while he was at Ischia. People sometimes accused him of loving the limelight, playing up to the press. But I know it was just – just his way.

He knew how to treat them so they'd bug him as little as possible. If he didn't give them stories now and again they'd come looking. But he never even bothered to read the stories, you know. Really.'

I found that difficult to believe; but then possibly mine was the natural reaction of one whose name had only appeared once in the newspaper ('Twelve year old J. Esposetto (sic) played Macduff's son' – *Radney Local Advertiser*).

'And anyway,' she went on, 'it was a pretty smart move on his part to look like he loved being out front. I mean, if he goes out of his way to be interviewed about his villa on Ischia, who'd suspect him of being involved in bust-ups and break-ins on the island? You know he fixed to have that interview himself, and he fixed it up just then deliberately – just before going to Ischia, even though he'd been in Naples for some weeks. And I reckon it worked as a system. I know he did the same thing in Bangkok and in Rio. In Rio all the papers ran a couple of pages on him and the jungle while he was – he was, well, I'm not sure exactly what, but it involved hoodlums. Some of the bust-ups got reported in the same issues, but of course nobody made the connection.'

I thought of Raffles, who boasted about the fact that his cricketing triumphs were reported on the same page as his burglaries, but I thought it better not to mention this precedent. It struck me too that Raffles had acted with the same arrogant assurance that charm and a public school accent excused all.

'OK,' I said, 'but you'd have thought, I mean, with something like this, he'd have glanced at the papers at least. I mean – '

'Remember he was fairly sure that Amedeo had had the deal cancelled. So he probably didn't feel things were that urgent.'

Something started to hammer in a corner of my mind, something urgent and sinister connected with what she'd been saying, but I couldn't work out what it was.

We drew up at Torre Annunziata. Franco waved a hand at the view and said, 'Home.'

Sarah said, 'Wow, it's just down the road from Pompeii.'

Franco said, 'And if you knew how this cheers up the inhabitants. Every afternoon they all go for a visit to the *scavi* with their guidebooks.'

'I was just making a remark,' Sarah said.

'I'm sorry, I know. In fact, when I was a kid, it's true, I often went and played there. We knew the *custode*; he let us in without to pay. It was wonderful for – for *nascondino*.'

'Hide and seek,' I said.

'Yes, hide and see. You know, I think I liked the houses better there than at Torre, even if they let the rain enter a little.'

Most of the people on the train, Neapolitans and tourists alike, got out at Pompeii Villa Misteri, the next stop.

'Hell,' Sarah said, looking down the crowded platform, 'this could be difficult.'

'Let's go to the entrance up the road by this way,' Franco said. 'We can see if we can enter there, you never know. If it's the same *custode*.'

Outside the station everyone was going towards the Porta Marina, where the royal visit was to commence – or, given that it was now ten past ten, probably already had commenced. One couldn't really tell; the terrific noise could be that of massed cheery welcome – or just the normal noise of an expectant Neapolitan crowd.

Franco led us off in the opposite direction up a hill. Vesuvius rose threateningly ahead of us. On our right, Pompeii looked like a mass of untidy, bombed council houses. We passed a camping site on our left and then a motel. There were cars parked all along the road, but their occupants had clearly all long since gone off to gawp at the royal arrival. We reached another entrance to the city where a few bored-looking Carabinieri stood around chatting. A man with a postcard- and guidebook-stand looked at them moodily, as if realising they were not going to be his best customers.

'No, we can't get in here,' Franco said. 'It was only an idea.'

'Hey!' Sarah said, pointing back down the road, 'who do I see?'

I turned. Gigi and Jameson were running along after us.

'What the hell – ' I said as they arrived. Jameson, I saw, had changed into more conventional schoolmastery clothes.

Gigi shot one quick glance at the Carabinieri and then said in quick urgent tones, 'You guessed it then, we've had no luck, we can't – '

'What are you talking about?' Sarah said.

I said, 'I know. I've got it. 'o Rauco's here.'

'Course he is,' Gigi said, 'you mean you hadn't – '

I turned to Sarah. 'Brendan got the bloody day wrong, like you. I knew there was something – '

Twenty – three

I clearly should have thought of this long before. After all, if I remembered the conversation on the cassette correctly, Brendan hadn't been able to stipulate any specific day – just a period of days and the place (presumably the Naples area). So in those last choking moments of life he'd said Sunday simply because he thought it the earliest possible day for the assassination. As I'd said to Sarah, slapdash. Criminally so. I turned back to Gigi and Jameson. 'So where is he?'

'I don't know,' Gigi almost shouted, and then looked nervously at the Carabinieri. They were paying no attention to us. One of them was pointing at one of the postcards – presumably a reproduction of one of the obscene wall-paintings – and the others were laughing. The postcard seller was still scowling. He knew they weren't going to buy it. Gigi went on, 'This shit said we'd find him easy, and I believed him. We've been running around, and when we saw you, down there by the station, we fought – '

Jameson said, 'Now we mustn't panic.' He was holding a small but thick red book with a map that opened out.

'Give me that,' I said suddenly. I snatched it from his hands and opened the map out fully. It was a map of the excavations.

'Is my book,' Franco said suddenly, 'my Touring Club guide. You took it – '

'Yes, sorry,' Jameson said, 'but you do see, it was necessary, we – '

'Of course, of course,' I said slowly.

'What?' Gigi, Sarah, Jameson and Franco said (Franco in fact said 'Cosa?').

'This is the map I saw in Amedeo's office. I thought it was a city – well, it is a city, of course, or was, but you know . . . Hell, why didn't I – ' I stopped. 'There was a mark on it.'

'Where?' Gigi, Sarah and Jameson said. ('*Dove?*' said Franco.)

'At the top somewhere. Along – along these walls.'

Sarah said, 'We must tell someone.' She was looking at the Carabinieri.

'You out of your mind?' Gigi said. 'Come on. We can get there in time.'

Franco said, 'We'll go round the fields. I know all this zone. Follow me. Don't run. The Carabinieri will watch us.'

'But,' I said, 'we ought to – '

'You try it,' Gigi said, surprisingly vicious all of a sudden, 'you bloody try it.'

We set off at a brisk walk down the road in the direction of Vesuvius. Once out of sight we started running. We passed another set of ruins which, if I hadn't looked at the map, I would have taken (at our speed) for a sprawling farm house, but which was the Villa dei Misteri, and then we climbed a fence and were in the fields. Vesuvius suddenly seemed more threatening, as if it were echoing Gigi's words. We ran quickly round to the right, through a vineyard, and then across a field with lines of squashy green things – I had no idea what. Behind a screen of trees and bushes at the far side of the field the northern walls of Pompeii were just visible, with squarish but jagged towers jutting up at regular intervals. By now Franco and I were ahead with Sarah just a little behind; Gigi and Jameson were lumbering along some way back. I was developing a stitch and the ache in my neck was beginning to throb again in sympathy.

Franco stopped and pointed. 'You see that big tower?' He spoke in Italian.

'Yes.'

'That's the observation tower. From there you can see the whole city.'

'Hang on a moment.' I had another look at the map. 'It's Tower 11,' I said. 'At the end of Via Mercurio.'

'And so?'

'Nothing.' I was remembering one of the entries in that

engagement book of Amedeo's: 'Via Merc. Tor. 11.' 'Do you think 'o Rauco's up there?'

'Don't be stupid. Can't you see there's a Carabiniere up there?'

I squinted. He was right. The Carabiniere was at the far side of the tower, obviously looking down at the city. After all, on this side there was only Vesuvius and a few fields to look at, on the other side he had a view Italian news magazines would pay millions for. 'So?' I said. Sarah joined us, panting heavily.

'They'll certainly go up that tower and look at the view. So . . .'

'I get you. He'll be somewhere among those trees.' From a view to a kill.

'I think so.'

We ran across the fields, possibly ruining the farmer's cabbage/asparagus/aubergine crop for that year. We could now see that between us and the trees was a fifteen-foot wire fence. We ran desperately along the edge. On its other side was thick undergrowth. At one point a tree had toppled and had smashed through the undergrowth. We could see that behind the undergrowth was a deep wide ditch, and the walls rose sheer out of the ditch.

I halted, and the others did the same. 'If he's in these bushes and wants to pick them off on that tower, he's got to be some way along to the left or right. Let's split.'

Franco ran off to the right and I kept running to the left. Sarah followed me, which I found a comfort. A glance behind showed Jameson and Gigi dithering about which way to go. I didn't look to see how they decided.

We were running along, instinctively bent almost double, peering into the tangled mass of undergrowth on the far side of the fence with quiet desperation. It was so thick that I knew I might have passed fifty concealed snipers. Then suddenly I caught a glimpse of something black that triggered off a memory: I remembered that dripping English wood, the dawn chorus, and Gigi lying on a *black* groundsheet. I jerked back and looked again. It was just a few square inches of shiny black stuff, seen through a particularly thick tangle of bushes – an almost unnaturally thick tangle.

'Hey,' Sarah said in a dramatic whisper, 'look on the tower.'

I swivelled and saw the Carabiniere coming to attention. 'Quick, give me a leg-up.' I shoved the guidebook into my coat pocket. She put her hands together, I stepped up, managed to get a footing on a horizontal bar half-way up the fence, and from there managed to grab at the top of the fence. I pulled and found myself in a sort of drunken sloth position, with one ankle over the top of the fence and the other hanging loose, and no idea what to do next.

'They're there,' Sarah suddenly said, and I swirled my head crazily round and saw well-known silhouettes against the blue sky, gazing at the volcano, no doubt saying how much it reminded them of the view from Balmoral. At this sudden movement my neck felt as if it had been twisted in two contrary directions at the same time, and this pain was the stimulus for me to do something I not only would never have dared to do otherwise, but would not even have been physically capable of doing: from that desperate clinging position I heaved myself in a kind of vault over the fence and crashed down into the bushes below me.

Somebody uttered a cry – almost a grunt – and it wasn't me.

I was mixed up with a hell of a lot of sharp vegetation and wondering whether I was in one piece, but was still aware enough to grab out at this human shape to my side. My right arm touched metal and I jerked it savagely. The metal object came away and I threw it out of the bushes.

I could now see a thin face, smeared with brown make-up, within inches of mine – and it was looking vicious. I found my left hand was free and I placed it on top of the head and pushed; the face spluttered hoarsely into the groundsheet. We stayed like that for fifteen seconds or so and then I heard Sarah saying in an urgent whisper, 'They've gone, they've gone. Are you OK?'

'They've gone,' I repeated. 'Done the view. Done the view.'

The human shape squirmed out of my grasp and rose to its feet. The apparently impenetrable undergrowth just split to either side. I lay there without the strength to do anything. I was afraid I'd disintegrate.

'o Rauco was dressed in green and black combat gear; he was slight of build but looked active. Far more so than me at any rate.

'Don't let him get the gun,' Sarah said. She was pressed up close to the netting in the shade of a pine tree, no doubt in order to avoid observation from the tower.

I found I was just about capable of one last action: I squirmed over and shot my arms out and grabbed the gun; I swivelled it and aimed it at 'o Rauco's belly. It was a long complicated thing with telescopic sights; there was an overturned tripod on the groundsheet. No thermos flask, however.

'I don't need these sights,' I said in Neapolitan, 'not at this distance.'

'o Rauco didn't raise his arms. He stared out behind me. I heard Jameson's voice speaking in his ludicrous Italian, 'We've come to help you.'

I turned momentarily and saw Franco, Gigi and Jameson all pressed up close to the netting next to Sarah.

There was a sound like the start of an eruption, and then I realised it was 'o Rauco speaking. 'The netting's cut there,' he said. 'Come on through.' He pointed at the fence just next to himself. They found the place where the netting opened like a cat flap and filed through. Presumably 'o Rauco's escape route. They were all clustered now in front of me.

'So now what?' he said in Neapolitan.

'I don't know,' I said in English. 'It's up to you, Sarah. You're the one who wanted him. You can come and pull the trigger if you like.'

'I'm not a killer,' she said.

'Let's go for 'o Rauco,' I quoted, 'you remember? Now you've got him.'

Gigi said, 'Let me see that gun.'

'What?' I said nervously. 'Wait a moment – hang on – '

Gigi came and took it off me, as easily as that. He threw it to 'o Rauco and then took a pistol from inside his jacket. I felt a trifle silly.

'o Rauco swivelled the gun and pointed it at Sarah and Franco. 'Down in the ditch,' he said in heavily accented English.

'Gigi,' I said, 'have you gone completely mad?'

'Look, Jan, I'm sorry about this, I really am, but, well, just obey, all right?'

We found a point where it was reasonably easy to descend, and all three of us stood there at the base of the city walls. 'o Rauco, Gigi and Jameson remained up top; they moved just a few paces to the left where a tree rendered observation from the tower impossible. 'o Rauco held his gun with casual ease, Gigi his pistol kind of apologetically and Jameson stood with a certain nervous eagerness between them. He was saying in Italian to 'o Rauco, 'Amedeo's dead, he's dead, and you remember my – my offer: how I'd be pleased to act as your manager if anything should happen to him. You remember?'

'I remember,' 'o Rauco said briefly without looking at him.

'You know, Gigi,' I said, 'I don't think I'm going to forgive this. I mean, never.'

'Jan, you've got to understand. This is my chance, my chance for the real big time, you gotta see that.' He turned to 'o Rauco. 'You remember me, don't you – Luigi, back in England, you remember . . .'

'Pasquale,' I said suddenly. And, absurd though it may seem, I remembered those stinging nettles of some fifteen years back and I was instantly twice as scared. I said again, 'Pasquale. You mean, Gigi, you knew who 'o Rauco was – you never intended – '

'Shit, Jan,' Gigi said, 'it was a chance in a lifetime. I mean, I heard of how Bren was actually on the hunt for Pasquale. Well, a chance like that – I mean, without Bren's money how could I hope to get to find him?'

274

'You were using Bren,' Sarah said, 'you were using him all that time.'

'Look Sal, I was gonna help Bren find Pasquale but, I mean, you couldn't expect me to want to kill an old mate, someone I knew as a kid.'

'Come on now,' Jameson said, 'we can't stand around talking.'

'You want to be a killer,' Sarah said. 'I can't believe it.'

'I didn't – I mean, until Bren died I didn't know what I wanted. I just fought, it's a chance – and I mean, look, now it's me only chance, you gotta see that – '

Pasquale said in English, 'We waste time.'

'Yes,' Jameson said, 'we really must go.'

Pasquale went on, 'Before we go, Gigi – ' and there was contempt in his use of the diminutive that only family had ever been allowed to use, 'show me you are worth to stay with me. You down there,' he said peremptorily, 'sit down.'

We stepped back towards the wall and sat on the ground against it. As I did so I felt the heavy bulk of the guidebook tugging at my jacket pocket.

Pasquale's cement-mixer voice went on, 'Shoot them down there. All three.'

'Yes, yes,' Jameson said eagerly, 'it really would be best, you do see – ' I half expected him to turn round and explain apologetically the necessity to us.

Sarah let out a half gasp which might have been a word.

Gigi said, 'Shoot – shoot them?'

'You start,' Pasquale said. 'And I'll continue. Don't worry, we can run to my car before anyone comes.'

Gigi lifted his gun slowly and then made a sudden half turn. Pasquale had obviously foreseen this possibility and his gun turned too and fired. Gigi spun backwards and fell.

Even while Pasquale's gun was swivelling my hand had grabbed the book from out of my pocket and in the same movement sent it hurtling through the air – with an accuracy I'll probably never repeat in my life. It struck Pasquale on the head and knocked him sideways. I scrambled up the side of the ditch, vaguely aware of Sarah and Franco behind me, and a distant shouting above us all.

Jameson was crouched over Gigi and was prising his gun from his fingers. Gigi was moaning. Jameson looked at Pasquale who was lying still and he said, 'Don't – don't come any nearer.' We all halted where we were, clutching at the roots and branches at the top of the ditch. From the tower a voice was shouting, '*Cosa succede? Cosa succede?*' They clearly couldn't see anything.

Jameson said, 'I'm – I'm leaving now – you must – you must stop here – if I hear anyone follow, I shoot, I swear, I shoot, you see that, don't you, I have no choice.' He held the pistol two-handedly, but still aimed at me. He lowered himself to the bottom and then started running along the ditch. I suppose he felt more protected down there.

We pulled ourselves up to the top. Sarah and Franco went over to Gigi and I pulled Pasquale's gun once again from his grasp. He came to with a sudden guttural cry and sat up. He heard Jameson's running footsteps, and with one venomous glance at us all, he leapt down the side of the ditch and followed Jameson.

There was another gunshot and we saw Pasquale staggering back like a silent film comic who had banged his head. Then he collapsed. Jameson further down the ditch was staring at what he'd done. He gave a sort of feeble whimper and then kept running. I said to Sarah and Franco, 'Get Gigi away – take him across the fields – get out of it – '

Franco said, 'I know these fields, don't worry – and you?'

I descended the ditch in a couple of leaps and a slither (only thinking at the bottom that it would have been pretty silly to have broken my ankle at this point in the whole affair) and I said, 'I'm going after him.'

I started running. If I had stopped to think I'd have realised that what I was doing was pointless – and unnecessarily dangerous too. Jameson had already shown his readiness to shoot; but as I leapt over Pasquale's body, all I thought was, the bastard's not going to get away with it again.

Jameson was running steadily some twenty yards ahead of me. I could see his long strands of hair streaming out behind him like a single rabbit ear. I passed a gate into the city – covered with scaffolding and inaccessible – and I saw Jameson look back. Without stopping he fired again; I didn't bother to dodge; it would only be a fluke shot that hit me at that distance, so I would be as likely to dodge into the bullet as away from it. He disappeared round a bend; the wall and ditch curved round to the right; there was a long stretch leading to another main entrance of the city – the Porta di Nola if my memory of the map was correct – where there was another railway station. Jameson was running unflaggingly. Suddenly he scrabbled up the side of the ditch. I did likewise and we were in an untilled field. He ran straight across it.

I heard the sound of a train approaching and so did he. He was visibly forcing himself now. He presumably hoped to get aboard the train at the small station we could see to our right – it was no more than a simple platform next to the entrance booth at the Porta di Nola. There was a hedge between us and the rails. Jameson had undoubtedly chosen this cross-field route to avoid any Carabinieri or officials there might be at the Porta; we couldn't see anybody from here, but they might be on the other side of the booth.

The train was getting closer. So was I. I was within ten yards now.

He whirled round again and fired. I felt the bullet – or the wind of the bullet's trajectory – tug momentarily at my right sleeve.

I don't know how he did it, but suddenly he was over the hedge. I could just see his top quarter running along the side of the rails. The train hurtled into sight, rocking the hedge. It was clearly not stopping at this station.

He swivelled to face it, waving frantically, the gun still in his left hand. I saw his face working with desperation and his right hand shot out impulsively as if trying to halt the train. Maybe he was remembering films where John Wayne leaps on to the running board.

The next moment I saw his arms and head flip over, like clothes in a spin-dryer, and I heard him give one sudden sharp shriek; then there was a crunching sound just audible above the sound of the engine – and then the screech of the brakes.

I turned round, bent low, and ran up the length of the hedge until I reached another field. I straightened up, but I kept running.

Twenty – Four

A couple of hours later I rang Franco's doorbell. Franco's voice, over the intercom, sounded pleased to hear me. He opened the door and Sarah was at his side.

'And Gigi?' I said.

Sarah said, 'His shoulder was a bit of a mess and we wanted to take him to hospital, but he said he knew a guy in the Spanish Quarters who'd fix it up, no questions asked.'

'He would,' I said. 'So he wasn't actually dying or anything?'

'No, the guy'd fired too quickly, just hit his shoulder – it looked real nasty though.'

'Yes, I'm sure,' I said, 'a gun that size.' He was very lucky – if getting your shoulder shot to pieces twice in one week can reasonably be considered lucky. Anyway, I felt a great sense of relief. We went towards the living room.

'I didn't like the look of the place,' Sarah said, 'not my idea of a doctor's house, but he insisted.'

'No,' I said, 'I don't suppose many doctors live around there. But how did you get him to Naples?'

'Luigi took us to where he'd parked the car. He was even managing to walk normally.'

'But he was in much pain,' Franco said.

'Yeah, but nobody noticed,' Sarah said. 'We covered him up, you see. But anyway, what about you, what about you? We've been listening to the news, but they just mention a shoot-out with two people killed. They say the tour won't be affected. That's what Franco tells me they say, anyway.'

'Do you mind if I sit down?' I said. 'I'm exhausted. Miles across country till I managed to get a bus into town.'

'Do you want a drink?' Franco said.

'Love one. Anything. Yes, a Martini.'

Over the Martini I told them of Jameson's end. I finished,

'And I don't think anybody saw me. I mean, all their attention was on this lunatic trying to stick the train up with a gun.'

'What a way to go,' Sarah said. 'Do you think he'd flipped?'

I remembered the way his body had suddenly, yes, flipped over and I suppressed a shudder. 'You mean, gone crazy?' I said. 'I don't know. I think he was half crazy anyway, only happy when he was scheming. He'd probably have schemed against himself if he hadn't anyone else, just you can't scheme against trains.' I was very tired, and was talking a little crazily myself. 'Tell me,' I said, 'did Gigi, er, apologise at all?'

'You know Luigi,' Sarah said.

'No, I don't think I do really.'

'No, maybe you're right,' she said, 'but, well, he didn't actually say sorry in so many words, but he kind of acted it.'

'I think your brother was a little crazy too,' Franco said. ''E really thought that this killer, Pasquale, would want to work with 'im because they played together when children. That was what 'e kept to say, saying, in the car – "But Pasquale was my friend, my friend . . ."'

'Just a sentimentalist,' I said. So he *had* been reading Christopher Robin.

Sarah said, 'You know, Luigi likes to give this impression of being the only one who really knows his way around and that, but he's pretty mixed up himself, I reckon. You know, all this "I'm the pro" – '

'The big-timer,' I said.

'Right.'

I had to agree. The big time (or clout, or whatever he called it) had obviously become a bit of an obsession with Gigi, presumably because he was basically aware of being out of it, of not possessing it. So perhaps the career of his old friend, being so clearly an example of the biggest of big time, had been raised to a kind of mythical level for him – a level where ethical or moral questions were either simply forgotten or considered irrelevant.

'You know,' Sarah said, 'he did make a kind of apology. He said that once he'd got working with Bren he'd started to give up the idea of going over to Pasquale. He got to like Bren and so didn't want to turn round and slap him in the face like that; he liked the idea of going on working with him. I don't think he'd made any definite decisions on what he'd do if Bren got really close to Pasquale – maybe he planned on giving Pasquale a tip-off. He was obviously a bit confused. But anyway, he was pretty sure he wasn't going to go over and join him.'

'I suppose Brendan Cullop was big time enough,' I said.

'Yeah, maybe. At any rate it was only when Bren died that he started to go back to his original plan. And of course he got talking with Jameson, who persuaded him that if he helped him get away he'd fix things up with Pasquale for him. And he fell for it.'

'Gigi, the pro. Did he leave any message or anything for, er, family?'

'Just said you'd hear from him sooner or later.'

'At this moment I hope later. I need to forget certain things about today,' I said.

'Yeah, I'm sure.' Sarah got up and poured herself another drink.

'And you?' I said. 'Have you started thinking about what you're going to do? I mean, once they start looking into Brendan's disappearance, they're going to start looking for Sarah Ryan too.'

'Yeah, well, let them. Sarah Ryan doesn't exist.'

'Sorry?' I said.

'My name's Felicity Fanshawe – no, really. It was Bren's idea when I got together with him that I should take on a new identity, something nice and simple for the Press to get hold of and be happy with. So, you know, if, when, things changed between us I wouldn't get hounded, he said.'

I'd never heard of anyone starting an affair with anyone by talking about the end of it. I was clearly out of touch with the times.

She went on, 'I think he was thinking of a situation like this too. Me being left to face the – the investigations.'

'But surely you've been photographed, interviewed, etc.'

'Not that much. Bren takes – took care of that. I'm sure all I have to do is change back my hairstyle and no-one'll recognise me as Brendan Cullop's old girlfriend. I know no one ever spotted their old friend Felicity Fanshawe on Bren's arm. After all, who's ever really noticed me next to him?'

'Well, I have,' I said.

'Thanks, but you know what I mean. I agreed to it all because I guess I always knew this was just a, well, a break in my life. A year of being someone else. He even got a fake passport for me, you know that? But I'll leave Italy as Felicity Fanshawe, and I'll go back to – '

'Not to your adman,' I said. Then I added, 'That is, if he ever existed.'

'Oh, he existed, sure. Still does, I guess. No, I'll go back to – well, no, I won't go back. I never go back.'

'Sing it,' I said, 'and you've got yourself a new career.'

'Sorry?'

'Nothing.'

'Anyway, I guess I'll go to New York. Always wanted to spend some time there. It'll be a change, and that's what I need.'

Franco said, 'I'm Neapolitan and I'll never leave Naples. But per'aps I'll go to New York too. Also I need a change.'

'Is everyone determined to make cryptic remarks today?' I said.

'You can live very easily in New York without leaving Naples,' Franco said. 'I 'ave an uncle who 'as done so for thirty years.'

'Well, that's you two fixed up. I don't know about me.' I thought that as a reaction to Sarah/Felicity I ought to say that I'd go back to my cosy little flat in London, never to leave it again. But I didn't really feel like it, I had to admit.

We had lunch together, but our conversation was aimless. At one o'clock Franco turned the television on for the news. The report was brief and confused and mostly insisted on the unlikelihood that it had anything to do with the royal visit. It was said to be most probably a *regolamento di conti* (settling of old scores) in the gang world, and the killers were said to have taken advantage of the confusion surrounding the royal tour for their purposes. Neither corpse had been identified. No reference was made to the high-powered marksman's rifle. I got the impression that they hadn't the faintest idea what to make of it all, and so had chosen a nice reassuring line for public consumption. No connection was made, of course, with recent events on Ischia.

After lunch I humped my rucksack on to my shoulder and made towards the front door. I said to Franco, 'I'll be in touch' and shook his hand. Sarah said, 'So long, Jan, it's been good knowing you,' and we kissed on both cheeks, Italian style.

I said, 'Yes,' and wondered whether to add, 'See you again some time, in New York perhaps', but I didn't. She'd be another person then – and she never went back. Instead I said, 'I'll remember you,' and I set off down the stairs.

On the way to the station I felt the rucksack sticking clammily to my back and I suddenly remembered the wet clothes that I hadn't thought of hanging out to dry. I debated on whether to have recourse now to a Sarah-type solution and chuck them (and my boring old identity) into the nearest bin. I didn't, however. They stayed sticking to me, as a proof that I was stuck with being boring. Perhaps even now the dampness was laying the foundations for a premature condition of rheumatism, which would keep me tediously but safely sedentary in future.

On an impulse at the station I rang up one of my aunts in town. Perhaps this stirring of family affection was yet another reaction to Sarah: even Gigi had said 'Sooner or later'.

I fought off the invitations to come and eat (explaining that I was still in Rome), then my aunt said, 'I've heard from Peppina in London. She says your – your *fidanzata*, Valeria, is back from America. She's looking for you.'

'Oh yes?' That was quick work.

'So are you going back to London?'

I said, without needing to think about it, 'No, I think I'll be in Italy for some time yet.' I said my goodbyes and then made towards a train for Rome.

Or Florence. Or Venice. Or an Apennine village. Anywhere really that had a clothes-line.

Afterword

In this story I realise I have dwelt on the more sensational aspects of Naples as a city. I suppose I am writing what is sometimes called 'sensational fiction', but all the same I wish I had managed to communicate more of that spirit of warmth and generosity which strikes every visitor to the city. Naples might, for example, have the worst traffic jams in Europe, but it's also perhaps the only city where a traffic jam can become a party – not to mention an outdoor market. Maybe if they didn't have this ability to make something out of the confusion there would be less confusion, but then it wouldn't be Naples which, thanks to this ability (and I suppose to the confusion), is not only one of the most interesting cities I know but also one of the friendliest.

Perhaps I should apologise too for the liberties I have taken with the geography of the south side of Ischia; here, however, my alterations were mostly carried out with the aim of providing my characters with wider, less built-up spaces to throw themselves around in, and I can only say, considering the canker of concrete on the island, that I wish Ischia were more as I've represented it.